In the
SHADOW
of the GODS

In the
Shadow
of the Gods

A BOUND GODS NOVEL

Rachel Dunne

HARPER Voyager
An Imprint of HarperCollins *Publishers*

IN THE SHADOW OF THE GODS. Copyright © 2016 by Rachel Dunne. All rights reserved. Printed in the United States of America. No part of this book may be used or reproduced in any manner whatsoever without written permission except in the case of brief quotations embodied in critical articles and reviews. For information address HarperCollins Publishers, 195 Broadway, New York, NY 10007.

HarperCollins books may be purchased for educational, business, or sales promotional use. For information, please e-mail the Special Markets Department at SPsales@harpercollins.com.

FIRST EDITION

Harper Voyager and design is a trademark of HarperCollins Publishers L.L.C.

Designed by Paula Russell Szafranski

Library of Congress Cataloging-in-Publication Data has been applied for.

ISBN 978-0-06-242813-4

16 17 18 19 20   OV/RRD   10 9 8 7 6 5 4 3 2 1

To my parents,
for every single reason

IN THE SHADOW OF THE GODS

797 Years after the Fall

The Parents wept when they saw what their children had wrought, and they cast the Twins forever from the world so that their stain would be spread no further.

—The Tale of the Fall

CHAPTER 1

Mount Raturo lurched above the forest like an ugly thumb, throwing its broad-shouldered shadow over the trees. Its sides were crisscrossed with hidden paths, crawling all the way to the snow-shrouded peak. Tunnels bored deep into the mountain's heart, entrances disguised by a long-lost magic. Death lurked in the shadows of path and tunnel, waiting for those who didn't know the proper words, for those who didn't speak quickly enough. Dark, hidden eyes watched from every egress, waiting patiently. Bones, human and animal, lay scattered among faint rust-brown stains, among pitted black scorch marks, beneath heartless rockslides. The mountain knew nothing of forgiveness, of mistakes, of second chances.

For Joros, the sight of Mount Raturo sent a rare stab of warmth through his heart. Few enough things could put a smile on his face, but the sight of home after a long journey was one.

"This is it?" the boy, Ranick, asked, a faint quaver in his voice as he stared up the sheer mountain face.

"Do you see another mountain?" sneered the woman, Verteira, eyes gleaming eagerly in their blackened sockets. The smattering of bruises across her pale flesh was fading, but slowly. She bore them with pride.

Odaro remained silent as always, his broad face thoughtful.

Watching his chosen three, Joros was pleased. Mount Raturo *should* bring fear and awe to those who gazed upon it, as it did with Ranick and Odaro. But Verteira . . . she saw Raturo's existence as a challenge as much as a wonder. Joros had been lucky to find the woman. The Ventallo would be pleased with her, and with him, he had no doubt.

"Come," he said, and walked toward the mountain. Odaro followed, tugging the reins of the mule on which Verteira perched, wincing, the fingers of her broken arm clutching at her swollen stomach. Ranick came last, his shoulders hunched as if he could feel the watching eyes. They had come too far, these three, to let fear turn them back now. Their pasts were dead and buried, their only hope the spire reaching up toward the sky to brush the clouds. They followed Joros as he began the long climb, because they had no other choice.

It was hours before Joros paused. His lungs burned, his breath wheezing through his mouth and nose, a stitch sending stabbing pains through his side with each step. His legs were useless lumps, feet slapping clumsily down, teeth rattling with each footfall. Every part of him ached—and he'd never felt so alive. He remembered his first ascent, his feet torn to bloody shreds, hands clawing at his neck with the desperation of too little air. Sweet memories, his finest triumph.

He stopped a moment to let his chosen catch their breath.

Odaro was heaving in great bellyfuls of air, a hand pressed to his chest as if to assure himself his heart still beat. Verteira clung grimly on to the mule's back, face pale, blackened eyes wide, not so fearless as she'd been at the base of the mountain. Ranick toiled a ways behind, half crawling, hands leaving behind red smudges as he dragged himself up the mountain steps.

Joros looked down at the forest, a dark blanket far below, swallowed up by the night. The ground was gone, a distant memory, a legend overheard, a tale to terrify children. The two red points of Sororra's Eyes hovered above the horizon, glaring over the world as Joros did. He looked up and up, to the light of the moon gleaming off the peak of Mount Raturo. They had a long way yet to go, and he was eager to be out of the cold. "Come," he said to the three, and he turned his eyes back to the steps and to the black shape that appeared before him.

The Sentinel loomed over him, blotting out the peak, blotting out the moon, a shape made of darkness itself save for its eyes, which were the blue-tinged color of stars in the night sky. "Speak," it grated, voice like crashing stones.

Shock gripped Joros for a brief moment. The black shape twisted, a shadowy limb rising up, fist poised to crush him. The words fell from Joros's mouth in a rush: "*Tevarro borine.*" *Long journey,* in the Old Tongue. The Sentinel's head dipped ever so slightly in acknowledgment.

"*Tevarro borine,*" Verteira repeated, voice half whisper, half prayer. From behind came Ranick's high-pitched wail: "*Tevarro borine!*" Silent, gaping Odaro stared and said nothing, and Joros smelled the sharp stench of urine.

The shadow moved *through* Joros, chilling him to the bone,

twisting his guts into miserable knots. The Sentinel's raised fist swung, suddenly terribly solid; Odaro flew, crashed into the unforgiving face of the mountain, and exploded.

Gore flew in every direction, chunks of meat and bone raining around Joros, covering him with a sticky red warmth. A severed hand hit the mule squarely on its nose and it reared, screeching, and tossed Verteira sprawling down the stone steps to fetch up against screaming Ranick. The mule twisted and plunged over the side of the mountain, and Ranick screamed louder. *"Tevarro borine,"* the Sentinel murmured, and melted back into the mountainside.

Joros straightened as sick relief flooded through him, and hurried down the steps to help Verteira. If she was dead, it would send all his hopes bursting like Odaro. She lay on her side, but she was already struggling to rise, alive and angry. "Are you all right?" Joros asked, hauling her to her feet.

"No more battered than before." She reached out and gave Ranick a sharp slap across the face, cutting his scream off abruptly.

"Then we carry on. You'll have to walk the rest of the way."

Ranick was shaking badly, and his voice even more than usual. "It killed Odaro!" he whimpered. "Killed him, *killed him*—" Cut off as Joros pressed the point of his knife against the boy's throat.

"Yes," Joros said evenly, holding Ranick's wide-eyed gaze, "the Sentinels of Raturo found Odaro unworthy, and he paid the price. You, in your infinite luck, have been spared." He pressed ever so gently forward, the knife's tip pricking into Ranick's flushed neck. "For now. I brought you here because *I* judged you worthy, judged that you had the tiniest trace of a spine." A slow twist to the knife, a drop of blood trailing down the boy's neck and into the sweat-soaked collar of his shirt. "I thought you had more courage than some wailing woman." Verteira sneered at his words, pursed her cracked lips to hawk a gob of spit at Ranick's feet. She had a sense for theatrics; she'd fit well, inside Raturo, should she make it to the end. "Was I wrong?"

Ranick's head twitched, trying to shake a negative with as little movement as possible.

"Because if I was wrong," and Joros twisted the knife back the other way, digging deeper, drawing a choking sort of whimper from the boy's throat, "I can spare you the trouble of having to climb hours more only to die at the hands of a different Sentinel. If you're as much of a coward as I'm beginning to suspect, that's the only way this will end, after all. So tell me, Ranick." He held the boy's eyes, watching the panic wash through him. "Are you a coward?"

For a moment Joros thought he would start wailing again, and tightened his grip, ready to plunge the knife home. But the boy's eyes hardened and his back straightened, the knife jerking a shallow slash through his neck. He didn't flinch. "No. I'm no coward."

Verteira spat at him again, and Joros was almost tempted to do the same. But judgment was not his to make, so he pulled the knife away, wiped its bloody tip clean on Ranick's shirt, and returned it to his belt. "Then we carry on."

"When do we sleep?" Verteira asked.

Joros laughed, and the sound of it tumbled down the

mountain like the mule. "Raturo never sleeps. Best if you don't either."

"Food, then? We haven't eaten since last night." She splayed her fingers pointedly against the bulge of her stomach.

"If you feel like searching for the mule, I'm sure you can cook yourself a fine feast."

She looked up to the mountain's peak, so far away; then down, back the way they'd come, not so terribly far when compared to the way ahead. Not too late to turn back.

Joros turned away from her and back to the steps, lifting his aching feet and setting them ever upward. He heard Ranick behind him do the same, scrabbling at the stone. And after a moment, Verteira's ragged breaths, following.

They climbed as the sun touched the outer edge of the great forest; as the sun beat down mercilessly upon them, not quite enough to burn away the chill that began to seep into their bones; as the sun disappeared once more behind the distant peak, wreathing Mount Raturo in brilliant fire. Joros stopped then, panting, hands braced on his thighs, and gazed out over the southern lands of Fiatera. The forest spread out far below, leagues and leagues of it, trees eventually giving way to the nameless plains beyond, a vast sea of sere grass that slowly faded and died and became the Eremori Desert, a lifeless, blighted wasteland.

Fiatera, the fire lands. Lovingly shaped, as the priests would tell it, by the hands of Metherra and Patharro, the Divine Mother and Almighty Father. Joros heaved in a breath of air and spat over the edge of the mountain. That, for all the Parents' hard work.

Ranick was drudging behind, of course, but not nearly so

far behind as Verteira. Joros sat down on the narrow-cut steps, back resting against the mountain's face and legs dangling into open air, and glared out over the world. The sun cast Mount Raturo's shadow farther and farther across the forest, reaching, reaching.

As the sun set, Ranick finally caught up to him, sprawling inelegantly along the steps. Joros cuffed him, growled, "Stand." Ranick dragged himself whimpering back to his feet, slumping against the mountain but standing nonetheless.

"What do you see?" Joros asked as the last traces of sunlight leaked away.

Teeth chattering, Ranick sniffled, "The w-world. It's s-so b-b-beautiful. I f-feel like a g-god."

Night closed its hand, and all was silent halfway up Mount Raturo save for Ranick's clicking teeth. The forest, plains, desert—all were shapeless, colorless, indistinguishable. A solid black, spreading out in every way to the ends of the world. The mountain cold sank through Joros, blood now creeping sluggish through his veins. His heart thumped slow, steady.

"Fecking mountain," Verteira wheezed as she sagged next to Ranick.

Joros breathed in deep, the frosty air searing his lungs. "What do you see?" he asked her.

She stood at the edge of the mountain, the edge of the world, and was silent for a long moment. "Darkness," she whispered. "Glory."

"Glory?"

She didn't look at him, just stared out over the blanket of the night. "There was a man who visited my village, years ago. He called himself a preacher of the night, just like you.

Said Metherra and Patharro were doomed, that their Twins would be unbound one day and rise to destroy the Parents' tyranny. That they would bring down Metherra's sun and cast darkness over the world. That the heart of every man would be laid bare and judged. That we'd all be made equal under the Twins' rule." She shivered, wrapping her good arm tight around herself. "They drove him out of town, of course, but I always remembered his words. This far above the world, and this dark . . . it almost feels like he was right."

A chill, deeper than the night air, ran down Joros's arm. A voice murmured in the back of his mind, *Her.* Joros didn't bother hiding his relief, lips twisting into a smile. He reached, his cold fingers wrapped around an ankle, and he *flung*.

Ranick screamed as he tumbled past Verteira, screamed as he fell through open air, screamed long after they stopped hearing him, if Joros was any judge. It didn't matter.

Verteira gaped at him, eyes wide in their blackened sockets. "One," he told her as he rose to his feet. "Only one is allowed in. You are judged worthy." His fingers tingled, blood racing into cold flesh. He pressed the other hand against the mountain, and a hidden door of solid rock cracked open to reveal the black mouth of a tunnel. Old magic, woven when gods still walked the earth.

Verteira looked up at him, hard exterior melted away, fear written plainly on her bruised face. "What is this place?"

"Don't you know yet?" He stepped into the darkness.

They walked through the blackness, a dark more solid than any night, until he could hear Verteira's short sharp breaths hissing shallow through her teeth, her feet stumbling, her hands clutching at his back. Smirking, Joros stopped to light one of the torches placed evenly along the wall. Verteira gasped in relief, shaking hands clutching at her stomach.

"Scared?" Joros asked her.

"No," she lied quickly.

"There are many who find the *idea* of a darkened world appealing, where all are blind and equal. In practice, though?" The harsh sound of his laugh echoed around them, leading the way as he continued down the tunnel, torch held high, Verteira close on his heels.

Time was meaningless inside the tunnels of Mount Raturo. He was tired, so tired. Three days, at least, they'd been walking. No food, no sleep. Verteira was flagging, bruised ankle dragging, blowing like a hard-ridden horse, black-ringed eyes standing out in her pale face. Joros couldn't afford to show weakness, couldn't afford to be weak. He was hollow, empty, legs screaming, stomach clawing at his rib cage. He always forgot how exhausting the return journey was. Forgot how many people died making it, even the ones who'd done it hundreds of times before. The bones were a good reminder. Full skeletons, curled up into helpless balls. Stretched out flat, bony hands reaching toward salvation. Torn apart, scattered, broken. Charred piles of splinters. Fools who'd been too slow to speak, too tired to think. Joros didn't intend to become just another warning; he was better than that. *"Atora beyan,"* he murmured with every footfall, weary eyes flickering at every shadow, every noise. In the Old Tongue, *safe passage*. In case the shadows moved, solidified, tried to turn him into a lingering reminder for caution. *"Atora beyan."*

"Seeker Joros," a deep voice murmured.

"Atora beyan!" Joros shouted instinctively. As a low laugh

sounded, his weary brain remembered that the Sentinels gave no warning. He shoved the torch forward and the light reflected off a doughy face. Sagging jowls, drooping cheeks, piggish little eyes sunk into rolls of flesh. "Fraro Borghen." Joros's lip curled. "A pleasure."

The fat man waved his words away, thick fingers made heavier by a king's ransom in jewelry. "The Ventallo wished me to conduct you into their presence with all haste. They have been waiting most . . . *impatiently* for you to arrive. What have you brought them this time?"

Joros stepped in front of Verteira. "I answer to the Ventallo alone."

Borghen's layers of fat shifted in what might have been a shrug. "Politeness, brother, politeness. It is a skill you could cultivate."

Joros spat at Borghen's feet and pulled Verteira behind him. He barged past the fat chancellor, who followed with a chuckle.

The tunnel grew gradually brighter, light creeping along the floor, until it opened onto an enormous cavern, ceiling lost in shadow far above, tunnel-speckled walkways spiraling lazily up and down the perimeter. The hollowed-out heart of Mount Raturo. Torches were placed at even intervals, just enough to alleviate some of the gloom. Black-robed men and women walked here and there, all far enough away to make Joros feel like the only living thing in the vast space. He shook off the feeling, and said to Verteira, "Welcome to your new home."

"We'll see about that," Borghen murmured.

It was another long walk down, though not so long as the

walk up. Raturo was smaller within than without, though one would hardly think it. Verteira looked ready to collapse with exhaustion when they finally came to the end of the spiraling path, the floor of the great cavern.

The walk across the chamber was a sobering one, as it was intended to be. They didn't speak, and the only sound was the press of their feet against the floor. Verteira walked with her head craned back and mouth hanging open, gaping up at the specks of torches flickering far above, circling into oblivion. Joros kept his eyes fixed straight ahead, on the carved archway. Three times the height of a man, it depicted the Fall of the Twins: Fratarro on the left, reaching up as he fell, pleading for mercy; Sororra on the right, falling headfirst, refusing to look back; and above, haughty and pitiless, the Parents. Joros pressed his fist to his brow as he passed beneath the arch, a gesture of obeisance—not to the sneering Parents, but to the ill-fated Twins. Borghen echoed the gesture, but Verteira's eyes were fixed on Sororra's hard, ascetic face.

Beyond the arched doorway was a circular room, claustrophobic after the huge cavern. A curved table dominated most of the room, twenty carved-stone chairs facing the entrance. Nineteen stern faces gazed out at them, nineteen men and women in robes the color of darkest night with the red sparks of Sororra's Eyes sewn over their hearts.

Borghen stepped forward and swept his low bow. "Exalted Ventallo," his voice boomed around the chamber, "I bring you Shadowseeker Joros, returned from his foray."

The old man sitting at the apex of the table waved a wrinkled hand in dismissal, and Borghen bowed his way from the room. Joros dropped to one knee, fist to his forehead, and saw

Verteira from the corner of his eye laboriously assume the same pose.

"Stand, stand," the old man called querulously. Delcerro Uniro, first among the Fallen, was not a patient man. Joros rose, and Verteira glared up at him as though she expected some sort of help. He let her struggle to her own feet. "What have you brought us this time, Seeker Joros?"

"A woman, Reverence. A woman the world has turned its back on. A woman who has nowhere else to turn." He pulled Verteira forward, was pleased at how she clutched at her stomach. "This is Verteira. She was cast out by her village, beaten, left for dead."

"And why, Verteira," Uniro asked, "is that?"

To her credit, she held her chin high and met his glare. "The midwife said I would bear twins."

A rustle of clothing shivered around the table, a few murmurs, eyes brightening.

"Twins?" Uniro asked, and a slow smile stretched his wrinkled face. "You are welcome to stay here, Verteira, for as long as you may wish. This shall be your new home." He made a discreet motion, and a servant hurried forward to touch Verteira gently on the arm. "Tomo will show you to a chamber where you may make yourself comfortable. A midwife will attend to you"—and he chuckled, the dry sound of rustling paper—"better than the previous one." Verteira looked wide-eyed at Joros as the servant led her from the chamber, an expression almost like fear. Joros turned his eyes back to the Ventallo.

"You have done well, Seeker Joros," crooned Ildra Setira, an ancient crone, seventh among the Fallen.

"*Very* well," put in Dirrakara Quindeira, fifteenth among

the Fallen. At thirty years of age, she was one of the few young members of the Vantallo, her skin glowing with health and a mane of red hair tumbling around her face.

Etengro Duero, second among the Fallen, creaked to his feet. "You may have noticed," he said, walking slowly around the table, "we are short one member." His bony tight-skinned hands rested on the back of the last chair on the left of the half circle, the empty chair.

"Poor Tisaro," wailed Saval Septeiro, seventeenth among the Fallen, then winked at Joros.

"He was old," Uniro snapped.

"We have been watching you, Joros," Dirrakara Quindeira said, dark eyes fixed intently on Joros. "*Very* closely."

"You have done great deeds," said Shuro Noviro, ninth among the Fallen, bouncing with excitement. "Brought many new initiates, spread the old stories far and wide, and now . . . *this*!"

"Twins!" Setira said wonderingly. "You have been a shadowseeker, what, three years?"

"We are pleased with all we have seen," said Valrik Trero, third among the Fallen, though he sounded less than pleased.

"*Very* pleased," Dirrakara added.

"Oh, so *very* pleased," Saval mimicked with a broad grin.

"The Ventallo need a new member," Uniro said impatiently. Joros felt his mouth going dry, his hands beginning to shake. He clasped them quickly behind his back.

"And we are thinking," said Deuro, pulling the empty chair scraping back, "that it should be you."

Uniro didn't smile, but his wasn't a face for smiling. "What say you . . . Joros Ventiro?"

"Will you join us, Joros Ventiro?" Dirrakara purred.

"A mighty responsibility," Valrik Trero cautioned, "and one not all are capable of taking."

"We think you are, though," Saval said. "Twentieth doesn't do much anyway. Mostly cleaning chamber pots and the like."

Uniro glared down the table. "Fraro Septeiro jests, of course. But we are wasting time. What is your answer, Joros?"

Joros swept a graceful genuflection—the one he'd practiced. He pressed his knuckles to his forehead, trying to suppress the grin that threatened to split his face.

It was about damned time.

"Exalted Ventallo," he said formally, "I am honored by your offer. It has always been my greatest wish to serve the Fallen, and it would be my deepest pleasure to continue serving in a higher capacity."

"That's that, then," Uniro said, pushing back his chair and rising to his feet. "Who will stand for him?"

"I will," Saval said quickly. Joros and Dirrakara Quindeira both gave him a faint glare, though he seemed oblivious to it.

"Very well," Uniro said as he hurried around the table and toward the great archway. "We're finished here," he called over his shoulder as he left.

The rest of the Ventallo shuffled out, some pausing to offer congratulations. Quindeira gave him a look that promised they would see more of each other.

Saval Septeiro fidgeted impatiently until they were alone, then puffed out his cheeks in a mighty sigh. "As you can see, meetings are all terribly boring. But bureaucracy is what it is, eh? There are other things that keep us busy. Come on, then."

There was a wooden door fitted into the wall behind Uniro's

chair, hidden in shadow. Saval pulled a dull metal key from the neck of his robe and inserted it into the lock. "Only the Ventallo are allowed in. You'll have your own key, of course. Don't let anyone else know about it, and don't *ever* let it out of your sight. They're so very serious about secrecy. That's the hallmark of the Ventallo. *Poroshen*, newest brother. *Secrecy*. Though I'm sure you know enough about that, with all your shadow scouring."

"Does the door actually open?" Joros snapped. "Or does that key just open your mouth?"

Saval laughed, a startling sound in its sincerity. Joros couldn't remember the last time he'd heard a real laugh anywhere near Mount Raturo. "I knew I was going to like you," Saval said, and swung the door open.

Joros could feel a headache building. Whoever had carved out the innards of the mountain had had an overreaching fondness for circular chambers. This one was low-ceilinged, lit by a single hanging brazier, the fire whispering in the quiet of the room. Below the brazier was an enormous, unadorned stone block, hip-high and at least as long as Joros was tall. Just visible within the brazier's circle of light were a number of doors set into the wall. Twenty of them, Joros soon saw, each carved with an unnecessarily large numeral. The closest on the right, which Septeiro went to, was numbered 20.

"Yours," Saval said.

"My, how complicated things are here."

Smirking, Saval pulled a key from the hook set above the door. It was strung onto a dirty, fraying piece of rope, and Joros wrinkled his nose as Saval offered it. "Paryn, the former Ventiro, is a . . . very austere man, shall we say? All about simplicity. He has one robe he's worn his entire life, and has never washed it once. You'll want to make sure to stand upwind of him. Come on, take this, put it on a nice chain or something. It's yours now, your most sacred possession. At least until one of those corpses decides to completely fall apart and you move up to Nodeiro. Then you get a slightly shinier key. They say Uniro's key is made of solid gold, though I doubt old bird-neck could carry it around if it was."

Grinding his teeth and doing his best to ignore the incessant babbling, Joros inserted his key into its lock. The heavy wooden door swung open on squeaking hinges to reveal a small room lit by a pale blue glow. A desk was the room's only furnishing, not even a chair to sit in. There was a book on the desk, thick and dusty and older than death, and quill and ink. And there was the source of the strange light: a tall, translucent candle burning with a steady blue flame. This flame, too, seemed to whisper, a soft hissing sound that slowly grew louder, more insistent. The throbbing in his temples deepened, not quite pain but annoyingly close.

"The ice candle," Saval said, walking to the desk. "Valrik made it when he was Quindeiro, years and years ago, but it's not ready yet for wider use. There are advantages to leading the Fallen—we get shiny things before any of the others. The light will help with all the reading you'll be doing." He patted the thick book, smirking. "This lists all the farmers and hunters and fishers who keep Raturo fed. You'll be overseeing them all, making sure they send us enough food and in a timely matter. You'll also send preachers out to remind the farmers of their duties, if they get lax. And they will—they always try to take advantage of the new Ventiro. Don't show them any bend and they'll straighten out."

Joros could feel a cold disappointment creeping through his stomach. A decade of dedication to the Fallen, and this was his reward? He put a hand to his forehead, trying to press back the growing headache. "So I'm a clerk now?" he growled.

"Oh, nothing so banal as that. You're an important cog in the machine, brother. That's all anyone is. You've gone from a tiny cog to a slightly bigger one, take heart in that. You can only grow from here. And it's only a matter of time until one of the Ventallo finds their dinner poisoned, or a knife to their neck. We're a constantly squabbling little family. *You* have nothing to worry about right now, of course, but once you move up . . . well, you learn to place your trust carefully and keep your back to the wall. Anyway, you'll rise faster than you think. Just scribble and count for a while, and know that it's all toward the greater purpose."

"The greater purpose," he mocked, but the whispering was too distracting to formulate more of an insult.

Saval grinned, a feral gleam in his eyes. One had to be crazy, Joros supposed, to be able to laugh inside Mount Raturo. "Oh, goodness me, did I forget to mention that? Oh yes, littlest brother, there is a greater purpose. The *greatest* of purposes." He flipped open the cover of the giant ledger, crooked a finger beckoningly at Joros. "It's written here, a constant reminder so you know what you're working toward. So you know what machine you're propelling, little cog." His finger tapped against the page, and Joros leaned over, squinting to read in the pale light.

The page was artfully illuminated, a colorful depiction of Sororra and Fratarro. In every other portrayal of the Twins, they were either falling, cast from the heavens by their holy Parents for the sin of wanting more to their lives than they had been given, or wrapped in chains, bound in a place deep beneath the earth. This, though, showed them free, broken chains dangling from their wrists and ankles, Sororra swallowing the Mother's sun, Fratarro holding the Parents by their throats. And in bold, flowing letters across the top of the page was written *Freeing the Bound Gods*.

Joros looked up at Saval, frowning. "You act as though this is some great revelation. They've been chanting this at me since I got to the top of Mount Raturo. The Bound Gods are a . . . a symbol—" Gods, his head hurt, and that damned whispering. "Something you can shout about to keep the sheep in line. They're not real."

"Oh littlest brother, oh tiny cog, you have *so* much to learn." Saval turned and walked from the room, back into the antechamber and straight to the stone slab; Joros remained in his new chamber, frowning down at the ice candle. It wasn't the candle flame whispering, he could see that now, but try as he might, he couldn't find the source. His attention was pulled away by a new sound, low and grating, and he turned to watch Septeiro in the antechamber.

The man had his hands pressed against the stone block, and Joros soon saw it wasn't a solid mass of stone, but a box. The top slid effortlessly aside, seemed to lower itself gently to the floor, and the whispering grew louder, fiercer, a babbling of soft, desperate voices. Saval smiled, that crazy light in his eyes again. Joros's head felt like it was about to split, and he thought, *There really is no dealing with fanatics.*

"Come, brother," Saval murmured, his voice carrying

under the whispers, eyes fixed on whatever was in the box. "Come see the glory entrusted to the Ventallo."

"This is ridiculous," Joros said, but the voices that were just beyond hearing were pulling at him, the throbbing in his skull pulsing in time with the incomprehensible words. His feet moved, and he stood next to Saval, and he looked down into the box.

Charred black and as long as the box, longer than a man, it was hard to recognize. But there was an ankle, there the smooth curve of muscle, there a toe the size of his hand. A leg. And the raw, rent flesh where it had been torn brutally away. The voices coalesced, crescendoed, broke over Joros in a single wave that commanded in a voice deep and desperate and lonely, *Find me.*

Into the silence that left Joros reeling, Saval whispered, "And thus did Fratarro shatter upon the bones of the earth . . ."

" . . . his limbs flung to the far horizons," Joros finished, the words learned so long ago, a child's parable.

"Not so far after all," Saval said, smiling that mad smile, and impossibly, Joros felt his mouth matching shape.

CHAPTER 2

A pounding at his door awoke Kerrus, and his breath formed a heavy mist before his face as he let it out in a frustrated sigh. "Can't sleep a whole night through, gods help me . . ." he muttered as he swung his scrawny legs over the edge of the bed, toes quickly finding his fur-lined boots. "Coming, coming!" he groused as the pounding continued. He pulled on his thickest coat and mittens before setting his hand to the door's cold handle, but the thing wouldn't budge. Grumbling more, he put his shoulder to it, and after a few hits that left his old bones feeling bruised, the snow that had been keeping the door shut gave up its hold. The winter air rushed in to swallow what little warmth had built up, and snow crept in to touch the toes of his boots. An eye peered at him from the darkness beyond the cracked door, and thin fingers helped Kerrus pull the door wider.

Mora, with her hair wild as the nest of a psychotic bird and her eyes almost as wild, said in her low voice, "You gotta come, Parro. There's trouble."

Kerrus sighed again. The Parents' work was never fecking done. He took a bracing breath before joining Mora out in the snow that fell so pretty and in such a deadly way. Together they shoved his door closed again; Kerrus wasn't going to let the winter get any tighter a hold inside his home.

They turned together down the line of orderly huts, and Mora clanked as she walked. She could still walk faster than Kerrus even with the iron chain stretched between her ankles. She was a runner, was Mora, foolish a thing as that was. The chains kept her to a quick walk.

"What's the trouble?" Kerrus asked her, tucking in his chin against the cold.

"Patrol come back, yeah? Brought somethin' with 'em they found in the snows." She licked at her teeth, eyes fixed ahead, body straining forward faster than her feet could bear her.

Excitement was low in Aardanel, locked in by snow and high palisades; Kerrus couldn't fault her her for relishing a little drama. "What did they find, Mora?" he pressed.

She looked at him, and her smile was made as much of fear as anything else. "A boy."

Kerrus pushed his legs to go faster, the camp courtyard coming into view and shouting voices beginning to reach his ears.

A group of wardens stood gathered in a circle of torchlight, hands jabbing, voices raised in varying degrees of fury. Chief Warden Eddin stood silent among them, the torchlight casting shadows on his practiced mask of composure. He caught Kerrus's eye and beckoned him closer, and the priest squeezed with relief into the warm press of bodies, leaving Mora to lurk behind in the shadows, too cautious of the wardens to get any nearer.

That was when he saw the boy.

No more than eight perhaps, he stood at the center of the group of wardens, thin-faced, wide-eyed, half naked. His clothes were little more than rags, and the exposed skin was, Mother help him, even dirtier than the rags themselves. The boy's hands were tied before him, fingers tinged blue, and another rope wound tightly around his ankles. He was trussed up tighter than most of the prisoners who came to Aardanel, eyes wide as he watched the dozen wardens shout over his head.

Kerrus sucked in a breath, feeling the cold burn in his lungs, and let it out in a bellow, "What in all the hells is this?"

The wardens fell silent, staring at their feet like chastised children, and Eddin nodded approval. One of the wardens finally spoke up. "My patrol found this Northman bastard wandering the snows. Brung him in for questioning."

"And I say throw the brute back to the snows he come from!" another warden shouted, not to be outspoken.

Someone muttered, "Ill luck, to have a Northman about."

Kerrus looked at the boy, and the boy looked back at him. Blue eyes like ice over a lake, and Kerrus supposed his lank hair might have been blond, given a few washings. Stocky, thick shoulders, skin tanned from the sun glaring off snow. Northern blood, no doubt of that. "He's small enough," Kerrus said. "I can't imagine he'll bring too much ill luck. Untie him."

"He's a bloody Northman!"

"He's a bloody child!" Kerrus bellowed back, and reached out to snatch the ropes from the wardens' hands. The priest knelt down in front of the little Northman and untied the ropes. "The Mother and the Father love all the world's children," he told the wardens sternly. "Northern and southern, young and old, highborn and low, everyone from the king right down to you dolts. This poor soul has clearly suffered enough to have earned the Father's protection, and I'll hear nothing more said about it. Do I make myself clear?" There was muttering and grumbling and shuffling feet, but no disagreement.

They drifted away, some with backward glares, until it was just the priest, the boy, and the chief warden. "You'll care for him, then, Parro?" Eddin asked.

Kerrus sighed. "It seems I will. I'm bound to offer succor to all the Parents' children. Or at least that's what my old master made me swear." Eddin clapped him on the shoulder, gave the boy a last, thoughtful look, and then went to join his men in the squat stone building that housed the wardens.

There was something eerie about the way the boy stared. He didn't blink nearly as often as he should. Some of the more superstitious convicts told tales of wolves in men's skin, big Northern brutes who could change into animals and tear you to shreds, beasts with no souls. It was cold out, but not quite cold enough for the sudden, violent shudder that took hold of Kerrus.

The priest looked away from those wide blue eyes, and became very aware of the other eyes staring. Prisoners and their families were crowded into doors and windows, braving the cold to gawp at their dirty visitor. Frowning, Kerrus held his hand out to the boy. "Come then, little lad. Let's get you cleaned and fed." The boy looked at the proffered hand, at Kerrus's face, back to the hand, and then stuck his own hands in his armpits. Kerrus snorted. "As you wish." He turned back toward his hut, and the boy slunk along behind him.

It took three scrubbings with the roughest sponges Mora could find, but the boy cleaned up well enough. Bundled in borrowed furs, skin shined raw, hair plaited at the back of his head—he could have passed for some young Northern lordling, if they'd had lords in the North. He had a healthy appetite, shoveling porridge into his mouth as fast as he could swallow the muck. Hard to tell if he hadn't eaten in a while, or if he just had a boy's voracious appetite. It amounted to the same thing.

Kerrus sat at his small table, waiting patiently until the boy had finished, then folded his hands and, with his most fatherly look, said, "Well, I imagine you'd best tell me what brings you to our neck of the woods."

The boy stared.

Kerrus tried it again in the Northern tongue, which he'd learned the rudiments of a few boring winters ago, and got the same response. That exhausted Kerrus's knowledge of languages. "Not much of a talker, eh? I can respect that. Man needs to know when to keep his mouth shut. You'll have to learn to trust me, though, little lad." He fished around in his pockets until he found one of the sweets he kept scattered about his hut and person. He set the sweet on the table in front of the boy. "I daresay I'm the best friend you've got now."

The boy picked up the sweet, sniffed at it, gave Kerrus a strange look, and popped it into his mouth. He sucked at the sweet, and stared, and kept quiet.

Kerrus was awoken for the second time that night, this time by a soft but persistent noise. His groggy mind thought at first it must be one of the camp dogs scratching at his door, but he remembered Fat Betho had put the last of the dogs into a stew two nights ago. No recent supplies, poor hunting, and all that. Patharro made the beasts to serve the men, and they served best here by filling hungry bellies.

And there was the scratching again.

Kerrus sat up and squinted around the dim interior of his home. The boy lay in front of a guttering fire, huddled in the nest of blankets Kerrus had made before the fireplace, sleeping soundly.

Scritch. Scriiiiiiitch.

Not sleeping after all.

"Boy?" the priest called softly. The little shoulders stiffened under a blanket, but the scratching didn't stop. Kerrus kicked off his own blankets and padded over to the boy. Propped up on his side, with one of Kerrus's small knives clutched in his hand and chips of wood scattered all about, he'd clearly been at it for a while.

It must have been a stride across, both ways, and cut deep into the floorboards. They never did do anything halfway, these Northmen. It was a huge design of gentle curves and sharp angles, intertwining lines, all made up of the same shape, repeating and overlapping. One of their runes, the world's oldest writing. *Scal*, in their ancient tongue. *Fire*.

"Aye, little lad," he murmured. "You've unraveled the mysteries of the world. This is, beyond a doubt, a fire."

The knife stuck quivering in the floor, so sudden Kerrus hadn't even seen the boy move. But there it was, at the center of the design, in the deepest-carved *scal*. The boy looked up at Kerrus with those eerie, unblinking eyes, and slowly raised his hand, pressing it to the center of his chest.

"That's you, then, is it?" Kerrus asked. He pointed from the rune to the boy, who gave a solemn nod. Kerrus sat back and chewed the inside of his cheek. "Well, Scal, I'll admit I've had some better conversations in my days, but I can't say I object to your way of speaking either. We keep talking like this, and I'll soon have the prettiest floor in all the North."

The boy was Parro Kerrus's shadow, and much like a shadow, he didn't do a lot more than follow.

It was a touch disturbing at first, being constantly and silently followed by the little lad. No matter where he went, there was Scal, a step behind Kerrus's right elbow. Boy got himself a bloody nose for it more than a few times, for Kerrus was, in his defense, not particularly used to having to watch for elbow-high followers. Scal was persistent, though. What exactly he was persisting in, Kerrus hadn't the faintest clue, but the Almighty Father loved determination, so Kerrus couldn't fault the lad for it. The boy learned to stand farther back, and the priest learned to tuck his elbows in.

The exiles were a different matter. Aardanel was, on the best of days, inhospitable. Most days the environment tended more toward hostile, and that was when it came to other Fiaterans. Even with such a small Northman, Kerrus could see murder in some of their eyes, and was grateful once again for the chains binding the most dangerous prisoners. These, the scum of the earth, sent to its farthest reaches, were not a trusting folk.

"It's a strange new home you've found for yourself, Scal," Kerrus said to the boy as he picked through his dwindling root cellar. As usual, the boy stood silent, but that had ceased to bother Kerrus. Most of the people he talked to said a good deal less by opening their mouths than the boy did by keeping his shut, and the priest was used to talking at unreceptive vessels. It came with the cassock.

"Sometimes I wonder if you Northmen don't have a better concept of justice than we civilized folk. Fight to the death, and the one who comes out alive is the one who's in the right. You've no prison camps, and I certainly can't say as that's a bad thing. But it's not a cheery life here, little lad." He glanced back over his shoulder at the boy. Food was still scarce, but Scal was already filling out some. "Can't imagine it's too cheery a life out in the snows either, though, is it? Ah, well, few of us are given the choice when it comes to hells, and for myself, I'd say living in this little hell is a good sight better than dying out in a wide-open hell, eh?"

Kerrus hoisted himself to his feet and pressed the vegetable basket into Scal's hands. The boy never offered up any help, but neither did he refuse whenever Kerrus asked him to do something. He still wasn't sure how much the boy understood; he got the same blank look even when he spoke the Northern tongue. He seemed an agreeable enough lad overall, Kerrus had decided.

The kitchen was as bustling as ever, with Mora and Fat Betho screeching at each other while a handful of children scrambled around underfoot, trying to do as told while attracting as little notice as possible. Parents help you if you caught Betho's attention when he was in one of his moods.

"Sodding whoreson," Betho growled in Kerrus's direction. There was a bloody carcass lying on one of the long tables. Looked like it might have been an elk. Fresh meat always put Betho in a good mood.

"Messenger come in earlier," Mora explained as she sorted through Kerrus's small offering of vegetables. "Eddin tol' him he ain't got supplies for us, he can walk back." Ah. Horsemeat, then.

"What'd the messenger have to say?" Kerrus asked.

Mora just shrugged. "More prisoners comin' in soon, but no supplies comin' in with 'em. Same old 'feck you' it always is."

Kerrus nodded glumly. A chunk of horsemeat apiece was as good as they would eat for a long while, until all the snow melted or until the sun fell from the sky, which was just as likely to happen. Kerrus hadn't seen grass nor good meat in the nearly two decades he'd lived in Aardanel, and he'd learned never to expect either.

Fat Betho glared, and hawked a slimy pile of spit onto the floor, narrowly missing one of the scampering boys. "Northman prick can feed his fecking self. Ain't wasting good meat on a craven little arsespittle—" He came to an abrupt stop as he tumbled off his stool, and then the kitchen was full of shouting. Betho hollering, the boys cheering, Mora screeching like a harpy. It took Kerrus a moment to realize why, and then he became very occupied with trying to drag Scal and his flailing fists off the much larger prisoner. Scal was growling and snarling, mindless animal noises that made the hairs on Kerrus's neck stand up. He was only a boy, but a strong boy at that, and seemed pretty damn determined to keep smashing his fists into Betho's face. It was all Kerrus could do to keep his arms wrapped around the squirming lad and stumble slowly back toward the door.

Blood poured out of Betho's nose as he scrambled to his feet with a bellow. There were chains between his wrists, but if anyone could figure out how to land a punch while chained up, it would be Betho. He hit Scal in the stomach with enough force to knock the air out of Kerrus as well, and priest and boy went tumbling to the floor. Through misty eyes Kerrus saw Betho pull his boot back for a kick, and then a dozen other boots filled the cramped kitchen as wardens rushed in to pin Betho down. Wheezing, Kerrus grabbed Scal by the back of his coat and started crawling for fresh cold air.

When Eddin found him, he was sitting against the outer wall of the kitchen, on top of a squirming little Northman. The two men watched as the other wardens dragged Fat Betho struggling and roaring away, likely to be thrown down in the Dark Box. Lucky for him they'd been on low rations lately; he hadn't fit last time they'd had to stick him down there, so they'd just chained him up outside the walls for a few nights. That had put the terror in him right enough, and he hadn't caused any trouble for a good long while.

Chief Warden Eddin watched Scal thrashing about underneath the priest for a while, then sighed. "I can't have him causing no trouble, Parro. I'm in enough shit with the men as it is, and I can't blame 'em. If there's a devil of a Northman tearing around the place . . ."

"He's no devil," Kerrus said firmly, and smacked the boy on the side of the head to get him to stop squirming so much. "Betho deserved a good punching. Hells, Betho deserves a good killing. He's a right bastard, and I likely would've punched him myself if he kept flapping his lips much longer."

"No, you wouldn't've."

"Aye, you're right, but I would've thought about it real hard." Kerrus shrugged, and now that Scal had settled down some, he pushed himself off the boy. He sat up, leaning back against the wall next to Kerrus. A calm shadow once again. Kerrus rested his hand on the boy's head. "He's a good lad, Eddin. I know he is. Every man in the world has the Father's fire within him, and I can't blame the lad for letting some of his out. But we've all the Mother's heart, too. The boy just needs time to settle in."

Eddin studied the boy for a good long while, and then sighed again. "Keep your eye on him hard, Parro. Anything else like this, and it's the snows for 'im."

The new prisoners arrived a few days later, and as always Kerrus took it upon himself to help them adjust to life in Aardanel. The families of the condemned were his especial concern, those wives and husbands who'd chosen to stay by their loved ones in exile. A perfect example of Metherra's gift of love, Kerrus's old master would have said, and Patharro's steadfastness. Idiocy, Kerrus called it, especially when the loyal fools brought their children with them. The camp was crawling with children, innocent children who'd likely know no other life because both their parents had bollocks for brains. They'd each be given the choice, when they reached their majority: stay in the camp and continue the life of labor their parents had chosen, or walk empty-handed out the gates, into the snows, and find whatever life or death awaited them beyond. It was a week's walk to the nearest Fiateran village, with nothing but snow in between. Most chose to work, to live the life they'd known longest, to die a death they could at least see coming.

Aardanel was no place for a child.

Kerrus watched them march in, a dozen or so skinny,

bedraggled-looking folk at the center of a company of guards. Six in chains with their heads shaved and a big bloody *X* carved into their left cheeks, convicted criminals who chose a slow death in hell rather than the speedy neck-jerking drop straight down. Four children, wide-eyed and crying, like as not to die before the week was out, all thanks to their parents' crimes.

The wardens separated prisoners from families, marching the convicts into the main hall so Eddin could tell them what was what. A few other wardens herded the sobbing families toward Kerrus, standing in the doorway of the chapel. He spread his arms wide to them, welcoming the two wives, the husband, the four children into the Parents' loving embrace. "Be welcome, child," he murmured to each in turn as they shuffled past him, into the meager warmth the chapel had to offer. After a week's cruel march through the snows, Kerrus didn't doubt they were grateful for any warmth at all. They all went to huddle round the everflame, pressing shaking hands as close as they dared. One of the wives began to pray, holding three black-haired children close. The fourth child, who stood at his father's side, edging nearer for warmth, was elbowed away.

Aardanel was no place for love.

"Well, priest?" the man asked, glaring at Kerrus. "What words of comfort have you got for us? What've you got to say t' convince us this situation's less of a feck-all than it looks?"

Kerrus shrugged. "Nothing. It is a feck-all of a situation you're in, and there's nothing I can say to make it any different. You chose to come here, knowing what this place is, and I won't tell you lies to warm your hearts. It's been called hell, and I can't imagine any of the real hells being too much different." The women were crying again, and the one had stopped her praying. There was little enough kindness left in Parro Kerrus's heart, little room for sympathy, for comfort. He'd been here too long, seen too much.

Aardanel was no place for hope.

"You'll each be assigned a duty—everyone does their part here. The wardens will give you yours, and show you to your huts. My hut is right next door here, if you need to talk, need advice, need anything. I hold prayer every eightday, but the chapel is always open. The best advice I can give you now is to keep your heads down, keep the Parents in your heart, and make the best of the choices you've made. It's scant comfort, but it's the most you're like to find here." Yes, Kerrus always took it upon himself to help the newcomers adjust to life in Aardanel. To teach them as quick as possible that it was a heartless and unforgiving life they'd put themselves in. "Now, if I may, I would like to speak to the children. You may wait for them outside, or the wardens can show you to your huts, and I will return them to you."

"Why?" the mother of the three demanded, holding them all closer. The father walked to the door without a backward glance, leaving his son huddled by the everflame.

"Children have an especially hard time adjusting to life in Aardanel. I would speak to them, put them somewhat at ease."

The childless wife snorted. "Aye, you've a real talent for that," and she followed the father out the door.

"I ask only a moment," Kerrus assured the mother, who clung still to the last familiar things in her quickly changing life. But finally she released them, handing the smallest to the oldest and heading out the door with a last, suspicious glance at the parro.

With popping joints Kerrus lowered himself onto the ground, sitting near the everflame. "My children," he said softly, looking at them each in turn, "I wish I were not speaking to you right now, for it would mean you were not here." He reached into a pocket and produced a handful of sweets. The children grabbed for them eagerly, eyes bright, as though they hadn't seen food in days. As though they hadn't seen kindness in years. He sighed. "What I said to your parents is true. This is not a pleasant home, and it will not be an easy life. You are innocents, brought here by the choices of others, and for that I am sorry. But know that Metherra still holds you close in her heart, that Patharro still shields your back. *I* will watch over you, do all that I may to see you each safe and comfortable. If you have need of anything, I beg you, ask me and I will do what I can. Aardanel is no place for children, but I would see that your lives are made as good as they can be." He handed out another sweet to each, murmured a brief prayer. "Be on your way now, children. Keep the Parents' kindness in your hearts."

The three black-haired children fled, their cheeks bulging with the sweets. The youngest was sniffling, her nose running, death a shadow on her pale cheeks. She would go to the flames, and soon, too, Kerrus thought sadly, and her delicate siblings not long after. They weren't made for the North, and Aardanel was no place for compassion.

The single boy lingered, staring at the ground, shuffling his feet, holding tight to something strung on a cord about his neck. He was young, but his face was hard, sharp, grim, a face that had seen too much bad and not near enough good. His eyes, when he lifted them to Parro Kerrus, showed the only softness, a plea that burned through him. There was a fire in his heart, one that would not be extinguished as easily as in those softer children. His hand dropped to his side, revealing the painted flamedisk around his neck, the symbol of the Parents' endless compassion.

"They say the Mother's turned her back on this place," the boy said quietly, a quavering note winding through the words. "That Patharro's closed his eyes on us. Is it true?"

That was a question Kerrus had not been asked in a long while. Most of those who came to Aardanel had given up or turned away from the Parents long since, and any seeking spiritual guidance were few and far between. "What's your name, boy?"

"Brennon."

"Well, Brennon. They say, too, that the Parents only turn away from silence. I've spoken to them every day these past forty years, lad. They'll not turn away from this place so long as I have breath left in me." He gave the boy an assessing look, and a pointed glance to the flamedisk. "Will you pray with me, child? Help me keep the Parents' attention on this sad corner of the world?"

They knelt on opposite sides of the everflame, and as Kerrus began his prayer, Scal ghosted out from the shadows and knelt between them, ever to Kerrus's right, hands folded like a practiced penitent. Brennon gave him a startled look, then snapped his eyes shut as Kerrus raised his voice sternly. "Divine Mother, Almighty Father, shapers of the earth and keepers of the flame, we ask you hear our hearts. Gentle Metherra, we offer you our fears and beg you soothe them. Stalwart Patharro, we give our hearts unto your keeping, and beg you keep the darkness at bay. Holy Parents, we give you all that we are, and ask only for your shelter, now and for always. We are the tenders of the flame, and we keep it burning in your honor. Mother preserve us, and Father shield our souls." He threw a small packet of herbs and kindling into the everflame, sending up a fragrant puff of smoke, and gave one each to Brennon and Scal. The boys, equally solemn, threw in their own packets, Brennon murmuring softly. Kerrus rested a hand on each of their shoulders, adding a silent prayer. *Keep them happy, Tender Metherra. Keep them from breaking, Loving Patharro. Let them find some joy in this cold, dark place.*

"Thank you, Parro," Brennon said quietly, rubbing smoke from his eyes.

"Any time, lad," Kerrus said, giving his shoulder a squeeze. "And remember what I said. If you need anything, even just to talk, come to me. And Scal here, too. He's a fine listener. You're not alone, Brennon." He gave the boy a gentle push toward the door. "Best get back to your parents now, lad."

At the door Brennon paused, eyes lingering on Scal, and the little Northman stared right back. It had been too long since Kerrus's childhood, and he couldn't decipher the look matched in each set of young eyes; not quite a challenge, not exactly unfriendly. Sizing each other up, perhaps. Brennon was the first to turn away, sliding out through the doorway, and Kerrus almost thought he saw a trace of a smile on the boy's face. Impossible. Aardanel was no place for a smile.

With a dozen new mouths to feed, Kerrus found himself scouring his root cellar much more often, loading up Scal's basket with stunted carrots, miniature cabbages, and shrunken onions. The saddest part was that everyone would be grateful for a nibble of any unripe sprout, and likely fall over themselves with joy for a taste of onion broth.

"Sad state of affairs, my boy," Kerrus grunted over his shoulder at Scal. "You might have waited to find your way here until spring. Not that the food would be much better, but there'd at least be more of it. Though I daresay there'll be fewer mouths to feed soon enough." The mother of three had turned up sobbing at his door early that morning, youngest child clutched in her arms, begging him to save her. He'd bundled the girl up near the everflame, said what prayers he could, but the rattle in her chest when she pulled in each laborious breath told him it wouldn't be too long.

Kerrus levered himself to his feet, turned to take the basket from Scal, and found to his great surprise that his shadow was missing. The vegetable basket rocked gently on the ground, no sign of its holder. After a few weeks of Scal's constant presence, his absence was more than a little disturbing. Kerrus quickly scooped up the basket and hurried out from behind his hut, out into the busy main thoroughfare of Aardanel. Busy being a relative term, of course. A dozen adults at most, hurrying here or there on an errand; perhaps twenty children scattered along the street, alone or in small groups, doing their own little jobs. There was a small knot of children, staring down at something on the ground; suspicious, Kerrus sidled over to the group.

Two boys were flopping around on the ground, grappling clumsily at each other, fists and feet flailing. Brennon's face swam up out of a tangle of elbows, and then, to Kerrus's horror, a shock of blond hair butted into Brennon's nose. Brennon fell away snorting and coughing blood, and Scal rolled onto his knees; Kerrus drew in a deep breath, but before he could loose his bellow, Brennon began to laugh. "Good hit!" he said, grinning with bloody teeth, and pounced at Scal. And they grappled again, grinning and snarling at the same time, both soon smeared with blood from Brennon's bleeding nose. A brief glimpse of Scal showed the little Northman's solemn face split into a wide grin.

Kerrus stood frowning down at the fighting, smiling boys, and it took him a moment to fit the pieces together. Not fighting. *Playing*. Playing like normal children. Playing, and smiling, and *laughing*.

It sent an unexpected stab of warmth through Kerrus's heart. He couldn't remember the last time he'd seen children at play in Aardanel. The children gathered around were smiling, too, quietly cheering one or the other. Children who had been in Aardanel awhile, children who he would have guessed had long since forgotten what play was, forgotten how to smile.

Quietly, he slipped away from the group, leaving them to their play. He went straight to his chapel and spent an hour kneeling before the everflame, thanking the Parents from the depths of his heart. *Let them find some joy*, he'd asked of the Parents. Never had they answered his prayers so quickly, or so thoroughly.

Scal still spent much of his time at Kerrus's elbow, though whenever the boy ghosted silently away, Kerrus knew he had only to follow the sound of children's laughter and he would find Scal and Brennon, and as many other children as had flocked around them that particular day. They were fast friends, and though he couldn't for the life of him understand why, Kerrus couldn't say he disapproved of it. Brennon was a good boy. What's more, he proved to be a very devout boy, spending much of his time in the chapel or Kerrus's hut. As a result, Scal became intensely pious himself, and Kerrus spent more time preaching than he had in the last decade.

Neither boy could read—or, if Scal could, he certainly wasn't telling—so Kerrus recited all the old stories, and answered all of Brennon's unending questions. Scal sat there, seeming to absorb it all, eyes rapt.

Kerrus was in the middle of his most chilling rendition of the Fall of the Twins when a question brought him sputtering to a halt: "Why?" It wasn't the question itself that took him so by surprise, for he'd answered it a hundred times before; it was the voice that asked the question, a soft, rough voice that had, without a doubt, come from Scal's mouth.

Kerrus saw that Brennon was gaping at the little North-man, realized he was gaping, too, and quickly snapped his hanging jaw shut. "Why?" Kerrus repeated, certain he'd imagined it.

Scal's mouth opened, and there was that raspy voice again, in passable Fiateran. "Why did Mother throw her children down?"

It took Kerrus a moment to get his bearings, and once he did, he stammered like a tongue-tied parro just out of appren-ticeship. "Well, you see . . . they were, ah, they didn't like the way the Twins—the Parents! The Twins didn't like how the Parents were, ah, running things. How they treated people. The Twins were . . . jealous! Yes, they wanted to have the same power as the Parents. And they tried to steal it . . ." Kerrus's voice carried on in the familiar recitation, but behind the words his mind was whirling. Two months of living elbow to forehead with the boy, and this the first he'd spoken! "Enough for tonight," he finished lamely, and Brennon wandered from the hut looking as dazed as Kerrus felt.

Scal was poking at the hearthfire, and Kerrus's knees popped as he crouched down next to the boy. The silence settled over them, but different now that they both had a voice. Kerrus finally cleared his throat, needing to say something, but not sure what. "So." Well, that was a start. "You've finally found your voice, eh?" Scal shrugged, still staring into the fire. "Or did I fall asleep in the middle of a story again?" Scal flashed him a smile—a more and more frequent sight since Brennon had been around. A bashful smile, an apologetic smile. "Eh? Was I just dreaming my silent little lad spoke to me?"

"No." So quiet it was almost swallowed up by the crackling of the flames. "I talked."

"I'm glad, Scal," Kerrus said, and for some foolish reason his throat went tight, pressure building behind his eyes. Stupid old man, near ready to weep like a woman.

"I too."

802 Years after the Fall

Even the best dog will bite if given loose rope.

—Northern Proverb

CHAPTER 3

Aro was crying again. Rora put her arms round him, trying to hush him before any of the biggers heard. Showing any weakness in the Canals was like asking for a shiv to the stomach. She hugged him close, but it only made Aro cry harder. "I miss Kala," he whimpered. It was dark, but Rora didn't need to see: she could hear the biggers rustling, grumbling. She clapped her hand over Aro's mouth, making him quiet. She could feel his scared breath wheezing over the back of her hand, but she didn't let him go until she heard Twist snoring. Twist was the mother for the Blackhands pack, and he hated most of the pups he watched over, but it seemed like he hated Rora and her brother extra just 'cause they were new to the pack and Aro cried too much. Rora didn't want to give Twist any more reason to hate them.

Aro hiccuped and nuzzled into her shoulder, finally quiet, maybe even sleeping already. It was good, if he could get some sleep. Rora couldn't, not with the water lapping, splashing up through the warped boards. She missed Kala, too, mostly for her house's solid floor. If she'd had anything to give, she would've handed it over for a packed-dirt floor to sleep on, far away from the Canals.

When the sky started to get light, she shook Aro awake and they crept to the edge of the raft, trying not to rock it too much. Aro jumped first, falling on his hands and knees on the canal's muddy bank. Rora landed next to him and hauled him up, sneaking off before any of the pack woke up and saw them.

They stopped a ways away, where there weren't any rafts nearby, and crouched down in the mud. "I don't want to," Aro complained, but Rora ignored him, shoving her hands into the mud and running handfuls of the goop through Aro's hair. Kala had cut it short, so the mud dried fast, leaving his hair sticking up in near-black spikes. It made him smell awful, but it was the only way to stay safe. She smudged more mud on his face, then pulled him to the canal, both of them peering into the murky water.

It was still like seeing two of herself. Even with her hair long, and Aro's short and different-colored, their faces were the same. The mud wasn't that great of a disguise. It just made him look like a dirtier version of Rora. But it was the best she could do. She dunked her head into the water, scrubbing the dirt from her own face and hair with fingertips that weren't much cleaner. Not that the water was any cleaner'n she was either, but this was as clean as she was going to get with Kala gone.

They walked along the edges of the canal, Aro holding to the back of Rora's shirt. With sunlight poking down, there were more Scum out and about now, and they all avoided each other like snarling cats. Rora stayed pressed up hard against the wall, staring at anyone who went by, her eyes daring them to attack two pups, while inside she prayed they wouldn't. You had to be tough, in the Canals, or at least look tough. It was the only way.

"Where're we going today, Rora?" Aro asked, rubbing the back of one filthy hand at his running nose.

"Sparrow," she corrected automatically; he always forgot to use the new name. "To the market. It's fiveday, so there should be plenty of people round. You wanna beg today?"

"You always get to do the stealing, it's not fair!"

"You're no good at it."

"Only 'cause you don't let me try."

"You're begging," Rora said firmly.

The Canals had been built a long time ago to bring in water from Lake Baridi, but they hadn't been built right. Over the years, the water'd worn down the bottom of the canal, eating away the dirt where the canal makers hadn't put down stone, and even sneaking under stone in time, the water digging down deeper than it should've. The water was down too low for any of the topsiders to know what to do with it, so they'd just decided to ignore all the waterways winding through Mercetta. They'd left the canals to the Scum, who scraped out a living on and around the water. The Scum made paths alongside the new canal bottom with wood planks and pried-up brick and anything sturdier than mud; they'd made the place as livable as they could.

The canal walls were mostly mud now, with brick starting where the canal bottom had originally been, higher up than Rora was tall. She boosted Aro up, and the boy hauled himself onto the ridge of bricks that the water'd left untouched. She had to jump to do it, but she got her fingers hooked over the edge and planted her feet against the soft mud wall, shimmying up to join her brother.

There were fewer Scum up on the high paths, since they were closer to topside, but every once in a while they had to sidestep around one of the other Scum, Rora growling curses and shoving Aro ahead of her. They finally got to the West Bridge and found the ladder—little more than holes where bricks had been pried out of the wall. Rora went up first, telling Aro to hang back in case there was any trouble.

It was a long way up. The people of Mercetta didn't like having to look at their trash, and the Scum were definitely trash. "Out of sight," Kala used to say, "out of mind." A lot of the bricks were crumbling, too, making Rora's bare feet slip, almost making her scared she was about to fall a few times. As she got closer to the top of the ladder, in the shadow of the West Bridge, she started to hear talking, whispers. There were people, at least a handful of 'em judging by the voices, waiting for her at the top.

"—waiting a hell of a long time . . ."

"*Shh!*"

"Gotta be close."

"Mace'll shit if we don' bring 'im more copper."

"We'll get more, I'm tellin' ya."

"*Shhhh!*"

There were biggers in the packs, too old to be pups but they hadn't been given any jobs yet, so they had nothing to do but bully pups. They were big, sure, but usually pretty slow and stupid—otherwise they would've got a job to do already. All you had to do was be a little faster and a little smarter, and biggers weren't any kind of problem. Rora tipped her head back and leaned as far away from the wall as she dared, fingers and toes curled tight around the bricks. "Your ambush needs practice," she called up.

There was rustling and hushing; one of them murmured, "Feck's an ambush?" and then a head poked out over the top of the wall. A bigger, sure enough, and he was scraggly-looking but with a thick enough face that he probably ate pretty well. Dirty, but no dirtier'n anyone living in the Canals; he might even have seen a real bath in the last year. Still Scum, though, and you could never trust a bigger.

"Hullo, girl," he called down, trying to sound friendly. "Need some help getting up?"

"That's so nice of you," she said, smiling sweetly. "But I think I'm okay."

The bigger grinned down at her. He was probably trying to look nice, but it only made him look like an animal about to attack. "No, no, let me help." He stretched an arm down toward her, fingers wriggling. She was just out of reach. "Gimme your hand, I'll pull you up."

Rora let go of the bricks with one hand and reached up toward him. When their hands were just about a finger apart, she curled her hand into a fist and slammed it into his palm, crushing it against the wall. Not enough force behind it to do any real damage, but enough to make him yelp and pull his hand back up real quick. He disappeared from view and she heard swearing from above, the others trying to figure out what'd happened. She took their moment of distraction to scramble up the last stretch of the ladder and jump onto solid ground. There were seven of 'em, all biggers, all gathered round the one who'd been talking to her. He saw her around the shoulder of one of his friends, and there was murder in his eyes.

Rora took off running. All she had to do was lead 'em off long enough for Aro to get up topside, then she'd lose the biggers and meet him at their normal spot. She'd done it more times than she could count, and it would've worked again if she hadn't got her foot tangled in something. She went sprawling, scraping her hands, forehead banging against stone, and they caught up to her before she could scramble away.

One of them stomped on her arm, pinning her in place, and another kicked her in the stomach. Groaning in pain, she curled herself into a ball as the blows rained down, one arm still stretched out with the bigger grinding his foot down. She could feel the bones in her arm shifting, twisting, *please, gods, don't break, don't break* . . . A foot, a *boot*—what Scum could afford boots?—slammed into the side of her head, rattling her teeth, making spots of light dance behind her squeezed-shut eyes. She tasted blood, cried out as a sharp *snap* echoed through her skull, hot fire shooting down her arm as the bigger twisted his foot, splinters of bone dancing under her skin.

"Stop it!"

The beating faltered, stopped. One of the biggers laughed. "Run back t' your momma's tit, brat."

"Leave her alone!"

Rora groaned. There was no mistaking that voice, even high-pitched and full of fear. "Don't," she tried to tell him, but the word came out as a cough, blood splattering from her lips, ribs aching with every movement.

There was more laughter, and the boot tramped down on her arm again. She screamed, and then it was like the world was screaming around her, more voices and terror and pain, and a sound like the world ripping in half. Something heavy fell across her, crushing her against the ground. She whimpered, felt tears sneaking through her eyelids. There was something else running down her cheek, too, running warm and fast and filling her mouth with the taste of iron.

She could hear sobbing, close by. Her? No, not Rora, but her voice doubled, projected back at her. "I'm so sorry, so sorry, so sorry . . ." The weight lifted off her, and she drew in a shaking breath, not caring that all her ribs bent and twisted and stabbed. She forced her eyes open, though they tried to stick together, red bubbles dancing at the edges of her vision. Aro's face loomed before her, face streaked with mud and blood, two clean trails carved down his cheeks as he sobbed. She tried to reach out, to comfort him, tell him everything would be okay, but nothing worked. All she could do was make a sharp wheezing noise, and that only made him cry all the harder. "Rora, Rora, I'm so sorry." He reached for her, and the world tilted and dropped away in a burning crash.

It was night, and she was in Kala's house again. Too quiet; why wasn't Kala in the kitchen, singing as she made food? A whimper, a sob, and she followed it to Aro, sitting in a puddle of blood, crying, "She knew, she knew, she knew." And Kala lay on the floor, twisted and broken, but it wasn't quite Kala; she had the face of the mother Rora'd never known, and she frowned. "Take better care of your brother."

"I don't know how!" Rora tried to tell her, but Kala turned her back and the floor vanished and Rora fell through the sky, Aro falling with her, crying, crying.

"How could you let this happen?" Kala yelled after her.

"I'm sorry!" she said, and Aro echoed her, "So sorry, so sorry."

The earth was rushing up at them, a gaping black pit. "Rora, help me!" Aro yelled, but she couldn't reach him, he was too far away, and the world swallowed her up, filling her ears and mouth and nose, twisting her bones, crushing her into pieces, and she could hear Aro crying but she couldn't find him. "Help me, Rora, help me. *Find me.*"

"Please wake up." A hand rubbed gently at her shoulder. "I promise I'll be good. Just please wake up." Rora groaned as she opened her eyes, and she heard a choked sound of surprise. "Rora, thank the gods!" Fingers squeezed around her own hand, and her eyes slowly fixed on Aro, bent over her, eyes glowing bright.

"What—" Her voice came out an ugly rasp as it clawed its way up from her bruised chest to her cracked lips.

"You're safe, Rora," he said, and there was pride in his voice. "I'm keeping you safe. But don't move," he added quickly as she tried to sit up and fell back gasping. "You've been sleeping a real long time, and you're still hurt. I . . . I did what I could."

It left a sour taste in Rora's mouth, when she remembered. The beating, and . . . the thing that'd happened after. No wonder she hurt everywhere. It'd been stupid, beyond stupid . . . "Are you okay?" she croaked.

"I'm okay." Aro lifted a battered tin cup to her lips, and warm ale trickled down her throat. It was the sweetest drink she'd ever had. "I—I'm sorry about the biggers," he said, tears starting to prick in his eyes, and her ribs twinged in remembrance. "I just saw them hurting you, and I didn't know what else to do . . ."

For a moment she saw blood, spattered everywhere, dripping onto her face. She blinked the memory away. "It's okay, Aro. You . . . you kept me safe. We do what we have to."

The fog was clearing from her head, little by little, and she started to take stock. They were in an alley, that much was clear, sandwiched between two different piles of trash. It smelled awful, but not near as bad as anywhere in the Canals smelled, and that got her worried. They weren't in the Canals, and the Canals were about the only place Scum could hope to be safe. "Aro, where are we?"

He beamed as he looked down at her, proud of himself. "Topside. Off the West Market, far away from the . . . the bridge. Far enough from the market, too, no one really comes by here. Did I do good, Rora?"

"Yeah, little bird," she said, trying to smile even though her stomach was clenching up with fear. "You did real good." His smile made her heart hurt.

"I been stealing some, too. I told you I could do it! I just need to practice some, and no one's caught me yet. I got some food, and some bandages . . ." His brow furrowed, and he frowned down at her arm. She frowned at it, too, where it lay throbbing on the ground, wrapped up in bandages dirtier than Aro. Even bulky-looking as it was, she could tell it wasn't shaped right. She choked back bile and looked away, staring up at the sky, willing her stomach to settle down. "I didn't know what to do with it. I'm sorry, Rora." And then he was crying, and she held her good arm out to him. He curled up tight against her side, wrapping his arms carefully around her, crying into her bruised shoulder, shaking against her aching ribs.

"We'll be okay," she said against his hair, tasting mud, the maybe-lie tasting worse than mud. "We'll be okay."

Time went away for a while, leaving Rora lost in the middle of it. She slept restlessly and woke up in a cold sweat, sometimes during the day, sometimes at night. Aro was there most of the time, but not always. The times he wasn't, she lay awake shaking and sweating and—much as she hated to—crying as her mind thought up all the awful things that could've happened to him, all because she couldn't take care of him. When he finally showed back up, she always clung to him, blabbering like an idiot, and she could see the worry in his eyes.

He took the bandages off her arm one day and she puked at the sight of it, not that she had much in her stomach to puke up. The lower part of her arm was all bruised, black and green and ugly, and it looked flat almost, definitely more flat than it should've been. It was bent, too, just enough that you could tell it wasn't straight. She couldn't look away, even though it made her stomach roll. It was a sick sort of pull, and on an impulse she tried to lift the arm up.

When she woke up back up, Aro'd wrapped new cloth around her arm, even tied a stick to the side. That was good thinking. It made it look straighter, at least. The whole alley smelled like sour puke. Aro hauled her up, putting her good arm around his shoulder, and dragged her a little ways down the alley, burrowing in between two different trash piles. They didn't talk about her arm, and Aro didn't change the bandages anymore, at least not while she was awake.

She slept a lot more. Even when she was awake, sometimes it still felt like she was dreaming. Aro cried a lot more, but she couldn't even do anything to stop that, couldn't get her mouth to say the words crawling around inside her head. It made her want to cry, too, but it was just easier to close her eyes.

Aro's face swam up out of a dream and said, "I'm going to find help." She tried to tell him, beg him, to stay with her, but he was gone, and the blackness pulled her back down.

She floated for a while. She and Aro used to talk about becoming birds, but if flying hurt this much, she didn't want to be a bird. She floated, and cried for the ground. She could hear people talking far below, thought she even heard Aro, but none of them would help her. Then the bigger was stomping on her arm again, and she plummeted screaming from the sky.

Sunlight danced on her face. She could feel it flickering over her eyelids, softly warming her skin. It brought a smile to her lips, and she could almost taste the sun, too. Kala would start banging on the pots soon to wake her up, so she enjoyed the little moment of peace while she could.

"Rora!"

Aro stood above her grinning, scrubbed clean, face glowing and hair shining like polished bronze. He looked like a boy-god, without a care in the world; Rora would have to remember to thank Kala for the hundredth time. Aro threw his arms around her, and she hugged him back—and froze as pain shot up her right arm. As she gaped down at her black-speckled arm sandwiched between two slabs of wood, the illusion broke.

The biggers, and the beating. Aro screaming, blood

everywhere, her whole body hurting. A whispered, "I'm going to find help." Wasting away slowly in an alleyway that smelled like vomit.

And now she was lying in a bed—a *real* bed, with soft blankets and a mattress that curled around her body—in some room, probably as far as you could get from a pukey alley. It was about the fanciest place she'd ever been in, and there wasn't even that much stuff. The bed, a big chair Aro'd been sitting in, a desk, two windows, trinkets and things scattered all around. Her first instinct was to get up and grab as much as she could fit in her pockets, but maybe Aro had learned enough to already do that.

"Where are we?" she asked. Her voice was scratchy, but it didn't feel too bad. *She* didn't feel too bad, almost normal except for the arm.

Aro grinned and said, "I *told* you I'd find help! He saved us, Rora, he even got your arm fixed! He says we'll be safe now, forever. Did I do good, Rora?"

"Who's 'he'?"

His face fell a little, when she didn't tell him he'd done good, but he brightened right back up. "I'll go get him! He'll be so happy you're awake, he's been real worried." Before she could tell him to wait, ask him more questions, he was out the door.

Rora sank back into the mattress, trying to plan, but she didn't even know what to plan for. Aro was too trusting, she knew that; if it wasn't for her, he'd probably've been lured into working in a dozen whorehouses by now. But she hoped, for both their sakes, that this time he'd done good.

The door opened and Aro bounced back in, followed by a tall man wearing all black. He didn't look at all happy to see that she was awake, but he had the kind of face that she didn't think ever looked happy. He was pretty old, older'n most Scum got to be, though that wasn't saying much. Some gray in his black hair and beard, wrinkles on his face, enough to know he'd seen a good deal of life.

"Welcome back to the land of the living," he said, his voice a deep rumble.

"Thanks," she said, instantly cautious, just like she was every time she met someone new. Aro might trust everyone, but Rora trusted no one. "Who're you?"

The man bowed from the waist, but his eyes never left hers. "I am Nadaro Madri, humble merchant. Your brother asked for my help, and I am honor bound to help those in need. You, dear girl, were in dire need."

"So what d'you want?" No one, especially not grown-ups, ever did anything nice without wanting something in return.

Aro's face looked pained. "Rora . . ."

Nadaro smiled, but it didn't go to his eyes. They stayed a flat gray, unblinking. "You're a smart girl, Rora. Nothing is ever free. It's a valuable lesson, and I'm pleased you've learned it early. Everything has a price."

"So what d'you want?" she asked again.

"I am a lonely man. I have only servants to keep me company in such a big house—it is a big house, isn't it, little Aro?"

The boy nodded eagerly. "It's *huge*!"

Still smiling that dead smile, Nadaro rested a hand on Aro's shoulder. "I wish for company. That is all. Stay here while you continue to heal, dear girl. You two, I think, have not had an easy life. I would make it somewhat easier."

There were truths, and there were lies, and Rora could tell

them apart pretty well. But there was a space in between a truth and a lie, a space where the words weren't either. Rora could tell when it was a half-truth, too, and those were even more dangerous than a lie.

Aro was near bouncing with excitement. "It's perfect here, Rora! It's so nice, so much better than Kala's. Can we stay, Rora? Can we?"

She looked from her brother back to Nadaro, still staring with his flat eyes. Almost like it was a challenge. "Yeah, Aro," she said, even though the words tasted like mud and left a heavy feeling in her stomach. "We'll stay."

CHAPTER 4

Ankle-deep in the river, arms flung wide as he faced the mob, Keiro begged yet again, "Please, don't do this." Another rotten fruit flew through the air, hitting his knee this time, bursting with a sick squelch and dripping red into the water. "They've done nothing, they're innocent." There was uproar at that, shouted denial. A rock—small but still a rock, hard and unyielding as Keiro prayed he could be—hit his shoulder and spun him half around in a stumbling step. "Just give them to me, please!" he cried as the hands reached for him. They dragged him stumbling and sobbing from the river, the same three men who'd spent the days since his arrival watching and glaring and hefting their cudgels. They pulled him away to let the others surge forward, the mob and their sacrifice.

Two of the big men held Keiro's arms, keeping him from collapsing or running, and the third grabbed a handful of his hair, yanking his head up so he would be sure to see it all. Aya stood there, not far away, in her blue gown, the same color as the sky, streaked with terrible red. She spat toward him, said clearly, coldly, over the chanting and the roaring and the desperate wailing, "This is your fault. You done this." Venna, who had sat with him in the night and heard his words and said she would follow him, wouldn't look at him now. She stood with the rest of the crowd, her face a mask.

"Please, no!" Keiro begged, his heart crumbling as the midwives stepped forward, into the river, carrying their burdens like so much trash. "I'll take them, you'll never see them again. Please!"

The oldest of the midwives, the heartless one, held the boy upside down by one leg, the babe's face as red as the swollen fruit that had splattered against Keiro's knee, his fragile body shaking with the force of his wails and his fear. The youngest midwife held the girl as far away from herself as she could, her face rigidly composed as the tiny fists clutched at air, at anything, at nothing.

The midwives knelt, and the mob roared, and Keiro whispered, "Fratarro forgive me."

And the babes' wailing stopped, cut forever from the world, as the midwives plunged them beneath the water.

A jagged cry of grief tore loose from Keiro's throat, swallowed by the cheers of the mob. Aya watched with stony eyes as they drowned her newborn twins. Keiro, a stranger in this place, was the only one who cried for the innocent ones, the only one who could cry.

After the midwives had risen and walked away, leaving their burdens floating pitifully in the shallow water, the three big men laid into him with their fists and their clubs. Keiro curled into a ball on the unforgiving ground, and through the merciless rain he prayed to his gods, not for salvation or for succor or for love, but for forgiveness, and for them to do what they could for their poor, lost avatars.

It was later, much later, after the sun had gone down and the stars had given their sultry light to the world, after the two bright points of Sororra's Eyes had cast their red gaze out over the Parents' earth and driven all god-fearing folk inside, that Keiro pushed himself slowly to his hands and knees. He crawled achingly to the water's edge, where the two bone-white mounds still floated, caught up by the reeds and weeds. He had tears for them yet, enough tears to last him to the end of his days, all the tears they would never shed. With an aching tenderness he pulled them from the river, from the green ropes that had caught them, and held them close, cradled them to his chest as he whispered the words of love they had never had the chance to hear in their unbearably short lives.

"None of it's true, is it?"

The words were soft, the voice familiar. They had sat whispering together under the stars, and her quiet voice had swelled with hope. That note of hope was gone, now. Gone as quick as a breath cut off.

"It is, Venna," Keiro said over his shoulder. He didn't want to let himself look away from the poor pale babes, whose deaths he would carry with him always, but he made himself look up at her. She stood in the shadow of a tree, barely visible, where none of the townsfolk would see her easily should they come looking. "It's all more true now than ever."

"How?"

She was so young, so new to the world that she didn't yet see the way of things. She had probably never been more than ten miles outside her small village in her whole life. Knowing so little, but so eager to learn. Her eyes had gone wide with all the things she'd never known, and endless questions had poured out of her as she and Keiro had spoken beneath the stars. She'd heard all the answers he'd given to her questions, heard them and taken them into her heart, and begun to believe. Instead of giving her another answer, now, he asked her a question: "What kind of loving god would call for the death of two innocent babes?"

She didn't answer, not right away. "The priests would say they're not innocent. That they've the taint of the Twins. Born for evil."

"The priests would say that," Keiro agreed tiredly. "What would *you* say, Venna? Did these children deserve the death they were given?"

"No one *deserves* death . . ."

"Some people do. People who commit such wrongs in the world that they cannot be allowed to walk its surface."

"Like people who kill babies?"

A soft sigh escaped Keiro. Truly, he was too tired for this, too tired to guide this poor girl when he still had the babes to tend to. He was a Preacher of the Long Night, sworn in ice and blood, but he was so very tired.

"I don't know how you can do it," Venna said finally, and Keiro could hear the tears behind the words. He hadn't been the only one crying that night, though the thought hurt more than it comforted. He wanted to reach out to her, to offer some comfort, but his arms were full of the babes.

"It's not easy. But I know the world can be made better. That people can be better than this." She wouldn't look at him, her hands twining in her skirt. "I can bear this because I know, one day, it will not be this way."

"Once the Twins are freed."

"Yes, Venna. They will set the world to rights, and no more children will die needlessly."

She slipped into her silence again, until finally she looked up to meet his eyes. They had gone hard, older than her fifteen years. "They say Aya would've had just one babe if it wasn't for you," she said, her voice raw. "They say you brought poison here. That it's your fault this happened."

"That's not true, Venna." He couldn't bear the accusation in her eyes, and so he looked back down to his arms. "These children were meant for this world, regardless of me or you or Aya or any gods. They were given life, same as the rest of us. And that gift was stolen from them."

It was quiet for a time, waves lapping gently at the shore, wind flicking leaves lightly against each other. A breeze ruffled the baby girl's hair, plastered to her brow in sticky curls. Keiro shifted the babes awkwardly in his arms so that he could brush the girl's hair back from her pale, sad face, so the starlight could see her as she was. It was part honor, part recrimination. This, all of this, was a thing that should not have been.

"Abomination," Venna said, just loud enough for Keiro to hear, and her steps moved away from him forever.

Three lost this day. The number grew so quickly, far faster than the number of those he had saved.

Sororra's Eyes watched him as he got slowly, painfully to his feet, cradling the cold, limp bodies in one arm. He found his walking stick at the edge of the river, where he'd dropped it chasing the mob. He carried the twins upriver, away from the town and into the shelter of the trees. Turning from the water, away from that which had taken them too early to the gods, Keiro walked deeper into the forest, not knowing where the heartache ended and the physical pain began. He walked until he stumbled and fell, walking stick slipping from his fingers, catching himself against the ground with one arm and keeping the other tightly about the babes. Above, Sororra's Eyes watched still, dim and distant through the forest canopy. It was a good spot, as good a spot as he could give them. Gently, so gently, he laid them down on the ground, and he began to dig.

With his hands bruised and his body weak, it was slow going, but it was the least he could do for them. The last he could do for them. The ground didn't give way easily, and his nails shattered against the dirt, his hands scraped raw and bloody. Sororra's Eyes watched him work, and as the shallow hole grew slowly deeper, he almost heard a voice, as if on the edge of consciousness, the edge of reality. Just a breath of sound, not even a whisper, nothing so substantial as that. But as his bloody hands scraped away the earth, he heard it sigh, *Find me,* and when he glanced over at the poor dead babes, he noticed for the first time that the boy's eyes were open and staring sightlessly into the night sky.

Keiro laid them to rest in that small open space beneath the sky, under the watch of Sororra's Eyes. He cried for them again as he scooped the dirt over their pale flesh, and he stayed kneeling next to that saddest little grave until the stars and the Eyes faded from the sky and the sun touched his cheek. Only then did he move again, pulling his cowl up to hide his face from the sun that had watched the babes die and done nothing. He rose, and could not bring himself to say farewell to the babes he hadn't saved. "I'm sorry," he told them instead, and would tell them until the end of his days. With his back to the sun, he began to walk. And he left them, the poor babes he had never and would never know, alone as they could always only ever be.

CHAPTER 5

It must have been cold. Scal could see the wardens' breath frosting in the air. Thousands of little crystals forming and dancing and disappearing. They were shivering, the twenty wardens. Chattering teeth loud in the still air. Gloved hands scraping against rough coats as they chafed arms. Four fires, and the wardens huddled as close as they could without burning their boot tips. Scal had told them they should not build fires, though they had not listened to him. For them, fire was life in the cold. It could be death, too. They knew it. They would chance that, for the warmth.

Scal was thirteen, nearly a man, and he sat alone. A distance from the fires, the warmth a faint caress against his skin. He did not need the heat. Parro Kerrus said it was the Father's fire that kept him warm. The wardens said he was a demon in man's skin. Brennon would always scoff and say, "You're North-born. Of course you can handle the cold."

Scal wished Brennon were here now. Brennon had a way of making the mood light, and it was lonely on these patrols. Lero was friendly during the day, when chance put Scal and the light-footed scout together. Once they made camp and the others were around, he never as much as looked at Scal. Joined the others in their disdain. Athasar spoke to Scal most, after Lero. Talking was the only way to give orders. To the wardens, all of them, it was easiest to simply act as though he did not exist. Scal had learned long ago to not bring attention to himself. Had learned to live with solitude. The wardens had stopped actively hating him, though it had taken months. They had not wanted to bring a Northman on their patrols. The group of scouts was meant to find Northmen, keep them from getting too near to Aardanel. Kill Northmen, if they could.

Chief Warden Eddin's trust had made Scal glow with pride. With the joy of being useful, of helping and learning. It had lasted only a few moments, until Athasar had begun shouting. He had heard them arguing long into the night, though he had hidden in the chapel. Prayed to the Parents, again and again. Until the words had grown blurred in his head. Until he did not even know what he prayed for. Even after living side by side with Scal for six years, the wardens still expected him to turn wild. Eddin and Parro Kerrus were all that kept them from throwing Scal to the snows. Here he was anyway, in the snows. Sitting in the deeps of the Northern Wastes. Kerrus would have laughed and said the Father had a healthy sense of humor.

Brennon had joined him in the chapel as the sun began to poke at the windows. Prayed for a time, from the other side of the everflame. "You'll do fine," he had finally said. Eyes willing it to be the truth. "I'm sure you'll learn plenty, so that's good. It's only another year until I reach my majority." He had flashed a smile then. It was harder to stop Brennon smiling than it was to stop Fat Betho cursing. "Then we can face the snows together and get out of this place, hey? There's gotta be somewhere your piss doesn't freeze on the way out."

Brennon had been right; there was much to learn from the wardens. They did not teach Scal much of it, not willingly. He watched, though. Watched and learned, so that when Brennon was old enough to be given the choice to leave Aardanel, Scal could keep them alive through the cold journey south. So they might find a better place, a better life. A free life.

"What's that?" Monarro said, voice rising high with sudden fear. He had the sharpest ears in the patrol. The camp fell silent in a hurried hush.

Scal strained his own ears. Only the wind swirling through the trees. The fires biting at the cold air.

Thump.

The wardens, almost as one, drew in a sharp breath and held it. Hands inched toward swords, bows, knives. The wind slowed. As if it, too, strained to hear what sounds the night held.

Thump.

They scrambled to their feet in a rattle of weapons and chain mail, hissing for quiet. Scal rose slowly, quietly. Hands clenching and unclenching at his sides. That had been one of Athasar's terms. That Scal be allowed no weapon. As if one boy could kill twenty wardens with a knife. As if he knew what to do with a knife. He had never felt the absence of a weapon until now.

Thump.

Some of them were looking at him. Eyes wild with suspicion. Forcing his hands to still, Scal looked to Monarro. The warden's head was swiveling slowly, eyes tight shut. Scal could almost see his ears straining to pick up sound. Athasar, stood near Monarro with his greatsword clutched in one meaty fist, motioned the others to silence.

Thump.

Monarro's hand shot up, one gloved finger pointing. Without a moment of hesitation Athasar set off in that direction, the others ghosting after him. Passing close by, Lero hissed at Scal, "Stick near me." Scal did not need to be told twice.

Their feet crunched on the hard snow, making stealth useless. They might have done as well charging forward, screaming battle cries. But they snuck. Moving forward slowly. Orderly. The light from the fires faded too quickly, leaving only the faint moonlight to guide them. Scal had good eyes—it was why Eddin had made him a scout—but fear had his gaze jumping at every sound, every flash of movement. The wardens sometimes startled at nothing out here in the wilderness, but even Scal knew this was not nothing.

Around the bundled bodies of the wardens, Scal glimpsed a faint flicker of light. Low to the ground. Not moving. A small point, growing larger as they crept up to it. A few of the wardens split away, circling around to either side. Trying to surround what they were approaching.

There was nothing special about the spot. A small space between the trees, a torch stuck into the crust of snow. Nothing of note. Until Scal saw why the torch had been left. Whoever had done this had wanted to make sure they would find it. That they would see all of it.

Radis, one of the sentries, was—had been—one of the worst among Athasar's company. Still, Scal would never have wished this thing upon him. He had been nailed to the tree, big spikes of metal stuck through his shoulders—*thump, thump*. His throat slashed. A deep cut that left his head lolling grotesquely. Scal could not tell if that had been before or after his stomach had been cut open. Guts spilling out all over the snow. Blood dripping slow from both gaping wounds.

Scal bent over and heaved. His meager dinner splattered over the snow. Looked like Radis's guts. He heaved again. Lero joined him. He was dimly aware of others making the same helpless retching noises all around the space.

"Pull yourselves together, boys," Athasar growled.

With great effort, Scal straightened up. Swallowing sour-tasting spit, fixing his eyes on a distant tree.

"Why?" one of the men was muttering. "Why? Why?"

"Iveran," the captain said in answer, and one of the wardens began to retch again.

For all its poverty, Aardanel was a stronghold by Northern standards. Northmen made raids when they could—rarely on Aardanel itself, but on the supply and prisoner chains that flowed into the camp. It had been worse in the last year, worse than Kerrus said he could remember, and he had been there a long time. There had been no new prisoners for nearly a year, when they had typically arrived every other month. They were all killed on the way. Supplies stolen. Bodies left to freeze in the snow. Meals had been even more slim than usual in Aardanel. More and more dying of hunger and cold. No one asked Fat Betho where he had found meat. No one wanted to know. Aardanel was crumbling.

All due to Iveran. A Northman chief whose tribe was picking slowly and ruthlessly away at the prison camp.

Grimly, Athasar said, "Back to Aardanel. Now."

"Why?" one of the wardens asked again, the only one who had managed to find his voice, weak as it was.

"Because Iveran already has a head start." With that, Athasar set off, away from the direction of their camp and its four fires.

Scal made himself look at Radis again, swallowing down the bile that threatened to rise. A torn-off branch had been nailed to the tree next to Radis's shoulder. Stuck straight out, his arm lashed to it. One finger—the only one that had not been cut off—pointed straight at Athasar's back. Straight toward Aardanel.

The storm clouds hung low above their heads as they trudged through the trees. Threatening snow but without so much as the scent of water to support it. It was an altogether different smell. The smell of a cold night. The smell of Kerrus's chapel. The smell of smoke, and fire. He looked up at the sky and felt sick. Not storm clouds. Smoke clouds.

Athasar, looking grim, called them all near to say, "We're close, boys, but I'm not sure what we'll find. It don't look good." He sent Lero and two others ahead to see what had happened. That left Scal with no defense, though Lero's near-friendship was little enough protection. The others soon turned to stare at him. Some fingered their weapons, the same look in their eyes as the convicts' sometimes had. The look of needing to tear. To destroy. To kill, because it was the only thing that made sense. "If you had anything to do with this . . ." one of them muttered, but Scal could not pick out who. He wished for a knife again.

The scouts came back pale-faced and shaken. "Wall's gone," Lero said, sounding like he could not believe his own words. "Burned down, some still burning. Few of the buildings are on fire, too."

"Any sign of Iveran?" Athasar asked.

Lero shook his head. "No sign of no one but birds. Place looks—" He stopped, going paler. Scal knew what he had been about to say. They all did. *Dead.*

Setting his face, Athasar said, "We move in slow, boys, and stay together until we know . . . well, until we know. Weapons ready, eyes sharp."

Athasar did not tell Scal to come with them, nor did the captain tell him to wait behind. So Scal went slow, sneaking through the trees with the rest of them. The smell of smoke was stronger now. Filling his lungs, filling his stomach with heavy fear. He prayed as they walked. Reciting every prayer Kerrus had taught him. Begging the Parents for mercy. For things not to be as bad as everyone thought. For everything to stay the same. *The Parents are always merciful,* Kerrus had told him a hundred times. *Sometimes it just doesn't fecking feel like it right away.*

The trees surrounding Aardanel had long ago been cut down to build the camp, so Aardanel stood in the center of a wide swath of open ground. They were coming from the east, and they should have had to circle around the tall wooden palisade to the main gate. But there was no palisade, no gate. Melted snow. Burned dead grass. Ashes. A still-burning section of wall to the north holding out. Flames tickling the sky. Smoke boiling up to mask the clouds.

Fire is the most powerful thing there is in this world, Kerrus had told Scal, hovering his hand above the everflame. *It speaks its own language, and "mercy" isn't a word it knows.*

"Steady, boys," Athasar said, his face as drawn as any of theirs. "Eyes sharp."

They moved forward again, leaving the trees behind. Scal's back prickled. Expecting at any moment to be hit with one of Iveran's distinctive white-fletched arrows. For a group of fur-wrapped Northmen to come screaming toward them. As Lero had said, though, there was no sign of anyone.

Dead.

Ravens cawed as the patrol picked their way over the ashes and entered what was left of Aardanel. Smoke hung low, making it hard to see. Not hard enough that Scal did not see more than he would have liked. From so far away, even sharp-eyed Lero had not been able to see beyond the smoke. This close up, it was red. Red everywhere. Not so long ago, the patrol had found one of the prisoner transports Iveran had butchered. Scal had seen more of it than he had wished, and this was just like it. Only more. All red. All death.

Bodies lay like a carpet along the main street through Aardanel, wardens and prisoners alike. Men and women and children. Most of the faces familiar. Some faces too bloody or beaten or cut up to recognize. Arms and feet and heads lay scattered around with none to claim them. Those white arrows, fletched with feathers from the snow eagle, stuck out of many bodies. But most were cut open or smashed up. The smell of fire was not enough to cover up the stench of blood and death, of guts and bowels and urine. Scal's stomach roiled, but nothing came up. It was too vast, too horrible, to be real.

They were near the barracks where the wardens slept, and Monarro pointed to it with a shaking finger. A body had been nailed to the door. Cut up like Radis, only this one was missing a head. None of them needed a face to know who it was. Only Chief Warden Eddin wore black-dyed uniforms. A raven perched on his shoulder, plucking at the gaping wound of his neck.

Others were heaving now, adding more mess to the scene. Scal could not find it in him to join. What was the point? This was no more than a nightmare. He would wake up soon, and tell Kerrus. The parro would tell him how even bad dreams were a gift from the Mother. *Glimpses of what-might-be*, he would say, *or what-might-have-been. We should all be thankful we only see a small portion of what Divine Metherra could show us—that, my boy, is mercy.*

His feet were moving. He did not know when he had started to move. That was the way of dreams. Running. Jumping. Slipping over the bodies and gore. His boot punched through bone, a skull, blood and brains spraying up his breeches. It did not matter who it was, had been. Not in a dream. He only kept running.

The chapel was gone, too close to the palisade to escape burning. Even with the snow red-spattered all around, it was not hard to pick out Kerrus's red cassock. He was on the ground in front of what was left of the chapel, lying there in his thin old robe like he had had no time to put a coat on. Not that a coat would have done him any good, then or now. Fur could not stop a sword. There was no point in trying to stay warm after the sword had gone through and the blood had gone out. He had always told Scal he would be smiling when he went to meet the Parents. But there was no smile on his wrinkled face. No joy in his fixed eyes.

Next to him, Brennon was not smiling either. He had found a knife somewhere. It was clutched still in his fist, unbloodied. It had not done much good against the arrow sticking out the side of his neck.

Scal's knees were cold in the few inches of pink snow. He did not remember kneeling down. His hand shook as he reached out and wrapped his fingers around the snow-eagle feathers. Yanked the arrow out of his friend's neck, arrowhead scraping against bone. The arrow came free, bloody almost half the length of the shaft. Little chunks of meat sticking to the arrowhead. *Mercy,* Kerrus had told him as they had watched the wardens burning a dead child, *has nothing to do with fairness.*

The shouting came dim to his ears, and the sounds of metal against metal. Unimportant. He could not pull his eyes from the arrow. His thumb smoothing down one of the white feathers, the vane rough against his skin. A single sluggish drop of blood collected slowly at the tip of the arrowhead, stretching out until it held on by a thread-thin line, and fell gently onto his thigh.

It was silent inside the shell of Aardanel. Silent as the dead.

"Ruuli?" a gruff voice called out, searing through Scal like an arrow. His fingers tightened around the fletching, crushing the delicate feathers. "Ruuli, where are you?" The rough Northern tongue. The language of Scal's forgotten childhood. The memories were gone, but the words stuck, somehow. "Ruuli!" Closer now. "There you are, Ruuli. What are you—"

Scal stood. The arrow in one fist, Brennon's knife in the other. He faced a big, gaping Northman, twice Scal's size, wrapped in blood-spattered furs. A big sword hung down by his side, dripping with blood. Lero's blood, and Athasar's, and Eddin's, Brennon's, Kerrus's.

"You are not Ruuli," the Northman said, eyes narrowing. Scal shook his head, silent. The man drew in a deep breath and bellowed, "To me!"

They came running. Nearly twoscore Northmen. Dressed in furs. Covered in blood. Bristling with weapons. A dozen arrows were aimed at Scal's heart. Swords and axes and maces were hefted ready to bash and cut. They had already killed a few hundred today. One more life would be as nothing to them. Scal did not know if his own life was worth much at all anymore.

A man stepped through the battle-ready crowd. Small for a Northman—little bigger than Scal, half grown as he was. A thick yellow beard framed his face, beads and bones braided into it so he rattled with every step. The crew wore a motley of colors. Brown bear and black wolf and gray fox. But this man wore only white. Thick snowbear pelts, wrapped with bleached leather, spotted with dirt and blood. A snowbear head snarled from atop his own head, a hood whose muzzle was brown with old blood. An enormous cloak of purest white. Scal had never seen the man before, but he knew. Iveran Snowwalker. Iveran-of-the-ice. Iveran the Coldhearted. Chief of the Valastaa Clan. Scourge of Aardanel.

"Well," he said gruffly. "Eddin had a Northman." Iveran paced slowly toward Scal, placing his feet carefully around the bodies. He carried a short spear in his left hand and a curved sword in his right, both held at the ready. "You speak, *ijka*?"

Scal stared flatly. Fingers flexing around the shaft of the arrow, the hilt of the little knife.

"Boy is an idiot," one of the Northmen muttered.

Iveran waved his sword for silence. "Idiot or no, he is one of ours. I will not have his blood spilled. *Ijka.*" He shuffled closer, eyes fixed on Scal's face. The unfamiliar word sounded like both comfort and command. "Why not put down that knife, eh? We will have a talk. Your blood is come to claim you."

My blood? Scal wondered dimly. North-born. Northman devil. Yellow-haired and blue-eyed, just like Iveran and the others arrayed behind him. He shared their blood. Numbly, he shook his head. "I am not one of you." His mouth formed the hard sounds of the Northern tongue without any thought, as if he had been speaking it all his life. The very act betrayed the words, and he could feel his cheeks start to burn with shame.

Iveran grinned. An eerie echo of the snowbear's snarl. "Of course you are, *ijka.* Too much time with the southerners, is all. We have fixed that problem."

The shame vanished, swallowed up by a rage that boiled through him. There was a snap as the arrow's shaft splintered inside his fist, head and fletching falling to the ground; the knife burned in his hand, a screaming demand. Iveran's grinning face swam up before him. There was shouting. Hands grabbing at his heated skin. Unbelievably, laughter.

The fury drained away slowly. He lay belly down on the ground, his arms twisted up behind his back. A great weight across his legs. A boot pressing one side of his face into the snow. He caught a glimpse of Iveran, the little knife buried in his shoulder. He was laughing as he pulled the knife out, its tip red with blood. He said, smiling, "Not one of us? You lie to me, *ijka.*"

They trussed him up like a pig. Lashing his wrists and ankles around a thick branch that took two of them to hoist. Scal's rage was gone, leaving only a festering shame behind. Even that did not burn so badly as his muscles after the first few hours.

He had put up with much abuse in Aardanel, but Kerrus had always told him that insults were no more than drops of water. Water could never harm a flame. *Violence is weakness,* he had said, *and the best way to fight is with compassion. Let your grace be your shield, and your generosity your sword.*

Well. Parro Kerrus had been good all his life, and what had it gotten him? A sword through the chest. A cold and lonely death. Scal had tried to be good, too, to prove he was more than a barbarian Northman. To make Kerrus proud. To make some kind of good life for himself. And it had gotten him strung up between two Northmen. Hanging-down head staring right at one fur-covered arse. All the people he had ever cared about dead and gone.

"How goes, *ijka*?"

Scal twisted his burning neck to the side, where Iveran paced along, grinning. The white furs on his left shoulder were faintly pink, but the chieftain showed no lingering pain. Scal turned his head away. The choice of which arse to look at was an easy one.

"No hard feelings, eh?"

It was not easy to manage, but Scal filled his mouth and spat to the side. The slime hit Iveran's hip. Slid slowly until it froze. One of the Northmen growled, but Iveran lifted a hand. He was smiling still, but his eyes were as cold as the air.

"You will thank me one day, *ijka*," he said, and jogged away to the head of the twisting column.

Never.

They made camp in the light of the sinking sun. Scal's two bearers untied him long enough to lash him to a tree. Arms stretched back, wrapped around the trunk, twisted so the pain in his shoulders was a constant, aching throb. They kept his ankles tied together, too, as though he could rip the tree from the ground and run off. Not too likely. He was a distance from the main camp, where they gathered around a big cook fire and traded stories and songs. Just as it had always been with Athasar's patrol. He was even farther from the camp than the supply sledges and the bushy, half-wild dogs that pulled them. The message was clear enough.

Not far enough away, though. He could hear everything they said, clear as light. He listened to the Northmen brag of how many they had killed that day. How many exiles and wardens they had taken down. Stories of their last moments, their begging. Laughter. Scal felt that hot fury start to rise again. One of them brought over a battered wooden bowl of some kind of steaming stew, held it to Scal's lips. The boy took a mouthful of the thick broth and spat it back in the Northman's face. The big man started bellowing, hands clawing at his face as the hot stew dripped. The stew cooled quickly in the night air. The man's hands went instead for Scal. One curling through his hair, holding his head still. The other forming a fist. It fell once, twice, before the others could drag him away. He took a fistful of Scal's hair with him, leaving the boy with a bleeding scalp and mouth. Iveran stood before him, arms crossed over his thick chest, frowning.

"He does not belong, Iveran," the man with a handful of Scal's hair shouted. "His blood is cold. Leave him for the snows."

Iveran ignored him, crouching down next to Scal. Holding the boy's eyes. "Too much time with the southerners messes your head," he said, tapping a thick forefinger hard between Scal's eyes. "Makes you think backward. You got your head wrong, *ijka*. We are your people. You are where you belong."

"You killed my people," Scal said, the words thick around a mouthful of blood.

Iveran's fist thumped into Scal's forehead, the back of his head bouncing off the tree trunk. Colors danced in front of his eyes. "Wrong, *ijka*."

Bloody spit dribbled down Scal's chin, and Iveran's face wove in and out of focus. Scal forced the words to come out clear. "I will never be one of you."

"That is what you want, eh?" Iveran held something in front of Scal's face, and Scal forced his eyes to cooperate, to focus. It was the little knife. Brennon's knife. The knife he had stuck in Iveran's shoulder. It was still dotted with blood, or rust. Hard to tell. "We have seen what southerners do to their prisoners. You want to be a southerner? Then you are our prisoner."

The knife swam closer until Scal's eyes could not follow it. Iveran's hand grabbed his aching jaw, held him still as the knife cut, once, twice. Deep cuts. All the way through so Scal could feel the knife's point scrape jarring against his teeth. He could taste the blood as it washed down his cheek from the prisoner's cross. Scal drew a sharp, surprised breath, but he kept his scream trapped behind closed teeth and his eyes on Iveran's face.

The chieftain stood slowly, his expression hard to read. It may have been because Scal was still dizzy from all the blows his head had taken. But it seemed like Iveran meant to say something.

"I have *vasrista* with the boy." It was the man who had attacked Scal; red welts ran down his face from the stew. The killing rage was gone from his eyes, but he looked no kinder.

Iveran pressed the bridge of his nose between two fingers. "Leave be, Einas," he said with a tired sigh.

"Honor will not wait," the man said sternly.

The chieftain was quiet for a long time, and Scal could feel the eyes of the whole clan on him. His eyes were working better now, but he let them stay unfocused. Not looking at any of the Northmen. He had no idea what they were all waiting for, but he did not expect to like it. The cold air sucked through the cross on his cheek as he breathed. It was the wrong cheek, for a prisoner. He was not a true prisoner.

"Make the ring," Iveran said at last. A small cheer went up from the men before they turned away. Iveran squatted down next to Scal once more, but Scal kept his eyes far away. "Listen to me, *ijka*. You have insulted Einas. Warm blood or cold, he will not stand for that. He has claimed *vasrista* on you. You know the word?" He paused, waiting, but Scal showed no sign of hearing. "It is a challenge against honor. You insulted his, so he calls for satisfaction. You will fight him, hand to hand, body to body, until one falls." Iveran's eyes passed critically over Scal. "He will beat the shit out of you, no doubt of that. Might even kill you. It would save me the trouble." Iveran stood, spat onto the ground next to Scal, and walked away.

The two Northmen who had been carrying him all day

came over to untie him from the tree and march him to a clear patch of ground. The others had kicked the snow away, exposing the brittle dead grass beneath, and now gathered in a ring around the spot. They parted to let Scal get shoved through, then closed the gap.

Einas was there, on the other side of the ring. About three good paces away. Stretching his arms and back, loosening his legs. Scal stood still, waiting, arms hanging heavy at his side. His fingers tingled with the blood rushing to them. His shoulders were aching lumps. Blood filled his mouth, the cross like a fire in his cheek. The pains felt right, matching the hurt that rumbled low inside him.

From somewhere around the ring came Iveran's voice: "Begin."

Einas did not move fast, but he did not need to. Scal was not going anywhere. As the big Northman rushed bellowing toward him, Scal stared flatly and thought of all the things Parro Kerrus had ever told him. *Inaction can be a man's wisest course of action.*

Einas barreled into him, leaning down to ram his shoulder into Scal's stomach. Wrapped his arms around the boy, propelled him backward into the living border of the ring. There, crushed between Einas and other Northmen trying to shove them back into the ring, breath gone in a mighty whoosh, Scal remembered, *Violence is the answer of a small mind.*

They were pushed away by the ring of Northmen. Einas stumbling back a step, Scal trying to draw in breath. Then Einas stepped close once more, fist jabbing against the side of Scal's ribs. *Revenge is a fool's game with no end.*

"Fight, boy!" Einas shouted in his face, spittle showering

from cracked lips and rotten teeth. The rest of the Northmen took up the cry. Scal stood still, if slightly bent, torso aching and breath coming hard. Einas's big fist thumped him in the center of the new-carved X on his cheek, sent him stumbling to the side and seeing stars once more. *He who provokes a fight is weak, but he who retaliates is weaker still.*

Einas brought his fist up against the bottom of Scal's jaw, snapping his head back, lifting him off his feet, and sending him into the barrier. Arms caught him, steadied him. Shoved him back toward Einas, whose fist connected solidly with Scal's nose. Bone crunched and blood poured. *If a man should break your arm, extend to him the other one.*

Scal thought at first that his eyes were bleeding, washed with red. His heart thumped loud, painful within his bruised chest. Someone was bellowing a wordless, endless animal noise, full of mindless rage. His throat hurt, and his hands as they sang through the air to be met with the solid thump of yielding flesh. The pain in his arms melted away, escaped through his knuckles that tore and bled but did not hurt. He spun like the wind, and his fist against a jawbone felt to him like a breeze. A blow caught him on the ear, another pounded against his ribs. But Scal was fury itself, anger given physical shape, and his body kept moving without being told. Until something terribly solid hit him between the legs and brought him and the screaming both to a shuddering stop.

Scal lay curled on his side in the snow, bleeding and bruised and shaking and hating himself. He blinked up through watering eyes to see Einas bent over him, mouth moving but his voice a mouse's whisper. Blood flowed from his nose and mouth and a split eyebrow, the same blood that covered Scal's knuckles.

He squeezed his eyes shut, pressed his face against the frozen grass. The cold ground cooled his blood, soothed his battered body. He wanted to sink into the earth and disappear forever.

Love your enemies, for they teach you what you'll never become.

The world rushed back in. Voices talking and laughing. Feet crunching on snow. The sigh of blood running across his skin. He tried to open his eyes again, saw Einas crouched before him. Grinning.

"Sorry for that, boy," the big Northman said cheerfully. "Could think of no other way to stop you." He held a hand out to Scal, to pull the boy to his feet. Scal kept his hands cradling his delicate parts. Einas did not seem to take offense, and grabbed Scal by the back of his coat instead. Scal's knees were weak as Einas set him on his feet, but they held. He kept his eyes down at the ground, watching the blood drip from his nose to splatter on the frosted grass.

A hand clapped him on the shoulder, nearly knocking him back down. Iveran said, "We will warm that blood of yours yet."

CHAPTER 6

The damned children found Joros in the halls again. They didn't move like children—more like shadows, fading when it suited them and springing up in places they shouldn't have been. Joros would almost compare them to the Sentinels, though that was probably unfair to Mount Raturo's guardians.

"Good morning, cappo," the girl said in her sugary voice. She always smiled when she spoke, but Joros couldn't help but feel the smile was more aggressive than pleasant. She should have been too young to even know what aggression was, but Joros had always maintained they were unnatural children.

"It's not morning," he growled, trying to sidle around them. He'd received contact from one of his shadowseekers that he was eager to follow up on. The blasted children stood in the middle of the tunnel, not more than hip-high, but standing shoulder to shoulder they took up too much space to get around without touching them.

"Is, too," the boy piped up. Avorra was obnoxious, with her chattering and her smiling, but Joros had decided he hated

Etarro more. The boy was always staring, wide eyes taking up too much of his face, and he spoke so little it would have been easy to forget he was even there, if it wasn't for his stare like a knife between the eyes.

They weren't even five yet, but Verteira's twins gave Joros the shivering shits.

"It's not," Joros said again. He reached out with two fingers and pressed them carefully against the boy's forehead, putting more pressure behind the touch until, frowning, Etarro was forced to take a step back. Joros quickly sidestepped around the children and hurried down the tunnel, hoping they'd find something else to do, or at least that their legs were too short to follow him.

They kept up well enough, unnatural as they were, trailing after him like kittens after a string. "It is," the girl said, carrying on as if it were an entirely normal conversation, and as if the subject were something Joros cared about. "Wanna know how we know?"

"No."

"We saw it," Avorra said, her voice barely above a whisper, like a breath over stone. "We saw the sun."

Joros hesitated a moment, his stride faltering just enough for Etarro to run into the backs of his legs. Joros sprang away with a growl, then turned to glare down at the children. They at least had brains enough to look a little scared then, though he'd never trusted Avorra's expressions since he'd found her practicing them in a mirror.

There were no other adults around, certainly none who'd take the beasts off his hands and give them the parenting he'd so very carefully avoided providing since Verteira had died birthing them, and so he gave an internal sigh before demanding, "How did you see the sun?"

They were silent, shared a glance that he couldn't read, though he could practically see the words moving between them. Finally Etarro looked back at him with those too-innocent eyes and said, "It's a secret."

Joros growled again; the one question had exhausted his store of patience for the children. He crouched down before the boy; the girl made spiders crawl up his spine, but he knew how to deal with the boy. Etarro was quiet and weak, easy enough to control with a firm hand. So Joros reached out and pressed his palm just below the boy's throat, pressing back until Etarro was against the wall and his already too-big eyes looked ready to swallow the rest of his face. "How," Joros said levelly, "did you see the sun?"

Etarro scrabbled weakly at Joros's hand, and his sister stared with jaw hanging, but the boy finally gasped, "She found a tunnel."

Joros let go of the boy and stood, wiping his hand briefly on his robe. "You will show me."

They grumbled and sulked, and Avorra glared at him with that particular glare she had, the one that belonged on the face of an older woman who had seen more of life than the dark innards of a mountain. They led him, though, good beasts that they were.

Joros was annoyed by the diversion, but the Ventallo had near-unanimously agreed on how the twins should be raised after their mother had died. One of the key points of that child-rearing plan had been that the twins not see the world outside the mountain. Should things come to pass as they were meant to, it would be best if the children didn't have any fear of the dark, or any great attachment to the sun. More practically, which was the part that mattered to Joros, it would keep them from scarpering off and getting themselves killed like so many other twins by the fanatic followers of the Parents. The children had been easy enough to keep contained when they'd been younger and stupider, but since growing some and figuring out that brains were a thing to be used, they'd proved distinctly less easy to contain. They had an eerie way of seeming not to follow the natural laws of walls and doors. It had been harder to keep their existence a secret from the other preachers, what with the fecking spooky little shits popping up in places they shouldn't be, strolling through the tunnels like they owned the world, and so the Ventallo had agreed to stop trying. Let them wander, let them roam—so long as they stayed within the spire of the mountain.

For all that Mount Raturo was enormous, it only had the one central path up and down the mountain, so it was exceptionally hard to avoid running into other preachers. And for all that their numbers swelled year after year, the Fallen were still a small group, rattling around inside Raturo like a handful of peas in a communal cookpot. All considered, it wasn't necessarily surprising that Dirrakara should cross his path; though Joros cursed it as another minor annoyance, she had the strangest effect on his ability to breathe.

She flashed him a sly grin, her hair curling like fire around her face. Joros gave her as much of a smile as he ever gave, a tight curving of the corners of his mouth. Dirrakara swept her arms wide and said, "Why, if it isn't some of my favorite people."

Honestly, Joros didn't know what she expected. A hug from the children, most likely, but that would be a ridiculous thing to expect and he couldn't bring himself to think so lowly of her. Avorra and Etarro didn't like being touched, and that topped the very short list of things Joros agreed with them on. So Dirrakara stood with her arms spread and a smile plastered on her face until she realized they weren't getting her anywhere. She hastily cleared her throat and crouched down in front of the twins; Etarro flinched slightly, and she noticed it, of course, her eyes going all mothery. She'd tried so hard to fill Verteira's place, for the children who'd never known a mother. They'd gotten along well enough without one so far, and they hadn't shown any sign of wanting that to change. Joros knew it hurt her every time they rebuffed her, but she kept trying. He saw her hold back the hand that tried to reach out and brush at Etarro's hair, and instead she put that smile back on her face. "What are you two doing with Cappo Joros, hmm?"

They glanced at each other, briefly at Joros, and then at the floor. They didn't seem inclined to answer, and so Joros did it for them: "They're showing me something they found."

Dirrakara looked up at him with eyebrows raised. "Is that so?" She looked back to the twins, though she still spoke to Joros. "And what have they found?"

Joros shrugged. "You know children."

Still not looking at him, she nodded. "I do. And I'm still wondering what they're doing with you."

He bristled at that, though he did his best to hide it. Usually he found Dirrakara's perspicacity and boldness refreshing, but not always. She'd come to know him well in the five years he'd served the Ventallo, better than anyone else could claim to know him. He was still trying to decide whether that meant he should marry her or kill her. "Perhaps I'm taking an interest in their lives. They're finally of an age where they can almost speak in coherent sentences. One day soon they might even say something interesting. It would be a shame if I missed such a groundbreaking event."

She smirked, eyes flicking playfully up to him. "It would be, wouldn't it?" She rose and stepped smoothly around the children, resting her hand lightly against Joros's arm. Her eyes were the deepest green he'd ever seen. "I have a present for you, once you're done with them. Come find me." She leaned in tantalizingly close, lips just brushing against his jaw, and then moved away, smirking again as she strode up the path behind him. Joros watched her until, from the corner of his eye, he saw Avorra trying to slip away. He set the twins marching forward again, and they went without grumbling now, resigned.

They took him all the way to Raturo's floor, where the wide space gave a perfect view of the great arch that led into the Ventallo's chambers. It was hard to notice anything besides the two falling gods, but the twins didn't even seem to notice their stone counterparts, walking instead to the two tunnel mouths leading farther down. There was the path leading to the Cavern of the Falls, which Joros had to visit fairly frequently for ceremonial reasons, and the other path led down to the sorts of rooms necessary to keep a large place full of many people fed and clothed and clean. Kitchens, baths, storerooms; the kinds of places Joros had managed to avoid, save when he needed cleaning. The children took the latter path, of course, strolling deep into the mountain's foot, going lower even than the Cavern of the Falls reached. It was darker there, below where most of the mountain lived, far removed from the labored gasps of life crawling through Raturo's tunnels.

The storeroom they took him to was near freezing, cold enough for his breath to make a cloud before his face. It was full of meat, carcasses hanging from the ceiling, dark pools of frozen blood dotting the floor. They wove through the room to a back corner, pushed aside a hanging pig, and knelt down before a pile of bones, shaved of their flesh. As the twins began to root through the bones, Joros felt a strange twisting in his stomach. The children were unsettling enough on their own, but there was something especially troubling about the casual carelessness with which they dug through bones and flesh and blood.

The storage room began to slowly grow brighter.

Through the tunnel they revealed, tight to the floor and barely big enough for a full-sized man to fit through, daylight stretched its fingers.

There were a great number of things Joros hated, and the children being right was most certainly one of them.

"See?" Avorra said with a grin that was half superiority and half disdain. "Told you it was morning."

Joros stepped forward and took the smile off her face with the flat of his hand. The twins gaped up at him with matching expressions of shock, Avorra's hand slowly rising to touch her reddening cheek. It took a great effort of will for Joros not to raise his hand again; he even managed to keep his voice low, calm and deadly, as he told them, "You will never come here again. You will never speak of this place." He glared at them a moment longer, letting them soak in his anger. "Go. Now."

They went.

When he was sure they were gone, Joros turned to regard

the tunnel. He would ask the right questions to the right people; he was confident he would know within the week who had thought of making a tunnel to discard refuse, who had been too lazy to drag carcasses up through the mountain to the gate. There would be proper punishments. But the tunnel . . . he wasn't sure what to do about the tunnel itself.

Carefully he rearranged the bones in front of the tunnel mouth, the sunlight fracturing against the far wall, dimming piece by piece until the storeroom was once again near dark, lit only by a single candle. There were always candles scattered throughout the mountain, since there was no other way of tracking time in the darkness. The initiates were constantly replacing them, precisely trimming and lighting them. Joros found himself staring at the flame much too long and shook himself, making his way from the storeroom and back up the path through the mountain. Not all problems had an immediate solution; this one would take some more thought.

He thought about ignoring Dirrakara's earlier invitation, of going instead to his own room and attending to his shadowseeker business. But Dirrakara was a nightmare when she was angry, and taking a bit of time now to make sure he didn't have to deal with her bitter anger for a week was an easy enough choice to make.

He entered her room without knocking; after so long, there wasn't any point in knocking anymore. She was at her worktable, where she was often to be found these days, wearing only a simple linen shift. Her discarded robe was a crumpled pile on the floor, likely cast aside in a flash of inspiration— she'd often complained that the robe's sleeves weren't made for rolling and just got in her way. A soft crunching sound filled the room, pestle grinding seeds to powder, holding all her bright-eyed attention. Joros almost didn't see her manservant, Haro, standing dutifully nearby in case she needed anything; the man was so innocuous he might as well have been a wall. Haro noticed Joros before Dirrakara did, but the man never did anything without his mistress's command.

Joros didn't like catching her like this—focused, forehead wrinkled, her thoughts swirling behind her eyes. She was useful, and a good enough companion, but he didn't always like to be reminded that she was more as well; that she had ambitions of her own beyond the ones he'd aligned her for. It reminded him that he didn't know her nearly as well as she knew him.

Absorbed in her work, she didn't even notice him staring, waiting. Finally he cleared his throat and she looked up from grinding seeds, smiling broadly. "There you are. I was starting to worry you'd forgotten about me." Joros shrugged noncommittally and dropped into the room's single chair. She had piles of cushions scattered around that she swore were more comfortable, but he'd persuaded her to have Haro find him a chair. "How are the children?"

That earned another shrug. "No smarter than they've ever been."

"What did they have to show you?"

"They found a storeroom full of string. Just piles and piles of balls of string."

She laughed at that; her face always lit up when she talked of the children. "I'm sure they had a tale of why the string was so important, didn't they?"

"Something about spider eggs. I told you, they're still idiots."

She threw a shelled nut at him with a snort. He threw it

back to her, knowing better than to eat anything that came off her worktable. "Strange, that they would want to show you of all people."

"I was just the first poor fool they stumbled across. They would have shown anyone they could find. You said you had something for me?"

It took a moment for her to answer—she was likely balancing whether or not to pursue the topic. "I do," she said after a beat, smiling again. "Haro, would you?" The manservant bowed slightly and drifted into the adjoining room. Dirrakara wiped her hands against the front of her shift as she walked around the worktable and came to stand behind Joros, her hands resting lightly against his shoulders. It made him slightly edgy, the touch combined with not being able to see her. Her breath tickled against his ear, and her hair tumbled down over his chest, and a slow shiver worked its way up his spine. Joros could feel her smile against his cheek as Haro returned and she said, "Here he is. Your present."

Haro dragged in the tallest man Joros had ever seen—stick thin and wearing soiled clothing, and there was a burlap sack over his head that muffled his cries somewhat, though not nearly enough. "Help me please help me I'll do anything please please please." A mindless gibbering that set Joros's teeth on edge.

Haro set a foot to the back of the tall man's knee, toppling him like a tree. He certainly fell with an impressive crash. "Please help please please I didn't do anything help me." His wrists were tied behind his back, but it was more complicated than that—strips of cloth were woven between his fingers, twisting and immobilizing them. That was a strange thing.

"What's happening help me oh please please let me go." Haro knelt on the tall man's back, keeping him pressed to the floor.

Joros twisted around to face Dirrakara, eyebrows raised. "What is this?"

"This is Anddyr." She walked to stand at Joros's side, and he saw she held a hand-sized earthenware jar. "And this is skura." The jar's lid came away with a twist, and a sharp, pungent smell filled Joros's nose. The jar was full of a thick black paste that looked as unappetizing as it smelled. "We're going to see what happens when the two mix. Give me your hand."

Joros hesitated; there was something distinctly eerie behind her eyes, and he had a healthy amount of mistrust for her even when she wasn't showing him tied-up men. She kept looking at him expectantly, though, and he finally held his hand out to her. For that kindness, she jabbed a knife into his palm.

"Bloody fecking hells!" he bellowed, and yanked his hand back. She managed to catch some of his blood in the jar, not that he could have done much to keep it from her. "Twins' bones, woman, you could have asked." She ignored him, eyes intent as she mixed his blood into the black paste with the tip of her little knife. "What is this?" he demanded again.

"Watch," she said, and went to kneel at the man's head, the jar held in one hand, the knife in the other.

Haro pulled off the burlap sack, revealing greasy black hair around a pale face and pale eyes, the latter of which were panic-wide as he continued his steady stream of pleading. Haro reached around the tall man's head, pressing thick fingers against his cheeks until the wailing stopped and his mouth popped open. Joros winced as Dirrakara put the knife into his open mouth. She drew it out, the black paste wiped off on his tongue, and Haro let go of his face. The wailing flared again, and Dirrakara watched him intently, fluttered a hand at Haro until the servant rose from the tall man's back. Joros watched, too, not sure what he was looking for. "Please help me help please help help—" The tall man's pleading ended with a strangled noise, and his pupils grew rapidly wider, the black eclipsing the pale blue. He stared at nothing, jaw slack, the sudden absence of his words making the silence greater. Joros was about to fill the long silence when the tall man began to shriek. It was a raw, nightmare sound, and his lanky body convulsed along the floor, great spasms that jerked his limbs in every direction.

Joros was half out of his seat before Dirrakara reached a hand toward him, not taking her eyes from the tall man. "Wait," she said breathlessly, and the man gave a final shudder as he fell silent and lay still on the floor.

"What in all the hells did you do to him?" Joros demanded, and the tall man's head snapped up with unsettling speed, those wide-pupiled eyes fixing on Joros.

Dirrakara grinned like a proud mother, rested one hand on the tall man's greasy curls. "I've made him yours."

That set off a twinge in Joros's gut; it sounded just like one of the spooky things the damned boy-twin would say. "I don't understand." He hated admitting that, hated her a little for bringing him to say it.

She deftly untied the ropes and cloth that bound the tall man's hands, letting his arms flop to his sides as he contin-ued staring disconcertingly at Joros. Dirrakara rose and knelt beside Joros, reaching out to wrap her fingers around his wrist. He resisted, not at all convinced she wouldn't stab him again;

there was enough blood dripping into his lap that he didn't need her help adding more. "Anddyr, love," she cooed, "the cappo is hurt. Won't you help him?"

The tall man rose, taking a long time to gather his long limbs beneath him. Once he got to hands and knees, he wavered as if a gentle breeze would topple him back over. He crawled until he knelt before Joros, who tried to shy away as the tall man reached out, but between Dirrakara, the tall man, and the damned chair, he was blocked in. Long fingers touched his bleeding hand, and the tall man fluttered the fingers of his other hand, weaving them haphazardly in the air as though he were at a loom that was trying very hard to dodge his touch. A coolness flowed from his fingers onto Joros's hand and, amazingly, the blood stopped oozing. Beneath a film of red, he watched the sides of the shallow puncture knit themselves together, and the pain faded almost entirely.

Joros had seen a mage only once before, and that man had called fire from the sky.

"What is this?" he asked once more, and this time his voice was a whisper.

Dirrakara was beaming, one hand on Joros's shoulder and one on the mage's. "This is what I've been working on for years. You must understand why I had to keep it such a secret. Uniro was firm on that. I'm calling it skura," she said, and pressed the jar into Joros's hand. "He'll need it three times a day, at least, to keep him calm. Less, as time goes on—just enough to keep control over him. The most . . . significant effects will be apparent over the next few weeks. After that, it's simply a matter of keeping him in the proper state."

Joros examined the jar so she wouldn't see his face. He had to clear his throat twice, swallowing the faint taste of bile, before he could speak. "How does it work?"

Her shrug was purposely casual. "I've been developing the recipe for years. There are a few ingredients that react most curiously with Highlands blood. Docility, susceptibility to suggestion, acute attention . . . really, qualities anyone could hope for in an assistant. There are side effects, of course—hallucinations, a period of uselessness after dosing, as you can see, but I think I've almost perfected the recipe."

"And the blood?"

Another shrug, and she wouldn't meet his eyes, though a smile played on her lips. "Necessary. Anddyr is yours now, attuned to you."

"Like a seekstone?"

"Something like. More a reminder that leaving you or your valuable blood would destroy him." Joros waited, letting the silence stretch until she hurried to fill it. "The skura will change the way his mind works over time, I believe. All my testing has suggested it. If he tries to stop taking it, he'll drive himself mad. He won't leave you for fear of it, and it will teach him . . . restraint, in dealing with you."

"He's dangerous, then?"

"Of course, love. That's the point. But that's what the skura is for. It will keep him controlled and safe as a kitten. Look at him."

The mage still knelt before Joros, a vacant smile on his face, hands folded docilely in his lap. His eyes flickered at any slight movement Joros made, but he otherwise seemed the consummate simpleton.

"He'll be the first of many mages to join our ranks," Dirra-kara said, pride burning in her voice.

Joros stared at the jar, turning it in his hands, felt the mage's eyes following the motion. She'd been working on this for years, she said, and this the first he'd heard of it. Secrets were the lifeblood of Mount Raturo, the currency of the Ventallo, and yet, somehow, a soft smile had made him think otherwise. He was very careful in how he said, "I wasn't aware the Ventallo were looking for slaves."

Silence stretched out. The mage's breathing was loud, even. Haro stood against the far wall, his eyes alert, muscle-thick arms flexing over his chest.

"There are many things you're not aware of, *Octeiro*," she said softly, turning the title into a faint insult. "You would do well to remember that."

Joros met her eyes, and didn't break the contact as he inclined his head ever so slightly. "As you say, Tredeira."

The silence stretched again, their eyes locked, and she was the first to weaken. He'd known she would be. Her face shifted into a pout, and she draped herself across his lap, finger tapping against his chest. "Why do you have such trouble accepting gifts?"

Joros bit back the first three replies that came to mind and said instead, "He seems like more trouble than he's worth." His hand moved up her back, fingers burying in her thick hair. Across the room, Haro silently drifted away. The mage still knelt before them, eyes flickering.

"He's a good boy. I'm sure you'll find use for him." Her hand flattened against his chest, the smile returning to her lips. "And I'm sure you can think of some way to thank me properly."

The mage, Anddyr, was a mumbler. He ducked through the doorway to Joros's chambers, peering into the corners and muttering to himself before settling his back against a wall and curling his long arms around his knees. He sat there, staring and mumbling and flinching, and the only time he did anything different was when Joros would move. No matter how small the motion, the mage's eyes would focus on Joros with the intensity of light through a pinhole.

It was unsettling, to say the least, and it put Joros strongly in mind of the damned boy-twin. The only difference was that this particular maniac could tear him to pieces with a twist of his fingers. Dirrakara had assured him that her skura would keep Anddyr docile, but Joros didn't like the risk of the mage gaining his mind back and turning first on his new master.

He had to pen a quick reply to his shadowseeker in the capital, Mercetta, before he could turn his attention to the mage, and by the time he sealed the missive, the muttering was already beginning to grate. Joros reminded himself of the mage who'd called fire from the sky, took a calming breath, and said in the most pleasant tone he could manage, "Anddyr, why don't you come here."

The mage startled, blinked owlishly, and then slowly rose to his feet. He walked like a new-birthed foal just learning the skill, tottering to Joros's side and standing there blinking like he'd just woken. "Sit," Joros said, gesturing to the other chair nearby, and the speed with which the mage hurried to comply reminded Joros of Dirrakara's words, *a susceptibility to suggestion* . . . He settled into the chair, and almost looked like a normal person again, something small changing in his face. "How did you come to be here, Anddyr?" Joros asked, still trying to sound pleasant. It didn't come easy to his voice, but he considered it worth the effort—a small amount of kindness might be enough to stay the mage's powerful hand should he ever fly into a maniacal rage.

The mage blinked again, opened his mouth. Nothing came out right away, but Joros resisted the impulse to prompt him. Finally he managed, "I was accosted." His voice was rough, likely from all the screaming he'd done under Dirrakara's supervision. "On the West Road. Where am I?"

"Ah . . ." Joros gave his answer some thought. He wouldn't have chosen to keep a virtual slave, but it seemed he had little choice in the matter, and this would be the first step in breaking the news to the broken man. Potentially, the first chance to see what explosive form the mage's anger took. "You're from the Highlands, yes?" An easy question with an obvious answer—something in the Highlands blood made mages. Any children born of mixed Fiateran and Highlands stock had a tendency to not make it to the Academy quick enough to tame the boiling of magic that came on young mages so suddenly. With his powers already proven, this mage had clearly trained at the Academy. Anddyr nodded a vague affirmative to the question. "You've seen the Tashat Mountains?" Another nod. "This is a mountain as well, though more impressive than any of the Tashats. It's where you'll be living now."

The mage's wide eyes fixed on Joros with an unsettling clarity, and though he spoke only one word, it was layered with understanding: "Why?"

It was rare that Joros ever spoke with full honesty. Past attempts had taught him that doing so rarely worked to his own benefit. There was a crackling in the air, though, a strange hazing between Joros and the mage that made the hairs of his arms stand. So while he didn't speak with *full* honesty, it was with more than he afforded nonmages, who couldn't set the very air afire. "I don't know why you were taken, or why I was chosen. I don't know why we've been thrown together, and that's the honest truth." Claiming something as true was more likely to make the listener believe it—that was a wonderful trick he'd learned. He claimed all sorts of things were true. "I know it's a poor lot you've been given, and I'd set you free if I could, Anddyr." Saying the mage's name seemed to sharpen his eyes, and Joros wanted the mage focused on the sincerity he made sure was dripping from his words. The tone was just as important as the words themselves. "But we're bound together by something beyond my understanding, and I don't think there's any getting away from it. We'll both just have to make the best of the shit hands we've been dealt." The mage was still staring, the air still crackling; a voice in Joros's mind whispered, *a susceptibility to suggestion* . . . "I'd like us to be allies, Anddyr." That sharpening of the eyes again, and then a softness spread through the mage's face, the dry air dissipating like a storm.

"Yes," he said in his scratchy voice, and after a beat added a whispered, "cappo." The title meant *master,* in the Old Tongue. He wondered where the mage had learned to use it.

"Good, Anddyr. Excellent." He didn't know if this had been enough to save him from the mage's fiery wrath, but it felt a start. "There's something we should do, if we're to be true allies." Joros rose and found a pair of attuned seekstones, one of the old magics lost to time. They seemed a simple enough thing, allowing the holder of one stone to see through the eyes of the one who held the other. Easy to use, yet apparently impossible to reproduce; in the centuries of history covered by the ancient tomes carefully stored in the bowels of the mountain, none had ever been able to create a new seekstone. Luckily, those long-ago Fallen who'd had the trick of making the seekstones had thought far enough ahead to fill a literal vault with the things, so there was no shortage; still, the knowledge would have been nice.

Joros hesitated, not sure how this would go. He held a small knife in one hand, sharp-tipped, not unlike the one Dirrakara had stuck in that same hand earlier. "Anddyr," he said softly, "I need your blood." The mage's brows knit, but he showed no other reaction. "Give me your hand," Joros tried instead, and the mage promptly stuck out his hand. Useful, that. Joros pierced the pad of Anddyr's thumb with the knife, pressed his thumb briefly to each seekstone—a smear of blood to spark the magic, the red dissipating into both stones with a swirl. The magics of those original Fallen seemed to rely heavily on blood.

Stringing one stone on a leather thong, Joros passed it to Anddyr and, still using the pleasant tone, commanded, "Put that around your neck, and cast a spell so it stays there." Joros narrowed his eyes briefly. "Something so complicated even you can't undo it." The mage did as he was told, muttering and waving his fingers around, and by the end of it Joros couldn't pull the seekstone from around his neck no matter how much force he put behind it; nearly strangled the mage trying.

Perhaps there was some value in Dirrakara's gift . . . He wouldn't say he was thankful for being a part of her experimenting, but the mage might have some use, and there was a simple way to put him to the test. He rose, and the mage stumbled along dutifully in his wake.

Deep within the mountain, the impressionability still proved useful enough; at a word, the mage was scrambling to move the pile of bones until he knelt before the tunnel mouth, gaping like a fish in the faint wash of sunlight.

"Anddyr," Joros said, speaking slowly as he would to a child, "seal up this tunnel."

The mage's brow furrowed, eyes staring hard at the tunnel. Finally he raised his hands and began moving his fingers. It was like watching him weave on an invisible loom. The Highlanders guarded the secrets of their magic jealously, so Joros had no idea whether the finger-waving was actually doing anything, or if the mage might just be playing him for a fool. He jumped as a loud grinding noise filled the storeroom, chains clanking and carcasses shaking as they jolted on their hooks. The rock itself seemed to melt, flowing down like mud to cover the tunnel opening, and then the room slowly settled back into silence. The mage looked up to Joros, face hopeful. "Like that?"

"How did you do that?" Joros demanded.

The mage flinched, trying to curl in on himself. "It's a simple merging," he whimpered. "Like calls to like."

Joros glared distrustfully down at the mage—true, Anddyr had done exactly as he'd asked, but Joros hadn't really expected it—until those words bumped up against something in Joros's brain and set off a small cascade of ideas. A single, shining thought dropped into place.

For the first time in many years, Joros laughed.

CHAPTER 7

All of Keiro's life had been walking.

Walking with his father, from town to town to town, looking for work, any work that would put coin in their pockets or food in their bellies. Walking the same roads and same towns even after his father died, until he'd realized his feet could walk him where he pleased instead.

Walking alone, more often than not, though there were companions, for minutes or hours or days, as long as their feet happened to walk the same roads. A tinker, who had taught him how to put an edge back on a knife so dull it couldn't cut soup. A scribe, who'd patiently taught him his letters. A mercenary, who'd taught him all the bawdy songs she knew, just to watch Keiro's cheeks flame red. A carpenter, who'd taught him how to make the best sort of walking stick, one that could be used as a weapon if it came to it on the long lonely roads. And then there was the preacher, who'd taught him his life's true path.

Pelir, his name was, and they'd met the same way it always

went. Feet coming together on the dusty road, pleasantries exchanged, conversation started. He was an old man, Pelir, wearing a black hooded robe that dragged around his feet, so that the hem was swirled brown and red with dirt, and he wore a black cloth bound about his eyes. Keiro thought he was blind, but the old man laughed at that. "I'm not brave enough, boy, or learned enough, not yet," he'd said, and Keiro hadn't understood. But the road had kept them together, and Pelir had spoken of his gods, the ones trapped beneath the earth, and Keiro had listened, and learned, and began to understand.

They had walked together, all the way to the foot of Mount Raturo, where Pelir had told him he must make the rest of the journey alone. A stone door had opened at his touch, and closed after him before Keiro could do more than gape. Then Keiro had walked alone again for a time, the long and twisting journey up the mountain, armed with the ancient words to send the Sentinels back to their sleep, with naught but the cold and the whistling air for company. His feet and his sturdy walking stick had brought him safely to the top, and Pelir had been waiting for him within.

Walking, then, the twisting halls of hollow Raturo, learning from all who would teach, learning all he could, until they sent him back out into the world with a black robe and a small seekstone strung around his neck.

Walking as a preacher, with Fratarro's gentle heart and Sororra's unyielding purpose held close. Walking, again, the same paths he'd walked with his father, though it was different now, more different than he could have imagined.

He'd gotten used to the scorn and the mockery, the petty cruelty, had even come to accept the blind hatred. "They are who they are," he would tell himself on the long road out of town, "shaped as they have been shaped. It is not their fault." It didn't make the jeers and the beatings any easier, but it made the too-rare spark of understanding, of recognition, that much more precious.

He would never, though, get used to the drownings.

The first one he'd seen had sent him walking farther than he'd ever walked before or since, to the edges of the Northern Wastes, as far as he could get from Mount Raturo and all those within. He'd gone as far as he could, trying to escape one faith that could drive a village to drown two innocent babes for the crime of being born together, and another faith that couldn't stop it. But he had walked back, eventually, because he believed still—and more, he believed that the drownings could be stopped. That the Long Night would come, that he could help bring it about, and that no more twins would be drowned thereafter.

But still the sun rose, and still twins were born, and still they were drowned by the heartless followers of the Parents. And still, staring eyes danced in his memories, eyes too big for such tiny faces, eyes full of terror and innocence.

His feet took him home now, as was his habit after a drowning. By his count, it had been nearly two years since he'd last set his feet inside the mountain—he preferred the open places, where a man could always walk toward the horizon and never touch it. His heart was heavy, though, like a stone dragging down a fishing net, and there was a comfort to home. His feet took him through the trees and the fields and the wild places, far from the kind of people who could kill an infant and call it holy. Through the farmlands where preachers lived a simple life, tending the flocks and fields that kept Raturo's storerooms stocked. He heard them call out as he passed, greet him in the name of the Twins. It would have been welcoming, another time. Now, though, he only wished to be done with walking for a time. He finally reached the only place he could name home, Mount Raturo, and he began the climb with Sororra's Eyes watching him, and all the babies' eyes haunting him.

The mountain knew him, remembered Keiro's scent and the blood he'd shed on his first ascent, but it took long hours of climbing to find a door that would open to his touch. The doors were keyed to ranking, and Keiro was a preacher of no great repute: a preacher who couldn't bear the darker side of that which he preached, who crumbled inside at the sight of tiny pale bodies bobbing in the water. It was a wonder the Sentinels had ever let him pass to begin with. "You've a gentle heart," Pelir had said, but he'd said it sadly, the night before he sent Keiro back out into the world with his new black robe and his black eyecloth. Keiro hadn't understood the sadness in that then.

The halls of Raturo were dark, dark as they always were, with lights the barest glimmer. Keiro's feet knew the way to his old teacher's room, and he watched them take it, unable to lift his eyes for the shame and the grief that swirled within him. He didn't knock at the door, but simply entered; Pelir turned his cloth-bound eyes up as Keiro stepped into the room and knelt before the blinded man. Leathery, unshaking hands rested on his head as Pelir murmured a greeting, a blessing, and it was the simple kindness as much as anything else that broke Keiro.

More tears still for the dead babes, for all the staring eyes he could never forget, for all the tiny twins he'd laid to rest over all his walking years, and through the tears he managed to say, "I will do it, brother. I will make the sacrifice." He didn't know he meant to say the words, but there was a rightness to them. It was a small thing, after all, and a fitting punishment for all the babes he hadn't saved. Perhaps he would finally stop seeing their eyes, staring with a simple grief that was harder to bear than recrimination would have been.

Things moved quickly, then, in the sacred halls of Mount Raturo. No one could fault the disciples of the Twins for being ill-prepared. With Pelir at his side, and as many preachers as could hear the shouted news trailing behind, Keiro made his way down and down to the deepest parts of Raturo.

The Ventallo were waiting in their black robes with Sororra's Eyes blazing over their hearts, as many of them as could be found or bothered to attend. Seven sets of their feet, Keiro counted, and it was more than enough. Uniro himself was there, Delcerro Uniro with his thin neck and shaking hands, who had lasted as Uniro longer than any had expected. Keiro supposed it was an honor, but still his eyes stayed on his feet. He couldn't seem to bring himself to look at anything else.

The assembled Ventallo parted, making way for Keiro to walk through their ranks and into the cold chamber beyond. The ghost lights flickered there in the big cavern, their icy light making the air seem even colder. The others followed after him, the Ventallo and Pelir and all the others who had come to bear witness. They walked until they came to the edge of the frozen lake, and then Keiro walked on alone, watching his feet take him across the ice. They stopped before the Icefall, water long ago frozen midtumble, and Keiro reached out to wrap his fingers around a cold spine. It came away with a snap that echoed throughout the cavern, the sound of a bone shattering. He carried it before him in his two hands, as the youngest midwife had carried the girl-child, and he knelt before the black robes and held it up for their inspection.

"I dedicate myself to the Twins," he said simply. He couldn't remember the worlds Pelir had used, years ago, but he didn't think it mattered. "I am theirs, and they shall guide me through the dark."

"Let it be so," Uniro said in his high, querulous voice.

Finally Keiro turned up his face, looking into the dark heights of the cavern, and he raised up the icicle, and with a sigh of relief brought its tip down into his right eye.

For a moment, a moment only, there was joy. Never again would he have to see the sad bodies floating in rivers, never again see the sun shining its torment down on the little graves. He was free, finally, of the staring eyes.

And then came the pain.

Through the thrashing and the screaming and the streaming blood, through the hands trying to hold him still, through Pelir's sonorous voice beseeching Fratarro, through it all, somehow, Keiro's eye opened, the one eye, the one he had left. It opened, and he saw something he had never thought to see.

Standing there, nearly hidden among the swirling black robes, were two children, a boy and a girl, holding hands firmly as they stared back at him. Two children that were mirror images of each other. Twins. Alive and grown and old enough to walk, to talk, to look back at him with comprehension. A woman knelt before them, put her hands on their shoulders, tried to shield Keiro from their sight. They were real, as real as Keiro, as real as life. And the tears burst from him then, one eye sobbing blood, as he washed his conscience clean, wiped away the guilt and the staring eyes and the tiny graves. For here they stood redeemed, all the drowned babes through all his walking years.

"Finish it, brother," one of the Ventallo rumbled.

"No," Keiro gasped out, a smile breaking across his face. "Don't you see?"

"We see," the man said sternly. Squinting with his one eye, Keiro saw that his face was sharp and unforgiving, uncompromising. "*You* should not. You've been given to the gods. Finish it."

They didn't see, none of them. Living twins! They meant that it was possible, all of it. The Long Night, and a time when there would be no more drownings, no more tiny hand-dug graves. They meant that Keiro could bear the sight of the world for a while longer, knowing that it would change. They meant that he would need his sight, to guide them, the beautiful living twins, to their destiny, to the salvation of all.

And looking at the twins with his one eye, he heard the fluttering of a voice again, no louder than the blood leaking from his empty socket: *Find me.*

"No," Keiro said again, not to the whispered voice but to the hands that held the bloody icicle out to him, to those who wanted to take his eye that had, finally, seen living twins.

They took his seekstone, cutting him off from the mountain, but they let him keep his robe and his eyecloth and his walking stick. Those were, really, the only possessions he'd ever valued. They let him keep his title, too, though they argued heatedly over it. He was a preacher still, a Fraro of the Fallen. They took him to the very top of Mount Raturo and pushed him still bleeding out into the waist-deep snow that blanketed the peak.

"Away," the hard-faced Ventallo intoned formally, filling the doorway he'd thrown Keiro from. "Be gone from this place. Apostate." In all the arguing, Keiro remembered, this man, this man he didn't even know, had called for his death. For dishonoring the gods. Because he was blind to the truth. And half blind, sprawled in the snow, banished, Keiro let out a little laugh. "You are given a chance," the Ventallo continued. "A hope of redemption. It's more than you deserve, but there it is. You may use our words still, and spread our teachings, and pray that the gods forgive you. Should we see your face again, it shall mean your death." He stepped back, into Raturo, and the mountain closed shut, swallowing him whole, and leaving Keiro so very alone.

His hands were cold, near frozen, but he managed to tie the eyecloth around his face, hoping it would slow the bleeding if nothing else. Behind his blind eye, he saw still the faces of the dead babes, all the drowned children he'd laid in the earth; but in front of his good eye, all he could see were the faces of the living twins. His redemption.

Perhaps he could not stand at their sides, lead them to the glory they were meant for. But he could prepare the world for them, as best he could.

Keiro used his walking stick to lever himself to his feet, and he began the descent, down the steep slopes of Mount Raturo. He had a long way to walk.

CHAPTER 8

There was a servant named Mayga who took care of Rora, not letting her get out of bed and—when keeping her in bed failed, which it did—not letting her leave the room. She was pretty closemouthed, Mayga, especially when it came to Nadaro.

"*Cappo* Nadaro," she said, putting on the emphasis like she expected Rora to give him the same respect, "is a good man. He does well by us all, and he'll do the same for you. Now get back in bed." She would yell at Rora for not calling him cappo, but sometimes, when Mayga didn't know she was there, Rora heard her call him "Seeker Nadaro," and she said it more scared than respectful.

More troubling than Nadaro was her brother, who was gone most days. "Cappo Nadaro is showing me the whole city!" he told her excitedly, burrowing into the bed next to her. "He lets me come with him wherever he goes, and it's so . . . so *wonderful*, Rora! It's a hundred times better than the West Market . . . there's so many things to see!"

She didn't like Aro hanging around the man so much, didn't like it at all. "I don't trust him, Aro."

He looked like she'd given him a whole pile of sweets and then snatched it away. "He's nice, Rora. He saved you." Unusually solemn, he looked her in the eyes and said, "I couldn't've saved you on my own, and if you'd . . . if you'd *died*, I would've been nothing. We owe him, Rora. And it's not so bad, not at all. Once your arm's better, you'll see."

She felt guilty doing it, couldn't look him in the eyes as she said it, but she had to. "I just . . . I wish you'd stay with me more. I get lonely here."

Aro hugged her tight. "I'm sorry, Rora. I'll stay tomorrow, promise. And I'll talk to Mayga, too, she likes me. I'll get her to let me show you the rest of the house. There's so much stuff we never even knew about, Rora . . ."

Mayga did let them go exploring, and the house was just as fancy as Aro'd said. She let him show her everything, but also kept her own eyes sharp, looking for a way out, just in case. And stuffing her pockets whenever Aro and Mayga weren't looking.

Her arm got better pretty fast, and Mayga said it was because kids healed quick, and because Nadaro had taken her to the best chirurgeon in the city. Rora didn't know what that was, but Aro said it was like the cutters that took care of sick and dead people in the Canals, only much better. It didn't matter to Rora, so long as her arm got better; soon as that happened, she was going to get her and Aro out of the house. There were a few doors to the outside, but they were locked all the time. If she could figure out where the keys were . . .

Nadaro didn't talk to Rora much, but it sure seemed like

him and Aro were fast friends. It made her angry, but at the same time she couldn't remember the last time she'd seen her brother so happy. Even when they'd been with Kala, he hadn't smiled so much. Every time she started to feel guilty about wanting to take him away, though, she'd see Nadaro's dead gray eyes, and know it was for the best. She still didn't know what he really wanted, but she knew she didn't want to give it to him. Especially not if it had anything to do with her brother.

Mayga took the splint off and put her arm in a sling. It still hurt a little, but not so bad as long as she held it still against her chest. Not too long after, Aro came whirling into the room carrying a pile of cloth near as big as he was. Clothes, she saw when he dumped them on the floor in front of her. Fancy clothes.

Aro was beaming, his cheeks red with excitement. "Look what Cappo Nadaro gave us!" he crowed.

Awkward with her left hand, Rora plucked up one of the pieces of clothing. It was yellow, the pale color at the edges of a candle flame, and the funniest-looking tunic she'd ever seen. It took a few moments for her to realize it was a *dress*. She wrinkled her nose in disgust at it. Not even Kala had worn dresses.

Aro was already stripping out of his clothes and tugging on the new fancy stuff, but Rora kicked the dress under the bed. Trapped halfway into his tunic, Aro gave her a sad look.

"I'm not wearing that."

"But that's what girls wear."

"So?"

"Cappo Nadaro's throwing us a fancy dinner. We have to dress fancy, too."

Rora sat resolutely on the bed and folded her good arm

over the bad one. "I didn't ask for a fancy dinner. Sure as hells didn't ask for a dress."

Rora had been taking care of both of them for most of their lives, and she'd gotten used to Aro doing what she told him to, even if he complained sometimes. So she was a little surprised when he straightened up and crossed his arms, too, a mirror of her. "There's two things I know," he said, his voice an exact match for hers whenever she had to talk him into something. "One thing is, if it wasn't for him, you'd be dead. The other thing is, I know he wants something from us. I'm not dumb. I know how biggers work, and adults are just bigger biggers. But he saved you, and that means we owe him. It's simple, Rora. Whatever he wants, we have t' give it to him."

There was a part of her that knew he was right, but there was a bigger part of her that knew that honor and fairness didn't really matter outside of kids' stories. "You don't know what you're saying, little bird."

"Yes I do."

"What if he wants to turn you into his slave, huh?"

The tears welled up in his eyes, but he didn't blink or look away. "Then it's worth it, 's long as you're alive."

Rora shook her head. "I won't let that happen. Ever."

"Then let's find out what he *does* want. If he really just wants us to stay awhile, keep him company . . . that wouldn't be so bad, Rora, would it?"

It's not that simple, she thought, but she kept the words behind her teeth. She couldn't really think of anything else to say, so she fished the dress out from under the bed. Aro's smile was all the answer she needed.

Aro had shown her the eating room a few days ago, and

she'd thought the long table was a dumb idea then; seeing it again didn't much improve her opinion of it. It was long enough that she and Aro could have laid down on it with their arms stretched up, hands to feet, and neither of 'em would've been able to touch the ends. Judging by the chairs, it could've sat a score of people. If Nadaro was so lonely, what'd he need such a big table for? And Rora would be the first to admit she didn't know a thing about fancy stuff, but it just looked dumb with only three places set at one end. Nadaro was already sitting at the head, his hands folded and that smile on his face that didn't go to his eyes.

"My, don't you two look lovely," he said as they sat to either side of him. "Rora, you clean up very nicely. In just a few years, I imagine you'll be setting young men's hearts to racing."

She grunted, glaring at all the stuff laid out on the table. The plate she knew, and the knife, even if it was dull and pretty useless looking. Then there was a two-spiked poker and a little bowl on a stick, and she was damned if she knew what those were for. They were made of silver, though, that she was sure of. There was enough room down the front of the dress that she could probably sneak at least one of them away and keep her and Aro fed for a few weeks once they got back out on the streets.

"I'm so glad you've decided to stay," Nadaro went on. He said the words, but there was nothing behind them. Rora'd seen a few acting troupes—the crowds were the best places to filch a few coins, with everyone paying so much attention to the actors—and you could tell when an actor was good, and when he was just saying his lines. Nadaro would've made an awful actor. "I hope you'll forgive an old man his prattling, but it's so refreshing to have company, especially such charming children." Aro was grinning like he couldn't hear the blankness in the man's words. He probably couldn't. Rora loved him, but she worried he was a little simple when it came to some things. He just trusted everyone and everything they said. Lies were as impossible for him to understand as flying. "I look forward to getting to know both of you better. I daresay Aro and I have already made a good start on that." And he and her brother smiled at each other in a way that made Rora's fingers itch for that knife. It was dull, but it was something. "But I'm afraid I don't know much about you yet, Rora, save for what your dear brother has told me. It simply won't do. Please, tell me about yourself." Everything about him said he was actually interested in her . . . except for the eyes. Gods, did his eyes ever move or change?

"Not much to tell," she mumbled.

"I hardly believe that. You managed to keep yourself alive for, what, ten years? In the quaint little hellhole everyone likes to ignore? And kept your young brother alive as well, no less. You're a remarkable girl, Rora."

There was a loose thread on the skirt of the dress, and to keep her fingers away from the knife, she let them tug at the thread, tug and tug, until there was a wad of thread and a ragged line running parallel to her leg. "We do what we have to."

"Of course," Nadaro said as servants marched into the room with tasty-smelling platters of food.

She'd eaten pretty well so far, thanks to the meals Mayga'd brought her, but never like this. The servants piled her plate high with things she couldn't even recognize, and even though she didn't want to accept any kindness from Nadaro, didn't want to dig her debt to him any deeper, her stomach growled like a wild dog and she grabbed a handful of some kind of meat. It didn't taste like anything she'd ever had before, and it was delicious.

Nadaro cleared his throat softly, and she looked up. He had the dull knife in one hand and the strange poker in the other, using the two to hack at the food on his plate. Aro was trying to copy him, but not doing too good at it. A servant stepped forward to help him. Rora met Nadaro's eyes and lifted the handful of meat to her mouth. They stared, and Rora promised herself she wouldn't be the first to look away. Bluffing, playing tough, just the same as she did every day in the Canals. She might not've known how to use a food-poker, but this she understood.

"Rora's real good at everything," Aro burbled around a mouthful of food, as if the conversation'd never stopped, as if there wasn't a little war going on. He didn't know fighting, didn't know toughness. If someone spoke to him too rough, he was as like to cry as anything.

"So I've heard," Nadaro said. "You seem a most resourceful girl, Rora. A useful friend to have. I do hope you consider me a friend?"

"Friends are people you can trust."

"Caution can be a virtue. But I would dearly love to earn your trust and friendship."

With all the innocence in the world, Aro chirped, "You're my friend," and Nadaro finally turned his eyes from Rora, gave her brother that dead smile.

"I'm very happy to hear that, little Aro."

Rora stayed as quiet as she could for the rest of the meal,

eating with her good hand and pulling at the thread on her dress, glaring at everything as Aro and Nadaro chatted as easily as if they'd known each other for years. And still Aro couldn't see what a bad actor the man was, couldn't hear the strangeness in his voice. As soon as Rora could, she announced that she was tired and pushed herself away from the table.

"Healing is a tiring process," Nadaro said, nodding. "I have enjoyed our time together. Sleep well. I hope you'll allow me to keep your dear brother for a while longer?"

"No," she blurted, fear and anger stabbing together at her heart. Aro frowned at her, and Nadaro smirked, the first thing that came close to touching his eyes, and it sent prickles up her back.

"No?" he repeated, faking shock just like a bad actor would.

"I . . . I need him."

"Need him?" Nadaro repeated again, and it almost felt like he was mocking her. "Whatever would you need him for? He'll be right here, with me. I had Cook prepare a special dessert, and it mustn't go to waste. It would break the poor woman's heart."

Aro's eyes lit up at that. "I'll be up later, Rora, I'm not tired at all."

Rora wanted to tear at her hair, to stamp her feet, to scream in Nadaro's face. Stupid Aro, why couldn't he see how things worked? "I . . ." There was still that smirk on Nadaro's face, and Rora knew with a simple certainty that she couldn't leave her brother with the man. Couldn't. "I . . ."

"You . . . ?" Nadaro prodded, and she *knew* this time he was making fun of her.

Her cheeks were burning, but she looked to Aro, trying to

talk to him with her eyes, to get him to understand. "I can't sleep without you." She saw his face soften, could almost see his heart reaching out to her, and she pounced on it. "It's just . . . we've always been together. It feels wrong going to sleep without you there. I can't sleep if I don't know you're safe."

"I'm safe here, Rora, we're both safe. I'll just be right here."

She shook her head, and glanced at Nadaro. *I'm a better actor than you are.* "It's not the same, though. My mind's always gonna be worried about you." The best actors were the ones who knew exactly what to do and say to get the best reactions from the audience, and Rora knew her audience better than anyone else ever could. "I'll just have to get up every few minutes to check on you. I won't get any sleep at all."

Aro's face was softening more and more, and as he gave Nadaro an apologetic look, she felt triumph well up inside her. She gave Nadaro the sweetest smile she could pull up.

"Can you tell Cook that we'll have her dessert tomorrow?" Aro said. "And tell her I'm real sorry. Everything else was real good."

Nadaro nodded, and his eyes were flat and hard again. "Of course. I wouldn't dare come between the bonds of sibling attachment." He waved his hand in dismissal. "Sleep well, dear children."

Rora took Aro's hand and pulled him up the stairs to the relative safety of their bedroom. Not that she really felt safe there, but it was better'n being around Nadaro. She yanked off the dress with its long tear and wadded thread, clumsy with her arm in the sling, and found the plainest clothes she could instead. Her old clothes, the ones she'd worn since Kala's, were long gone, probably burned. All the clothes Mayga'd brought her were a little small, but at least they were simple wool, and not dresses.

"What's wrong with you?" Aro demanded.

"I don't like it here."

Aro puffed out his cheeks, blew air at her. "You're being dumb."

"I'm not!" She rounded on him, trying to shake her finger in his face until the pain reminded her not to move her arm. It just fueled her anger anyway. "You don't even know him. You shouldn't trust him. You trust too much. We can't trust anyone but each other."

"We trusted Kala."

"Yeah, and look what happened. She would've had us killed, and now she's dead. That's why you can't trust anyone!" The tears sprang into his eyes, and guilt hit her like a punch. She went to him, wrapped her good arm around him, held him as he cried against her shoulder. "I'm sorry, Aro. That was mean of me."

"I didn't mean to . . ."

She hushed him gently, stroked his hair the way their father had always done in her dim memory of him. "I know, little bird, I know. But don't you see? We've got each other. We don't need anyone else. Other people just . . . they make things messy."

He sniffled, wiping his nose across his sleeve. "I thought . . . thought we could be happy here. I just want us to be happy."

Rora made herself smile. *I'm a better actor,* she silently taunted Nadaro. "We'll be happy so long as we stick together, hey? I'll always keep us safe."

She waited until it was dark and the house was quiet. Aro

had fallen asleep, but he woke up easy enough. "Do you trust me?" she asked him as he blinked away sleep, and he nodded with all the seriousness in his little body. She grabbed a few trinkets that looked valuable, and then she and Aro ghosted down the stairs in the darkness. There was a door off the kitchen that Rora figured was their best bet, even though it meant creeping past the servant boy who slept in front of the kitchen hearth; he slept like a lump, so she wasn't too worried. He wasn't even there when they snuck by, probably gone to sleep with the other servants since the night was warm enough, and Rora thought how lucky they were.

"Where are you going, little birds?"

Rora near jumped out of her skin with fright, and Aro let out a small yelp. The fire was low, but as her eyes darted around the room, she could make out a shape in front of the kitchen door, blocking the way to outside. Nadaro, she saw as she stared hard as she could, sitting in a chair that was leaned back against the door.

"Aro was hungry," Rora quickly lied, and stomped on her brother's foot before he could get a word in.

Nadaro chuckled, a low sound that felt like it echoed all around her. "You're a poor liar, Rora."

She bristled. *Better liar than you are.* "I'm not a liar."

"And there you go, doing it again. We'll have to train that out of you, my dear, if you're going to be any use."

The fire was low, but it gave off enough light that Rora could see his eyes, glowing in the darkness like they were the flames. Moving slow, she pushed Aro behind her, making sure she was between her brother and Nadaro. "What d'you mean?"

"You owe me, Rora. Or have you forgotten already? You

owe me your arm, and you owe me your life. What's more, you owe me your brother's life. No debt goes unpaid. How many favors is your arm worth? What value do you put on your life?" There was a low scraping sound, and though the fire was low, she saw its light gleam off metal. A long dagger, held across his lap as he dragged a sharpening stone across it. "You're young still, of course, too young. But you'll grow, and you will repay your debt, both of you."

Rora wanted to stand her ground, to show him she wasn't afraid, but she was shaking inside, every part of her screaming. In the Canals, you listened to anyone with a knife or you got your throat cut out. Those were the rules. Even this far from the Canals, it seemed like a dumb rule to break, and that was the biggest dagger she'd ever seen, too.

"I think we understand each other," Nadaro said, and there was a smile on his face. His eyes were still made of fire. "I told you when we met that nothing was free. But allow me to give you some advice, little Rora. You don't want to defy me. Now go back to bed."

She couldn't see any way around it, so she started backing up slowly, pushing Aro back out toward the hallway, never taking her eyes off Nadaro. She was nearly back into the shadows when he called out softly, "Oh, and Rora? You might do well to remember that I hold your life—both your lives—in my hands still. Even if you did get out, how far do you think you would get once I started shouting that I'd spotted twins?"

Rora went cold all over, and behind her Aro made a strangled little whimper. *"She knew, she knew, she knew,"* Aro sobbed *from the middle of a puddle of blood.* "We're not—"

Nadaro cut her off. "Yes, you are." The smile almost reached his eyes as he said, "You could at least try to hide it better. Do you even know what your names mean?"

Girl and *boy* in the Old Tongue, their father's favorite joke until his laughs turned to coughs and he didn't wake up. She just stared at Nadaro, numb with fear.

"You will stay with me," he went on, "and serve me, and in return I will keep your secret. I'll keep the whole city from tearing you both limb from limb. But only if you pay off your debt to me. Do we understand each other, Rora?"

Her stomach was spinning in knots and it felt like her throat was closing up, like someone was squeezing a hand slowly around her neck. All she could do was nod and shove Aro away, pushing him ahead of her as they fled back up the stairs. It took a while, but she got the big desk pushed in front of the door before she went to sit on the bed where Aro was curled up in a miserable, crying ball. "I can't do the bad thing," he sobbed. "I'm sorry, Rora, I can't, I can't . . ." She hushed him, stroked his hair, soft and clean, and told him she would take care of things, to trust her. He fell asleep eventually, but she stayed up staring at the door until light peeked in through the windows. Aro woke up puffy-eyed from so much crying, but Rora's cheeks were dry, and though it felt heavy as a chunk of metal, her heart was hard and full of purpose.

She left Aro sleeping in the room when she snuck out the next night and retraced her steps, tiptoeing down to the kitchen. The servant boy was in his usual place before the low-burning fire, but he slept hard, snoring, not so much as twitching as she moved through the kitchen like a ghost. She glanced at the outside door, just once, but she couldn't leave Aro behind.

The cook was a very organized woman; everything had its own place, and the Parents help anyone who didn't know her system. Rora'd only been in the kitchen once, outside of these two nightly trips, but she hadn't needed more'n a moment to memorize the location of the most important things. She had to climb up onto the chopping block to reach, but her groping fingers found a bone handle and pulled. The sharp-pointed carving knife came free from its slot with a whisper, a sturdy blade twice as long as her hand, and Rora looked at it with awe, a slash of her face reflecting back at her, one brown eye, the side of her nose, the corner of her mouth. She'd never held a real knife before, never held any weapon more'n a sharp piece of metal she'd found half buried in the Canals. It was dangerous, and intoxicating. It was power, pure and simple, something else she'd never had before.

The fingers on her right hand were still a little stiff, not moving too well, and with the arm in a sling it wasn't like she could do much with it anyway. So she kept the knife in her left hand, awkward as it felt, and curled her fingers tight around the handle, holding her new power with reverence and excitement as she crept back up the staircase.

Nadaro's room was the one place in the big house she'd never been into, but she didn't hesitate outside the door. It was unlocked; all the doors except the ones outside were always unlocked. She nudged it open real slow, just far enough so she could slip in all quiet, the knife held out in front of her. Her heart was pounding fast, so fast inside her chest, a mix of thrill and terror. The door closed just as quiet as it had opened.

The fire had burned down to coals, giving off a dull red glow. A bit of moonlight leaked in through the window, enough light that she could make out the furniture, not too different from her and Aro's room. Big bed, taking up most of the space, and deep sleeping breaths coming from it. She moved forward on the balls of her feet, fingers twitching nervously on the knife's hilt.

Sleeping, he didn't look so bad. Just a getting-old man with a stern face, and even that wasn't so mean when he was sleeping. But he *was* mean, she told herself, said it over and over in her head, called up all the things he'd said last night, all the threats. He'd kill them, maybe not soon, but one day, and treat them worse than slaves up until he put a knife in them. He'd kill her sweet Aro, unless she did something about it. She lifted up the knife, clumsy in her left hand, and stared at a spot on his chest, the spot right above where she could almost swear she could hear his heart beating steady. *For Aro,* she thought.

But the knife wouldn't move. Her hand started to shake and she felt that awful pressure behind her nose, the one that meant she had to fight back the tears. Crying was for weak people. Aro was weak, she knew that, but she had to be strong for him. She clenched her fingers tighter around the bone hilt. *For Aro!*

Her hand dropped, bearing the knife down with it, and fell dangling at her side. Her head drooped forward, those damned tears pricking at her eyes. She couldn't do it. She was weak, too.

"Do it!"

Nadaro's eyes were open, shining black in the darkness, and his face was all twisted up. It was a smile, she realized, taking a scared step back. A smile that actually reached his eyes, and it was awful.

"Do it, you coward," he hissed, baring his teeth at her like a wild animal.

Even though her mouth tasted like fear, she still held the knife tight in her hand, still had power. She tried to summon any courage. "I could," she said, her voice like a frog's croak. She forced her back straighter, glaring with a bravery she was nowhere close to feeling. "But I'm sparing your life instead. A life for a life, that's how we do it in the Canals."

"My life," he said slowly, "for yours?" That horrible smile stretched back over his face, made her knees feel like jelly. "Then go, Rora. Leave. Your life is yours. But I only have one life, silly little bird. You need two."

Aro. She could go, but Nadaro would keep her brother. That was no kind of choice at all. "No. Aro comes with me. I—I could still kill you." She shook the knife at him, as if that was any kind of threat.

He moved fast as a snake, sitting up to face her, grabbing her hand that held the knife. She squawked in surprise, but he brought the tip of the knife to rest against his own chest. "Then *do it!*" His fingers were tight around hers, both his hands wrapped around her hand wrapped around the knife. She gaped up into the black pits of his eyes. "Kill me," he hissed. She tried to pull her hand back, pull the knife away, but he was too strong. "Kill me, or I'll go kill your brother." One of his hands let go of hers and suddenly there was a second knife, the long dagger he'd been sharpening in the kitchen last night. He pointed it right between her eyes, then waved it in the direction of the hallway, the blade flashing a hairsbreadth from the tip of her nose. "Could you live with that for the rest of your life, Rora? Knowing that you're the reason he died?"

His hand squeezed around hers, around the carving knife. She couldn't breathe, panic pounding through her whole body;

her hand would've shook if Nadaro hadn't held it steady. "I can't, I can't, I can't," Aro sobbed, except it was her voice.

Nadaro's face twisted with hatred, and he started to stand.

The panic flowed through Rora, a burst of mindless alarm—*Aro!*—and her hand moved.

The dagger dropped from Nadaro's fingers, clattered to the floor.

His fingers slipped from hers, hers slipped from the carving knife, and she scrambled back. The knife stayed where it was, in the middle of a spreading circle of red.

Nadaro looked at the knife in his chest, looked at Rora, and started to laugh. A high, crazy sound, the sound of every bad thing in the world, a sound that wasn't really human.

"The shadows know you, girl," he gasped in between spasms of laughter, blood dripping down the knife's pale bone handle, plopping to the floor. "The darkness knows your name, and it never rests. My brothers and sisters will find you." He slumped forward, falling onto the floor, falling into the pool of his own blood, and still he laughed. Still his black eyes stared into her. "They will follow you to the ends of the earth. The darkness never sleeps. You will never find peace. The shadows know your name."

The dagger was in her hand. She couldn't remember picking it up, but it was in her right hand, the hand he'd saved. It barely even hurt as she planted the tip into his neck. The mad laughter stopped, cut off, changed to gurgles. She pulled the dagger free and stared down at him, watched the light go out of his eyes, waited until the breath stopped wheezing out through the hole in his neck.

Her fingers flexed around the hilt of the dagger, and she

held it up in front of her. A slash of her face, reflected for just a moment, until Nadaro's blood leaked down the blade.

She went to wake Aro, and smashed a window open with the big blue gem set into the dagger's pommel. They climbed out of the window into a moonless night, and ran.

CHAPTER 9

Valastaastad seemed to hang in the empty air. A floating island held up by a broken cliff of stone and ice—a
jagged arm of the Faltiik Mountains, reaching out to cup the
clan-home in its palm. It was like something out of the fairy
tales Mora the cook had sometimes told him and Brennon
when they were younger. Valastaastad would be the home of
an evil ice-giant who, through ancient magics, had raised his
fortress high above the earth so that no one could rescue the
princess he had stolen. For a brief, sweet moment Scal could
imagine himself as the avenging warrior in shiny clothes,
come to scale the impossible heights and free the beautiful
princess.

Then a ragged cheer went up from the Northmen, and
Einas leered at him, rotten teeth thrust out from his matted
beard. The moment broke. If anything, Scal was the princess
who had been captured by the foul ice-giants. It was a dampening thought.

"Welcome to your home," Iveran said. Beneath the shaggy

yellow beard, his cheeks were bright and a smile stretched his lips.

Scal shook his head. "You burned my home."

"That was no home for no one, *ijka*. Just a prison. For you especially."

One of Scal's former jailors, Uisbure, threw his arms wide. "Breathe the freedom!"

Iveran nodded wisely, drew in a deep breath. "You will see one day," he said to Scal. "Soon, I hope. That is all this is. Us setting you free. You will see, *ijka*."

Scal shook his head and, out of pure stubbornness, held his breath for as long as he could, until spots danced at the edges of his vision and his feet stumbled on the crunching snow. Iveran was there to steady him, grinning, as his lungs reflexively filled themselves.

"You understand," Iveran said.

Scal had used every way he knew of telling the man he would never understand. Never accept. He just shook his head and stared at the ground, refusing to look as they drew nearer to his prison.

He could not help but look, though, when they came to the solid wall of ice.

Staring straight up, the cliff dwindled away to blend almost perfectly with the grim sky. And hovering between the icy peak and Scal's craned neck was Valastaastad. Not floating in the sky, but built on a shelf of ice that hung out dangerously far into the open air. It must have been at least a dozen lengths up to it, and the shelf looked no more than a few lengths thick, with houses clustered all along it. Scal could not help gaping. It was a mind-bogglingly stupid place to build a village.

"Impressive, eh?" Iveran said, grinning.

Scal shook his head, groping for the right words to describe just how foolish it was. "The ice will break," he said. "It is a miracle it has not already. The whole shelf will crumble away."

A full-bellied laugh boiled up out of Iveran's throat. "Have some faith, *ijka*! Valastaastad has stood such for five generations. We may have thick skulls"—he rapped his knuckles sharply against the forehead of a passing Northman, who grinned in return—"but the ice is thicker."

Scal shook his head in mute denial, but Iveran and the others were already moving away, tramping under the ice shelf. The dogs raced ahead, barking eagerly. The sledges jouncing dangerously across the rough ground. The dog handlers racing alongside and laughing with the joy of it. Only Uisbure remained, bushy eyebrows raised high. He held a long spear in one gloved hand, its tip glimmering like a fallen star as he waved it toward the backs of the clan. Scal hunched his shoulders, fixed his eyes on the ice, and set his feet one before the other. Into the wide pool of shadow cast by the ice shelf. Trying not to think about the weight of ice above him. Wishing it were more so it would crumble and fall. Wishing it were less so that it would not crush him so bad when it did fall.

He ached still, from the beating two days ago. Each breath sent jabs of pain through his chest, from the bruises and a few cracked ribs. He had to breathe heavily through his mouth, his nose broken and useless. With every breath he could hear a strange, faint whistling noise. It had taken him a while to understand that: the ragged edges of his new convict's cross were starting to knit on their own, but his tongue could not leave the bloody edges alone, keeping the X in his cheek open enough for the wind to whistle through.

His legs felt like the bones had been replaced with fire-fresh iron pokers, burning with every step. They let him walk, at least. Pain was better than the shame of being carried like a trussed pig. *Pride is a fool's refuge,* Kerrus whispered at the back of his mind, and his body wanted to agree. But he would not give Iveran the satisfaction. The cold was starting to seep into his skin, too, and he walked hunched over with his arms wrapped futilely around his chest to hold the heat in. To hold himself together. The rest of the Northmen had thick furs to fight off the cold, and even their cheeks were rosy. None of them had offered him anything warmer than his own clothes. He was not about to ask for any. *We endure,* Kerrus had said. *Sometimes just getting by is a great accomplishment.*

"Hey-o!" Iveran's voice carried across the ice in ripples, bouncing off the cliff walls, the ice ceiling. His white-gloved hands were cupped around his mouth, his head tilted back as he shouted into the air. *"Riikar drith,"* he called, the sound of the words unfamiliar to Scal's ears. Not the Northern tongue at all.

Scal tilted his head up as well, confused, just as a wood-and-rope ladder tumbled through the air.

The men all stepped back, clearing space as the falling end of the ladder clattered to the ice. Another joined. And another. Six in total, draped in a neat half circle wider than three men could spread their arms. Gaping up, Scal finally saw it. A hole cut into the ice far above, the ladders dangling and, dimly seen, a score of faces peering down.

Ropes followed, and the sledge men set about unhitching

their dogs from the cargo and stringing the snarling beasts up by the ropes instead. Scal watched in a mix of horror and amazement as the dogs were lifted into the open air. Wailing and snarling and thrashing, feet clawing desperately at nothing, twisting to try to bite the ropes. Moving up span by jerking span, terrified yowling voices bouncing from the walls and echoing down until they disappeared over the lip of the distant hole.

The ropes dropped back down, and they did it over again.

Scal's jaw ached from clenching his teeth, his head pounding with the sound of blind dog-fear. The Northmen were just starting on the sledges when Uisbure nudged Scal with the butt of his spear, then pointed to the hanging ladders. Men were beginning to make the slow climb. Scal's stomach sank at the thought of dangling in the air like one of those dogs. Blown around by the uncaring wind. Fear aside, his fingers were cold and stiff, and he was not sure they would be able to grip the wooden slats. That his legs could make such a swaying, upward climb.

Uisbure poked him with the spear again. "Up," he said, and his eyes darkened when Scal shook his head. Uisbure's mouth was hidden behind his thick beard, but Scal did not need to see the frown to know it was there. "Go, boy," he growled.

Scal stood perfectly still, arms wrapped miserably around himself, and shook his head again. *Stand behind your decisions; if you won't defend yourself, no one else will.*

His ears rang and spots danced before his eyes; he did not realize Uisbure had hit him until the man's hand was already back at his side. Blood filled Scal's mouth. The prisoner's cross, broken open once more. Uisbure's face was no kinder, but there was a hint of something in his voice—reason? sympathy?—as he said, "I am telling you, boy. You do not want to make this hard for you."

There was sense in that. In choosing the easy path. Close his eyes and climb the ladder, fingers gripping cold, and give himself into this new life. Stick his head up through the ice-cut hole and smile at all the faces so like his own. Cheer and laugh and celebrate homecoming. Belong.

Gingerly, Scal bent his legs and sat in the snow at Uisbure's feet. He should have felt the cold seep into him, but he did not. It was beyond his concern. Uisbure kicked him, but he sat stern and solid. Belong? No. Never.

Three Northmen joined Uisbure, and the four of them hefted the boy and hauled him toward the ladders. A smile tugged at the corners of Scal's mouth. Did they think they could make him climb? Foolishness. But they did not set him by the ladders. They set him by the last sledge, by the empty dangling ropes. Three of them held him still, so by the time Uisbure began looping the rope around his chest and he thought to struggle, it was too late. They tied him as they had tied the dogs, a rough harness of scratching rope, and tied his hands as well. The rope tightened around his chest, and the Northmen released him, and he began to rise into the air.

Rope dug into his shoulders and his chest, scraping painfully as he was lifted. Iveran looked up and laughed as Scal rose slowly above them span by span, and soon the rest were laughing as well. Scal, raised like a dog into Valastaastad.

Panic did not take long. The Northmen grew smaller, the ropes dug deeper. His breath wheezed through his teeth and the prisoner's cross. He twisted and kicked, aching for the solid feel of ground beneath his feet. His hands fluttered use-lessly behind his back, denied even the dogs' scared scrabbling comfort.

There was a small noise, almost lost in his terror. A creak-ing, a protest, a strained groan. The sound of a rope harness made to hold the weight of a dog. Not a man. Not even a boy.

High above the Northmen, still laughing. High enough that he would break when he fell. Shatter into pieces like a block of ice. He would fall, and he would die. He knew he must stay still, keep the rope from weakening. *Fear is natural*, Parro Ker-rus had said, *but so is pissing yourself. A man must learn to control both.* But Scal's fear was a wild thing. He flailed and howled, like a dog, and the rope wailed with him.

Fingers touched his skull. A hand, wrapped through his hair, hauling up. Hands on his shoulder, under the ropes, pull-ing. Thrown limp, landing with ice beneath his back, a desper-ate joyous sob rising in his throat. They laughed at him, too, a ring of broad blond faces staring down. He did not care. There was solid ground beneath him. No matter that it was a sheet of ice hanging high above the real ground. For now, it was enough.

Scal kicked out as he woke from his dreams, and was rewarded with a sharp yelp of pain. A smile with no joy tugged at his mouth. The dogs had been bothering at him all night, trying to steal his boots. They still smelled of the animal they had come from, no doubt. Kerrus had glowed when he had given them to Scal. Good boots were a luxury in Aardanel, new boots even more so.

The kicked dog slunk away growling, eyes fixed on Scal.

The others were watching him, too, the whole pack. A mixture of hatred and terror and hunger. One snarled as he met its eyes, baring its sharp teeth. The rest soon joined in, and the kennels were full of a barking and howling and snapping bedlam. Scal sat in his corner, and endured.

A fist pounded against the wall of the kennel, a rough voice yelling fury. The dogs' anger changed to fear, their crying bouncing around the kennel until it subsided to whimpers and a few growls, and the pounding stopped.

It had been Iveran's idea. The Northmen of Valastaastad had kept a close eye on Scal after hauling him up through the hole, though he had had no intention of moving. Then the chief had loomed over him, humor and anger and disgust and disappointment all playing over his face as he looked down at Scal. "You have much to learn, *ijka*," he had said. "My dogs may teach you more lessons." He had turned away then, and a group of Northmen had dragged Scal away. Thrown him into the kennels with the dogs. It was a long low stone building, not unlike the other buildings in Valastaastad he had glimpsed, although built to an animal's stature. A small open doorway in each wall so the dogs could come and go freely. A fence, twice the height of the biggest dog, circling the kennel to keep them from running off. Scal had huddled against the fence, watching the dogs watch him with wary eyes. Watching as they had fought and played. Watching as Paavo Dogmaster had fed them, as they had fought for the best scraps. Watching as one hulking brute of a dog had torn out the throat of another that had come too close to its food. Paavo had laughed at that, and laughed more as the dogs had crept forward to pick at the body of their dead fellow.

It had grown cold, though. There had always been fire in Aardanel, and even on patrols with Athasar there had been campfires. Scal had known cold—the chill, biting cold that crept up on toes and fingers and cheeks. He had known it, and never been much bothered by it. But that had not been real cold. Not the cold of the true North, the cold that blew pitilessly off the Faltiik Mountains. This cold was brutal, merciless. It crept through the cracks and hunted down any hint of warmth. Smothered it. There was no withstanding it. Scal, in tunic and breeches, had crept freezing into the kennels, ignoring the growls that challenged him. Found an empty corner and claimed it. The dogs' breath misted in the air as they watched him all through the night. He had stayed there, having nowhere else to go. Not wanting to lose the space he had claimed. Listened to the cold whistle through his cheek.

His stomach rumbled, though. He had refused most of the food Uisbure had tried to give him on the journey, and he had been offered none since being thrown into the kennels. He had known hunger in Aardanel. It had been a constant thing, as familiar as Brennon's smile. He had lived with the faint gnawing hunger, and survived. But this hunger . . . it was like a live thing. Curled up in his empty belly. Fingers clawing at the insides of its prison, leaving deep aching gouges. Howling and snarling like the dogs, loud enough they growled in return. Leaving him weak and slow and shaking.

Paavo's voice rang in the yard, and the dogs moved as one, rising and rushing into the cold air. Food. Scal's hands scraped numbly along the ground as he crawled out to join the dogs. Paavo was tossing hunks of meat, laughing as they fought over the fatty morsels. Raw meat, but the sight of it made Scal's stomach roar. Still laughing, Paavo threw a chunk toward him and the dogs turned as one, teeth bared. Scal pounced before they could, grabbing the piece of meat and stuffing it into his mouth. Sharp teeth snapped shut on empty air where the meat and his hand had been seconds before. Scal bared his own teeth as he chewed and chewed, the raw meat sliding slimy down his throat. The dogs had moved on to the next piece of their meal falling from the sky.

The meat hit the ground a pace or two away from Scal. A big piece of it, enough that Fat Betho could have used it to make meals for a week, stingy as the bastard had been. Scal jumped at it, but the dogs were faster. Jaws locked around the steak, pulling it away, but Scal reached still. Teeth sank into his hand, into the thick flesh at the base of his thumb. The dog shook his hand as it would a rabbit. Pain shot tearing up his arm and he cried out. Tried to yank his hand back, felt the teeth rip deeper. He brought his other hand up, pounding it against the dog's skull until its teeth opened and the beast slunk snarling away. Scal cradled his bleeding hand against his chest. Felt the cold seep into the deep punctures and run through his veins. He ground his teeth, and air hissed sharp through the cross on his cheek.

Laughter flowed over the cold air. Paavo, of course. And next to him, wrapped in white, Iveran. Teeth and eyes flashing. Not so different from the dogs still watching Scal with wary eyes and curled lips.

"Come here, *ijka*," Iveran called, waving a lazy hand.

Scal used his good hand to push himself to his feet. He was slow, unsteady. Two days of sitting and crawling had taken their toll. He shook and stumbled like a new-walking babe. The dogs pressed their bellies to the ground, slinking away from him. Weak as he was, he was Man now, and Paavo had taught them well to fear anything on two legs.

As he made his slow way through the yard, the dogmaster continued to feed his beasts. The chunks of meat fell near to Scal's feet, so that dogs darted in snarling and snapping at his ankles, near tripping him as Paavo chortled. One of the dogs closed its heavy jaws around the toe of Scal's boot. Tugging and shaking, and Scal fell backward. Instinct set his hands down to catch his weight, and he cried out as his wounded hand took the brunt of the impact. His arm crumpled, and his elbow and tailbone connected sharply with the ice. Something slammed into his chest, pressing him all the way back as teeth snapped near his nose. He threw up his arm to shield his face, and so the dog took a firm grip on the offered limb. More teeth took hold of his shoulder. Fangs scraped along the sole of his now-bare foot as he kicked out. Barking, so loud it drowned out the sound of someone screaming endless terror. Strange, that someone nearby could sound more scared than he felt.

Barks dissolved to yelps. The weight lifted off his chest, teeth scraping against bone as the dog refused to let go its prize. The teeth held on until they passed bone and met in flesh, but still they pulled. Dragging, tearing, until finally the connection was severed. Paavo threw the beast into the wall, and it fell to the ground with a mindless cry and a crunch, and then lay silent and still. The other dogs swarmed to its body, filling mouths and dashing off with bloody muzzles. One carried a small mouthful, the edges of the meat pale around the blood. The size and color to match the dent in Scal's arm.

He managed to roll himself onto his side before throwing up.

Paavo dragged him up, set him on his feet. Gave him a hearty thump on the back. And together he and Iveran roared with laughter.

Bandaged, bruised, and limping, Scal trailed in Iveran's wake. All of Valastaastad stared. The men with disapproving frowns. The women with concern, or perhaps pity. The children with the same hard, incurious eyes as the children of Aardanel. Even the buildings seemed to stare. Square-cut empty windows with flapping hide covers tracking their progress down the town's single street. If it could even be called a street. A strip of ice, lined by ice-seamed stone houses. The gaping hole through which Scal had been hefted was the center of the town, with lowly hovels stretching toward the lip of the ice shelf, clustering together as though afraid of being blown out into the great emptiness. To the other side of the hole, the houses became grander, if homes of stone and ice could be called grand. They were bigger, for the most part, and had spaces in between their neighbors' walls. A few raised up on platforms. Some even built two stories high. The grandest was at the end of the street. Stilts raising it up near man-high, and three uneven levels piled on top of it. It looked as likely to crumble as the shelf on which Valastaastad was built, which was fitting enough. Real glass filled the openings in more than half the windows. Scal did not need to be told that this was Iveran's home.

"My home," the Northman said anyway, his face bright with pride.

A ladder as rickety as the rest of the place was the only way up. Scal managed it one-handed, though his bitten shoulder burned with the effort. Once up, Iveran clapped him on the back and swung the door open wide. "Your home," he said. "Until you make a place for yourself."

A fire burned in a wide pit at the center of the room, fighting off the chill that hung in the air. A woman tended the big pot hanging over the fire, and she turned as man and boy entered. Her stomach bulged hugely ahead of her. She had a pleasant face. A faint, wary smile. "This is the boy?"

"Aye. This is Scal." Iveran's fingers wrapped around Scal's unbandaged arm, drew him forward. "*Ijka,* this is my wife, Hanej. And"—a smile split his face, pure and bright, unlike anything Scal had seen since Brennon had wished him luck before the patrol left—"our son Jari."

Hanej rested a hand over her broad belly, her smile softening to match Iveran's. "He is sorry he cannot meet you yet."

"Soon enough." Iveran stepped forward and wrapped her in a gruff hug. Scal stared at his feet. At the one boot with a gaping hole along the instep, puncture marks all around. Paavo had brought it to him as the midwife was wrapping his wounds. Thrown it at his feet and told him to remember. As though the holes in his flesh were not reminder enough.

Iveran led him limping up a creaking flight of stairs. The second floor was a narrow walkway, no more than two steps across, a hole in the center that smoke from the fire lazily climbed through. Looking up, Scal saw a similar hole in the ceiling, and another beyond, open to pale blue sky.

There were three doors, hides stretched over the frames. "Mine," Iveran said, pointing to one with a snowbear's head hanging above. His finger moved to the doorway across. "Yours. Go sleep, *ijka*. We will talk more later."

Stepping around the hole in the floor, Scal pushed aside the door covering. The room was small, sparse. A pile of furs for a bed. A rough-hewn stone chest. A window, real rippled glass, looking out onto the edge of the ice shelf and the endless snows beyond. Inside the chest, a neatly folded pile of fur and leather, a set of boots. Some candles, a flint. A small, sharp bone knife for eating.

There was an ease to the exhaustion and pain that filled him. It was a simple matter to collapse onto the pile of furs, drag one around himself with his clumsy bandaged hand. He closed his eyes, and there was a comfort in the blackness. In not having to think, or to feel.

He dreamed of Brennon, of the easy smiling innocence that seemed to warm the air where he walked. He dreamed his friend's laughter, the simple heart-lightening joy of it. He dreamed of Brennon smiling, smiling as arrows and swords and dogs' teeth tore at his body. Of his happy laughter ringing out as he bled into the earth. He dreamed of Parro Kerrus, making the sign of the Mother over Brennon with one hand while the other tried to fit his guts back into his belly. Of the parro's soulful voice intoning, *"And thus did Fratarro shatter upon the bones of the earth, his limbs flung to the far horizons, and a shard of ebon did pierce his immortal heart . . ."*

"And so did Sororra vow vengeance," Scal whispered into the furs as he woke, his head aching and tears drying on his cheeks, fresh blood leaking slow and warm from the rent in his arm.

It was dark, dark as the woods on a moonless night after Athasar's fires had all gone out. He went to the chest, crawling along the floor like a lame dog, his wounded arm folded close. A low rumble filled the house, a rhythmic noise, achingly familiar. Parro Kerrus had snored like a bear in winter. It was not Kerrus, though, because Parro Kerrus was dead. Killed, murdered. He reached into the chest, groping blindly. The edge nicked his fingers, but it helped him to find his way. His cold aching fingers wrapped around bone, and drew the knife from the chest.

It was dark, but the little blade seemed to glow, a single curving line of fire. Righteous fire. Vengeance, and salvation. He crept to the hide door and pushed it aside, leaning his back against the frame, staring across at the white bear hide and snarling head. Watching. Waiting. *Patience is the Mother's gift; the wisdom to use it is the Father's.*

CHAPTER 10

It was, Keiro decided as his feet took him once more through the forest around Raturo, the third hardest thing he had ever done.

The first twins, the first he'd had to bury—always, they would be the hardest. His first failure, and his first true taste of what the world was like when civility was peeled back by blind fear.

There was the blinding, that had seemed such a good idea until the pain had brought him crashing down from his cloud-like grief. He could, he thought, have finished the blinding, appeased the Twins, if he hadn't seen the young twins. He had been ready to do it, even through the pain. It had been harder than he would have guessed to put a stop to it, once his eye had seen.

And so the twins. Walking away from them was hard, almost the hardest thing he had ever done. But they were safe, in the safest place they could be. Keiro could do nothing for them inside Mount Raturo that was not already being done.

Keiro had been made for walking, and though it was hard to leave the living twins, visible hope, his feet were happy for the road.

The exile hurt, to be sure, but he didn't let himself dwell on it. He had walked all his life, and if the rest of his life was to be walking as well, then that was as it should be. He turned his one eye north, and went to the best place he had ever walked.

Many preachers, after they ventured once more into the sun out of the darkness of Raturo, chose to go to the Tashat Mountains. The Highlanders, with their One God, were heathens who could be converted, shown the truth of the world. It was a good place to start, for it often taught preachers failure. That was an important lesson, for preachers by their nature would face it again and again. Keiro had found his own first failure among those snowy peaks, in the places where Fiateran blood and culture had hardly touched the deep-set Highlands ways. But he had also found his first success in the lovely, sprawling valleys scattered among the mountains.

He hadn't seen Felein for a long while—she, too, had been made for walking, and their paths rarely crossed. But he remembered her fondly, she with her faith already shaken by long mixing with Fiaterans. She had listened to him beneath the stars that were strung so beautifully above the mountain peaks, for she had a quick mind that wanted to learn all the world would give her. Her blood, too diluted by Fiateran stock, had none of the spark of magic that lurked in the Highlands, and so she was denied the Academy. "There are books there," she'd said, with the same sort of reverence with which Keiro spoke of the Twins, "more books than there are stars. More books than anyone could read in a lifetime. In five lifetimes!"

Books she would never see, because she had been deemed inferior.

"When the Twins rise," Keiro had told her, "it will be different. All will be equal under their rule. You will never be denied a thing that another is given. Without Metherra's sun, in the darkness, no man is different from any other."

Her eyes had blazed with joy, but then the fire had died. "You can't read in the darkness."

He'd thought it another failure, another in his growing count. But when he'd left the village a handful of nights later, another set of feet had left with him. "There's a way," Felein had said with confidence, the stars glowing in her eyes. "There has to be a way." And so it was a success, after all.

They welcomed him, the Highlanders of those little valley villages. They welcomed him same as they would any traveler, eager for news and trade and a face they had not seen a thousand times before. They stared, of course, at the raw socket of his lost eye, but it was healing, and he learned to wear the eye-cloth crossed over the one eye only. They didn't always listen to him, when he spoke of his gods trapped beneath the earth, but neither did they chase him from the village, throw rocks at him, beat him with clubs. It was, in all, the best place he could think of to spend the first few weeks of his exile.

"God is good to us here," Terron said, sipping the spiced drink the Highlanders called hacha. "Why should I ever want to leave this place to wander, reviled wherever I go?"

"It's not like that," Keiro said, though the half lie made him uncomfortable. He preferred honesty when he spoke of his gods and his people, but Terron had already proved to be just as devoted to his own God, though increasingly curious about the Twins. "Fear is a strong motivator throughout the world, and we fear that which we do not understand. The world, generally, is a frightened place."

"Frightful, more like."

Keiro waved a hand to encompass the mountains that ringed them in all around and asked, "Have you never wondered what's beyond your comfy peaks? There's a whole world you've never seen, and places just as beautiful as this in their own ways."

"'In their own ways,'" Terron repeated, smirking into his hacha. "That's a kind way of tying a bow on a pile of shit."

The village was called Two Rivers, a small place. A gentle place, so far from the cruelty of the world, and close enough to the Academy that they were well educated. Terron, himself a failed mage, had greeted Keiro eagerly and immediately drawn him into a theistic debate. It was a good place; Keiro could not and would not argue that point. If he had not been made for walking, he might almost have been tempted to stay a great deal longer than a few days.

"Don't sneer at things you've never seen," Keiro said, a gentle chiding in his voice. "For all you know, your heart could beat in time with the Great Ocean's waves, or the crowded steps of Mercetta's streets. There are things a man cannot know about himself until he has traveled beyond the circle of the places that make him feel content and safe. And, more, a man who does not know himself cannot truly begin to guess at what hands shape and guide our world."

"Ah, so you say because you have seen more water and hills and fields than I have, you know the face of God?"

"Not at all," Keiro said, taking a sip of his own bitter hacha. "I merely say that I *have* seen more water and hills and fields than you have, and I have heard all the myriad voices that whisper in places of beauty to those who will listen, and I know the voice that calls to my heart."

Terron's eyes fixed on him, the gentle, friendly mockery replaced by something Keiro could not quite read. It was a long, quiet moment before Terron asked, "You claim you have heard your gods?"

Keiro shrugged, hoping to banish the sharp suspicion in the other man's eyes. "I claim only to be a very good listener."

Terron shook his head in flat denial, his mouth open to argue, and then his eyes went strangely distant, fixed on a place over Keiro's shoulder. There was a crackling in the air, a dryness like the moments before a strike of lightning, and behind his missing eye Keiro saw again the eyes of all the babies he had let die.

"Something's wrong." Terron rose so abruptly he bumped the table, their earthenware mugs of hacha trembling and tipping, spilling the spiced drink with a sharp scent of cloves. In the silence, laced with a nameless sudden fear, the sound of one of the mugs shattering against the ground was unspeakably loud.

Two Rivers, small as it was, did not have much of a village square. The people gathered, when they needed to, in the green space behind the elder's hut. That was where they found the crowd. Terron had told him, in their long talking, that though the Academy had cut away his power, he still had his senses, sharper for a mage than for the average man. Average a man as could be, even Keiro could feel the fear and anger, battling like live things in the air.

There were as many of the villagers as Keiro had yet seen, more than he'd thought had lived in the small collection of huts, and it seemed as though all of them were shouting. Their target was a woman, wearing the same black robe as Keiro, and his stomach knotted.

Terron touched a man's arm, made himself be heard over the crowd's fury. "What's happening?"

The man said only a single word, but it took all the color from Terron's face: "Lethys."

Standing on his toes, Keiro tried to see above the heads of the villagers. Vaguely, he could make out a form at the preacher's feet. Nothing distinct, until a shift in the bodies revealed a hand, reaching from the huddled lump to clutch at the preacher's robe. Using his elbows, stomping on feet, Keiro forced his way through the press of bodies. His hair stood on end, the invisible storm close to breaking.

There was true fear in the preacher's eyes, her face pale but hard. She clutched a staff in one hand, not so different from Keiro's walking stick; her other hand rested on the matted hair of the man kneeling at her feet. His eyes were wide, almost entirely pupil, staring uncomprehendingly as his lips moved. He could have been shouting, but still his voice would have been lost in the crowd. There was an older woman, crumpled and sobbing, and a straining man being held back by others. And there was the shouting, too many voices to be words, no more than a primal scream shaped by many throats.

Keiro stepped forward, into the half circle of space between the preacher and the mob, and hoped he would be heard over the shouting. "Sister, what happens?"

Relief flooded her face for a brief moment, replaced just a quickly by horror, and then a blind hatred that mirrored the faces surrounding her. Clearly, over the shouting, he heard her spit, "Apostate."

Out of the pressing crowd, Keiro could start to hear individual voices. The old woman sobbing, "What've you done to 'im, what've you done?" The man fighting against those who held him, two words repeated again and again, "My son. My son." In the incoherent shouting, occasionally one sound emerged, that name: "Lethys." Each time, the man huddled at the preacher's feet flinched, as though the word were a physical blow, but his lips never stopped moving.

"Please," Keiro said to the preacher, "I can help." Behind his missing eye, the small eyes swam, wide and blank. "Please. Let me help you."

He would never know if the rock was aimed at him or the female preacher. It hit him, though, high on the shoulder, hard enough to spin him half around and send him stumbling. The preacher stepped back from him as he fell, letting him sprawl in a heap near the muttering man, and he saw the second rock fly over her head, a narrow miss. The third didn't miss. It hit her arm, and her staff fell from numb fingers, and her other hand clenched in the man's hair as she cried out in pain. The man's lips stopped, opened wide in a long scream that made the tendons stand out stark on his neck, and somehow over it Keiro heard, *"My son!"* The preacher fell heavily near Keiro, borne down by the weight of a father's fury and his fists, and all around they were shouting, "Lethys. Lethys. Lethys," and through the battering fists the preacher shouted with bloody teeth, "Lethys, help me," and the man's hands danced in wild patterns. Lethys cried out as a light burst from his fingers, and the smell of burned meat came strong to Keiro's nose. The preacher pushed the man off of her, and Keiro saw the hole that went through him, from one side of his chest to the other, the edges of the wound a deep black.

In the Highlands, they told tales of the first mage, blessed by their God with powers beyond human reckoning. Garen Three-eye, who had stood atop a mountain and torn lightning from the sky.

The older woman who had been sobbing now screamed, high and piercing, and there was a screaming in Keiro's chest, too. For mages, using their powers to kill another brought a fate worse than death. The Academy had strict laws, and little sympathy.

"Shield us," the female preacher said thickly. Her lips were bleeding, one eye already swelling shut. Lethys, the mage, quickly began to weave shapes in the air, and a faint prickling shivered across Keiro's skin. The crowd surged forward in fury, but they were halted by some kind of barrier that Keiro couldn't see.

The preacher rose slowly to her feet, using Lethys for support. When she stood, the mage clung to her robe as tears streamed down his cheeks, his wide eyes fixed on the dead man lying near his feet. His own father.

The preacher reached into her robe, brought out a little jar, and from it scraped a black paste across the tongue Lethys eagerly stuck out. His eyes closed as he swayed on his knees, still clinging to the preacher as though he would tip over.

It was all too much for Keiro to understand. "What have you done to him?" he asked softly.

The preacher didn't turn to look at him, just gently stroked Lethys's hair as he swayed. "There are things you do not know, broth—" She stopped herself, amended: "Apostate." She was quiet for a time, eyes on the ground, carefully avoiding the crowd battering against the shield Lethys had created. Her hand faltered against Lethys's hair, and there was a different note in her voice when she spoke again. "I didn't mean for this to happen. I didn't know this was his village . . ."

"What has been done to him?" Keiro asked again.

Briefly, her fingers tightened, clutching at hair. "He's mine. I was given permission." Her fingers loosened, straightened, smoothing once more. "He is helping me." Finally she turned to face Keiro, and the look in her eyes did not match the hardness in her voice. "You should leave this place, apostate. I am bound to kill you on sight, for whatever your crimes might be. But . . . there has been enough death here today. I will say you were never here, if you leave now."

"Please, just tell me—"

"Go, apostate. Go far from here. Go farther than anyone can ever find you."

Keiro could hardly breathe around the lump in his throat as he stepped from the shelter of Lethys's protection. The crowd grabbed at him, hands and fists and feet, looking for anything on which to vent their fury. He knew he would have suffered worse than those few strikes if the preacher hadn't drawn Lethys to his feet and begun to walk in the direction they had come. The shield stayed tight around them as they walked, though the villagers certainly tested it, with fists and rocks and their own angry bodies. They left Keiro standing alone, aching, near the sobbing and screaming woman, who crawled slowly to her dead husband. He could not stand to watch it.

He turned away from the preacher and the mage; away from the villagers he had come to know in so short a time, their kindness peeled back in layers by one cruel act. The Highlands, a place that had mingled so deeply with Fiatera, a place that had still been shaped by the hands of the Parents, were no longer a good place for walking.

"I'm sorry," he said aloud, to Terron and the other villagers, to Lethys and his dead father, to all the dead twins, and the live ones inside Raturo. "I'm sorry," he said as he left them behind.

"You've a gentle heart," Pelir had told him, and Keiro's gentle heart could no longer bear this place. He would prepare the world for the young twins, and the Twins when they were freed from their prison, but Fiatera was too hard a place. Like Fratarro, he would find a corner of the world, a peaceful place, and quiet, and he would shape it for them. A place that was far from dead buried babies and their eyes that would not leave him. A place where he could hear the voices of his gods and know he had followed the right path. A place where, finally, his walking feet could rest.

CHAPTER 11

Joros found his mage talking to the children. That alone wasn't enough to send his anger near to boiling over, for Anddyr could often be found with the young twins—broken things had a tendency to drift together. It was the day that had come before, combined with the fact that the little beasts were *in his rooms,* that made Joros kick the chair.

It splintered against the wall, more force behind the kick than he'd intended, but Anddyr was the only one to flinch. The mage curled into a ball of fear, and the children turned to look at Joros with level eyes.

"You should really learn to control your anger," the boy said softly.

Joros wanted to kick something else, but there was nothing near enough, and his foot was throbbing. He settled for grinding his teeth. "I have told you," he said as levelly as he could, "that you are not to be in my rooms." Dirrakara had chided him for being too harsh on the children, told him he'd regret it if he made them hate him. He'd been making an effort to hide his distaste, but the monsters didn't make it easy.

Avorra sneered at him—she was working on perfecting that expression. "If you let Anddyr go out sometimes, we wouldn't have to come here."

"I have also told you that you are not to speak to Anddyr."

"But he's so lonely."

Joros glared at the mage, who carefully avoided his eyes. "You're not lonely, are you, Anddyr?"

"No, cappo," the mage said quickly.

"See? Now please leave."

Avorra sneered again. "It's not the truth if you say it when you're scared." She knelt down next to Anddyr and his eyes fixed on her face. "You're lonely, aren't you, Anddyr?" Her voice was a coo, startlingly close to Dirrakara's mothering-voice. "Don't you wish you could spend more time outside this room?"

The mage's eyes flicked from the girl to Joros to something he held in his lap. When he shifted, Joros got a clearer view of it: the lumpy, poorly made stuffed horse some preacher had given to Avorra when she was a baby. She'd carried it around everywhere until she'd discarded it a few months ago. He'd thought the stupid thing gone forever. And yet there it was, with his mage's hands wrapped tightly around its yellow body.

There was a story, one of the old stories preachers told of the times when the gods still walked the earth, of man's first death. Patharro had come down to visit the first man, Beno, one of his earliest creations; the man had grown wrinkled and bony, centuries old, but he still had the energy of a young man. The Father spoke with him for a time, until he grew tired of Beno's querulous nature; but when he went to leave, Beno followed after him, jabbing at Patharro with his heavy walking stick and demanding why the Father had not shaped him better—made his bones stronger, given him claws like a greatcat, made his eyes sharper, made his skin thicker, given him wings. Finally Patharro turned and tore the stick from Beno's hands, using it to strike down the first man. Patharro had made it so that no man would ever grow so old as Beno, so that death would take everyone before they could ever grow so tiresome.

Joros didn't always agree with the Parents, but he thought the Father's actions there had been justified. Joros could barely manage living with irritating people for a normal life-span; he couldn't imagine what an eternity would be like. Honestly, it showed a good deal of patience from Patharro that he'd allowed mankind immortality for even a short time.

He stalked forward and pushed Avorra aside, stood glaring down at the mage. "Give me that," he said sternly, holding out his hand for the stupid horse.

Anddyr's hands tightened around the horse's soft body, and something drifted into his wide-pupiled eyes that Joros hadn't seen before. A hardness, a sharpness, something that did not want to bend. "It's mine," Anddyr said, and the words came out almost a snarl. There was a crackling in the air, as brittle as the mage's eyes.

Joros's heart took a pause in its measured thumping. It had proved easy enough to put the mage in charge of his own drugging—he'd stare at a time-candle for hours as his mind melted like wax, counting down the marks until he could patch his sanity back together with black paste. He never took the skura too early, and certainly never too late, but there was a madness in his eyes that Joros was not used to seeing. "Anddyr," he said, gentle and careful, "when was the last time you took your skura?"

The mage moaned, eyes screwing shut, hands wringing at the stuffed horse. The stone beneath Joros's feet shuddered.

"We told him not to," a small voice said, soft but triumphant, and Joros rounded on the young twins, the young fools. They stared back at him with mismatched expressions on identical faces, the girl smug, the boy sad and resolute. Avorra went on, "He listens better to us."

There was something very close to fear rising in Joros, surging along with Anddyr's strident muttering, more frantic with each crackling moment. He nearly flew to the cupboard where they kept the skura, neat lines of little earthenware jars, seeds and roots and careful poisons mixed with his blood. He grabbed at one, knocked over others in his haste, scrabbled at the lid until it came away with the earthy stench of rot.

The very air seemed to fight him, thick and suffocating, as he stepped back toward the mage. Anddyr writhed on the ground now, eyes locked on the ceiling in blind horror, the stuffed horse clutched to his chest. The damned twins stood still and silent, watching, the girl with contempt, the boy with curiosity. The air around them was visible, a crackling haze that lifted their hair in strands like live things.

His heart raced, but Joros's legs hardly seemed to move, like walking through chest-high water. "Fire!" Anddyr screamed at the ceiling, and then a laugh tore through him, a horrible rending sound. "Fire, all fire, fire at the end." The air around the mage was hot enough to burn, made the skin over Joros's face feel stretched too tight. The jar of skura grew hot between his fingers, hot as a burning ember, and as he lurched toward the mage, some instinct of self-preservation made him give up his hold on the jar.

It fell, by some lucky fluke, directly onto the mage's face. That startled him into silence, long enough for the skura to drip down into his mouth, and soon a different kind of convulsing took the mage. The fire fell from the air, and the stone floor settled once more, and a choked sound emerged from Joros. Relief, perhaps.

It lasted only long enough for the fire to settle into Joros, and he turned once more to the twins. The anger was wild in him, reckless at the near escape of whatever horrors an uncontrolled mage could bring crashing down. "Never again," he snarled at them, and he reached down to tear the idiotic stuffed horse from Anddyr's slack fingers. The mage lay slack and useless, wallowing in the stupor the skura brought on. Joros shook the horse at the twins and said, "You will not speak with him again. Do you hear me?" He twisted the horse, the lumps of its body shifting under his hands, fabric stretching.

"It's mine," a voice behind him said, and that put pause to the raging anger. Usually it took Anddyr's shattered wits a good while to knit themselves back together, to make him almost human again, but his voice was firm, if not loud. It put a twisting chill in Joros's stomach.

"You begin to understand." The boy-twin stood facing Joros, face utterly calm and utterly unchildlike. His eyes had gone distant, staring at something far beyond seeing. "He is ours," Etarro said, his voice strangely inflectionless. "You will keep him for a time, but he will always be ours. You will keep him from us at your own peril."

Silence hung in the air after the boy's words, heavy as a fist, until his distant eyes finally blinked and returned, features smoothing once more into those of a wide-eyed child.

"We'll try not to bother you anymore, cappo," he said, voice soft as usual. He turned and walked from the room, and Avorra hurried to follow him. There was a strange look on her face, something between fear and wonder and anger.

The silence stayed after they'd left. Even Anddyr, who usually muttered incessantly to himself, sat quietly in the afterthroes of his skura. "It's mine," he finally said again, and Joros turned silently to offer the stuffed horse by one leg. The mage took it; intelligence had returned to his eyes but the madness was not entirely gone. Dirrakara said the drug would twist his mind over time, make the skura madness his reality, with the black paste offering the only relief from delusions. She'd also warned him, quietly, that the mage might not have a particularly long life. Anddyr had his uses, but Joros found himself praying earnestly that she was right.

Finally Joros went to sit in his chair near the hearth, flickering with bluish flame. It was a conceit of the preachers, a powder that changed the fire's color and little more; blue made for a softer light, and anyone found burning red flames inside the mountain would be severely punished. Still, the blue flame was as unnatural as those blasted twins. Years ago, when he'd brought their mother safely up the heights of Raturo, he'd been sure the children growing inside her would be his key and his crown. He'd grown less sure of it every passing year.

There was a stack of letters near his chair, and he shuffled distractedly through them until he saw the mark of one of his agents in Mercetta. The man had proved to be slightly unhinged over the years, but there was no arguing that he was a good seeker, and he'd had the most interesting news of late. Joros had taken over the shadowseekers five years ago; it had been easy enough to do, once he'd been elevated to the Ventallo. His old mentor, Chevo, had been none too pleased with being replaced, but the old fool hadn't been able to do anything about it—when a Ventallo spoke, all others knelt. Since then, Joros's days had been filled with reports and letters and a shelf of carefully organized seekstones. Tedious things, usually, but entirely worthwhile.

Joros skimmed the report and smiled to himself. *Twins.* For long years, Verteira's children had been the only viable option; but there was change in the air. Just because a thing had been so for a time did not mean it would always be so.

There were more reports; his seekers were scattered throughout Fiatera, but they were nothing if not faithful about sending in their reports. Reading through page after page of possible sightings and disappointments and drownings at least took his mind off Etarro and Avorra, gave his anger the chance to settle. Anddyr's muttering was a constant backdrop—almost comforting, strange as that seemed. Joros snorted, and growled at the mage to be silent.

It took some hours to read through all the reports and pen the necessary replies, the longest going to the seeker in Mercetta with that most interesting news. Anddyr sealed each letter, fumbling with the wax, his fingers growing clumsier with each moment. That was the trouble with having an assistant who saw things that weren't really there. The mage would grow convinced that Joros's seal was a spider trying to eat his fingers, the wax a piece of the sky that had fallen, and he usually ended up throwing one or both into a dark corner and had to be sent hunting after them. Finally Joros gave up on the correspondence and rose to his feet with a stretch. "Come, Anddyr," he called tiredly, and the mage's head swung around. "We still have our work to do."

Dirrakara often complained that Joros kept himself too busy; with his duties as Octeiro, heading the shadowseekers, and his newest project, he had little time to spare. That was well enough—he wasn't a man prone to indolence. He wasn't a man who wasted his time.

The Ventallo chamber was empty, as it usually was, or if any of the others were around, they were closed up in their private chambers. It was for the best; he'd rather none of them knew yet about his newest project. There were getting to be so many mages skulking through Raturo, their wits addled by Dirrakara's drug, that it wouldn't surprise Joros if one of his brothers or sisters shared his realization, but Joros was determined to have a head start, if nothing else.

Anddyr knelt down before the stone box, a creature of habit, though he forgot his purpose somewhere between standing and kneeling. A tired sort of disgust roiled in Joros's stomach, mixed with contempt; he had no patience for weak wills, but the mage had proved himself too useful to discard, and too dangerous to antagonize. He showed flashes of intelligence between his mutterings and his ravings, but they were rare; he'd settled easily into thralldom, and so Joros wasn't inclined to think he'd had much will to begin with. Still, he tried to be friendly to the mage—or as friendly as he was capable of being. "Do you even think of fighting anymore?" Joros asked, not bothering to hide his distaste, but genuinely curious.

The mage blinked, mouth dropping slowly open. His eyes

drifted sideways, flicked back, drifted away again. His lips formed the shapes of syllables, but no sound came out.

Joros's fingers curled tightly; he was wasting time, and there was none to waste. "Answer me," he growled, and without thinking he kicked at the mage. His foot connected lightly with the mage's shoulder, and for a small moment of terror as he remembered what Anddyr was capable of, Joros wondered if this was how his miserable life would end.

But the mage merely whimpered as his eyes snapped back to Joros, flashing with fear. "No," he blurted. "No. I don't think about fighting." He flinched, though Joros hadn't moved.

No. Not someone worthy of any respect, or of any fear. "Go, Anddyr," Joros said, hiding his deep relief as the mage sluggishly pressed his hands to the bier. "Find him." Anddyr's eyes drifted shut, and his fingers twitched against the stone, and Joros very quickly grew bored.

They had been at this for almost two months, and Joros was becoming impatient for results. He hadn't been so foolish as to think it would be *easy,* but he had expected it to be quicker. In one of his more lucid moments, Anddyr had tried to explain how his magic worked, how it was much more complex than simply "like calling to like," but Joros didn't care how it worked. He cared only about the answers it could bring him.

He stood for a moment, watching, his hand resting lightly on the stone box. He still wasn't convinced it was going to work, but belief, he had discovered, was not always such a straightforward thing. Belief could be learned.

Joros went to his door, *18* carved deep into the wood. There was another ledger book inside the room, identical to the ones he'd scribbled in as Ventiro and Nodeiro, though this one was filled with line after line of initiates' names. Whenever a new aspiring preacher stumbled into the darkness from the cold of Raturo's peak, the watchers stationed there would jot down names and answers to a few questions and bring these to Joros, who each night faithfully recorded them in his ledger. He'd once asked Dirrakara if any of the Ventallo did aught besides keep records; she'd laughed and smiled, but kept her lips closed.

It wasn't what he'd imagined power to be. And he'd imagined power often, as a younger man, the third son of a fifth son living in squalor on the outskirts of the capital. He'd been a boy, once, who'd dreamed of being a king until his brother had sneered and told him merchants couldn't be kings. Even the so-called merchant kings of Mercetta had little power over things of any import. There was little chance for a humble man to rise to greatness.

But there was another place, where men were not judged by their birth but by what they made of themselves. And Joros had known he could make himself a great man. He could make himself a king.

He didn't think kings spent so much time filling lines.

A gasp startled Joros, his pen skittering across the page in a blotchy line that obscured half the names he'd just entered. He scowled down at the page, his fingers tightening dangerously around the pen, until he heard the sound again.

Anddyr was on his back next to the stone box, eyes wide in his pale face, hands scrabbling at his throat as he gasped in shallow breaths. Joros grabbed him by the shoulders and shook him, demanding, "What is it? Did you find something?"

"I . . ." Anddyr pressed one hand to the floor as a brace and the other against his chest; Joros wasn't sure if he was short of breath or too addled to speak. "I . . . I *felt* something."

There was a beat of silence as the words registered, and then triumph surged through Joros. "Felt what?"

"I . . . I don't know. It felt like . . ." He reached a hand out toward the bier but stopped short, fingers curling like he'd touched something faintly slimy. " . . . like what's in there."

Joros almost laughed. His hands tightened on Anddyr's shoulders, a moment of shared victory. "Where is it? Can you take us there?"

Anddyr flinched, trying to twist away like a worm, and Joros tightened his fingers further as the joy began to slip away. "I only *felt* it," Anddyr murmured. "It . . . it scared me. Surprised me. I couldn't . . ." He whimpered and tried to twist away again.

"Go back!" Joros threw the mage against the bier, drawing a yelp as Anddyr's face scraped against the stone. Joros's hands were like claws as he pressed Anddyr's palms to the bier, and he heard the sniveling mage begin to cry. *"Find it again."* Anddyr wailed and struggled for a moment, and then his mind fled away in the manner of his searching. With an effort, Joros released the man, making sure his stickish body remained draped over the stone box. He paced restlessly, hands clutching air at his sides, glaring often at Anddyr's unmoving back.

Finally Anddyr twitched, shifted, slid down to the floor. Joros rounded on him, grabbing him by the neck and shoving him against the bier again. The mage didn't seem to notice; he was grinning wildly, and he crowed, "The North! It's in the North!"

Joros's hand didn't loosen from around the mage's throat.

"The North?" he repeated slowly, softly—and then with more incredulity: "The *North*? Do you have any fecking clue how big the North is?" With Anddyr held immobile between his hand and the stone box, Joros's fist connected solidly with the side of the mage's head. He let the mage fall to the floor, and when he didn't answer with a spout of flame, Joros aimed a kick at his stomach. The mage curled into a ball, but that didn't stop Joros's booted feet or balled fists. Joros vented his anger on the useless fool, spitting curses, until his breath came short and his hands ached. Anddyr lay whimpering and muttering, always muttering, and showed no signs of being any kind of danger to Joros.

"Get up," Joros snarled, all his disgust returned thrice over, "and find me something useful."

Slowly Anddyr drew himself up to his knees and pressed his shaking hands against the stone. The fingers of one hand were bent unnaturally, and his nose was swollen, leaking a steady stream of blood. The mage was wise enough not to utter a sound of complaint, and sent his magic out once more.

Joros stood panting, his limbs slowly relaxing, bloody-knuckled hands uncurling. The feeling of triumph gradually returned to stretch his lips into a smile. He was getting closer.

CHAPTER 12

They slept in an alley just off the West Market, behind a quiet baker's shop . . . or at least Aro slept. Rora couldn't get her eyes to close, couldn't pull them off the bright dagger, the blue jewel that looked like it was full of its own light. The knife was exactly as long as her forearm, from fingertips to elbow, like a smith had measured it just for her.

By the time the sun poked its fingers into the alley, Rora had scrubbed away every last spot of Nadaro's blood off the knife, using the edge of her shirt and then scraping with her thumbnail, once the blood got dried on. It was bright and shiny and beautiful, glowing in the sunlight, and it made her glow, too.

Aro didn't ask what'd happened. Must've been something in her face that told him he didn't want to know. He just rubbed a hand under his runny nose and asked, "What're we gonna do now?"

Rora'd been thinking about that, too, through the night. She had a few things she'd filched from Nadaro's house, enough to sell for them to live on for a while, but that came with its own set of problems. They couldn't stay topside, not unless she found them somewhere safe. That meant buying a room somewhere, which would keep them safe and cozy for a little while until she ran out of things to sell, or holing up somewhere secret, which was free enough but it meant dodging guards and biggers and anyone else who'd chase them back down to the Canals. Maybe they looked it now, and Kala'd argued it half a hundred times, but Rora knew in her heart that they didn't belong topside. They were Scum, clear and simple. Sure, they could probably pass off as topsiders for a while, but in the end, they'd wind up right back in the Canals, and worse off for having sold all their stolen valuables. So it was better to skip to the end, and find some advantage to it.

"We're going back down," she said decisively. Aro's face fell, but he didn't argue. It seemed like he'd learned his lesson about not listening to her. That was good. It'd make everything easier. She stood up and brushed the dirt from her clothes, rubbed some dirt in Aro's stubby hair to make it lighter, and then held on to the long knife for a bit, thinking. She wasn't about to leave it behind, but she couldn't really walk around just carrying it. Finally she ripped off some cloth from a stolen cloak that was too long for her or Aro anyway, and wrapped it around and around the blade. It wasn't near as good as a proper sheath, but it would keep the sharp edges away. She tied her belt off below the knife's hilt, stuffed the knife down the inside of her pants, hanging alongside her right leg, and looped the belt around her hips. It'd have to do.

She had to walk with a twist in her step, to keep the knife from bumping against her leg, to keep anyone from seeing it sway when she walked. Guards got twitchy about pups with knives, and she didn't want that kind of attention.

They went to a fence, a man who'd managed to make it out of the Canals and still had a soft spot for Scum. He bought up everything Rora'd stolen, no questions, and he even gave her a good price on a battered sheath for the knife. It was a little big, but it was better than rags. She and Aro stripped off the clothes Nadaro had given them and traded them in for plainer things, clothes that wouldn't get them noticed down in the Canals. The fence offered her a good price for their boots, but that was something Rora couldn't bring herself to sell, not with winter coming on. Still, after all of it, she had five silver gids and a few durames, and a pouch to keep them in. She stuffed the gids in her and Aro's boots, and kept the coppers in the pouch around her waist.

And after that, there was no more putting it off.

Sure, she took her time about it, taking the windingest route through the city, crossing all the way over to East Quarter, where the houses were just a little nicer, the people just a little meaner. They climbed down under a bridge, wedging fingers and toes into the torn-out bricks like they'd done hundreds of times before under a dozen other bridges. Mercetta was full of bridges, and full of the water that ran under the bridges, and full of the Scum that lived on the water.

Soon as her feet touched the ledge, a hand snaked out to grab Rora's arm. Stinking breath hissed into her face as a man said, "Gimme whatever you got."

"Rora!" Aro shouted, but by then the too-big sheath was rattling, and the knife was shining bright in her hand, her bad hand that maybe wasn't so bad now it'd been getting so much use, and the man let her go.

"No trouble," he whined, backing off with his hands raised, baring rotten teeth and looking like he was ready to give trouble soon as she turned her back. "No trouble with you, girl."

"You stay back," she said, shaking the knife at him.

He spewed reeking laughter at her, but he did stay back, watching with hard eyes from the shadows under the bridge. Aro dropped to the ground behind her and they backstepped together, Rora keeping her eyes on the man, but he stayed where he was. They turned a corner, leaving the man and the bridge behind, and Rora spat into the canal. "Welcome home." Aro just sniffled.

The Scum had done what they could as far as bridges went, but when you only had stolen goods and castoffs to work with, it wasn't too surprising the bridges were as few and poor-built as they were. The first one they came to was no more than two ropes stretched across the canal, one foot high, the other shoulder-high to Rora. The ropes were old and scummy and smelled like mildew, but there wasn't much in the way of options. There was a blue mark chalked onto the walls just ahead that looked something like a snake, and Rora was damned if they were going to go anywhere near the Serpents. So it was cross the shit bridge, or get drowned by the first Serpent to spot them, and that was no choice at all.

Rora went first. She was heavier, so if the rope was going to break, it'd do it for her, and she was a better swimmer anyway. Better shimmy-er, too, made it across in half the time it took Aro, once she finally got him to put his feet on the rope. Then it was down more winding, smelly canals, past lion-shaped yellow marks and red claws and shapeless green splotches and all the other pack marks, and across the first bridge they found once Aro spotted a black handprint on the walls. Finally they found a white mark that looked close enough to a snarling dog to put Rora somewhat at ease. They walked on, into Whitedog Pack territory.

It didn't take too long for an eye to stop them. He dropped down from above, probably perched and watching from the ledges, and nearly squished Rora. She landed on her back with his foot on her chest, all the air whooshing out of her. Aro screeched like a girl, and the eye laughed. He leaned down over her, his face swelling huge to her foggy eyes, and his stale, oniony breath washed over her. "What're you doin' here, girl?"

Rora managed to suck in enough air to gasp back out, "Come to be a Dog."

"Have you now?" He laughed again, and she gagged on the stench of his breath. Aro was whimpering somewhere behind her, too scared to do the smart thing and hide. Her head was still fogged up, but she made her hands start moving, one trying to push the eye away, the other reaching. "Scrap sees to the pups, and he don't have much use for whimpery pups at all, truth t' tell. Your boy there . . ." His chin jerked up, toward where Aro would be, and her fingers weren't moving fast enough, clumsy and weak. "He don't look too strong. Bet he don't swim too strong neither. Might be Scrap can find a use for you, girl, but your boy there ain't good for more'n fish food."

Finally her fingers found the gem, cold and hard, and she pulled the knife clattering from the too-big sheath and sliced it across the back of the eye's leg. Nothing deep, just enough to tear his breeches leg and some skin, and pull a yelp from him. He jumped back, which was all to the good, and Rora drew in a good and deep breath. Some of the fog crept back away from her, and she sat up carefully. Aro threw himself at her back, wrapping his shaking arms around her.

A laugh rang out, not the eye's laughter but a woman's. She dropped down next to the cursing eye, a tall dark woman with a flashing smile. "Best watch out, Cross," she said cheerfully. "This pup's got teeth."

"She won't when I'm done with her," he growled, stepping forward, but the woman held out a hand to stop him.

"Don't think so. The Dogshead likes pups with some fire to 'em. Your name, girl?"

Rora shrugged off Aro's arms and pushed herself slowly up to her feet, keeping the knife held tight but not quite so threateningly. Aro hovered behind her, trying to look small and worth no one's while. It was the best kind of defense he had. Rora looked the woman in the eyes and said, "My name's Sparrow." A little bird, plain and quiet but fierce in its own way. It was the name she'd been giving out since she'd realized her real name wouldn't do—Nadaro was just more proof of that.

"And the boy?"

Before Rora could even open her mouth to name him Finch, Aro's voice piped up, high and scared but determined, "Falcon." Rora choked back a groan but kept herself from elbowing Aro in the nose.

The woman snorted. "A nice flock we've got, eh, Cross?" The eye was still grumbling, didn't answer. "I'll take 'em, then. Come, pups." She motioned for them to follow her, and Rora did. It was that, or fight the eye, and she didn't see much chance there.

Aro stuck close to her heels. As they passed by Cross, she

heard him mumble at the woman's back, "So long as my hands are clean of it."

They passed by a few more dogs' heads chalked onto the walls, each one bigger and meaner-looking than the last. Deep into Whitedog territory. The longer they went without the woman knifing them, the more Aro seemed to trust her, and he'd soon scampered up to bother her. "Who're you?" he asked.

The woman smirked down at him. "I'm called Tare."

Aro's nose wrinkled. "What kind of a name is that?"

"The one I chose, same as you, *Falcon*." Tare's hand moved, and Rora had nearly planted her knife in the woman's back before she realized Tare'd just reached down to tousle Aro's hair.

"So *what* are you?" Aro pressed. "That eye listened to you. He was *scared* of you. You must be someone important."

She laughed. "Maybe you should learn from him."

"But you're not that scary. So that means you have to be important. Are you a mouth? Or an ear? You move real quiet, are you a foot? Maybe an arm?"

"Ar—*Falcon* . . ." Rora hissed at his back, but he ignored the warning.

"You, boy," Tare said, with a smile on her face but her voice flat as the stones they walked on, "are the loudest little falcon I have ever seen. Beak flapping that wide, you'll never catch any prey. Or secrets."

Rora grabbed the back of his shirt and dragged him to her side. He kept his eyes down on the ground, but not because he was scared or ashamed, like he should've been. He was thinking. Rora smacked him on the back of his head to try to knock loose whatever thoughts he was having. He shot a glare at her, but for once he kept his mouth shut.

Whitedog Den was smaller than Blackhand Den, where they'd lived before Nadaro, but fuller, too. There were people everywhere, felt like as many people as had ever filled the markets topside. Back with the Blackhands, Rora'd felt like a coin rattling around a burlap sack; it'd been easy to avoid everyone except Twist, who'd been mother long enough it almost seemed like he could sense his pups no matter where they were. Unexpectedly, Rora wondered if Twist missed them, if he was angry they'd gone. "You're a good pup," he'd told Rora once, stroking her hair like no one ever did. "You'll make a better foot, and maybe even a finger before too long. You're a special pup." But then she remembered why he'd had to calm her down, the blood dripping from Aro's nose and mouth and the handprint on his cheek, not black but red and shaped just like the hand touching her hair. She ground her teeth, and didn't care if Twist missed them. She rubbed the blue stone set into her dagger, and she hoped he died.

There were more people in Whitedog Den, but Rora and Aro were just pups, and pups didn't get second looks. Tare did, though, and sometimes the lookers flicked their eyes down to the two pups trailing behind her, and Rora saw curiosity in those eyes. She kept her hand tight on the dagger. Curiosity meant greed and wanting and blood and death.

There were two fists guarding the other end of the den, and a rotting dog's head stuck onto a pole. Flies buzzed around the empty, black eye sockets, and the tongue hung swollen out of the mouth like some huge fat leech. Aro half hid behind her, scared of anything he didn't recognize, but the head didn't scare Rora. The teeth, probably sharp once, were rotten, and maggots writhed around the jagged stump of its neck. It was dead, as obviously dead as anything could be, and you didn't have to be scared of dead things.

The fist standing closest to the dog's head nodded to Tare, and said through his nose, "Best send Brick out t' find a new dog." He drew in a quick sharp breath, and looked like he was about to be sick.

Tare chuckled. "This one suits just fine. Hasn't even started to fall apart yet." She clapped the man on the shoulder, and then walked past.

Rora hesitated, Aro with her as ever. "Where're you taking us?" she called at Tare's back.

The woman didn't even look back, but she said, "I told you, the Dogshead likes pups with fire. You got fire or not?"

You couldn't walk away from a challenge like that in the Canals, not if you wanted to be anything, and anyway it wasn't like they could just walk back out of Whitedog territory. So they left the stinking dog's head behind, and walked into the heart of the den.

"Rora," Aro whispered urgently at her side, "pups don't get to see heads, not *ever*. Where's she taking us?"

She didn't have an answer for him, and maybe he was right. Packheads didn't care about pups, didn't waste their time with them. You could make it all the way up to mouth, she'd heard, and never once see the head, so why should she, a pup, expect to? But she remembered Tare dropping down out of nowhere and saying, *The Dogshead likes pups with some fire to 'em,* and she had to hope, because all she could think of was Nadaro with blood leaking from his chest and hissing, *The darkness knows your name, and it never rests. My brothers and sisters will find you.* And if there was one thing the Canals had taught her, it was that when times got rough, a smart pup got protection.

The canal ended all of a sudden, a big brick wall stretching all the way up topside, and there was a door in the wall, the first door Rora'd ever seen in the Canals. You didn't have doors down here, because doors meant rooms, and rooms meant getting trapped when the Canals flooded, and *that* usually meant death. So doors were, all in all, a pretty bad idea. But still, there was a door, and Tare rapped her knuckles against it and swung it open in the same instant.

What happened next was a blur that Rora had a hard time following, but she saw knives flashing and thumping fists, and heard breath whooshing out in painful grunts, and then there was a man lying on the floor at her feet, gasping like a fish as Tare held two knives to his throat.

Then a voice inside the room laughed, and a man said, "He's getting better, I'll give him that."

Tare grunted and stepped back, putting both knives in one hand and hauling the man to his feet with the other. "Still too slow," she said, thumping him on the back.

"He almost had you, and you know it." Peeking around Tare's hip, Rora saw that the man inside was leaning against a tall table, a smile twisting up one side of his mouth. "Go on," he said to the wheezing man. "Get a drink, Tare can watch me for a spell. Least she could do for you."

As he hobbled gratefully away, Tare motioned the pups into the room ahead of her. Rora made sure her hand was on the blue gem of her dagger before walking in with Aro on her heels. She stopped just inside the door, gaping up in amazement. The room had no ceiling, and no walls except the one they'd just come through. There was a glimmer of sky way up above—a sinkhole, probably—and a broken-off canal trough dumped down water in an enormous half circle of waterfall that made like a wall for the rest of the room. The floor was slimy, slippery wet under her boots, and the air warm and misty, dampening her hair and face and clothes.

"What's this?" the man at the table asked, eyebrows raised as he looked from Rora and Aro to Tare.

"Pups I thought you might like to see." Tare walked over to a small cupboard off to the right, near where the waterfall disappeared beyond the edges of the floor, and poured a murky red liquid into some cups. She gave one to the man first, then brought one each over to Aro and Rora. Aro sniffed at his and lifted it to his lips, but Rora tugged on his sleeve to stop him; she waited until both Tare and the man had drunk from their cups before she let Aro's arm go.

The man at the table smirked again. "Cautious pup, eh? Don't see that often enough these days."

"Most pups have their heads so far up their asses they can't breathe without being given a go-ahead," Tare agreed. "Got a feeling about this one, though."

Rora flexed her fingers around the dagger's handle, gave the man at the table a good looking-over. "You're the Dogshead?" she asked.

He smiled the crooked smile again and asked, "Don't I look like it?"

Tare leaned her hip against the table and gave Rora a stern look. "Best show some of that fire, girl."

"Speak," the man prompted.

Rora'd never expected to meet the head of any pack, or that

she'd have to ask the head for protection at all. The arm, maybe, or even the face, if Whitedog was as tight as everyone said. She didn't know what to say to a head. But here she was now, so she'd better start talking. She squeezed the blue gem, and felt stronger knowing she had the dagger.

"We started out Rats," she said.

The man spit. "Fecking hate Rats," he muttered.

"Us too," Rora agreed. "Left soon's we could. Joined with the Serpents, they taught us how to beg and thief, but . . ."

"But Serpents are bastards, too," the man said, nodding.

"Right. We tried to make it topside for a while, but"—*Aro sitting in a puddle of blood, crying, "She knew, she knew . . ."*—"it didn't work out. So we went to Blackhands, 'cause we'd heard they were tough, figured they could keep us safe. But we had to leave there pretty quick, and I don't think they'd be too happy to see us again."

"So you need a new pack," Tare said. There wasn't a smile on her face anymore, or on the man's. "You're more boring than I thought, pup. What's to keep me from tossing you into the fall and seeing how deep the Canals go?"

"Everyone I've ever heard says the Dogshead loves to make deals," Rora said, thinking fast, fingers rubbing on the blue gem. She looked at the man, trying to sound like she knew what she was doing. His eyebrows lifted up, but he didn't say anything. "I've been a pup long enough to know how it all works. But I'm better than a normal pup, I can do more. I'll do whatever needs doing."

Tare tilted her chin up, asked, "And your boy there?"

"I don't want him begging or thieving. I want him kept safe."

The man laughed, a low sound that wasn't really a laugh. "Awful high demands for a pup to be making. You'd best have a good offer on the other side of that coin."

Tare didn't say anything, just looked at Rora's eyes, and Rora looked right back at her as she pulled on the blue gem, pulled the dagger out from its sheath and held it in her left hand to keep it steady. "This is what makes me better than a pup," she said. "I killed a man with it yesterday, and I'll kill with it again, if you tell me to." Before she could think better of it, she drew the knife down across the palm of her right hand. The arm was still useless, what'd it matter anyway? But she still felt the pain shoot up her arm as she cut into her hand. Aro gasped, but Rora kept her pain locked up tight inside as she held her hand out, dripping blood onto the slimy floor. "My life and my knife," she said, "for my brother's safety."

Tare and the man looked at each other for a long time, and then together they turned to look at the back of the room, at the center of the waterfall. "Your call, boss," Tare called out, "but for me, I'd take the girl."

Something poked through the waterfall from behind, a big stick, splitting the water in a triangle. And inside the triangle there was a woman standing, with serious, watchful eyes, and they were fixed on Rora. She stepped forward, through the split water, pulling the stick with her so that the water fell into place at her back and kept on tumbling down and down, just like there wasn't anything on the other side of it.

The woman wasn't young, but she wasn't old either. Still, she leaned on the stick as she walked forward, a little limp in her left leg. She walked straight to Rora and knelt down there, even though Rora saw it hurt her. She held her hand out, palm up, and Rora drew the knife across it, too. They clasped hands, shared their blood, and the woman's grip was strong, her eyes still serious as she said, "Sharra Dogshead takes your bargain, girl. You go with Tare—you're hers now. As for you, boy . . ." She let go Rora's hand and turned to Aro, and there was a smile in her eyes when she said, "I've always wanted a valet."

CHAPTER 13

The helm fit snugly over Scal's head. It was too big in places, the fur lining tickling down into his eyes. In other places it was too small, so that it felt like his brains were going to be squeezed out from his ears. Iveran had told him with pride that it was made from a snowbear's skull, but it must have been a very small snowbear.

He had healed, finally, from the dogs. Enough that he could bend his fingers, swing his arm. Enough that there would be no more delay.

Kettar Blademaster pressed a sword into his hand, and even though he had been expecting it, even though the edges were dull, Scal could not keep himself from being surprised. A sword, his own sword. From outside the ring, Iveran was grinning as he watched. Laughing at something Uisbure said, though his eyes never left Scal. Looking back, looking for a sign of challenge in those eyes, Scal saw none.

Across the ring, Arje was stretching his arms. His own dull-edged sword flashed in the bright sun as he moved. Scal stood still, unmoving, the tip of his sword against the ground. It was long and heavy and ugly. Kettar gave him a hard look. Measuring.

"The swords are dull," the blademaster said, "but they will cut still. Lift your hand." Scal did as told. He had learned in these weeks that defiance led only to beatings. He held his hand out, and Kettar turned it palm up. With his other hand the blademaster lifted Scal's sword. Pressed it down against the boy's palm. After a moment the skin broke, and blood welled up. Scal did not flinch. He was covered in such lessons after a handful of weeks in Valastaastad. Bruises and cuts and scars. His flesh a tapestry of Northern education. "You see?" Kettar said. "You let Arje get too close . . ." He pressed the blade against Scal's arm, against the sewn leather that covered him. "Will not cut here. But here . . ." He raised the blade to press against the side of Scal's neck. Enough pressure to spark a bit of real worry in Scal's gut. "Here, you are dead. You should not let Arje kill you. We have spent too much time on you for you to die so stupidly."

Scal said nothing. He had told them, Iveran and Kettar both, again and again, that he did not want to fight. That he *would* not fight. "You keep saying this," Iveran had observed the last time. "But each time you are attacked, you fight. When we found you, you fought me with your little knife. When Einas claimed *vasrista*, you fought him like a devil. When the dogs decided to eat you, you fought them as a dog yourself. So tell me now, why is it that you think you will not fight?"

Scal had not had anything to say to that either. *A man's life is worth only as much as he's willing to fight for it*, Parro Kerrus had said, but Scal did not think his life was worth fighting for any longer. Not with the parro dead. Not with Brennon's smile gone from the world. Not with his life crumbled to ashes. Not with his face cut like a prisoner's, his skin mottled black-and-blue, his flesh scored with Iveran's lessons. He had nothing left to fight for.

Kettar went to stand near Iveran and Uisbure and all the others who had gathered to watch. "Begin!" the blademaster called.

Arje charged forward with his battle cry. The boy a head taller and a stone heavier than Scal, a ram's horns curling atop his skull helm. His sword held up high, ready to split Scal open from neck to navel. Scal watched him come, and did not move. Watched his death come rushing toward him.

Watched as his own arm lifted his sword to block Arje's.

It's a hard thing, Kerrus had said, *for a man to face his own death with open arms.*

He tried to stop. Truly he tried, or he would tell himself later that he truly tried. To stop his arms and the sword and his feet that would not stay still. To stop and let Arje's dull-but-sharp-enough sword cut through him. To let his well-earned death claim him.

It's a much harder thing to die than to live.

So his feet moved him away from Arje, and his sword met Arje's sword, and he fought again. Fought, and hated himself for proving Iveran right once more.

Kettar called a halt to it, and the boys came to a quick stop. Arje, breathing heavily but grinning, thumped Scal on the shoulder. "You fight well!" he said joyfully. Not knowing his words cut deeper than his sword could have. Iveran vaulted over the fence and came with Kettar to give each boy praise.

With his eyes on the ground, Scal kept his lips tightly closed.

Violence is weakness, Kerrus had told them after Brennon had punched another boy. *It's the coward's way, and I know you're no coward. So stop fecking acting like one. The Parents gave us words for a reason. You can keep bashing your way through every situation like bloody knuckles are the only way to keep your tiny brains from leaking out your ears, or you can act like a real fecking person who doesn't think with his cock and his fists. Which'll it be, lads?*

"I knew we would warm your blood, *ijka,*" Iveran said, grinning. "You will train with Kettar every day, until you are as good a fighter as any Northman!"

"It will not be hard," Kettar agreed, smiling, too.

"But it is not only fighting you must learn." Iveran pulled the sword from Scal's hand and tossed it to Kettar. The blade-master caught it neatly and pulled Arje away. "Come with me, *ijka.*" Scal started to lift the squeezing helm from his head, but Iveran stopped him. "Leave it. You make a good snowbear." Laughing, Iveran led him into Valastaastad.

Iveran liked to walk. More, Iveran liked to talk. Parro Kerrus had been much the same, though it hurt Scal to think of them as the same in any way. Many a night, Iveran made Scal walk with him, in a long circle around the edges of the ice shelf, and he would talk and talk and not mind that Scal did not talk back.

"I have been thinking," Iveran said as they walked slowly down Valastaastad's one road. "From the first, you have reminded me of someone, but I have not been able to think who. I think I know it now. I had a friend when I was young. Not a brother, but closer than a brother. Maarin, his name was. You know the word?"

It was one of the Oldest Words, of the runes that belonged to the North alone. A rune like the one for which Scal was named. "Ice," the boy said.

"Ice," the chieftain agreed, approval warm in his voice. "Ice, as you are fire. It is no small thing, that, I am thinking. We grew together in this town, Maarin and I, closer than brothers. He was older by a hand of years, and so he taught me much of what it means to be a man. To be a good man." He stopped outside one of the houses and pulled back the door flap, motioning Scal inside. It was warm within, an old wrinkled woman tending a roaring fire. She rose when Iveran entered, and went into a back room. Iveran crouched down by her fire, warming his hands. "It is a lonely thing, to be chieftain. Lonely, too, to be the son of the chieftain. Maarin never treated me as more than another boy. He was my truest friend, and he saved me from being lonely. I would have such a friend for my Jari." The old woman returned, a white bundle in her arms. She gave it to Iveran, who unrolled it with an approving noise. He showed them to Scal. A cloak, a boy's cloak, made from a snowbear's pelt. As white as the cloak Iveran wore. And a pendant, made from a black snowbear's claw that was longer than Scal's hand, strung onto braided leather. "What do you think, eh? Good gifts for my son?" Scal nodded. It was the only response Iveran usually needed. "These will mark my Jari as the son of the chieftain. No one will ever know him as less. Still. I would have him have a friend. I do not know that you are Maarin's son. I do not know that Maarin had a son, for he left Valastaastad. But you will be a good man, Scal. I will teach you, and you will teach my Jari to be a good man in turn." Iveran pressed the snowbear cloak into Scal's hands. "This will be your gift to my son. That, and the gift of your friendship. I would have you be my son's better-than-brother. To keep him from being lonely. What do you think of that, *ijka*?"

Too much.

It was too much for Scal, who still kept the little bone knife in his boot, the knife with Iveran's death promised to it. Who bore the cuts of a hundred sharp lessons. Whose life had been torn root and stem from the earth by this man. Yet who was fed, and fed well, by the same man. Who was clothed and housed and kept warm. Who had been given a helm made from the skull of a snowbear.

Too much.

Instead of an answer, Scal asked, "What does *ijka* mean?" It was the only Northern word his mind could not place, the only word he could not remember from his forgotten first life before the swirling snows that had brought him to Aardanel.

Iveran's mouth quirked up in a smile. So unlike his normal grin, with teeth bared like the snowbears he mirrored. It made him look a different man, almost. "I have said it before. You are sharp, boy. Maarin was the same. Too sharp for the rest of us. *Ijka* is what we call the little bears. The cubs."

The children of the snowbears.

Too much.

Scal gripped the snowbear cloak in his hands, and stayed silent. At length Iveran rose from the fire, the pendant held loosely in his hand, and thanked the old woman. Touched Scal lightly on the arm, murmured, "Hanej will be wondering where we have gone." Together they walked from the house, the elder bearing a snowbear's claw, the younger bearing a snowbear's pelt, and they walked in silence.

So Scal learned to fight. He would not say he enjoyed it, never that. But he could not deny that his blood sang as he danced the sharp dance. That there was a sweetness to the swirling of the blades. That he swelled with pride at Kettar's praise, and at the sharp, beautiful sword the blademaster gave to him. That he found himself returning Iveran's bear-toothed grins.

So Scal learned what had been Maarin's idea of what it meant to be a good man. Iveran would tell him on their night walks. Long lectures that rambled and forked and never seemed to end where Iveran meant them to. But more, Iveran showed him, or he tried to. Helping the smaller and weaker, as when they helped a group of young children fight a snow battle with a group of older children, or brought food to the elders who could not make their own. Giving praise when earned, no matter how small the deed, as when bright-eyed Talud showed Iveran the little snowbear he had roughly carved from a piece of stone. Meting out appropriate punishment when necessary, as when Iveran had Helvi's tongue cut out for insulting Camad's ancestor, or when he threw Ueni from the ice shelf for kicking Iveran's favorite dog. Killing a man yourself, when his death was called for.

So Scal learned the harsh truths of the North. *Fair is a fool's dream*, Kerrus had told him, and it was more true in the North than anywhere else. They were a hard folk, these people of the ice and snow, hard as the place that shaped them. They were a folk that laughed as they watched Ueni fall screaming to the ground far below, yet prickled to rage at the slightest hint of dishonor. Honor was the most important thing, but it did not seem to mean to them what it meant to Scal. Honor was beating one who was weaker, even as it was helping one who was weaker. Honor was taking all that you could take by force, even as it was giving to those who had greatest need. Honor was in teaching, though teaching meant fists and kicks and cuts and sitting naked in the snow through a night.

So Scal learned to hate. These people who looked so like him, who spoke the words his heart had always known, they were no blood of his. No matter what Iveran said, he would never be one of them. He learned to make a mask of his face, to keep the hatred hidden away. He would lie at night in his pile of furs in Iveran's home and listen to the chieftain snore. The little bone knife in his hand. The lump of his hatred and his hurt held closest in his heart. He would wish for Iveran's death, as he had never before wished for a man to die. And yet he would stay wrapped in his furs all night, and sheathe the little knife only in his boot.

And so Scal learned a new kind of love, the love there was to be found in the North. To laugh with gentle Hanej, and take a simple joy in helping her cook and clean. To respond to the cuffs men leveled at his shoulders with cuffs of his own, and a bear-toothed smile to go with it. To play with the other boys of Valastaastad, wrestling and fighting and always parting with friendly words. To respect Iveran, for the chieftain was a good man more often than not, and kind to Scal when he had had no reason to be, and because he called Scal *ijka* still. To look at Hanej's swelling stomach, and the snowbear cloak he was to give to the baby, and wonder if Jari would be anything like Brennon.

More than anything, Scal learned that he no longer knew himself.

He learned, too, that like the followers of the Parents, the Northmen burned their dead.

Screaming split his dream in two. He had been talking with Parro Kerrus in his dream, as he often did, when a sharp sword sprouted from the parro's stomach, slicing him open, and he began to scream with a pain that was raw and pure and heart-breaking.

Scal came awake and leaped from his bed with the knife in his hand. Rushed from his room to the landing. And saw, there, Iveran laughing with joy as a group of women bustled past him into the room beneath the snowbear's head, where the scream-ing still echoed. Seeing Scal, Iveran threw his arms wide. "It is time, *ijka*! Soon we will meet my Jari!" And he laughed as Scal had never heard him laugh, laughed like a child finding his favorite toy.

The men all gathered out in the snow to wait and drink and celebrate together, as was tradition. Close enough to a man, Scal joined them. They drank the rough, burning ale the Northmen so loved. They drank, too, the wines and brandies they had taken from Aardanel. Scal did not drink those, for the sight of them set off an ache in his chest he had no name for. But the mood was joyful and infectious, and he drank the burning ale, and nearly threw it back up as the men laughed and cheered and made him drink more.

They waited, all of them, to greet the chieftain's son, the future chieftain.

They waited for a long time, so that some of the men began to grow restless. Iveran, as attuned as ever to his clan, started to pace as he pulled at a bottle of brandy, eyes darting toward his house at the end of the lane. The joy was gone, then, replaced by a restlessness that took them all. So it was quiet among the men when the keening began.

High and wailing as the wind that tore through the Faltiik Mountains on the coldest nights, the noise pierced through the real glass windows of Iveran's house. And the chieftain began to run.

Knowing, already knowing, the men followed more slowly. Scal waited outside the house with the rest of them. There was a cry, as raw and pure and heartbreaking as the one that had woken Scal, that rose over the endless keening. No one moved. No one breathed.

After a time Iveran came stumbling out. Face twisted. Eyes red, crying. White tunic streaked with blood. He pushed past them, running, running to the far edge of the ice.

And they knew, though they had already known. The keening of the midwives, the keening that was only for the dead. They went in to bear witness, the men of the clan. But Scal was not a man. He was a boy, a boy with too much grief in his soul, and his feet took him in the other direction. To the far edge of the ice.

He stood a dozen paces behind Iveran, silent. Alone high above the world, surrounded by barren whiteness. No wind, no sound to hide Iveran's racking sobs. Scal watched, and remembered. All the sobs he had held within himself. All the pain he had bitten back. His flesh remembered, would always remember, Iveran's sharp lessons. He wanted to feel joy. Joy that, finally, Iveran felt a measure of all the pain he had caused. Joy that, in a small way, perhaps Kerrus and Brennon had finally gotten some vengeance.

But his chest hurt, in that place that was for Kerrus and Brennon and Eddin and Lero. All those who had been kind to him, in his second life after the snows. The place where he kept their memories. Where he kept them alive. Since Iveran had killed them.

We rise above, he knew Parro Kerrus would say. *It is never a fault, to offer the Father's kindness, or the Mother's forgiveness.*

He hurt, for all the kindness he had known. In Aardanel, and in this remote place. Iveran had given him a home. A helm made from a snowbear's skull. The name *ijka,* marking him. Had wanted to give him a brother, a better-than-brother. To give him something to live for. His chest hurt, in that place he could not name, and he learned that Iveran, too, lived in that place.

So he stepped, a dozen steps forward, to kneel next to Iveran. He put his arms around the chieftain's shoulders, and held him as he cried his grief into the world.

There was a time, after the tears and the shaking slowed, when Iveran grabbed Scal's hand. Pulled it from his shoulder, held it palm up. Pressed something into it, something that was as big as Scal's hand. For once, Iveran had no words.

Scal tried to give it back, after the tears had stopped and they had risen to their feet. "No," Iveran said. "It is yours now, *ijka.*" He put it himself around Scal's neck, the snowbear-claw pendant that had been meant for Jari.

They burned them that night. The men knew what to do, and had done it without being told while their chieftain grieved. The pyre stood on the barren ground below Valastaastad, wood stacked careful, precise. Waiting.

Iveran could not do his part, when it came to it, so it was

left to Scal. With Uisbure and Kettar, he entered Iveran's house. Climbed to the second floor. Crossed into the room beneath the snowbear's head. The women had left, their duty done for now. Left the rest for the men to see to.

Had it not been for the blood, the blood over everything, it could have been normal. A mother, reclining on her sleeping furs, with her newborn held to her breast. But there was the blood, and they were too still, and too dead. Scal wrapped the baby, Jari, in the little snowbear cloak and carried him down. Kettar and Uisbure followed with Hanej. They laid her in a sled, to lower her down through the ice, but Scal kept Jari held close as he went one-handed down the ladder.

Iveran watched dry-eyed as they laid his wife and son on the pyre. Scal stood at his side as old Kaija the midwife chanted the songs of passing. But Iveran stepped forward alone, a torch's light shaking in his hand, and touched fire to the pyre.

It caught quickly, for the wood was dry and hungry. Iveran stayed close to the fire, closer than he should have, the torch hanging down by his side, eyes far away. Gently Scal took his arm and pulled him back, among the others. No more words were said, but the midwives began their keening once more.

They stayed until the last of the coals had cooled. Some sat, the children slept. But the midwives kept their keening, and Iveran kept his watch. Silently, through that long night, Scal, standing dutifully next to Iveran, prayed to the Parents. All the prayers Kerrus had taught him. Prayers he made up, too. Asking Patharro to give Hanej comfort, for Metherra to consider Jari gently. Asking them both for guidance, in this place where he felt so lost.

The sun rose, touching the embers of the pyre, and the

midwives fell silent. The Valastaa Clan rose, touching their brows in respect to the departed dead. And they started up the ladders to their homes. Iveran was the last to leave, and Scal with him.

There was another fire that day. After Iveran had emptied his house. Thrown out everything Hanej had ever touched. He burned it all. Recklessly, on the very ice shelf, in front of his house. He would have burned the house, too, Scal guessed, but the stone would not catch. When that second fire was blazing, Iveran left it and got sobbingly, roaringly drunk.

He had killed four men before the sun set on that second day. Ones who had tried to stop him, or help him. It did not matter. He killed them each in their turn, and threw their bodies over the edge of the ice. In a fit, he ripped his cloak from his neck, the cloak made from a snowbear's pelt, and threw that over the ice, too.

He was still drinking, still trying to pick fights, in the middle of that night. Scal left him to his grief, and made another descent down the ladder. Alone, this time, and carrying nothing but his clothes, and the sharpened sword Kettar had given him, and the knife with Iveran's death promised to it, and the snowbear-claw pendant. The only things he had. The only things that mattered. His boots touched the ground, and he began to walk.

He stopped only once. To look at the wreckage Iveran had made of four of his clansmen. Four loyal men. Good men. Or as good as any Northman. Once, it seemed like so long ago, he would have been on his knees retching at such a sight of human destruction. Once, in another life. His second life, after the snows that had sent him to Aardanel. In this third life, a life of hardness and cruelty and sharp, painful love, the dead men had no effect on him. His own flesh was too torn and scarred for theirs to matter.

One thing more he took with him as he left his third life behind. He bent to pluck it from the snow, from the ice already trying to suck it into its depths. Matted with frost and dead men's blood, he took it still. The North was cold and heartless, and the warmth of a snowbear's pelt might get him to his fourth life, wherever it lay.

810 Years after the Fall

Run all you like, but with enough time, everything'll come back around to find you.

—*Tare*

CHAPTER 14

Joros's anger was like a thing alive, clawing and howling and wanting to destroy. There was an ache in his jaw from keeping his teeth so tightly clenched, but that was distant, like his nails digging grooves in his palms, unimportant, only serving the boiling fury.

Thirteen years! Thirteen years he had served the Ventallo, and nearly a decade as a shadowseeker before that, serving the Fallen with all the faith he could muster. He had done everything right, exceeded all expectations, achieved the impossible—and *this* was his reward! In the absolute darkness within Raturo, he felt the brush of a passing preacher and, snarling, lashed out; there was a cry of mixed surprise and pain, but Joros was already moving on, anger driving him forward.

His chambers were as dark and cold as the rest of the mountain, but a single barked word sent Anddyr scrambling forward to fill the hearth with fire. The first thing he gave to the flames was his book of research, all the ideas and experiments meant to make the lives of preachers easier. The flames ate the paper as eagerly as the paper had eaten the ink. Then the piles and piles of letters and reports and rumors from his shadowseekers, useless fools who couldn't do the simplest tasks, a lifetime of records fed to the hungry fire. The flames burned bright and red, perhaps the first natural fire Raturo had seen in years. He could see, almost, why the Parents' priests thought fire sacred.

When he was out of things to burn, with his fury cooled to smoldering embers in the face of the roaring fire, he sat before the hearth and he began to think how he could kill the new Uniro.

Joros had quarreled with Delcerro over the years, and he would be the first to admit he hadn't exactly wept at the old man's passing, but he would give an arm to have that old bat back. Valrik Deuro, now Valrik Uniro, had revealed himself as something of a fanatic.

Though Joros had spent his thirteen years in the Ventallo doing everything to prove he was a faithful believer, Valrik still remembered him as the power-hungry young man fresh from the mountain, and the new Uniro had made quite clear his suspicions that Joros was still that same man. While Valrik was Uniro, Joros wouldn't be trusted with anything more complex than paperwork—and perhaps not even that, since paper was so good at carrying secrets.

Joros could have withstood Valrik's mistrust and his insults; he had long years of experience working in secret, working in the shadows, and he could have done it for many more years.

But for this latest insult, Valrik would have to die.

"You've done well, brother Sedeiro," Valrik had said flatly, regarding the five seekstones in Joros's hand.

The praise would have meant nothing even if it hadn't been empty, but Joros still gave a shallow bow. Praise was praise, and Joros would be the last to deny that he was due some. "I'll leave at sundown to begin the search." He'd need a few hours to prepare everything, to put his affairs in order, but with the seekstones finally made, he didn't want to let any more time trickle by.

Valrik snorted. "You'll do no such thing." He was an old man, but he was spry still; he snatched the seekstones from Joros's hand quicker than a blink. "You have too many duties to attend to here. I will send others." And he had sat silently and listened to Joros's screaming and cursing, turning the seekstones in his hands until Joros had stormed from the room.

Years of Joros's efforts, robbed from him in a moment. His greatest work, and unworthy others would reap all the benefits. He would see Valrik burn for it.

"Cappo." Anddyr barely breathed the word, knowing better than to disturb his master.

Joros had his hand raised to strike the mage when the flash of a black robe caught his eye. A hand rested lightly on his shoulder, and Dirrakara asked with careful nonchalance, "Are you out of that blue powder, love? The fire will hurt your eyes." She waited for a reply, and received none. She tried again: "Valrik has summoned us."

"Let him come for me himself, then."

After a moment's hesitation, she said, "I think you'll want to be there for this."

Finally he looked at her, saw how drawn her face was, her smooth skin pale even in the fire's warm light. He felt a flash of concern. "What's happened?"

They walked together through the halls of Raturo, Anddyr trailing dutifully behind as ever. The main floor was already full to bursting with black-clad bodies, but they parted to let Joros and Dirrakara through, recognizing the red Eyes stitched above their hearts. The stream of human flesh flowed into the Cavern of the Falls, where many of the Ventallo had already gathered before the preachers who'd been lucky or pushy enough to get into the Cavern early.

Valrik stood on a slight promontory at the edge of the ice lake, staring out over the press of bodies before him. Illo Deuro and Ildra Trera flanked him, the three of them together a walking exhibit of the dangers of aging. Joros joined the other dozen Ventallo who'd already gathered, his eyes hard on Uniro, trying to guess the man's motives and glare him to death in the process.

More and more preachers filled the room, bodies pressing in too tight. Anddyr nearly leaped back as someone pushed him too close to Joros, but there wasn't enough space for the mage to move away; instead he stood there trembling, nearly a head taller than anyone else in the room, his nervous-quick breathing stirring Joros's hair in a way that was almost intolerably annoying. Joros jabbed his elbow into the mage's stomach until he turned his head away.

There had never been so many bodies in the Cavern of the Falls, not that Joros had ever seen. The Icefall actually began to drip, slow droplets pooling at the tips of the fall's spines and falling heavily to the frozen lake. And still more preachers pressed in, filling the cavern with their unwashed warmth, panting their heat into the air.

Finally, *finally*, Valrik Uniro raised his arms into the air.

Silence rippled through the cavern, strangling noise to the far walls and up the tunnel, until the only sound in the wide room was the drip of melting ice. "Brothers and sisters!" he called out, voice still strong and carrying for such an old man. "Hear me now, and listen well. You have been misled, all of you." His hands fell to his sides, no longer needed to hold the attention of all the idiots listening with hanging jaws. "Our forebears, the first of the Fallen, would weep to see us as we have become. We have turned from our true purpose, the only purpose. We have become too focused on changing the world, trying too hard to shape it to the visions of gentle Fratarro and unyielding Sororra. I tell you now, my brothers and sisters, that is not what we are meant for. It is not the purpose held by the first Fallen, who built their mighty halls within the throne Fratarro pulled from the earth. We have been led astray for too long, caught up by the petty squabbling against which we were made to fight. No longer."

Valrik stepped down from the promontory, and the Ventallo parted before him like the tide around a stone. "Do you know our true purpose, my brothers and sisters? Our first purpose?" He stepped slowly through the gathered masses and they all fell back, heads bowed, hands clasped, utterly silent. "I tell you now, and listen well. We are not meant to shape the world for the mighty Twins. We are only human, and the power of true shaping is not ours to bear." To the edge of the ice lake, the preachers parted. Valrik didn't pause at the break between stone and ice, but continued his confident steps. In the heat of so many bodies, the ice groaned beneath his feet, a sheen of water over the ice. Valrik didn't falter. "We are meant instead to find them, to free them, to restore to them their stolen powers. *They* will shape the world, my brothers and sisters. We need only find them." The sound of ice snapping was unspeakably loud, and Valrik held aloft a long spear of ice from the Icefall. "Today marks our return to that purpose. Today marks our faith renewed." At the last word, Valrik lifted his icicle with both crabbed hands and brought its tip down into his left eye. In the resounding silence, Joros heard the wet squelch, the burst of blood. Valrik didn't hesitate as he pulled the shard free, blood steaming on the ice, and thrust it into his other eye. The icicle fell from his hands, shattering against the frozen lake, and Valrik looked out upon them with the red, weeping wounds where his eyes had been.

There was a pit in Joros's stomach, a gaping hole that threatened to swallow him down. Unexpectedly, his hands were shaking.

Valrik Uniro, first among the Fallen, newly blinded, raised his arms as if to embrace them all. "Fratarro shelters us still in this place of his power. By his mercy, we have been shown the path to our redemption. My brothers and sisters, I tell you this: the greatest task of our fellowship has fallen to us. The longest road shall be ours to walk, but the greatest reward lies at its end." He lifted his hands into the air, and between his fingers gleamed five seekstones. Joros knew them instantly, the ones Valrik had taken from him, and anger coiled in his stomach. "We have done it, my brothers and sisters. We have found them."

There was outcry, shock and denial and joy, all weaving together to make one swell of sound. Over the noise, Uniro spoke again: "I promise you all, we will go to them, and we shall restore them to their birthright. It shall be done, and done in our lifetime. Sororra and Fratarro shall once more walk the earth, and they shall bring their judgment." There was acrimony in the emptiness of his eyes. "I remind you that we, the faithful, shall be judged first. That even as we raise the Twins from the earth, they shall turn their eyes upon us, and they shall read our hearts.

"I pledge my faith to the Twins," Valrik Uniro cried in his ringing voice. "I shall face their judgment without fear. Who among you can say the same?" The blood flowed slowly down his cheeks, pooling in the wrinkles and folds, painting his visage a vengeful mask. "Today we begin anew. Today, in this sacred place of the gods, we cleanse our souls. To those of you who would atone for your transgressions, I call upon you to step forward. Receive my blessing as Sororra's, my forgiveness as Fratarro's. For those of you who would not fear judgment, I call upon you to join me." He stepped to one side, the lake creaking beneath his feet. Steady, unwavering, his hand pointed to the Icefall.

In the mad press of bodies that followed, Joros held his ground, his hand like a claw around Anddyr's arm. Dirrakara was swept away from him, her face burning with a delirious light, and the frozen lake howled louder than the frantic prayer that swelled to the ceiling and shook the spines of ice hanging there. He needed to be gone, away from this place. Joros pressed back through the surging crowd, dragging Anddyr with him, and he couldn't make his other hand stop shaking.

Stepping into the tunnel was like the first breath after drowning. Now that he was free of the screeching, crying crowd, his thoughts began to arrange themselves in some sort of order. He didn't like the paths they were taking.

"Cappo?" Anddyr's voice surprised him; the man was all but invisible more often than not. "Do you want . . . should I . . . ?"

The mage's question, half birthed though it was, at least turned his brain in a productive manner. "Yes," he said finally. "Follow Valrik, see what he does next. Don't be seen."

Anddyr swallowed hard, but he nodded resolutely. At his waist, his fingers wove a complex pattern Joros had long given up on deciphering. Like blinking, the mage disappeared from sight. Joros nodded vaguely, mind already twisting back to what he could possibly do.

Raturo had never felt hollow, though it was. Like an anthill, it boiled with hidden life, always a voice whispering, feet sliding softly across stone, the gentle flicker of pale torchlight. The place felt empty now, dead, all the life drained out from it. It was what all the priests of the Parents would wish for, the mountain cracked open and excised like a boil, darkness reclaiming all the places where life had dared to take root. The image stuck with him.

The fire was still burning in his hearth, though it was a dull shade of what it had been. A sad thing, compared to the brightness it had once held, all the potential. He watched it burn down to embers, watched it die its slow, flickering death. The red glow leached from the room, and the life, and Joros sat alone in the darkness. His hands, finally, had stopped shaking.

"Cappo?" Something clattered, followed by a curse. Joros didn't bother looking; Anddyr muttered something and a faint light shimmered. It drew closer, the mage kneeling down next to Joros's chair. "He's sending five of the Ventallo," Anddyr said, voice barely a whisper. The mountain had ears and eyes aplenty; it never hurt to be cautious. "They'll go searching, each with a small retinue. Report what they find, or bring it back, or—"

"Who." Joros didn't ask it as a question, his tone utterly flat. His eyes didn't leave the dead fireplace.

"Essemo Noniro. Saval Tredeiro. Dayra Quardeira. Ebarran Septeiro."

"That's four, Anddyr."

Still the mage hesitated. Joros knew the answer before he finally said it: "Cappa Dirrakara."

Joros nodded vaguely. It was fitting. He had dedicated his life to the Fallen, spent his finest years in service to the Ventallo—and they would leave him with less than nothing. If that was the way things were to be, then Joros would play that game as well. He was not a man given to losing—no matter the cost, no matter the end. And if there was a game he couldn't win, he would just as soon overturn the board.

He rose to his feet, eyes finally leaving the hearth where the red flames had gasped out their death. "Come, Anddyr," Joros said, the new purpose rising in him like a fanned ember. "We have much to do."

He was sure the mountain had been buzzing after Valrik's blinding, and all the other blindings that surely followed his speech, but the excitement had waned. The scattered time-candles had burned low, and the halls of Raturo were empty and dark, silent as death. Joros sent his mage to gather supplies, and though he was starting to show the twitch that meant he was close to needing his skura, Anddyr was too cowed to do anything but obey.

Joros walked alone to stand before the great arch, where

prideful Sororra turned away from spite guised as righteous punishment, and Fratarro wept for the beauty and the love that had been torn from him. Every day for nearly thirteen years, he had walked beneath that arch, but he had rarely paused, never stopped to study it. He stood close enough that he could see in Fratarro's eye, big as Joros's palm, faint, shallow traces of a paradise aflame, the ground cracked, and a horde of mighty creatures plummeting through the air as their wings burned. Fratarro had created his own worshipers when none would turn from the Parents, winged beasts he called *mravigi*. All the old stories said they had been beautiful, majestic, more worthy of a god's love than fallible mankind. When Patharro had burned all that Fratarro had created, it had included the living beasts. Reflected in Fratarro's other stone eye were the Parents' faces, brutal and uncaring as they watched their children fall. So high up, almost lost in the darkness, the likeness of the Parents lurked over all at the top of the arch. There couldn't be one without the other, twined together like a complex knot. The light and the shadow, fire and embers, blood and ice.

That was where the boy found him, melting out of the shadows. "Twins' bones, boy, you should make some noise." Joros waited for his sister to follow, but it seemed Etarro was alone. They might as well have been attached, for as little as they were apart, and yet the boy came to stand at Joros's side. Hardly even a boy anymore, grown nearly as high as Joros's shoulder. His too-big eyes gazed at the arch, traveling up one side and down the other, and came to rest on the floor.

"You shouldn't try," the boy said softly.

That was something to finally reach through the cloud that had swallowed Joros. "Is that a threat?"

"A warning." The boy looked up to meet Joros's eyes, his own earnest. "It won't be like you think. You won't be able to stop them."

"You don't have to pretend for me, boy."

"I wouldn't. Not for you."

Joros was the first to look away, back to the great arch.

"I know I can't stop you," Etarro went on, "but you should know you'll fail."

Joros could feel his teeth clenching, but it was a distant thing. "Did Valrik send you? Tell you to scare me, make sure I stay in line?"

"No one sent me, and I couldn't scare you any more than the doubts that eat at your heart. You have my mage, that's all, and I have to be sure you're taking care of him. You risk death with every step. But so long as you live, he lives. Tied together like a knot." Their eyes locked again, and the boy didn't blink. "Light and shadow. Fire and embers. Blood and ice."

A chill crept its way up Joros's spine. "The others might believe your little prophecies," he said quickly, "but you don't fool me, boy."

Etarro shrugged. "Some things are true whether you believe them or not. And lies aren't healthy, you have to be careful they don't nibble away at you until the lie is all that's left of what you used to be." A blink finally, slow and thoughtful. "Just take care of him. Good-bye, Joros." The boy turned away and the shadows took him once more. Joros looked back to the arch, but Fratarro's fire-filled eyes looked too much like Etarro's. He hurried under the arch, into the Ventallo chambers beyond.

The blue glow of the antechamber was almost startlingly

bright, its cast shadows making the doorways look like twenty gaping tombs. Joros went to stand over the stone box, staring down at it, trying to stare *through* it. There was a gnawing in him, one he hadn't felt in more than twenty years, since stepping inside the mountain. It was something empty, a sense of rightness leaching away.

There would be changes. Oh yes, Valrik Uniro would make great, sweeping changes—for the benefit of all, of course, all except untrustworthy Joros. He who had professed his faith since before he'd reached Raturo's peak, professed it twice as loud and actually begun to mean it after he'd joined the Ventallo. He who had worked tirelessly through the years, made strides where all others had failed. Still, he would be punished for it while Valrik remained.

Joros pressed his hands against the lid of the stone bier, and pushed.

Anddyr was waiting for him, shaking like a kicked dog, two travelsacks slung over his shoulders. The mountain opened to Joros's touch, sliding back to reveal the tops of tall trees and the stars hanging far above. Light again, as much as there could be on a no-moon night. They had to walk down still, down around the outside of the mountain to the forest floor, but they should reach it before sunlight swallowed the stars.

They stepped together into the night, quiet as a breath. Above, Sororra's Eyes glared down at him, burning like twin flames. Joros turned his shoulder to the red stars and began the long walk down, a travelsack over his shoulder and a heavy pouch hanging from his hip like a stone.

CHAPTER 15

It was bright and loud and full to bursting inside the tavern, and all of it bundled together really made Rora want to stab someone. The musician singing much too loud for how bad he was at singing—he'd be a good choice. Or the bruiser who kept grabbing for her arm; there was no denying a knife in his ribs would improve Rora's opinion of him. Any of the men or women, really, just standing blindly in her way. But the one who most deserved her knife—most often deserved it, but especially now—was the sandy-haired man—*boy*, not man; that much was clear—playing cards with a group of fingers and losing all her money.

She grabbed him by a handful of the hair he so lovingly brushed every morning and put a foot against the back leg of his chair, so that when she tugged back on his pretty locks, it sent him and the chair both tumbling. The fingers, who could see her, who knew who she was, all held their hands up, trying to look like the lice they were. Aro, though—always slow to think but quick to react—started shouting even as he was falling, "Stone, help!" And the bruiser, who didn't know who he was grabbing at and was too thick to notice the fingers' reactions, tried to wrap his meaty arms around Rora. It didn't work, of course, because he was as slow and dumb as his name, and Rora ducked easily away and came back up with her dagger in hand. While Stone was still looking surprised at his empty arms, Rora reached up—a stretch, damnit—and brought the blue gem down hard onto the base of his skull. She didn't have enough leverage to really knock him out, not with his height and her distinct lack of it, but it was enough to give him a lump and a headache and spinning eyes long enough for Rora to grab her brother by the back of his shirt and drag him through the milling, laughing crowd. They made way for her this time, though it probably had as much to do with Aro's flailing limbs as with the glare she kept flinging around.

She let him go once they were out on the street, and he quickly scrambled to his feet. Ever since he'd grown a head taller than her, he'd learned never to face her without standing. She usually let him, because he needed any advantage he could get. Not this time, though. Neatly, she kicked his feet out from under him, sending him back to the ground. She smiled inside at the thump and the poof of dust he made, but outside she kept her face grim and angry and full of the desire to use the knife she'd put away.

He tried to get up again, because he had a hard time taking hints when he drank, so Rora stepped down on the inside of his thigh and pinned him there. He used his only real defense, then, the big innocent eyes that'd always softened her heart. They still did, some things never changed, but Rora did her best to hold on to her anger. She used the voice

Tare'd taught her, level, deadly calm. "Burn tells me you've been here drinking these last three days." He nodded, still using the big eyes, still thinking they'd be enough to get him out of trouble. "These last three days," she repeated, "when I thought you were dead."

"Not dead," he slurred, "just very, very drunk."

She leaned down and slapped him then, only because she couldn't bring herself, despite everything, to punch him. She had once, a few years ago now, and knocked out one of his teeth. He'd moped for two days straight and hadn't talked to her for a month because of it, not until Slip had forced a berbiere at knifepoint to make him a fake tooth that looked just like a real one. Rora still got mad about that, sometimes, but not near as mad as she was now.

"We thought you were dead," she said, trying hard to stay as calm as her voice sounded, "all of us. The Blackhands said they did it, and sent a hand to prove it." She looked down to check, because she hadn't yet, but both his hands were still there. Bare, because all his rings were back in the Canals, pried off the flaking, burned hand they'd sent her. "I didn't believe it," she went on, "so Worm was nice enough to take me to see your body. *Your body.*" She had to stop, then, because the memory still made her sick. They'd burned the body, of course—Blackhands always did—but not enough that she couldn't recognize him, couldn't see parts of her own face staring back around the black, burned flesh. She'd killed Worm without even a thought, only the second man she'd killed outside a contract. She would've killed any other Blackhands she could, too, if Tare and Garim hadn't dragged her away.

Aro pushed at her leg, and she let him up this time. His

eyes had gone soft, and he reached for her, but Rora turned away, started walking. She knew he'd follow. She took them down a familiar alley, dark and quiet, away from the street, and when she turned back around he was there, arms wrapping her in a gentle hug. "Rora, I'm so sorry," he whispered against the top of her head.

She leaned against him for a moment, just a moment, but he smelled like ale and sweat. Pushing him away, gently now that there wasn't anyone around to see, now that the anger was mostly leached away by the memory of the burned body, she crossed her arms over her chest and looked up to meet his eyes. "Tell me what the hells happened, Falcon." She stressed the name; he still forgot sometimes, after all these years.

With a sigh he sat down, leaning his back against the wall. He patted the ground next to him and, feeling too tired to even stand anymore, Rora sank down next to him. "Me and Leaf were out drinking," Aro started, eyes closed, head back against the wall. *Of course,* Rora thought, but she didn't say it. "We didn't realize we'd gone too far till we were already there. Coro was waiting, with his thugs. They jumped us. Took Leaf down right away, knife through the eye. Very clean. You'd've been impressed." He was quiet for a while, and so was Rora. There wasn't much to say, not yet.

But the silence went on and she almost thought he'd fallen asleep, but she could see his throat working, swallowing hard, and his eyes squeezed tight shut. So she finally opened her mouth, needing to say something to let him hold on to. "Blackhands've been looking for an excuse to start a war for a while now. I suppose they wanted you to be it?"

He nodded silently, swallowed again, pulled himself

together. "That's about what Coro said. They started after me, and I got scared. I . . . it went bad."

Rora had to take a hard swallow of her own. "It happened?" When he nodded, she looped her arm through his, leaned her head against his shoulder. He leaned into her, and against her hair she felt his cheek wet with quiet tears. "They could've used any of the bodies, I suppose, once they found 'em . . ."

"You always said Leaf looked enough like us he could keep us safe in a pinch."

Rora nodded slowly against his shoulder. "I did say that." She'd liked Leaf. He'd been as good an influence as Aro'd had lately. "Why didn't you come find me, though . . . after? I'd've helped you. I always have."

His shoulder shrugged under her head. "It hurt too much. I just wanted to get away for a while. I . . . I guess I didn't think much beyond that. I'm sorry, Rora."

"It's fine." How could she be mad at him anymore, knowing now? "Just don't do it again." She meant for him not to disappear again, but it worked for the other thing, too.

"Can we go home now? Please?"

He was still teeteringly drunk, so she got up first so she could haul him to his feet. She wasn't much good as far as a crutch went, being so much shorter, but Aro was stick thin and she was strong enough to mostly hold him up with an arm around the waist. She kept to the alleys and back lanes—it wouldn't do either of their reputations any good to be seen like this. Well, maybe it'd add to the soused legend that was Falcon, but she wasn't much in the mood for feeding that.

Managing the ladders was more excitement than she needed on this already too-long night, but she got Aro down into the Canals without him falling too far. The bridges were another story, but the water was low enough and sluggish enough that the few times he tipped into it didn't do him much harm. Luckily, it wasn't too far to safe territory, and she made all the appropriate signs to keep the eyes and feet in their roosts. The den was quiet this late at night, full of sleepers on their rafts or in alcoves, a few fists on guard duty gently tossing dice. Rora wasn't halfway across the den before a woman materialized on Aro's other side, looping his other arm over her shoulder. "Mother be praised," the other murmured. It was too dark to see, but Rora knew Slip's voice well enough. The two of them together got Aro, already mostly asleep on his feet, settled into an alcove. "Garim's been waiting for you," Slip said as she tucked a blanket around Aro. "You better go see 'im. Don't worry, I'll stay here."

Rora hesitated, long enough that the other woman definitely noticed it, but that was a familiar dance between them. Rora'd never been able to bring herself to trust the older girl, mostly for all the trouble she'd got Aro in over the years. But she knew Garim had been just as worried as she was, and it'd be cruel to keep him waiting. She'd have to report to Tare, too, and there was no sense delaying that. So much as she didn't want to, she left Aro with Slip.

The fists guarding the entrance to the heart of the den, next to the rotting dog's head, knew her, of course, and let her by without a word or a look. She could still remember when she'd thought the walk took forever, back when her legs had been small—or smaller, really—and the whole den had felt like a maze. It'd taken her a year to realize Tare was *trying* to keep her lost, taking a different way every time. Tare'd laughed when

Rora'd finally accused her of it. "Took you long enough. I had to use longcuts that haven't seen feet in decades, fleece-for-brains." Now it was simple enough, the second left, the next right, and a long stretch to the circle room with three other channels branching off it. That's where she found them waiting.

Garim was pacing, like he did when he was nervous or angry, so it was hard to tell which one he was feeling most. Tare was leaning against a wall, sharpening one of her knives like usual. She saw Rora first and made the knife disappear—not even Rora knew where the hand kept all her blades. "Well?" Tare asked as Garim spun to face her, too.

"He's alive and drunk," Rora said. When it was just the three of them, she didn't bother with anything like an official report. "No worse off than usual."

Garim sagged with relief. "I may just have to make Bone a mouth for that," he muttered.

"Don't be ridiculous," Tare said. "His mouth's too big for him to be any good as a mouth."

Garim waved a hand like he was shooing away flies. "All talk for later. Come on, the Dogshead's been waiting."

They fell into line, Garim leading, Tare bringing up the rear, as they went down the left passage. Over a board bridge, taking a right, and then they came to the only door Rora'd still ever seen in the Canals. There was a knife on guard who gave the door two smart knocks before swinging it inward and letting them pass.

Sharra was at her desk, just where she always seemed to be. The packhead was *supposed* to be a mystery; most of Whitedog Pack didn't even know who their head was, and Sharra wanted it that way. There was a time, Tare'd told Rora once in a low whisper she'd hardly been able to hear, when it hadn't been that way, when Sharra had always been out among her pack, acting like any old fist. That'd been before her leg, and Rora still didn't know the whole story behind that—it was the one thing neither Tare nor Garim would talk about, and she wasn't about to ask Sharra either. But now the Dogshead spent near all her time in the waterfall room, passing all her words on to Garim, who saw they got to where they needed to go. That was how it was supposed to be, the face told her, but Garim always seemed sad when he said it.

"How's my boy?" Sharra asked, looking right at Rora. That intense gaze always made her feel like Sharra could see under her skin and straight to her heart and mind, and much as she liked and respected the Dogshead, that wasn't something Rora wanted.

She did straighten her back and clasp her hands for an official report this time. "Alive and unhurt," Rora said. "I found him in the Stinking Pit, just like Bone said he was. He's sleeping now; probably will be for a while."

"And did he tell you what happened?"

"Coro got him and Leaf in a bad place. They killed Leaf right off, but Falcon managed to get away before they took more'n his rings."

Tare was frowning. "Get away? Just like that?"

Rora shrugged; she'd gone over this part carefully in her mind, knowing they'd ask. "He's always had the dumbest luck. There were only four men, two of 'em green. He said it happened fast enough he couldn't remember it right, but he got away while they were fighting over his rings." She shrugged again. "Dumb luck."

No one said anything for a while, but Sharra was staring hard at Rora, and she supposed Tare was, too, but she didn't look away from the Dogshead's gaze. Didn't blink, didn't twitch, didn't even think in case Sharra saw her thoughts behind her eyes. Finally the head gave a small nod, let go of Rora's eyes. "And then?"

"He was scared. Sad over Leaf. He wasn't thinking clear, and didn't want to think at all."

"So he went and got drunk," Tare muttered distastefully.

Garim made a low, angry noise in his throat. "And I suppose he just lost track of time, is that it?"

Rora met the anger in the face's look. "No one's madder about it than you," she told him levelly, "except me."

"Did you hit him?"

"Twice."

"Enough." Sharra sighed, rubbing a hand over her eyes. Moving with practiced experience, Tare ducked through the waterfall and came back out, not much more wet, with a plain chair. The Dogshead sank into it gratefully, only a little stiff on the leg that didn't bend right. "The fact that Falcon *is* still alive only means the Blackhands couldn't manage to track him down a second time."

"Which means they don't know where he is," Tare said, thinking aloud with Sharra like they so often did, "or that he's even still alive."

"Or that we have him back," Sharra finished. Her eyes moved back to Rora, then away. "Tare, you mentioned a contract that came in tonight?"

She didn't see the dismissal until Tare was leading her to the door. They were always like that, thinking and moving faster'n Rora could keep up with. "Go find Goat," Tare said. "He'll give you the details." She paused a moment before closing the door on Rora. "You did good tonight, Sparrow. And don't worry. The Blackhands *will* pay . . . now we've just got more options for how." Then she did close the door, leaving Rora on the other side of it.

The knife was still on guard, and he looked like he was about to say something. The look on Rora's face must've stopped him, which was good because she was in no mood for talking. She understood it, that she was just a knife, not fit to talk politics and war with the head, face, and hand, even if it was her brother who would be at the heart of all their talks. She understood it, but it still made her gnash her teeth. "It's not that we don't trust you," Tare had explained the first time she shoved Rora unceremoniously out of the room. A minute later, when she'd swung the door back open and sent Rora tumbling forward, her ear pressed to the ground instead of the door like it had been, Tare'd grinned like a wolf. "It's just that we don't trust you."

She wanted to go back and find Aro, but she knew he'd be sleeping for a good long while, and not being able to yell at him some more would just make her angrier, until she was likely to punch him in the face while he slept. A contract would help get her mind off the night, if nothing else.

The knifeden was a string of quiet rooms, all propped-up boards and blankets hung up for doorways, and the common chamber with chairs and pillows and tables. It was full at this time of night, the nocturnal knives talking or drinking or dicing, but they were never a loud bunch. She spotted Goat easy enough—you couldn't miss that big a man in that small a room. He'd had Tare arrange it, the big divan that barely managed to hold him, getting all the fingers to work together to nip it from one of the classier parts of North Quarter. Rora'd stood with the rest of the pack, trying to smother laughter as they watched the dozen fingers trying to navigate the canals with the big divan propped on their shoulders. These days, Goat didn't leave the divan unless Tare made him.

Rora plopped down into the little open space between Goat's girth and the edge of the divan, and said, "Tare sent me to talk to you about a contract."

Goat gave her an appraising look. "This supposed to be a reward or a distraction?"

"Distraction, but not from what you think. Falcon's fine. Dogshead just wants me out of the way."

Goat nodded sagely, folded his hands over his considerable belly. Tare said he'd been skinny as a stick once, and the best knife she had; but years of being the hilt and just overseeing his knives had made him . . . not lazy, but he did too much eating and relaxing for how little moving he did. He was still a damn good hilt, though, there was no arguing that. "You're going topside, then. East Quarter, Fishertown. You're looking for a big boardinghouse with a blue door. Alley side, second floor, should be the second window, but if it's not a sleeping old man, best move onto the third room."

"Who's the mark?" Rora asked.

Goat fixed her with the same hard look he always did. "An old man. Old men already have death breathing on their necks, so I wouldn't spend much more time thinking about it. Go fill your contract, knife."

CHAPTER 16

The trees pressed close, silent and grim. Dobren had whined when Scal had said no fires, but Attemo had silenced his second. Scal had worked for Attemo before. The caravan master trusted him as much as was possible, though it was not much still.

They were no more than a day from Bastreri, the trading center of northern Fiatera. Not so close that they were safe yet. Not so close that any guards would come to their aid. Close enough to the snowy North that Scal knew the wagoneers would be feeling the cold. Such a thing did not touch him. He was thrice born of ice and snow, and these Fiateran autumns were little more than a brush of wind. They would be cold, though, the eight wagoneers and mercenaries. Cold men shot poorly, swung swords slowly. But they were alert. Cold men listened to the night crackle around them. Cold men would hear the step of a foot, the brush of a shoulder, the creak of leather.

Reports of bandits had chased them all the way from Corinn. There was a desperation that came with the cold winds, in the men who had to fight for a chance of food. A hope of shelter against the coming snows. There was a desperation, too, in men like Attemo. With winter closing in, this was the last trip his caravan would make for the year. The last chance at a purse full of coin before wintering in Bastreri. A small caravan, so they could move quickly. Few guards, so he would not have to take too much from his profit. It was a gamble, to travel so unprotected in these bandit-haunted lands. Scal had never understood gambling. Attemo said that a touch of fear was what made life worth living. Long ago, Parro Kerrus had told him, *A man who risks his life without need is a waste of Patharro's gift of breath.*

The roving bandits were bravest near Bastreri. An old mercenary had warned them a few towns back, his face scarred by old fights. All the caravans would be flocking to Bastreri for the last of the trading season. Pickings would be rich, for a few men brave enough.

So Scal stood among the trees, a distance from Verris and his mercenaries with their swords. Attemo and Dobren and the other wagoneers sitting cold atop their wagons and clutching at bows with half-frozen fingers. Scal stood alone, and waited to die. It would not be such a bad thing. He had been waiting for it, since the snows had spit him out into a fourth life.

A twig snapped—danger. Easy as breathing, Scal found the red anger, the fight-song rising in his heart, pulling at him. A step forward, to the left three paces. His sword bit smoothly into a creeping bandit. A gurgle, no more. Leaves rustled behind him, a quiet wind of movement. Scal turned, sword low, cutting up and through. Warmth spattered across his face and the body fell heavily to the ground. A scream, from the wagons, as strings snapped and metal clattered, the distant sounds growing in frenzy. An arrow sank into a tree at Scal's right. He moved forward to the camp, head low. It was dark, but the moon was high behind the trees. Enough to pick out friend from foe. His sword flashed before him, a star rising and falling in the night, bringing death where it landed. The mercenaries screamed as they fought, battle cries from men who knew the business of killing. Two of the mercenaries moving together like a storm, their staves whirling. Their sticks sent weapons flying away, knocked men from their feet, but metal-tipped sticks did not kill. It was Scal who sent the fallen men to their gods. And the red was over all, driving him forward. Hungry. Needing. The song of blood loud in his ears, and his heart.

There were, suddenly, no more foes. It ended. The same sudden way it always did. It left Scal standing with sword raised and red before his eyes, ready to face the next blow. There would not be one. He was never ready for the end of the fighting. The red glow faded too slowly. Left him feeling dizzy and lost. He could feel the others, staring. For a moment, his sword almost moved again. There were still bodies standing. Still blood flowing.

"Well done, boys," Attemo called from the top of his wagon, and there was cheering. "Let's get the place cleaned up and a fire started."

"No fire," Scal croaked through the red. It was dark, but Scal could see the doubt in Attemo's eyes. Almost, he threw his sword into the wagoneer's chest. It would take strength, but he could have done it. He stopped himself. Closed his eyes, hoping for the red to fade. Through his teeth, he said, "There may be more." It had not been enough. It never was.

Silence, for a time. Feet shuffling. Leaves rustling. The

moon, climbing through the sky. Attemo cleared his throat. "It's cold enough, we'll chance it. Ring up the wagons, we can keep the fire hidden. Verris, you and your men take shifts watching. We'll need wood. Let's get moving."

There was flurry. A foolish flurry, and the anger was deep in Scal's chest. Stalking away, sticks cracking carelessly beneath his feet. The first man he found had been crippled by a whirling stave. Finished by Scal, with the sword through his neck. It was easier, then, to remove the head. Gripping the hair, boot against shoulder, two sharp slices. He took the man's own sword and stalked into the trees, thirty paces from the wagons, and planted the sword into the ground. With some work, the head fit over the hilt. It stared as he worked. Accusation in its eyes. Mouth open in shock. It should not have been so surprised.

There were only six others. Enough, though, to make a ring around the camp. It might be enough to give pause, to any who would think of an attack. Attemo had hired him to keep the caravan safe. To keep them all alive. It was harder to do, when Attemo would not listen. This, at least, was something that could be done. In the night, fear was a powerful thing.

With the red fading from his eyes and heart as he planted the last sword, he sank to his knees. Blood dripped slow, small spatters against the ground. A faint glow from the hidden moon, turning the blood to a mirror. He did not like what he saw there. "Forgive me," he said softly, to the head and to the Parents. He reached up to touch his chest. His painted flame-disk hung there. He had spent all his money on it, after his first caravan, to mark himself a new man.

He had known a priest, once. A man who loved to see the irony in life.

"Parents guard you," Scal said softly, to the head before him and the others among the trees, "and keep your souls. I am sorry. There are things a man must do, sometimes."

Scal rose. Sheathed his sword over his shoulder. Worked his way back to the wagons. They did not look at him, Attemo and the wagoneers, Verris and his mercenaries. They would have seen the bodies without their heads. They would know. They would think it a Northern custom, an evil thing of the far snows. They would call him a demon. A beast. A monster in men's skin. Never would they think he had done it to protect them.

A man, the priest had told him, so long ago, *is never only one thing or another. A man's heart is much more complicated than that.*

It was silent in the ring of wagons, around a fire that would be seen easily, as Scal retrieved his old wooden bowl from his single pack. He filled the bowl with the stew they were cooking. It was his right. Food and passage and coin for the protection of his sword. He took his meal and walked back out of the wagons. Softly, they began to speak again.

He ate alone. Alone he sat through the night, with his sword across his knees. Eyes closed but not sleeping. Listening to the night around him. To the sound of celebration, among the wagons. The first battle on this journey, and they had all lived through it. Verris came upon him, once. Patrolling, but he smelled of wine. He turned, wordless, avoiding Scal's eyes. Through the rest of the night, the mercenaries would stop and turn before they reached him. An incomplete circle, to avoid him.

Softly, staring out into the snow with his hands folded and his eyes sad, Parro Kerrus had told him, *Even the best of men, sometimes, must do bad things.*

It had been seven years since his first caravan. Freshly

reborn from the ice and snow, a boy as big as a man. Looking wild as a bear. Heartless as a winter. They had hired him, hoping the sight of a Northman would keep bandits away. Mostly, it did. Always, though, there came a point. An attack, and Scal would do what he had been paid to do. Always, after, they would fear him. Hate him. Give him a pouch of coins and tell him to leave. Drive him away with their own weapons. It was never the same after the killing.

Alone he listened to the night. Mice in the brush. An owl, flying low. Somewhere in the trees, two mercenaries and the soft sounds of lovemaking. A log being thrown into the fire, sparks crackling in the cold. The night, spinning on around him. Steps. Light on the ground, creeping. Four, five. A pause. Soft voices, cursing, warding, as fear proved stronger than a desire for vengeance against the slain whose heads ringed the camp. Steps again, back the way they had come.

The only pride a man should take, the priest had said, *is in knowing that he's done a job, and done it well.*

The night was long, but all things end. As the sun touched the leaves, Scal rose. Sheathed his sword over his shoulder. Worked his way back to the wagons.

Attemo did not drive him off, or ask him to leave. Simply, they all ignored him. None would meet his eyes, as he took some of the cold porridge. Attemo would not look at him as Scal took his place on the bench of Attemo's wagon. One of the other mercenaries knew some Northern songs and would always try to get Scal to sing, but this day she stayed at the back of the caravan. They were close to Bastreri. They would be free of him, soon enough. If a man could pretend, long enough, that a thing did not exist, he might one day be proved true.

Sometimes, too, Scal remembered the words of another man. *Men are the cruelest of all the beasts*, that man had said, he with a bear's head atop his own.

A fourth life, the snows had given him. He wished, sometimes, that they had kept him instead.

Birds sang, and the wind blew. Among the rolling wagons, it was silence. The priest had told him, once, *It's hard, lad, to change a man's opinion of you. Earned or no, some men will always only see you a certain way.*

Scal pulled his sword from over his shoulder. Saw Attemo flinch. Laid the sword over his legs and pulled out his whetstone. The blade was longer than Scal's arm, so that the tip of it rested on Attemo's thigh. The caravan master stared ahead, eyes fixed. Tight lines in his throat, sweat on his brow. Scal whistled, loudly, as he sharpened the edge of his blade.

The other man, the one whose cloak Scal wore, had said, *It is a hard world*, ijka. *There is no place in it for soft men.*

They reached the gates of Bastreri before sundown. Stopped, to wait in the long line of wagons hoping for passage into the town. Without a word, Attemo set a pouch of coin on the seat between himself and Scal. Silently Scal took it. Jumped from the wagon to the ground and walked, without looking back, into the city.

There were things he had learned, things that would always be true. Always, men would fear him. And always, men would hire him because of their fear. There would be jobs waiting in Bastreri. There was always work for a man who knew how to kill and did not fear his own death.

CHAPTER 17

There was nothing like walking to cleanse the soul and the mind. It had always been one of the deepest truths of Keiro's life. His earliest memory was of walking, holding on to his father's pant leg with chubby fingers and coughing at the dust his feet kicked up. He'd walked with wide eyes, then, taking in everything, each sight something wondrous and new to hold in his heart. In the days after his first ascent of Raturo, when he'd gone back out into the world as a preacher, he'd been in the habit of walking with his eyecloth bound tight, honoring the Twins' dream.

It had been years now since he'd last worn the eyecloth. It served better wrapped about his brow, to keep back the hair that had grown long and the constant threat of sweat. And, too, it kept his eye free to absorb the new sights that came with each day. Seven years since he lost his eye, and he had never walked the same path twice. Seven years of his exile, and his heart had never been more full of joy.

He liked to think he now walked the same ground the

Twins had once strode, for the lands south of Fiatera had been theirs, in the time when they'd freely walked the earth. They had seen no steps upon this corner of the earth, and so they had claimed it, with their feet and their hearts and their love. Keiro did not claim the land with his feet, for it had been claimed by others after the Twins had left it, and, too, he wanted no lands for himself. But he worshiped the land and the gods who had walked it, worshiped with his feet and heart and love, each step a whisper of prayer. It was a pilgrimage of sorts, though his journey had no true ending. The pilgrimage was the walking itself, for his feet had taken him farther than the Twins' ever had, but the walking was truly all Keiro could ask for.

The first year he had gone west, and in the years that followed he'd gone as far west as west went. Truly, Keiro hadn't known the world was so big. He'd known of Bragia and Montevelle, the countries hidden behind the Tashat Mountains, and the hilly lands below them populated by the Shrevan nomads. The Bragians had been kind and welcoming, the Montevellese hostile. The nomads had been something else entirely; distant at first, nothing more than a retreating cloud of dust given life by their horses' hooves. The first to approach him had been a youth, full of bravado and bluster, pushing his horse in tight-stepping circles around Keiro until the mouth-sore beast had thrown the boy to the ground, and he and Keiro had both laughed about that. The Shurou tribe had welcomed Keiro in for a time, had eventually accepted him as a part of their sprawling, extended family. They'd given him the greatest gift among their culture: a horse of his own, a bright-eyed filly who loved a journey as much as Keiro. He'd cherished that horse, until he'd come to the wide river-that-ran-from-the-sun, which the nomads said stretched all the way to the sun's distant home, and he'd had to see if that was true. He'd never found the river's birthplace, but at the crossing he had found, far northwest of the Shrevan lands, the dark-skinned women who manned the crossing had given him passage in exchange for the horse—though the transaction was done in simplistic hand gestures and much jabbing of chests, for they used words Keiro had never heard before. The crossing was too rich a temptation for him to refuse, much as he loved the horse. Finally he saw the far bank of the river he'd followed for so long, and kept going west from there. The dark-skinned people had stared and laughed at him, until a young woman, grinning, had woven braids and beads into his hair and beard. They stared less, then, and the girl walked with him for a time. "Algi," she told him, holding one hand over her eyes, the other over her heart. He mimed the motions and named himself, but she always called him "Erokiyn." He would learn later that it meant "old man," and he would laugh at it. With the sun turning his skin to leather and bleaching his hair to near white, he could hardly say he didn't look the name. In time, once they'd learned some of the other's words, she'd listened to his talk of the Twins and their Parents, but had shaken her head and told him of her sun god. He sounded much like Patharro.

When west ended at the sea Algi named Forsaera—"poison water"—he had turned south, and Algi with him. Sometimes he regretted that he had gone south instead of north, for at length, following the coast, they had come to a desert—*the* desert, Keiro would learn, the same Eremori that lurked beneath Fiatera. Fratarro, when he had claimed a land of his own and built of it a paradise, had not felt the need to contain his creation to a small piece of the world; and Patharro had not been stingy in his fury, blighting all that Fratarro had built and all the lands it touched. Algi had no name for the desert, and she had terrible nightmares after Keiro told her of Patharro's destructive hand. When Keiro turned east to follow the edge of the desert, she turned north, to find and rejoin her people. She'd grown into a woman by then, and had kissed Keiro on the mouth before she left. If he'd gone north instead of south at the sea, she might still have been with him.

With the desert heat distantly shimmering ever at his right, Keiro had found a mighty forest where the air was so thick and damp it beaded on his skin, and long-armed furry creatures with faces that looked almost like his screeched down at him from the heights of the trees. A sleek bear had nearly taken off his leg before Keiro had scrambled up a tree, and then he'd been pelted with nuts and stones by the tree's residents until the bear had lost interest. An enormous spotted cat had chased him into a pool of water but refused to enter, stalking around the banks, swiping at him and snarling through the longest night he'd ever lived. The only signs he'd seen of humans in the forest had been a few picked-clean bones.

It had been months since that strange forest, months of rolling hills and plains and forests full of creatures he recognized. He thought of himself when he was a younger man, when he'd thought Fiatera had been such a huge place. He could walk from Raturo to the Northern Wastes in little over a month. It had taken him *years* to walk to one end of the world, and he intended to walk to the other end of it as well. Fiatera was no more than a drop of ink on the map that rolled through his mind; yet, still, his heart ached for the only true home his wandering feet had ever known. He was still a goodly distance from the southern reaches of Fiatera, but it would be good to again walk the land he had loved, to venture through the dense and sprawling Forest Voro, to gaze upon the sharp peak of Raturo over all . . .

But no, that was not how things were to be. "Should we see your face again," Keiro repeated the words that had been said years ago, by the Ventallo who didn't know him and wrongly hated him for a perceived betrayal, "it shall mean your death." Fiatera was forbidden to him, the land no longer his to walk.

No matter. The world was a wide place, and he imagined he would die before he could ever see all of it. That was the way of things. He had found acceptance, in the soft pad of his feet against the earth. He, a man with no home, was made for walking, and walk he would.

There were, though, some places that could not be walked.

It had been many years since he had seen the vast river, the river-that-ran-from-the-sun. It lay before him now, so wide he couldn't see the far bank, flowing steadily south as it fled the sun's home. The sight of it filled Keiro's heart with an unexpected fluttering, for it was the first familiar thing he had seen in all his long traveling. The river was wider here, and slower, than to the north, where he had first crossed it, the river having left behind its wild and reckless adolescence, grown into a steady adulthood, but it could only be the same river. He loved it, as much as a man could love a body of water, and he slept that night on the bank of the river-that-ran-from-the-sun with a smile on his face.

The smile was diminished by the sun's rising, though. It had taken Keiro months to find a crossing north of the Shrevan hills, and even the point where he had first met the river was far north of where he now stood. There was no knowing what life, if any, lay between his position and that lonely, faraway crossing. His feet itched to walk, but they itched for the far side of the river, for the lands nearer to his forbidden home. He might waste another year trying to find a crossing.

It was one of the few times in his life that Keiro chose not to walk.

His father had taught him how to swim, long ago, in rivers and lakes they crossed on their endless walking. Keiro had not swum for a very long time, for the rippling water always seemed to shape itself into staring eyes. He thought he still had the trick of it, though, and it would no doubt be the fastest way to cross the river.

Of what little he owned, he left most of it where he had slept, a strange collection from a wandering life. A thin grass pallet, so well woven it had lasted him years; his walking stick, less fit for swimming than walking; a lump of stone that threw off rainbows when the light caught it; the hollowed-out horn of some strange beast; a clumsily made journal of parchment and bark and leaves, anything he'd been able to use for writing. He was loath to leave the little carving Algi had made for him, her own face with the smile just right; she'd given it to him the day their paths had gone in different ways, before she'd pressed her mouth to his. He hadn't had anything to give her.

He stripped off his robe, ratty and half tatters, but he couldn't ever bring himself to part with it. He was a preacher still, after all. He knotted it into a crude pack for the few things he was going to keep, his flint, his eyecloth, a bone knife for which he had traded a strange piece of metal that would fly through the air to stick to iron. This he tied across his back, over one shoulder and under one arm, and then he waded into the warm river-that-ran-from-the-sun and began to swim.

The rivers of Fiatera where he had learned to swim were no match for a river that had spent its whole life racing ahead of the daylight.

The heat was the worst of it. The hunger he could stand, for he had gone hungry many a time in his wandering. But the heat was almost past the point of bearing, a smothering thickness that tried to crush him against the burning sand.

He had seen his death, many times, in the long, torturous tumble down the river-that-ran-from-the-sun. So gentle, the river had seemed, from that distant bank. It had proven to be a fierce river no more than a few strokes in, a thing that fought, a thing that did not like to be crossed. It had pulled him under and spat him up more times than he could count, dragged him down its center, where he could see both banks but reach neither, slammed him against rocks and crushed him between their weight and its own force until he thought he would never draw air again. And then he had opened his eye, with sun burning his face and sand burning his back and the river to the west, and he had thought if he could survive the river crossing there was truly nothing that could kill him. He had laughed with joy at life itself, until the laughter turned to sand in his mouth.

A river, no matter how fierce, was not the worst thing in the world.

Fire and water, the Parents had used to craft the world, light and life. He had abjured the Parents all his life, and now, wandering deep in the blighted desert, they were taking their revenge, slowly trying to kill him with their favorite weapons. It would not be an easy thing for them, with the river rushing ever at Keiro's left, but he had been thrown deep into the desert, and the Parents would have their time to try. He didn't know how long he'd been in the river, how far it had washed him from green lands.

This land had been Fratarro's once, empty as it now stood until the god had reached out his hand and named and claimed it for his own, built it into a thing of beauty and serenity. All the tales said it had been a paradise, more wondrous than anything the Parents had ever shaped. Destroyed now, all of it, burned by jealous fire so the very land cracked and crumbled beneath his feet.

There were echoes, though, echoes of the time before Eremori had been blighted. That, or delusion was settling in, but Keiro saw flickers of *something* behind his empty eye, something more than the staring babes that usually lurked there. He saw trees once, as grand and proud as the trees in that rainy forest he had passed through, but when he turned his good eye in that direction, there was nothing but sand. He would catch glimpses of enormous, black, almost birdlike creatures, hovering far above, but they always dissolved into sunspots. When the sun set and the night-cold bit as hard as the heat, he would hear laughter in the distance, a sound of utter joy, beckoning him away from the river-that-ran-from-the-sun and into the visions that hovered at the edge of his sight. He had been told, in a time long ago, that the blinding ceremony gave preachers a different kind of sight, deeper than what eyes alone were capable of, but if this was even half of that sight, Keiro was glad he hadn't completed the ritual. The visions alone were bad enough, but the beauty of them was like to break his heart.

Keiro had walked through many lonely places in his life, walked them all with deep respect and care, and treasured every step. Sometimes, before, he had heard whispers—the voices of those who had walked before him, or the voices of those who watched over the lonely places. Gods, a superstitious man would call them, speaking in the world's quietest places. Keiro always listened, for a wise man did not ignore a voice offered into silence, and old voices were well worth hearing.

There was only one voice he would have expected to hear in this loneliest of places, this blighted land that once had been beautiful and full of life and flying with love, this place that had been smote by jealousy, razed by fear. *Find me,* Fratarro whispered, voice a breath on the dry air.

"I am trying," Keiro said aloud through cracked lips, his voice a rasp.

Find me, and it shimmered through the reflections of the trees that once had been, echoed in the faint cries of the things that were not birds and were no more.

"See me through this, Fratarro, and I shall," Keiro promised, head swirling with the heat, eyes fixed on his dark feet so that he would not wander toward the illusions. "I swear I will find you if you let my walking take me out of this place."

So fixated was he on his feet and ignoring the distant visions that he almost missed the first bush.

It was a scrubby, half-dead thing, alive purely out of stubbornness. But it *was* alive, there in the midst of the endless sand and heat. It was the best thing he had ever seen, in all his long walking. A croak of a laugh burst out of him, and he stumbled toward the bush, falling and scrabbling on sand-burned knees, to cup its scraggly branches with both hands. The bush blurred in front of him, and for a moment he feared it was an illusion, a vision of the former land sent to taunt him. Then he felt the thorns piercing his skin, a sharp sweet pain, and he realized it was only tears blurring his sight.

There were more bushes over the next hours, singly, as starving as the first, firmly jealous of the ground they had claimed. As he walked on, the sand gave way to a green-tinged land, and the scrub became friendlier, more willing to share space with their neighbors, until Keiro was forced to walk at the very edge of the river to avoid the clustering thorny-brush. The sere grass was sweet against his hardened feet, and though his lips were still cracked from the heat, he found himself whistling softly.

As the bushes faded to yellow-green grasses, the hard dry earth beginning to roll into hills, a final current of unbearably hot air brushed against Keiro's face, enough to rob the breath briefly from his lungs, and it carried a whisper: *Find me.* It was not a plea, not a request. It was a command, as soft yet unyielding as the sand Keiro had left behind.

It was the only time he looked back at the Eremori Desert. It was distant now, trailing behind the scrub, but he could still see the sands swirling, the air rippling with heat. Keiro's hands began to shake entirely without his volition.

Priests of the Parents and preachers of the night alike agreed that Fratarro had broken apart when he fell to the ground, a mighty crashing that rent his limbs from his body with such force that they flew far and wide, landing themselves heavily enough to be buried deeply where they fell. Lost, unfindable, gone as surely as Sororra, wherever she had fallen.

It would be fitting, Keiro thought, if jealous Patharro had pushed his children from the godworld so that they would land at the heart of Fratarro's destroyed creation, the land he'd shaped and named Eremori. Fitting, to give Fratarro a grave surrounded by the husks of the mighty creatures he'd created, the winged *mravigi,* who had fallen burning from the sky at Patharro's wrath.

The grass rustled, the river-that-ran-from-the-sun burbled on its way, and birds—real birds—cried out overhead. It was too loud here for any god to speak to one who might be listening. The breath of desert air was gone, but the command remained, hanging heavy in the air. The desert shimmered at him, warning him away like a dog with its hackles raised even as the summons beckoned him back. His death waited there, a slow death, and painful. Keiro knew that as sure as he knew anything in the world. He had felt the brush of death on his back among the sands; it would certainly find him if he dared set foot on the sands again. Perhaps he could find more than death in the desert, find redemption before the heat made his blood boil—but there was no surety to the thought, and his hands still shook as he watched the hot air dance.

It was the hardest thing he had ever done. Harder than walking away from living twins, harder than the blinding, harder even than watching the drowned babes, their memories still so clear in his mind though it had been years since he had seen a drowning. Every piece of him cried out in protest.

Keiro turned, putting the deathly heat of the desert once more at his back, and walked deeper into the growing green. He walked with his shoulders hunched, for he would swear he could feel glaring eyes boring into his back as he walked away, shaking.

CHAPTER 18

The woman would not stop staring.

Scal had felt her eyes the moment he had walked into the tavern. Though if he was going to be honest, and he did try to be, he had felt *all* the eyes on him when he had walked inside. It was nothing he was not used to. There was the difference, though, for all the other eyes had looked away. Some more quickly than others. Some after looks of speculation or hatred or fear. All of it, he was used to. They had all looked away. They always did.

Except for the one set of eyes that he felt on his back even now as he sat in his quiet corner and cupped his hands around his mug.

He thought, for a moment, of standing. Turning. Walking to the table where she sat alone. Telling her to stop, or perhaps asking for a reason. He thought these things as he drank the ale that was warm against his tongue, and knew he would never do them.

A man must know himself above all else, Parro Kerrus had told him. All the paths of all his lives had given Scal more than enough time to know his own heart. He was not a man who would confront a staring woman. He was a man who would sit quietly with hunched shoulders until he finished his drink and could leave this place and her eyes. He knew what kind of a man he was. He was comfortable being such a man.

He looked up from his mug, and saw that she had moved. For now she sat across from him, her eyes no longer on his back but on his face. He was not an easy man to sneak up on, and it startled him badly. Smiling with one side of her mouth, she mopped up the spilled ale with the flowing sleeve of her yellow cassock. Scal stared with his mouth hanging open.

He had not spared her more than a glance when he walked into the tavern. One person among a sea of staring faces. He had not *seen* her. Not truly. Not as he saw her now.

There had been one caravan, one of the first he had guarded. One of the wagoneers had been a devout man. He had shown Scal his hand, where he had leaned too close to an everflame as the priest added his prayer herbs. "So much prayer," the wagoneer had joked, "that Patharro blessed me right then." The skin of his hand had been red and twisted where the fire had touched it.

The woman's face was much like the man's hand had been. Scarred by fire, deeply scarred, from her dark hair to the neckline of the cassock. Her nose was flat, the tip all but gone. One ear, too, was little more than a curl of skin, making her hair fall forward. There was one eye that seemed to have no lid, the same side of her face where the mouth did not move with her smile. Old scars, but scars that would not fade.

Scal realized he was staring and quickly looked down. Her

hand, where it rested on the table near his mug, was as badly scarred.

"Well met." Her voice was soft. The sound of a lute as a musician ran his fingers over the strings. Scal glanced up, and she was still smiling. As much as she could. He quickly looked back down.

"Well met, merra," he returned, though he could not say it with the same enthusiasm as he would usually greet a priestess. It was unworthy of him, he knew, to act so. But knowing did not make the sight of her easier.

Fingertips touched his cheek, the center of the cross only half hidden by his beard. He flinched away from the touch— more for the act than for the woman, he told himself. He did not know whether or not that was a lie. Her hand dropped back to the table. Glancing up, he saw sadness in her eyes. They were green, the color of sunlight on the leaves of a forest. Still she smiled, though, the half smile.

"I've been looking for you," she said.

Scal shifted uncomfortably. Held his mug tighter. Stared at the ale within. "Forgive me, merra," he said, "but you have the wrong man."

"I saw you," she said, "in the flames. It was a strange vision . . . the first I've doubted. A yellow-haired man with the convict's mark on the wrong cheek. I thought it impossible. I've been looking for you for a long time." She reached out, laid her hand over his around the mug. Her skin was warm, her palm smooth. Untouched, it seemed, by the fire that had scarred her. "Will you tell me your name? Please?"

Scal pulled his eyes up from the mug, from her hand over his. Made himself look at her. Beneath all the scarring, he saw that she was young still. She could not be much older than himself. "Scal," he said, deeply unsettled.

She grinned wider, even the stiff side of her mouth pulling up a very little bit. Her eyes lit with joy. *"Fire!"* she said, and she laughed. It was a sweet sound, a sound that did not belong with the ruin of her face.

Scal was learning that he did not know himself so well as he had thought.

Slipping his hand from beneath hers, he pushed his chair back and rose to his feet. Nearly he knocked the chair over in his haste. He looked down at the woman, looked at her shoulder so he would not see her face. "Forgive me," he said again. Choked on any other words he had been meaning to say. Fled.

Hevnje was waiting outside, eyeing the horse she was tied next to. She had spirit, this new horse. He had paid too much for her, near all of his wages from Attemo, but she was, so far, money spent well. She spun eagerly as he mounted, and ran into the wind.

He had been hoping to find new work in Bastreri. No caravans would be traveling, for the snows would come before they could find a bigger town. There should have been others, though—merchants traveling alone, musicians, families, all hoping to beat the winter on its way south. But Bastreri was close to the deep snows of the North. In Bastreri, they did not trust yellow hair. Two days he had spent, searching for work. Time enough wasted. Sivistri, some days to the south, he thought would provide better luck. And less staring women.

He was no more than an hour from Bastreri when she caught him up.

"You owe me five guilders," she said cheerfully as she appeared at his right. Hevnje snapped at her horse's shoulder, and the old nag nearly threw her as it twisted away. Despite himself, Scal leaned out to grab her reins, to still the horse. "Thank you," she said.

"The horse is not worth five gids," he told her. "It is not even worth five rames."

Pushing her hair back from her face, she smiled. The hair did not stay behind the twist of her one ear, but she seemed not to mind that. "That's what I told the farmer, but you didn't exactly leave me much time for haggling, did you?"

Scal shook his head at her. "I did not ask you to follow me."

"Men so rarely *ask* to be followed by priestesses. They teach us stubbornness, at the convents. I learned very well."

"I am not the man you are searching for."

"You certainly look like him."

Never argue with a priest, Parro Kerrus had told him. Though Scal had long suspected that particular aphorism to be more a tool to gain obedience than holy writ. He shook his head again, and tapped his heels against Hevnje's sides. Still the woman followed him. Her horse kept a careful distance from Scal's. Refusing to look at her, to acknowledge her presence, Scal kept his eyes fixed on the space of road between Hevnje's ears. Looked at nothing, said nothing. The silence was a space between them. Wide as her horse's fear of Hevnje. Thick as the lump in Scal's throat and heavy as the one in his stomach.

She was the one to break it. Softly, but in the silence it was not hard to hear her voice. "You and I, we're just different kinds of monsters." His hands were hard on the reins, and Hevnje rocked to a halt, tossing her head. Scal looked over sharply at the woman. She stared unflinchingly back. "Your horrors are easier to hide. That's all."

Never, Kerrus had told him, when he had been too young to understand, *let a woman know you too well.*

"Who is it that you think I am?" He spoke softly, too, though there was no reason for it. The road was empty. They were alone. Yet her eyes on him felt like a thousand eyes. He could not hold her gaze for long.

She shrugged easily. "You're the one I was sent to find."

"You do not know me."

"You're Scal. The Parents showed you to me in the flames. That's all I need to know."

"Why?" The word burst from him before he could bite it back.

Her smile now was soft, gentle as her voice. Barely a smile at all. "That," she said, "is what I'm here to find out."

There's no arguing with a woman who's made up her mind, Parro Kerrus had told him, and, *Sometimes a man's wisest course of action is to bite his tongue and bide his time.* These he took to heart as he put his heels to Hevnje once more. The woman, of course, followed.

There was little enough, between Bastreri and Sivistri. Some farms, some small collections of huts that could be called villages. No places that would smile at a Northman. Places, perhaps, that would welcome a merra, but she did not suggest any stopping. She did not speak at all, which Scal found a good thing. The sun began to lower, and there was a stand of trees that would shield them from wind, and perhaps from sight. It was a strange thing he had learned, in his years on the road—a man alone had little to fear from bandits. Often they would wait, for fatter prey than a single man. Two, even, was a safe number. Likely little enough between two travelers worth stealing. As Scal set up camp, he tried to make himself believe that the woman was merely setting up her own camp that happened to be near his. He could not deny, though, that she was competent. By the time he had finished brushing Hevnje, the woman had gathered a respectable pile of kindling and sticks. She had left her horse, though. The poor old beast still saddled. It looked as though she had no intention of tending to him. That made Scal angry, but not angry enough that he would let the poor horse suffer to prove a point. So he removed her saddle, and cared for her horse as he had done his own. When he had finished, the woman had a pot of roadstew bubbling over a fresh-kindled fire.

Scal stood by the horses, staring. Disgruntled. He did not like to share the road, to share a camp. Even when a job demanded it, he would build his own fire, his own bed, a distance away from any others. A long habit. He most especially did not want to share his camp with this woman who was following him. And yet the camp, as it stood, was more hers than his.

He did not know he made the sound, but a deep, unhappy growl rumbled up from his chest.

Resolute, he went to gather his own wood for a fire.

He set his first armful near the horses. When he returned with the second, the first pile was gone. The woman's pile of sticks was noticeably grown. He set his down again, and went for more. It happened the same.

There was a knot in his stomach. One he knew well. Twisting and grumbling. A boiling fury.

He stomped, though he knew it was the act of a child. He gathered half of her pile of kindling in his arms. A stick poked him in the eye, and he left a trail of sticks behind him that he could not keep hold of. Hunkering down, he began to build his own fire. He kept his back to her.

When the fire was burning well, he looked up to see that she had snuck up on him once more. It was a dangerous thing, that. She planted her cooking tripod over his fire, hung her pot of stew, and crouched down across from him. Staring again, over the flames.

"You," she said, "might as well get used to me now."

"I travel alone."

"You used to."

The knot twisted, fire bubbling up his throat. "I do not want you here."

"And I don't particularly want to be here," she said easily. "But I do as the Parents command me. That fire over your heart says you should be doing the same."

Instinctively he reached up to grab at his chest. Two pendants, strung on the same circle of leather. The painted flame-disk, to mark him as a different man than he had been. The other was a reminder from his last life. That he was, always, who he was. Usually he kept them tucked inside his tunic. Hidden.

"They have not demanded anything of me," he told her.

"Then you're not listening well enough."

He did not wish to speak with her anymore. The stew was boiling, and he was hungry. If she was going to force herself into his camp, he was not going to feel any remorse at eating her food. Retrieving his well-used wooden bowl from his pack, he dunked it into the pot. It burned the tips of his fingers some, where he was careless, but that he hardly noticed.

"My name is Vatri."

The stew was not bad. She had used dried meat, torn into pieces, and it was fresh enough that the taste was good. There were some berries he recognized, and leek and onion mixed in.

"We should know each other, if we're going to be traveling together."

The broth was thin, though. He could have made it better. Still, it worked well enough to soften the hardbread he pulled from his pack.

"You're going to talk to me eventually."

Scal licked his bowl clean and stowed it away. He pulled his snowbear cloak around himself. Lay down with his pack for a pillow. The fire would spend itself. It was warm enough outside that a fire was not needed for sleep.

The words were quiet, so that he almost thought he dreamed them among the night sounds. Cracking one eye open, he saw her staring into the fire, her eyes not on Scal as her words drifted into the dark night. He stared up into the sky, at the stars. She had a nice voice. Nicer when it was not matched with her face.

"I hate the dark," she murmured. "I learned how to make a fire almost before I learned to walk. My papa taught me. I was marked." Her hand lifted, touched the side of her neck where the skin was rough and ridged. "It's gone, now, but I was godmarked. That's why I was sent to the convent. The day I arrived was the first time Metherra spoke to me. That's not a common thing, you know. Priests say all the time that they hear the gods, but most of them are lying. She spoke to me, though, she really did. Welcomed me home. It was years before I heard her again. I couldn't sleep, went to tend the everflame.

I built it too big, but I heard her again. Nothing clear, nothing I can remember, but it was her voice."

The merra stopped, but she did not need to go on. Scal could see how the story would go. Building a fire, big enough to bring the voice of a goddess. Staring into the flames, hearing a whisper. Shock, perhaps, or rapture. Leaning too close, too eager. The voice drawing her in. The flames swallowing. Skin boiling and melting. Screams, dancing with the flames. He could see the memory in her eyes, alongside the reflected flames.

Her voice was small, scared, hardly even spoken. "I can never sleep at night."

Long ago, in a life he had long left behind, Scal had been a boy who could not sleep. There had been a priest, who softly sang his prayers in a voice not meant for singing. In another life there had been a woman, holding her swollen belly and singing her own songs before a night-fire, calling to the boy who crouched on the landing above and stroking his hair as she sang. It was those songs that came to his mind, as they did most nights. Softly, in a voice as ill-fitted for singing as the priest's, he began to sing the old songs of the North. Of cooking, and cleaning, and building. Of children, and children growing into men. Of quiet nights spent waiting for the men to return. He did not know when Vatri finally slept. It was before he drifted into his own sleep, leaving the stars to their silence.

CHAPTER 19

The wide world hadn't much changed in the thirteen years since Joros had last gone wandering. The roads were still packed dirt, winding in strange patterns, never taking a straight route if they could detour by a pond or an unusually large rock. The villages were still ramshackle collections of huts, hardly deserving of whatever name the villagers had branded the place with. The people, overwhelmingly, were still stupid.

It was much how he imagined things would be if he returned to his family's home. Disgust and disappointment from both sides, and an excess of sullen glares. At least in the villages, Joros wasn't causing his sisters to cry.

They'd run into a traveling merchant a few days ago, a merchant who'd looked so much like Joros's puffed-up, pompous father that his hand had gone instinctively to the sword at his belt. Wise men were better than their emotions, though, and Joros had made his fingers loosen. Instead, he'd had Anddyr weave a distraction while Joros had robbed the merchant blind, horse and all. It hadn't improved their traveling speed, with Anddyr still trudging along, but it had spared Joros's feet and given him clothing that drew less attention than his preacher's robe. His brothers would have laughed at the irony of Joros finally wearing merchant's garb.

He'd hesitated before giving Anddyr one of his black robes; the mage wasn't deserving of the black, but the days were growing colder, and he was starting to shiver in his simple tunic and breeches. Joros couldn't have his mage dying of the cold, but it stirred a small anger in him each time he looked back to see Anddyr plodding in a preacher's robe. Still, the mage would fare better than Joros if any of the villages should turn sour quickly at the sight of a black robe. Anddyr usually had enough presence of mind to hide himself before entering a village, a simple spell that directed eyesight away, but his stores of magic weren't endless.

Joros had considered having the mage attune more seek-stones, but it could take just as long as the first set—years of Anddyr's searching to even find the proper locations, and years more for the mage to devise a way to twist the seekstones' magic to affix a location. They'd be a waste of time, in the end, so long as Anddyr didn't get himself killed. The man was like a walking seekstone. He would cast his searching every few hours to see if they needed to turn from their winding road onto one that went winding off equally foolishly.

Waiting as the mage searched, Joros would brush his fingers over all the seekstones his shadowseekers had brought him through the years. The work of a lifetime, of many lifetimes; careful discoveries, and careful markers. They were the shadowseekers' greatest accomplishment and purpose: one seekstone matched to each set of twins they'd found hidden throughout Fiatera. The stones showed little different than they ever did, flashes of imagery and a faint tug in the direction where the matched stone sat, far away. His best prospects seemed to be in the capital, Mercetta, which was at once surprising and unsurprising: there were so many people living there that someone should have been able to recognize twins, yet so many people that it was easy enough to hide in a sea of faces. Joros only needed to find one set, and so—much as it made his skin itch—they were traveling toward the capital.

The villages became less scattered the closer they drew, but that was good for one thing, at least: inns. Warm taverns with beds that were soft, if also buggy, and enough food to make his stomach swell up. The first nights out from the mountain, they'd slept on the hard ground and eaten what they could, after they'd gone through their meager food supplies. It had been berries and roots until Joros had commanded Anddyr to kill them a deer or a bird or *anything*, and the mage had returned bawling with a dead rabbit cradled in his arms. The fool had burned away nearly half the rabbit with his killing blow, but the meat had been better than berries. Joros had to force Anddyr to eat his portion, and the mage had thrown it back up after two bites. That had earned him a royal thumping, but the uneaten portion had comfortably filled Joros's belly.

How Joros had ever survived as a wandering seeker, he couldn't remember. It had been over a decade ago, and truly he hadn't ever wandered far unless it was to follow a promising lead. Any time he hadn't spent inside cozy Raturo was likely spent in an inn after a day of walking, and for the times when no shelter could be found . . . he'd blocked those dark times from his mind, honestly. He'd survived them, and that was that. Joros wasn't a man prone to failings, or to admitting them. They were past camping now, for a while at least, and that was a blessed thing. There was nothing like a real bed for a man's health and happiness.

Anddyr, strangely, seemed to thrive in the outdoors. At the first inn they'd come to, the mage had sheepishly asked if he could be allowed to sleep behind the building. Joros had lost half a night of sleep to suspicion, but he'd kept all the skura jars in his bought room and slept holding the seekstone that was tuned to the matching one around Anddyr's neck. In the morning he'd found the mage dew-wet and curled into a ball around that stupid stuffed horse, sleeping as peacefully as a child who didn't know any better. It had been much the same all the nights to follow; Joros still had a faint chariness lurking in his mind, but the mage knew better than to run, and certainly wasn't brave enough to go anywhere without his skura.

They were perhaps four days outside of Mercetta, if Joros's memory was any judge, and the villages were slowly becoming veritable towns. It made his fingers twitch, the places starting to look too much like the town where he'd grown up. He was happy to avoid them when he could, happier still when he could find a crossroads inn between towns, full of travelers as dispassionate about conversation as he was. It was still a few hours until the sun would flee the sky, but there might not be another inn or another town in that space, and Joros wasn't about to chance a night in the brush when there was an inn standing right before him. He dismounted and waited for Anddyr to plod by.

The mage was so bound up in his own head that he walked

past Joros without even noticing, his eyes fixed on the ground and his lips moving as they always were.

Joros cast around until he found a good-sized rock; his aim was off, hitting Anddyr on the hip, but it was enough to get his attention. The mage trudged back to take the horse's reins and immediately began talking to it in low tones, pressing his forehead against the beast's nose.

Frowning, Joros reminded himself to check the skura supply later. It seemed to him that his pet mage was growing slightly more unbalanced with each passing day. He might have been dipping his fingers too deeply into the skura jar of late.

"Anddyr," he said sternly, to pull the mage from his reverie with the horse. The man liked that horse more than he should; it was the same as it had been with those blasted twins, an unhealthy relationship, but there was little Joros could do about it. "There will be a trough around the back. Care for the horse, and clean yourself up before you track any of your filth inside. I daresay the place has enough as it is." Joros left the mage to it, and ducked into the inn.

It was everything he'd expected: a dozen quiet travelers mostly sitting apart from each other and nursing mugs or plates of food, a roasting lamb spitted over the hearthfire, a pretty but sour-faced woman bustling about and showing no reaction to suggestive gibes or roaming hands, all watched over by a barman with an honest face and hard eyes. It was the same sort of inn that existed at every dusty crossroads across the realm, straight down to the hard-on-their-luck mercenaries eyeing his merchant's robes, and a musician glumly plucking at a lute near the fire. Truly, the world hadn't changed in Joros's absence from it. Some things simply were that way, as constant and unchanging as the sun in the sky.

Joros chose a table where he could overhear a few different murmured conversations and keep an eye on the mercenaries, and told the sullen maiden to bring him food and wine. There was no telling how long Anddyr would be out with the horse; the mage could find his own food if he took too long. Joros could only do so much to care for the man.

There was talk of bandits to the north, of increased killings in Mercetta, of a lake near Fozena mysteriously going dry. The food was good; warm and filling, which was all he had come to expect from roadside taverns. Altogether, it was nothing too enthralling . . . and yet, somehow, Joros didn't notice the hooded man until he already stood before the table.

"Cappo Joros." The man's voice was a deep rumble, sounding like rocks scraping together inside that hood. "Apostate. You have stolen something that is not yours to take." There was a faint flash, fire off metal as the tip of a knife poked from the man's sleeve. "The shadows have come to claim you."

Joros would later tell himself that it had been quick thinking that saved his life, but truly, it was the hooded man's stupidity in giving him a moment's warning combined with a surge of raw panic that made him throw his goblet of wine. The goblet grazed the hooded man's shoulder, spilling wine down the side of his robe. It did no lasting damage, but the man was as surprised by it as Joros himself was. In the moment of shared confusion, Joros had time to scramble out of his chair and wrap his fingers around the hilt of his shortsword, and then the hooded man leaped forward.

Joros backed into another table, scrambled sideways amid

the surprised curses of the table's occupants as a very sharp knife upset their cups. That was enough time for Joros to pull his sword free, and that got the attention of the rest of the inn.

"Hey now!" the barman called, voice ringing and stern. "I won't have none of that in here. Take it outside, lads."

The hooded man ignored him completely, cat-stepping toward Joros, the tip of his knife drawing patterns in the air like Anddyr's sigils. Joros stepped with him, his sword's length keeping the man at bay. Joros would be the first to admit he was a poor fighter; he'd never had the time to properly learn, and anyway he had the luxury of employing others to do his fighting for him. But he could swing a blade well enough when he had to—and with his blasted mage nowhere in sight, it seemed as though he had to.

"He's a fecking preacher," someone spat, and there were disapproving murmurs all around. Frightening words, at first, until Joros remembered he'd traded in his black robes. This would-be assassin hadn't had the same forethought. For the briefest moment, Joros hoped the crowd would do his work for him—drag down the hooded man and pummel him bloody for the crime of wearing black.

"Betrayer," the hooded man growled at Joros, loud enough for all the others to hear, and the rising tide of righteous anger flattened out to encompass both of them. There'd be no help from any of them.

"How did you find me?" Joros demanded, stalling, hoping Anddyr would amble in any moment.

The hooded man laughed. "You should know there's nowhere left to hide in this world." It was true enough; the shadowseekers were highly trained, thanks in part to Joros himself, able to track down a mark better than a hunting hound. Joros hadn't even considered he might have been marked.

"Who sent you, then?" Circling carefully, Joros got a table between himself and the hooded man. "Whatever they told you is a lie. I'm on important business for the Ventallo—for all the Fallen. You'll regret getting in my way."

It didn't give the hooded man pause. "Betrayer," he said again. He grabbed the edge of the table between them, gave it a sharp shove so it caught Joros's thigh, then flipped the whole thing toward him. Cursing, Joros scrabbled backward, though not quickly enough—the table's edge bit at him again, crashing down onto his foot with the crunch of small bones breaking. He twisted away to avoid the knife that followed the table down, ignored the pain as he tugged his foot from beneath the table, and got the length of his sword between himself and the hooded man again.

There was no room in Joros's life for hesitation; that was doubly true on the road. His mage was missing, and there were no friendly faces around. As far as the inn's patrons were concerned, one less Twin-worshiper was no bad thing, no matter which one of them lost. It made things simple. Joros was going to have to kill the hooded man.

Joros lunged forward, his sword leading him. It missed the hooded man's stomach, and Joros had to twist to avoid the swinging knife. He stumbled into a chair, hooked his crushed foot around the rungs, and let the pain leave him in a shout as he kicked the chair toward the hooded man. It hit squarely against one of the man's legs and Joros brought his sword swinging up and then down with both hands, aiming for the corner where the man's neck met shoulder beneath that hood.

Somehow, the man got his knife up in time, Joros's sword skittering down the blade and the man's arm; he at least took some flesh with that deflection, the hooded man bellowing with pain. But Joros was left off balance, his bad foot crumpling beneath the weight, and the hooded man's pain seemed to lend him strength. His left fist landed against Joros's ribs and sent him sprawling to the floor of the inn.

That was how it should have ended: with the hooded man falling onto Joros and plunging the knife into his heart, letting poor Joros's blood empty onto the inn's dirty floor. Instead it ended with a flash and searing heat, the hooded man screaming as he fell burning on top of Joros, his knife plunging by some fluke into Joros's shoulder. The knife wound, combined with the man's flaming arm pressed against Joros's neck and the side of his face, were enough to tear a scream from Joros's throat. Pain could lend him strength, too, it seemed, and he managed to heave the hooded man's form off. The man was screaming still, writhing, though the flames were flickering out on his red flesh. There was no hood left to him, not that Joros could have recognized the ruin of his face anyway. The flames faded, but the trails they had left did not.

Breathing heavily, clamping down his pain, Joros yanked the knife from his shoulder and gave it a better home—namely, the burned man's heart. "Bastard," Joros muttered.

The inn was silent, some eyes fixed on the dead man, some on Joros, but most on Anddyr, standing in the doorway with his face painted in horror and shock and disgust as he stared at his own hands. "I didn't mean to . . . I only wanted to stun him . . ."

Joros's vision was swimming, going black at the edges, and

it felt like the side of his face was still afire. He'd never had much cause to deal with such injury before, but he knew that unconsciousness would claim him soon; there was one last thing he had to do first. His left hand wouldn't cooperate—the knife must have nicked something in his shoulder, and his right hand shook so badly it was almost useless, but he methodically emptied all his pockets there on the floor of the inn where he sat bleeding and burned. The only seekstones were his own, all keyed to others, and there was nothing else suspicious he'd carried with him from Raturo . . .

His shaking hand found the cord around his neck. Over thirteen years, he'd grown so used to the weight of a key against his chest that he never thought of it. Never suspected the keys to the Ventallo's numbered chambers might be anything besides keys. No matter how he squinted at it, his blurring eyes couldn't make out anything suspect; but it was a thick key, thick enough it could have been shaped around a seekstone long, long ago.

It scraped against the burns on his neck, but Joros yanked at the key until the cord snapped. He tossed it, hoped it landed near Anddyr's feet. "Destroy that," he croaked, and then he finally let the pain pull him down.

CHAPTER 20

Rora watched the bodies come in and felt sick to her stomach. It never failed. She'd been surprised, the first time the dead had been brought back, that Tare hadn't laughed at her. There was no room in Tare for weakness, but she'd put her hand on Rora's shoulder and looked at her with serious eyes and not said a word.

It was like that with all of them. Rora hadn't learned that until Tare had given her her own little alcove in the knifeden. Tare'd told her it was so she wouldn't feel so alone, with Aro always holed up with the Dogshead. She'd seen how every one of the knives came back quiet after a contract, not talking, not looking at anyone. She'd seen how no one ever asked any questions. There'd only been one, a new knife come over from the Serpents, who'd bragged about his contract, eyes glowing as he laughed at how the woman had begged for her life and shit herself as he cut her throat. He'd wound up with his own throat cut, not long after. Goat or Tare didn't even ask who'd done it. The only thing Tare'd ever said about it was

"You don't talk about contracts. Ever." By then, Rora'd already known that.

The fists were all quiet, walking in with their arms full of the dead to lay 'em down in front of Garim. The face looked at each of them, the men he'd sent out to die without knowing it. Five and five and five had gone out, and they'd all come back, even though most of 'em were carried back. You didn't leave a brother behind. Five and four, lying at Garim's feet with their eyes staring up at the grimy walls. Five and one, kneeling there covered in blood, with their faces hard as stone.

It was harder to look at death when your own hands were so good at bringing it.

The whole den was quiet as night, until Garim, with his voice like a rock dropping in water, asked, "What happened?"

"Blackhands," one of the fists said. A low growl went through the den. They'd all figured that out by now, but it was something that needed to be said anyway. You had to give a name to a thing, to hate it right. "Caught us topside. Twice as many of 'em, like they knew we'd be there. We got back below, but there were even more waiting. All we could do was run." And pick up the dead as you ran. "They stopped chasing once we got across the Teeth."

"We'll get revenge for them," Garim promised as he looked at each of the dead fists again, like he was fixing each of their faces in his mind. His hand made a small motion, and Aro slipped away out of the shadows. He'd report it all to the Dogshead so she could start planning while Garim took care of the pack. "We'll give them the proper rites, too. Gods know they've earned it."

A long time ago, when she and Aro'd had a roof over their

heads and a real dirt floor to sleep on and a place to feel safe, there'd been a woman named Kala who'd said, "Do you know why they're called Scum?" She'd always been trying to tell them how bad it was everywhere but topside, like they didn't already know it. Like she thought they'd choose to go back there. "Whenever someone dies in the Canals, they send the dead bodies floating on the water, and eventually they rot and turn green." Sometimes Rora wished she could go back and tell Kala all the things she'd been wrong about, but Rora wished a lot of things that weren't ever going to happen.

They did what they could for rafts, but it was hard with so many. You could only fit two across at the narrow points, and there wasn't much spare wood lying around to make the rafts too special. "It's the doing that counts," Garim kept saying, and he was right, at least. He tried to make them go rest, the five and one who'd brought the others back, but they just said his words back at him: "It's the doing that counts." So they got four others, mostly other fists who'd known the dead, and they fitted some of the pups out with long sticks that took two of 'em to hold, so anyone could see the white hank of cloth tied to the top with a big circle painted on it in blood. Not even the Blackhands would go against the death flag.

As much of the pack as could went along, though some had to stay back to guard the den. No one would cross the death flag, but the flag wasn't hanging in the den. Rora thought about staying back, but Tare touched her elbow, flicked her eyes. She saw Aro, saw how he was careful not to look at a hunchbacked woman wearing a deep-hooded cloak and walking with a limp, shuffling along with the rest of the pack. It didn't surprise her too much, when she thought about it. Of course the Dogshead would want to be there to send her dead off.

Some of the pups with flags led the way, slipping on stones, leaping across the canals because they were still kids, even with death around. Then it was the fists with ropes over their shoulders, five on each side of the canal, towing the rafts down the center. Everyone else came behind, no order to it except for Tare and Rora and a handful of other knives who kept a careful distance around the disguised Sharra. They'd never talk about it later, but she knew all the knives'd all be thinking the same thing: how it was good to have something to do, instead of just thinking how busy their nights were going to be with killing. It was harder to look forward to revenge when you were the one bringing it.

All the canals of Mercetta flowed into the Sinkhole. It'd been there as long as anyone could remember, and it was why the Canals'd been abandoned and left for the drifting poor to claim. The water kept pouring in from Lake Baridi, but it always found its way to the Sinkhole, and no one knew where it went from there. All the Scum-made paths ended in jagged stumps where the Sinkhole'd opened up its mouth and swallowed anything in its way, and the roar of the pouring water was louder'n in the Dogshead's waterfall room.

Garim was up at the front, and Rora could see his mouth moving. He'd be reciting prayers to the Parents, probably, asking them to hold tight to the souls of their dead, or talking about the good each of them had done. Only the fists at the front, straining to hold the ropes against the pull of the Sinkhole, would be able to hear him, but it was the doing that counted. When he was done talking he stepped back, and the first set of fists let go of their ropes.

The raft rushed forward and was gone over the edge even before the fists' arms had dropped back to their sides. Garim watched it go over with a hard face, watched the first two dead disappear. Rora knew there were some faces he'd never forget. The next two fists let go, and the next. Rora couldn't make out much under Sharra's hood, but she could see tears on the Dogs-head's cheek. The next raft went, and Tare crossed her arms in front of her waist, her hands resting on the pommels of her two knives. They'd both be helping with the revenge Garim had talked about. Then the last raft, with just the one man, the last of the day's dead, but Rora knew he wouldn't be the last by far. Wherever the Sinkhole took the dead Scum, she knew there'd be plenty more to join them before too long.

They stayed awhile, some crying, some with faces that would've put real fear into any Blackhands. But the hand signs rippled up, Sharra to Tare and all the way up to Garim, who talked some more to the fists who could hear him. They turned eventually, the five and five, and the rest of the pack turned with 'em. The death flags swung around crazily as the pups tried to work their way to the new front of the group, to lead the way back home.

It hadn't been war before, not yet. But you'd have to be dumb, if you didn't think it was now.

Hanging by her fingertips from a windowsill three stories above an alley that smelled like piss and death, battered by a wind that was the very essence of rotting fish, Rora wondered if it was too late to reevaluate her life choices. She knew, though, as she twisted to bring one bare foot—boots left in the alley below, probably being chewed on by rats by now—up onto the sill, that the time for changing her mind had long passed. There was killing to do.

"There's a man," Goat had told her earlier. "He sells meat to the Blackhands. They can live on bread for a while."

Rora didn't know the Dogshead's plan, no one did except Garim and maybe Tare, but it was a longer game than Rora'd expected. You couldn't just march into Blackhands territory with fists and knives and hope to win, of course. That wasn't how Scum fought. "Sneaks and cheats," Kala'd said, "there's not a single decent person in the Canals." Still, Rora'd expected something more than killing a butcher. A butcher who wasn't even Scum, who wouldn't even know why he was dying. It didn't feel like revenge.

It sometimes felt to Rora—and she usually thought about it most on contract nights, when life and death were balanced like a coin spinning in the air—that there was a string stretching out in front of and behind her, guiding her along through her life on some path she couldn't see until it was already behind her. It all made so much sense then, everything falling perfectly into place. So very *convenient*, and she hated things that came out too easy. It usually meant there was a twist down the way, something bad lurking just around the next corner. Sure, maybe she could've changed her mind a long time ago, before Nadaro, before Whitedog Pack, before Tare had sent her out on her first contract, but it was too late now, she was too wrapped up in it all. There was nothing to do but let the string tug her forward.

There came a time, every contract night, without fail, when she thought about turning around, leaving it all behind, taking her life in her own hands. Sticking to the windowsill by sheer stubbornness alone, with one foot dangling in open air as the reeking wind pushed at her, that was when the thought hit her this night. It was easier to swing down than lever the rest of her body up, after all. The coin was still spinning.

With a practiced move, she pushed off with her one foot and grabbed on to the upper edge of the window frame, bringing her other foot up onto the sill and clinging there like a squirrel. It was lucky she was so small, Tare'd told her so often—it made sneaking that much easier. Gritting her teeth and silently mouthing the same curses she always sent toward Tare on contract nights, Rora let go with one hand and fished around inside her vest till she found her kit and the slim hook inside it. She stuck it between the shutters, found the catch, worked it carefully upward, and then began slowly pulling the far-side shutter open. Must've been oiled recently; it didn't squeak or make any sound. She liked working North and East Quarters, they always kept things nice and maintained, even in the fish-reeking Iceblood District on the shores of Lake Baridi.

She paused, then, with the shutter half open and the wind trying to push it shut, and listened. For any noise from inside the room, a sleepy question, an angry exclamation, a terrified shout. But it was quiet, safe as could be, so she stuck her legs in through the window and dropped down to the floor.

Buildings in Iceblood always seemed to hold on to the cold wind that blew in off Lake Baridi, and it was colder inside than it'd been even with the wind always blowing on her outside. It was still quiet, though, so she reached up to slowly pull the shutter closed. That made it dark in the room, but Tare and Goat had taught her patience, making her lie in a pit of snakes—little ones, they didn't have any venom, but they still had big teeth that hurt like a bitch—that'd get angry if she much as breathed wrong. So she stayed crouched low beneath the window, waiting till her eyes adjusted to the dark, and then she crept toward the dim outline of the bed. She pulled her dagger out as she went, the long knife with the blue gem in its hilt. She always felt calmer holding it, felt more like she was in control of everything, even if she had to use her left hand. Her right one, the whole arm, had never seemed to work right since it'd been stomped on.

"Where's your brother, Rora?"

Reflexively she dropped into a low crouch even as she spun around, eyes darting in the darkness. Blackhands, that was her first thought, some kind of ambush, but then her blood went cold when she realized what the voice had called her. Her name, the name no one but Aro knew.

There was a whisper of noise, and across the room in the fireplace, flames grew slowly to life—blue flames that hardly seemed to move, just flicker, an unnatural light. With it she could see a woman standing there, covered and cowled in a black robe, a small smile playing over her face, dancing with the light.

"Who're you?" Rora demanded, flexing her fingers around the hilt of her dagger. Something had gone awful here, but Rora would put up plenty of fight if it came to it.

The woman's smile widened. "I am the shadows," she said, "and I know your name."

It hit her like a punch, the words from so long ago that always came back to her on dark nights, in moments of fear, the words she could never forget no matter how hard she tried. *The darkness knows your name,* Nadaro had said with a knife in his chest, *and it never rests.*

"You didn't think we'd forgotten about you, did you, Rora?" The woman asked it like they were talking about the weather. Moving careful slow even though she wanted to run far as she could, Rora moved one foot back toward the window, her best escape. Across the room, the woman stepped with her. "Don't you remember? *'To the ends of the earth.'* You are marked, Rora. We know your name."

There was the part she hadn't even told Aro, the part that still gave her nightmares, jerked her awake covering her own mouth to hide the screams: *My brothers and sisters will find you.*

"You are ours, Rora." Another slow step toward the window, mirrored by the other woman. She was in front of the fire now, looking like nothing so much as a featureless shadow standing there, and a whimper crept up out of Rora's throat. "You've always been ours."

It was cold in the room, so cold, the fire that wasn't a fire not doing any good. Rora wanted to dash to the window, fling herself out through the shutters and drop three stories to the ground, anything to get out, but it was so cold her muscles were stiff, uncooperative. It was all she could do to take another crouched step toward the window. Through chattering teeth, trying and failing to use the tough voice Tare'd taught her, Rora asked, "Who are you? What do you want with me?"

"I already told you, Rora." She stepped forward this time, toward Rora, shrinking the distance between them. "I am the shadows. I know your name." Another step closer, the blue flames throwing her shadow across Rora. She flinched away, but the cold held her tight, immobile. "You have been given to us. Promised by blood. Promised by Nadaro Madri." A step, another, Rora's eyes fixed involuntarily on the woman's blank face as she drew closer, towering above her, blotting out the light and the world. "I have come to take you home," the shadow said, reaching out. "You belong to the shadows, Rora. Your life is ours." Fingers brushed against her cheek, burning like red-hot iron, and Rora screamed.

Somewhere, dimly, so very far away, a voice that was so like her own shouted, *"Rora!"*

Her knife seemed to move almost on its own.

There was the flash of it before her eyes, a silver blur, and then a burst of red, a scream to match her own. The hand bounced off her knee before it hit the floor, leaving a smear of blood. In the flickering blue light, Rora leaped for the window, flung herself through the shutters. She caught a clothesline halfway down, slowed her fall enough she could drop down the rest of the way with little more than a shot of pain from her foot up to her hip, but nothing that would slow her down now. She was running even as she landed.

Her life, after all, had never really been her own.

She ran all the way back to South Quarter, feet flying over the streets, gasping for air by the time she swung down into the Canals. She near leaped over the canals, didn't slow till she got to the edge of Whitedog Pack territory, and only then because she couldn't've answered any questions the eyes might ask. She made herself walk slow and calm, even though her heart was still screaming and she wanted to scream, too. She clutched at the hilt of her knife, held it like a prayer, and somehow made it to the den.

Aro was awake when she found him, his eyes as big as she thought hers probably were. "You're okay?" he demanded in a whisper. There was no one nearby, but you learned early on to whisper, just in case.

"We have to leave," she said for an answer, though the words came out more a scared sob than a whisper.

He didn't argue, bless him, he knew after all the years when to argue and when to just listen. There wasn't time for packing, wasn't anything to pack when it came down to it, but the screaming in her chest was making her desperate to get out. They took nothing more than what they wore, and they left. Back the way Rora'd just come and up the first ladder they came to. It didn't matter whose territory they came up on, not anymore. Soon as they hit solid ground, Rora was running again, and Aro at her side. They left Mercetta through the small South Gate and didn't stop running, because with every step Rora heard and reheard, *To the ends of the earth. To the ends of the earth. To the ends of the earth.*

CHAPTER 21

Work was hard to come by. Harder than Scal had expected. Though he could not fault himself, or the opportunities. It was late in the season, but there were always travelers. There were always men who felt the danger of the world, and chose to fight it with money and other men's swords. Few travelers, though, would want a disfigured merra trailing in their wake. Few men would wish to hire a guard followed by a burned woman.

He had made a decision on the ride to Sivistri. It had been partly because of the night when he had sung, though he did not like to think of it. Mostly, he told himself, it was because of the ride. With Vatri at his left and slightly behind, he had found his words easier, not having to look at her. He could answer the questions she asked. With few words, though. He always held on to his words, giving them out carefully. She had asked simple questions. Where he was going. Where he had been. What plans he had. She had not asked about his snowbear cloak, or the claw pendant, or how he had gotten his scars.

In Sivistri, he had spoken to her as he tied Hevnje to a post, so that he would not see her face as the words came. "There are men who are made to walk alone in the world. There are men whose lives are made harder when there is another. I am not in the habit of traveling with a companion." It was more words, almost, then he had yet spoken to her, all tallied. "I am not in the habit, also, of telling others what they must do. Or where they may or may not go." He had tied the last knot, and then looked at her eyes. "I do not wish to travel with you. I will not tell you to leave."

He had not been surprised when she had followed him still.

So she was with him, and he had said he would not tell her to leave. He was not a man to break his word. Yet, as a man keeping his word, he could not say that it was filling his coin purse.

She had said he did not need to work, showing him the bag she had that was full of coins. "I'm here to help you," she had said.

It was not his way. He had been told, many different times, that such was the way of the North. A man did not take things freely offered. He did not know if he had learned that from Iveran, but it seemed the right way. He would not take her money, or let her use it on him. A man lived by his own means. When his own coins were gone, he slept outside instead of at inns. He hunted for his food instead of buying it. Hevnje grazed instead of eating grain. That was how things went, in the life of a wandering sword. The merra did not like any of it, but she was not as stubborn as Scal.

They were west of Mercetta, the capital, and Scal was

beginning to grow frustrated. Here, at the center of Fiatera, there would be few men looking for guards: most noblemen and merchants so close to the capital maintained their own garrisons. Scal did not wish to bind himself so fully as to join one of those companies. He traveled alone.

"Where are we going?" Vatri asked, shifting uncomfortably in her saddle. She had said riding put an ache in her hips. Still, she did not complain of it often.

Scal sighed. "We go north."

She made a face at him. "We just came from the north."

"There will be no work here. It will take too long to reach the trading cities in the south." He gave her a glance, measuring. It was easier, now, to look at her. The hills and ridges carved into her skin grew easier to ignore, with time. "*I* go north. You should go to Mercetta. It is not so far."

She gave him a withering look. The same look she had given him each time he had suggested she leave. She did not need to say anymore that she was not leaving. The look spoke for her well enough. Still, he could try.

They did not take the same path they had just traveled. Such would be foolishness. They rode through the fields and forests for a time, going east. Toward the capital, though it made Scal's skin itch. He did not like cities. They seemed an unnatural thing to him. Too many men in too little space. Cities reminded him of a cold, walled-in place from another life, and the charred smell that covered those memories. The countryside gave way, though, to a road Scal knew. There would be a town, not too far away, with an inn where he had often found work. He had some coins left, from a barn he had helped a farmer to repair. Vatri, with her yellow hood pulled low, had blessed the farm without the man seeing her face. The farmer had counted himself lucky. They could stay at the inn for a night. Two, perhaps. He could make the merra stay in the barn, so that he could find a job for himself. The thought drew up one corner of his mouth.

They did not make the town by the time the sun began to lower, and so they made camp. It had been an unspoken thing between them, since that first night. To have a fire made before the sun was gone.

Vatri tried to read the flames, as she did every night. She had had little success. More success than Scal, who saw only red and yellow and orange dancing. This night, too, she ground her teeth in frustration. "It's the same damned thing," she said.

She had as foul of a mouth as Parro Kerrus had had. Scal had asked her if they taught cursing, too, at the convents and monasteries. She had sworn colorfully, cheerfully at him.

"White?" he asked.

"White," she repeated glumly. "All I see is white, with a lump of coal lying in the middle. It means nothing. It's never been like this before." She swore again, vehemently, and then growled a perfunctory plea for forgiveness to the Parents. "It doesn't make any sense! How can I be any help if I can't read what they're trying to tell me?"

Scal shrugged. "Things will happen as they are meant to." It was a thing Parro Kerrus had told him, long ago.

Stubbornly the merra shook her head. "It's not supposed to be like that." Her eyes narrowed at him, as if she were thinking. "I told you I was godmarked. Do you know what that means?" Scal shook his head. It was not a word he knew, nothing the parro had taught him. Vatri touched her neck, where the skin had formed hard bubbles. "I was born with the mark of a flame here, a darker spot on my skin. It means I was claimed by the gods, destined to be their servant. To serve them in ways no other could. *That's* why Metherra speaks to me, so that I can do the bidding of the gods."

Scal frowned into the fire. He had revered the Parents for most of his life, since Parro Kerrus had shown him the ever-flame and told him all the old stories. He had followed all the teachings. Said a prayer each night and morning. Carried their flame in and next to his heart. But never had he thought of himself as a servant of the gods. He could not imagine that the Parents could care so deeply about the life of one mortal. It was hard, sometimes, to understand what Vatri was trying to tell him.

"I can't help them," she said, still angry, "if I don't know where they want me to be, or what they want me to do! It's impossible. And you"—she jabbed a sharp finger into his chest—"are no help at all. I found you, but you're not *doing* anything! You're useless."

It was not the first time she had said such things. Scal did not bother to respond. He poured her a bowl of onion broth with the last stringy chunks of a rabbit he had caught some days ago. She ate, still growling angrily into her food.

There had been a space between them, in the beginning. A space as wide across as one side of the fire to the other. The space had gone, piece by piece. Even angry at him, she sat at his side. The days and nights were growing colder. Winter beginning to wrap its fingers around the trees, sink its toes into the ground, blow a small cold laugh into the wind. Vatri had only a threadbare cloak. She would sit with him, under the snowbear pelt, to share the warmth. She would not share it with him at night, nor let him give it to her. He would, though, once her eyes drifted shut, laying the pelt over her small form. She would protest, in the morning. He would do it again the next night. His blood was warm enough to stand the cold.

Twice more that night she tried to read the flames. Each time she threw up her hands and swore so loudly it woke birds, chattering down at them. Which only made her more furious. It made Scal laugh, to watch her screaming at the birds. He did not remember the last time he had laughed. She screamed at him, too, for the laughter, and then she went to sleep. It was her way, he believed, of spiting the Parents. He would never claim to understand her ways. He laid the pelt over her shoulders when she began to shiver.

They came to the town before midday on the next day. It was warm within the inn, too warm almost, though the merra huddled happily near the hearthfire. There was a fresh-cooked lamb whose flank they shared, and a strong, heavy ale that made Scal think of the ice and the snow and two bodies burning. They spoke little. Vatri did not like inns. Rather, she did not like the people one found at inns. Scal could feel the eyes on them. She would be feeling the looks more than he. She had said once, defiantly, that she did not care if people stared at her. It was not true, though. That was clear from the way she grew so quiet. Grew so small.

A hand touched Scal's shoulder. Shaking. So delicate so as to hardly be a touch at all.

Turning, Scal saw the man. He was tall, maybe taller than Scal even, though it was hard to tell when sitting. Hook-nosed, black-haired, pale-faced. There was a strange staining on his lips, black smudges and smears. Beneath the travel stains, the robe he wore looked to be black. A dangerous color. His entire body was trembling. Eyes huge as he stared at Scal.

"You're a fighter?" he asked. His eyes flickered to the sword hilt poking over Scal's shoulder, and he gulped.

Scal sized the man up. The same way he did every potential employer. He could not claim to be impressed, and he did not like the black robe. Still he said, "I am."

"And are you"—another hard swallow, a tremor that momentarily rocked him—"for hire?"

"I am," Scal said again.

"Would you please come with me?"

Scal nodded and rose. Vatri touched his arm. It looked as if she might have been trying to raise her eyebrows in question. He shrugged. He knew she would follow whether he asked her to stay or not. If she did not go with him, she would hide around a corner or crouch outside a door. She rose. Together they followed the shaking man up the steps, to one of the small rooms the innkeeper rented for much more than they were worth. The room was cold, the window wide open to the wintry breeze. A single man sat in a chair in the center of the room. Seeing him, Scal had cause to wonder what he had done to so vex the Parents.

The man waiting was burned. Not so badly as Vatri. More recently than Vatri. Still, it was not a pleasant thing to see. His hair was missing from the right side of his head, the skin beneath and around red and angry. He had recently shaved away a beard, for the skin where it would have been was pale where it hadn't been touched by flame. His left arm hung in a sling, the lump of clumsy bandages visible under the black cloth that covered his shoulder. His black robe was cleaner than the other's, a more obvious black. When his eyes flicked to the merra, his face curled. It was a look Scal had seen often, on the faces of those who saw her. His eyes did not stay on her long, though. The shaking man knelt next to his chair, mumbled words Scal could not hear. The burned man pressed a jar into his hand, and he retreated to a corner, cradling the pot.

"Do you know how to use that sword?" the burned man asked.

"I do." Scal was not a man to boast. He would be hired, or he would not be. Things happened as they were meant to.

The man sized him up, and Scal sized him up in return. The mumbling from the corner was distracting. There was a twist in Scal's gut. Different from the boiling rage. An animal instinct. A warning for caution.

A muffled scream. In the corner, the shaking man was writhing now. Head thrown back. Mouth agape. Tendons standing out like cords on his neck. Eyes wide and staring.

Scal stepped toward him, concern flaring. The burned man held up a hand. "Leave him." As he said it, the screaming stopped. The man sagged into his corner. Eyes closed. A smile playing over his blackened lips. Into the silence, there came a quiet humming. A child's sleeping tune Scal had heard sung before.

"Abomination."

Vatri stepped forward, and she was shaking almost as badly as the man had been. She, though, with fury. Her hands were clenched, spine stiff. Her face could not be said to be expressive, but the anger was there to see, more than clear.

The burned man faced the burned woman, and asked calmly, "And who are you?"

She did not answer. She spat at his feet, and went to the humming man. Kneeling, cradling his head. Feeling at his neck and chest.

"Anddyr." The burned man sounded annoyed. "Tell this woman you're fine."

"I'm fine," the man said. His voice was distant, small. The voice of a child. A simple child, who was not let out of the house for fear he would drown trying to catch fish with his mouth. There was still a smile on his face.

"You see?" And then the burned man dismissed Vatri. Turned back to Scal. "I find myself lacking in suitable protection. I need to hire someone who can keep me alive better than the mumbling idiot." From a pocket, he pulled a pouch, tossed it at Scal's feet. It hit the floor heavily. Scal knew the sound of coins.

"You can't," the merra said. Her arms were wrapped around the man, who was humming again. He did not seem to notice her at all. "Please, Scal. We should leave."

He looked at her for a time. The twisting in his stomach wanted to listen to her. He did not like the burned man. Did not understand what had happened to the shaking man. Had never liked the black-robed wanderers who spoke against the Parents.

Another pouch of coins landed next to the first. This one came open as it landed. Coins spilled onto the floor. Gold shimmered in the dull light. Arcettan royals, all of them. More money than Scal had ever seen.

"Half now," the burned man said, "and the other half when I no longer need your services."

There were few jobs Scal had taken that he had liked. He

did not like the long, boring caravans. He did not like killing men, strangers, only because his employer told him to. He would have left his sword at the side of the road, if he had had any other way to earn a living. But he did not. He took what jobs were offered, because it was the only thing there was to do.

Even the best of men, Parro Kerrus had said, *must sometimes do bad things. It's the way of the world, little lad.*

Scal knew the kind of man he was. He had made peace with it.

"You may go where you wish," he told Vatri softly. He could not look at her again as he bent to pick up the coins. "I will do as I must."

CHAPTER 22

Distant Raturo, tall enough, almost, to view all the wide world, was little more than a smudge on the horizon. Keiro had fallen to his knees when he'd realized what it was, hands clasped to his forehead in prayer. He didn't move until long after the sun had set, hiding the mountain entirely from his sight, though he knew where it lay as surely as he knew his own heart's beating.

"Should we see your face again," Keiro said softly, sadly, "it shall mean your death."

He rose in the darkness, pulling the night like a shelter around himself as he stood trapped between desert and mountain. He could not go farther north, for Fiatera lay there and was forbidden, and he would not go back south, where death lay among the burning sands and killing heat, where the refused summons would be waiting for him, ready to swallow him whole in retribution.

Slowly he turned to face west. His heart ached, and his body, and his feet, and for the first time in his life Keiro wanted to sit inside a firelit house and rest his callused feet on a stool. He could go west again, and find Algi. A year and more since their parting, and he still remembered the feel of her lips pressed gently against his. He was lonely, and tired, and wanting of comfort.

It hurt to turn again, to turn his eyes from the mountain, though not so much as turning from the desert's call. He turned east, away from the past, for there was another half of the world he had not walked. He was not meant for a house, or a wife, or peaceful comfort. He had been made for walking, though it had never felt so much like a curse.

It had been two or so moon-turns since he had left the course of the river-that-ran-from-the-sun, for its gurgling had sounded too much like an accusation. He had changed to an eastward-drifting north, carving his own fork from the mighty river, so east was not so sharp a turn. He had passed through the hills of the Shrevan nomads, though he had seen none of the horse-folk, and those hills had flattened even as the grass reached high around him, to his shoulders or higher. The Plains had no other name, but they were as good a place for walking as any. East took him deeper into the high grass, high enough, hopefully, to mask the distant point of Raturo by the time the sun rose.

It wasn't, he learned. Raturo still hung like a smudge over the waving heads of the plaingrass, and his left eye, his only eye, kept wandering toward the sight of it. Eventually Keiro had to change course slightly, turning a touch south so that Raturo lay just behind his left shoulder. It was easier, then, to walk and not think overly much.

Keiro spoke aloud, sometimes, his voice rising and falling

with the rhythm of his feet against the ground. He would have been surprised had anyone told him his thoughts were spoken aloud, but there was no one to tell him that, and that was itself the reason for the talking. He was lonely, since Algi had left him. He talked to her, sometimes, as if she were still walking at his side. It made the walking easier, somehow, though each step took him farther from where she was.

"You would like it here," he told the girl who wasn't there. "The grass would tickle under your nose, and the groundbirds taste almost like those red birds we loved."

There were footprints, sometimes, sunk deep into the rich dirt between the grass stalks. The prints were smaller than his own, and though the old stories, the tales of the gods that had been passed from mouth to ear long before they had ever been written down, said that Sororra and Fratarro had been giants among men, still Keiro liked to think it was their tracks he found, followed. After all, the Twins had come first to the Plains, when Patharro had sent them down into the world to wander and learn alongside mankind.

"You would almost believe, here," he told Algi. "Perhaps your sun god is Patharro, and maybe he's not. But I have to believe he would send his children, if he had them, to walk here, too. It's beautiful, in its own way. Peaceful. A good place for walking."

He thought, sometimes, of what his life had become, would be still. He was made for walking, to be sure, but was that all his life was to be? Often he remembered the words of the Ventallo who had thrown him out at the top of Raturo, the hope he had offered beyond Keiro's own hope of preparing the world for the young twins within the mountain. "You are given a chance. A hope of redemption." He'd thought for a while Algi was that chance, that hope, a heathen of faraway lands who heard all the old stories with wide wondering eyes.

"But you only liked the stories themselves," he reprimanded her gently. "*Any* story would do for you. You never cared for the truth behind the words, so long as they were spoken well."

He heard her voice, sometimes, the lilting tune, the playful tone. Her laughter. "A wonder I listened to so many of your stories, then, Erokiyn."

"Demon spawn," he said fondly, and then stopped, his feet falling still, for there was the point of a spear poking into his chest.

The man at the other end of the spear was short, made shorter by the ready crouch, with skin smeared by mud and pieces of grass. He was naked, wearing nothing but bands of woven grass around his neck and arms and legs. All this Keiro took in, and he smiled broadly, for this was the first human he had faced in over a year.

Keiro raised his hands, the universal supplication of harmlessness, and took a step back from the spearhead. Another point pricked his back. He didn't need to glance over his shoulder to know there would be another muddy man there as well.

"Peace," Keiro said, and though his voice was dry and rusty, the word came out clear. He could not stop the smile that stretched his face, his burned lips cracking. It had been a day, almost, since the last puddle of water among the grasses. "I mean no harm."

The man squinted up at him, as if sizing up Keiro and his words. So little was known about the people who called the

Plains their home. Keiro only hoped they might speak the same language. As he stood waiting, four more men stepped from the long grasses, each carrying his own spear. These were little more than sticks scraped into a pointed end, though the points looked plenty sharp. They surrounded Keiro, a ring of spears pointed inward, fixed at Keiro's heart. Still he could not stop smiling. He had been too long alone, much too long.

Finally the man before him turned and made a motion to his fellows, and the spear behind Keiro prodded him forward. And then it was naught but more walking, which Keiro understood well enough.

At length they came to a village, the first village Keiro had seen in his long wandering of the Plains. It was no real village, truly—the grass was flattened in a broad circle, and woven-grass sleeping mats were strewn about, a few grass mats propped up on sticks as shelters. There was a small fire pit, hardly any bigger than the ones Keiro had carefully made to cook his sparse meals, at the center of the village. The people who stared, and there were a great many of them, were all as small and as naked as his captors, their hair dark even beneath all the mud.

An old, wrinkled woman came forward to meet them, and the leader of the hunting band said, "We found him in the grass." Relieved beyond all telling that they spoke in a language he knew, Keiro laughed aloud.

The woman walked boldly up to him, hands planted on her hips. She stared, her eyes fixed on the empty space where he had once had a second eye, and looking back, he saw that one of her eyes was glossed over with a milky-white film. She grinned at him, showing missing teeth, and said, "We two, we know."

They called themselves plainswalkers, and though they were not arrogant enough to claim to be the world's oldest children, Yaket, the half-blind elder, proudly said their people had lived as long as the Plain's grasses had been sprouting from the earth. As they sat around the carefully contained fire, eating pieces of the cooked groundbirds Algi would have loved and a chewy root that grew beneath the grass, the young women of the tribe picked and plucked at Keiro, giggling, covering his skin with mud, winding grass bands around his arms, ripping away the tattered pieces of his clothes until he wore little more than his breechclout and the eyecloth over his brow. He stopped them, then, and wouldn't let them pull out the beads Algi had woven into his hair either. With the sun setting, the children begged him for a story.

It had been much the same with Algi. Young folk were the same no matter where one walked. It had taken a while, but once she and Keiro had found enough shared words, she had begged him to tell a story every night. He'd told her all the old stories, trotted out the entire preacher's repertoire of tales, but even that was not enough to fill four years of nights. She'd made him make up his own stories for her. She hadn't understood what a princess was, or a castle, but she'd liked hearing about the adventures of a mischievous young woman called Ilga—"Ilga!" she had exclaimed excitedly, patting her hand over her heart, but Keiro had shaken his head stubbornly at that and gently teased, "I really don't see the similarity."

He didn't think the plainswalker children would be as enthralled by the Ilga stories, and so he had only the old stories to fall back on. That was as it should be. Any story he chose would be new to the plainswalkers—he knew that no preachers would have traveled this far into the Plains, or even into the Plains at all. With enough work to be done converting the followers of the Parents within Fiatera, what point was there in looking to the primitive folk living within the sea of grass? "A hope of redemption," the Ventallo had told him at the top of Raturo. "You may use our words still, and spread our teachings, and pray that the gods forgive you."

He had a hope, a very small hope, the first in years, beginning to form within his heart, knowing that the plainswalkers spoke in his own tongue. He had worried that he'd shunned his redemption when he'd turned his back to the calling desert, that he had condemned himself to endless, hopeless, purposeless walking. But here, perhaps, was another chance. A better chance. People who spoke his words, and who were untouched by the ancient quarrel between two gods and their children. People who could be won over, who could see the truth, who could bring glory to the Twins and perhaps even help, in their small way, to free them from their prison beneath the earth. He could not read the trails of future and chance. He could not know what might come from such a small thing as a story told in the grass sea. But he could hope. This story might matter a very great deal.

Solemnly, he lowered his threadbare eyecloth for the first time in years, since the last of the old stories he'd told Algi. It was almost like a homecoming, the comfort of the preaching blindness and the well-loved words swelling his chest. "Do you know," he began, and he could feel them leaning toward him as the expectant silence fell, "of the burning sands and the killing heat that live to the south?" They didn't answer, they weren't expected to, but he let the pregnant pause draw on.

"The Eremori Desert is old, almost as old as this sea of grass—but not quite, for it was given shape after the rest of the world had grown. I tell you now how the desert was made. This is the oldest story.

"We all know"—belatedly he realized they wouldn't, but it was too late, the words had already been said—"how Metherra and Patharro shaped the world, and all the creatures to inhabit it, and in their joy they shaped two children of their own, a boy and a girl, who each were as a mirror to the other. The Twins sought to create as their Parents had, but they were young and untrained, and full of wild power. They were sent down from the godworld to wander our world, to learn humility and the way of things. Their first steps were taken on this very land. The lessons they learned, though, were not those that the Parents had wished."

Keiro had heard the priests and priestesses of the Parents tell their own version of the oldest story, and this was the point that marked the differences in the two teachings. "Sororra, seeing the petty squabbling that subverted mankind's perfection, sought to repair the humans that were Patharro's most-loved creation. Only, she thought, when all were made to see the power of the gods would they renounce their pettiness, and be equal under one firm and fair rule. She showed them miracles, and she shaped the very world around them. Thus did Sororra earn their fear, yet also their respect and devotion.

"Fratarro saw the great beauty his Parents had wrought in the world, and sought to create something fully as beautiful. He pulled a great spire from the earth upon which to look out over all creation, and from there he saw an untouched space, far to the south. There he created a place of unsurpassed beauty, pouring his love into the very shaping of the land. When it was complete, he led any who would follow into this place. Thus did Fratarro earn their love, and their devotion.

"But Patharro"—and Keiro pitched his voice lower, his words grave—"had not intended for his children to interfere in the world. He saw the land Fratarro had shaped, and he grew jealous of the beauty that surpassed his own creations. He called on the people who had followed his son, for they worshiped Patharro still, and he drew them from Fratarro's land, leaving it deserted, its beauty neglected. Fratarro grieved, but he poured his grief into a new creation: the *mravigi*, a living race to rival humans, peaceful and gentle and loving, and he gave them wings so that they might soar among the stars.

"Sororra, who was furious for her brother's sake at their father's jealousy, acted in a thoughtless rage. She reached out with her power to shape—not the world, but the very minds of her followers, to show the Parents the imperfection of their creations, and to reveal her own power as well." He felt the shudder roll through his listeners, the fear and caution that was Sororra's purpose.

"Metherra pulled the Twins back into the godworld, for she could not allow her power to be challenged. She saw in Sororra no repentance, and in Fratarro no relenting of purpose. The fire of her wrath burned the Twins, and Patharro sent a fire to scorch the land that his son had shaped, destroying the great beauty and killing the *mravigi*. It is the Eremori Desert now, a broken and lifeless place.

"When the land was dead, the Parents cast their children back down into the world, stripped of their powers but not their immortality. Fratarro wept and pled for mercy, but the

Parents turned their backs, and so Sororra turned her own back to them. And so they fell, and thus did Fratarro shatter upon the bones of the earth, his limbs flung to the far horizons, and a shard of ebon pierced his immortal heart, so that he would bleed for all his endless days." The silence shaped by the words stretched, fractured, bent to breaking, and just before it shattered entirely, Keiro opened his mouth for the last words, the ones to put a seal on the tale—and the moment before he gave them voice, the plainswalkers spoke, their own voices raised in solemn unison, to finish the oldest story:

"And so did Sororra vow vengeance."

The silence spun out once more, the thoughtful silence that every good story birthed, and within it Keiro sat dumbfounded. They should not have known the words, the words that were the anthem of the preachers. They lived here in the Plains, sheltered, primitive, unlearned. They should not have known.

The silence broke as a hand touched his knee, and Yaket said, "You tell it well, fraro."

And then the children were begging for more, the story of Sororra and the golden flower, of Fratarro's long sleep, of Straz, first of the *mravigi*. They knew all the old stories by name, it seemed. Each had their own favorite story. Keiro sat within their flurry of words, and had no words of his own. His heart broke, a very little bit.

That night he lay on the grass mat they had given him, which was too small for his long body, and he stared up at the stars. Sororra's Eyes were low to the horizon, hidden by the waving grass that surrounded him on all sides. He had had a hope of redemption, here among the rippling sea of grass, and it had been dashed as quickly as it had formed.

Keiro was not a man given to reflection; he did not spend overmuch time considering the paths and circles of life. His feet took him where they willed, and if he happened to walk the same path twice, he supposed it was as it was meant to be. But his thoughts that night took an unfamiliar turn, raising questions he was unused to asking or answering. How did these isolated people, a whole race of small folk the wider world disregarded, know all the old stories? He couldn't answer that on his own, and when he finally found the words to ask aloud, Yaket just smiled at the question and tapped a finger below her blind eye. "We two," she said again, "we know."

CHAPTER 23

Joros hadn't thought there could be a person alive more obnoxious than those blasted twins. Anddyr, who was nearly as detestable in his own ways, at least had the grace to be obsequious about it.

But the merra, the thrice-cursed priestess with her horror of a face—she may have been the worst person Joros had ever met, and that was an impressive feat, especially after only two days of traveling together. If she didn't have to pause to breathe, he doubted she'd ever stop praying; as it was, she rode her horse directly behind Joros's and chanted verse at his back. "And so shall the unfaithful be smote, and their souls denied a place among the eternal stars . . ." Someone so bloody ugly should have the sense to be quiet and let herself be forgotten.

The throbbing pain that lived on his left side, face and neck and shoulder, made his tolerance shorter than usual. Anddyr had been blubbering apologies since the inn, weaving his healing spells every day over Joros, but to begin with, it was harder for the mage to knit the wounds of another—he had some explanation that Joros had no interest in hearing—and he claimed burned skin like Joros's took time to mend, even at the accelerated pace Anddyr could provide. The short of it was that it hurt to move, but Joros wouldn't let a weakness like that affect him. He nursed his aches silently, as a man should.

When the merra wasn't praying at Joros, she was likely to be found speaking to Anddyr. That itself was an insult, and troubling to boot: she talked to the mage like he talked to the horses, gentle and encouraging. She'd tried to take the skura from him, their first day traveling; Anddyr had bit her, and that still made Joros smile to think on. It didn't stop her talking to him, though, likely whispering sedition into his impressionable ears.

Still, if she was part of the price to pay for the hulking brute of a Northman, he could withstand her. Scal's presence had already done wonders—with his stolen merchant garb too burned to wear, Joros had had to go back to a black robe, and there'd been many unwelcoming stares and unhappy mutters at the inns they'd stopped at. With the Northman sharing his table, though, it never went any further than staring and muttering. Joros would even allow that the burned merra made for an excellent deflection from his own wounds and the black robe. He'd rather not have the monster around, but there were worse things in the world than her, and there was no sense in fighting a losing battle.

So he withstood the burned merra and her aggressive prayer, and took comfort instead in the imposing presence of the Northman. He, at least, knew how to keep his lips together.

Near when the sun was at its highest, Joros turned his stolen horse toward a sad stand of trees off the road. The others followed, used by now to these occasional stops. It was growing harder to find places they wouldn't be seen, places far enough from any of the villages and towns; they were not much farther than a day outside Mercetta, and traffic was growing thicker on the road. Still, it was important to Joros to at least remain out of sight for the seekings. It wouldn't do to have villagers and travelers wondering why the evil preacher's servant got all glass-eyed and hang-jawed when Joros handed him a certain pouch.

Joros dismounted under the dappled shelter of the trees, letting the horse graze freely. It made Anddyr twitch when he did that; something about the reins or the bit, it couldn't matter that much. Joros took the pouch from his hip and handed it to Anddyr, settling his back against a tree as he waited for the mage to finish his seeking.

"What's he doing?" the merra demanded, just as she did every time. She and the Northman remained on their horses, him watchful, and she as full of glares as ever. Joros took great delight in ignoring her.

As had become his habit, Joros reached inside his robe and ran his fingers over the seekstones. Most showed him places on the far edges of Fiatera, scattered and distant; not exactly useless, but significantly less useful. Then there were the promising ones, the one at the center of Mercetta and the one at the city's borders—wait. The latter was different, showing him new images for the first time in years. It had always been dirty stone walls and running water, grim faces swimming in and out of focus, grimy hands holding out a dagger with a blue stone in its hilt. Always some variation of the same, never leaving the safe, suffocating embrace of Mercetta.

Until now. Now it was fields and trees and running feet, and a steady northwest pull.

The back of Joros's hand brought Anddyr out of his seeking, his mouth agape. There was no time. The mage was taller than any person had a right to be, but there was no weight on his bones; he was like a stick in shape and weight, and there was no resistance as Joros clambered astride the horse and hauled the mage up behind him. The horse would carry them both, or he would replace it with one that could.

Joros set his heels into the horse harder than he needed to and the beast leaped forward, crashing out of the copse. Startled travelers dodged out of the way, spitting curses at his back.

"What happens?" the Northman rumbled, his horse keeping pace easily. Dimly, Joros could hear the merra cursing as her nag faltered, but he couldn't even enjoy that through the pounding of his heart.

"They've left," Joros said, as much to himself as the Northman. "Something may have happened." He'd taken all the seekstones with him, ensuring the Fallen wouldn't be able to track down any of the twins, but his shadowseekers were clever. There were some who wouldn't need the help of a seekstone to monitor found twins.

And so they rode hard, Joros's fingers clamped around the seekstone, glimpses of another road swimming before his eyes, dirty and tattered shoes raising dust, the road before him blurred and indistinct, full of leaping bodies hurriedly fleeing his horse's hooves. They rode at a gallop until the Northman tore the reins from Joros's hands, pulling hard enough that the beast stumbled and reared. Anddyr tumbled to the ground, but Joros kept his legs clamped around the horse's middle and took handfuls of its mane to keep his seat.

"What in all the hells do you think you're doing?" Joros near shouted.

The Northman gave him a level stare, no emotions on his scarred face. "Wherever it is we are going," he said slowly, like he was drawing the words one at a time from a bag, "we will not get there faster on dead horses."

Scal's face grew more vague, overlaid with another man's face, wide-eyed, mouth moving quickly. Joros's fingers tightened around the seekstone, and the other face grew clearer. Young, still, but a man, with dirty hair past his shoulders and fear deep in his eyes. Joros had seen his face before.

"They need to be walked," Anddyr said blearily from the ground.

Joros let his fingers slip from the seekstone and turned his horse to pull alongside Anddyr. The mage was dust-coated and vacant-eyed, sitting propped up on one arm; he was at the perfect height for Joros's boot to connect easily with the side of his head.

The merra shouted curses at him, coming on too slow on her hard-breathing old nag. Joros dismissed her utterly, turning back to face the Northman. "We're wasting time," Joros said, fighting to keep his tone level, fighting to keep his fingers from the seekstone, his mind from trying to solve the mystery. He itched to lash out, to vent his frustration and anger against something solid again. But Joros was no fool—the merra's horse now shielded the mage from his reach, and something in Joros's gut told him that striking at the merra would be the same as striking at the Northman. His fingers chafed, but he touched them to the seekstone once more. There was still the road, still running, but it was no farther away. He let the seek-stone drop, and touched his fingers to the others instead. Still there, still where they always were, nothing changed. Joros still burned for an answer, one he would get even if he had to cut the Northman down where he stood . . . but there were always alternatives, should this one fail.

Joros closed his eyes, drew in a deep breath. Dirrakara had always laid a hand on his chest, felt the rise and fall of his breathing until she deemed him calm enough to speak again. That spot over his heart felt cold, empty—only for a moment.

He held out a hand, finger pointing down the road. Away from Mercetta, toward the running feet. He tried not to spit the word at the Northman: "Lead."

They had to wait for Anddyr, spitting out a mouthful of blood, to climb behind the Northman—the merra's nag could barely carry her alone, and Anddyr wouldn't meet Joros's glaring eyes, so that left the Northman's horse to carry him. Scal didn't say anything to dissuade or encourage the mage, his face the same blank it always was.

The pace the Northman set made Joros gnash his teeth, but with his fingers around the seekstone, he couldn't deny the pull was growing stronger, closer, the distance between the path they traveled and the half-glimpsed road to the north growing smaller. Joros called a halt for the night only when he was satis-fied his quarry had also stopped; he was tempted to push on through the dark, but the Northman rumbled a flat "no" when Joros voiced that thought. He and the merra built a fire before they did anything else, even leaving their horses saddled and grumbling while Anddyr fretted over them. It was strange, the way the followers of the Parents so feared the dark that they couldn't let any bit of it brush against them. He had expected better from Scal, but he supposed the Northman had been in Fiatera long enough for southern suspicions to taint him.

Joros sat before the fire while Anddyr and the merra tended to the horses, sweat-dark and tired-eyed. The Northman disappeared briefly, a shortbow in one hand and three arrows in the other; he returned just before the light had leached from the sky with all three arrows and a dead hare. He skinned it while the merra chopped up some roots Anddyr had dug up some days ago, given to her like a holy offering, while the mage went off to fill the dented cookpot with water from what amounted to little more than a puddle. It made for a poor stew. Joros hated traveling, he really did; he missed his bed, and warm meals delivered to him each night and day, and all the comforts of being a leader of the Fallen.

"What have they sent you to do?"

The voice seemed to come from the fire itself, but after a moment Joros picked out the eyes staring at him from the other side of it. Green eyes, amid skin warped with the patterns of flame.

"I have not been *sent* anywhere," Joros said stiffly. He couldn't say what made him answer her. The preachers held that in the darkness, a man couldn't hide anything; with no light, there were no lies, only truth. With only the fire holding back the dark, perhaps some of the truth was beginning to leak out of him.

"Then what vileness have you chosen to wreak?"

"Look closer into your flames," Joros suggested. He'd seen her each night, trying to draw truth from the fire and muttering over it like Anddyr. "If you lean close enough, I'm sure you'll find the answer. Right at the center . . ." Moving slowly, Joros stretched out his leg, and at the last word, he nudged a burning log with his boot. The fire jumped toward the merra, and she leaped back with a shout, and Joros's laugh rang into the night.

"You're an evil man," she said softly from beyond the fire.

Joros smirked; the skin on the side of his face had begun to heal enough that smirking no longer hurt. "You don't know the kind of man I am."

"I hope I never do."

"You're welcome to leave any time you wish. I have no need of you."

"I go where Scal goes."

Joros shrugged, tilting his head back to look at the stars. Silence, sometimes, could do better work than any words could do. The stars stared down at him, bright against the black sky. Though the two sects couldn't agree whether it had been Patharro or Fratarro who'd created them, all of Fiatera agreed that the souls of the dead went to live among the stars—one of the few things preachers and priests alike agreed on. Joros imagined it would make for an awkward afterlife, escaping the feuding divisions of the world only to have it carry on endlessly among the stars.

"You know you can never win," the merra whispered, her face dancing behind the flickering flames. "You have to know it's hopeless."

Joros pulled his cloak around himself and, still smiling, rolled onto his side. Briefly he brushed his fingers against the seekstone; the twins were still and unmoving. From the ground he said, "I, for one, very much hope that you're wrong."

It took the next day and most of another before they caught up to their prey, though they were too late. Approaching the village ahead, they could see the pinpoints of massing torches glowing against the dusk. Joros kicked his horse into a gallop, and this time no one gainsaid him.

The shouting and the torches led him; he found his quarry cornered in what must have been the town square, walls on three sides and a swarm of humanity on the fourth. The villagers were waving their torches, working up their courage, waiting to see who would be the first to throw their flame. Usually, the Parents' followers preferred to drown twins, but that was harder to do when the twins were more than mewling babes. Fire would do in a pinch.

The man was tall, the woman short, but their faces were much too similar to be mistaken for mere siblings. It was a wonder they had gone undiscovered for so long, if they took no care to disguise themselves. That was a question to be answered later.

"*Twins,*" the merra hissed, a lower echo of the angry shouts that filled the square. "Parents preserve us." She made the sign of the sun over her heart and spat on the ground twice.

The crowd hadn't noticed the arrival of Joros and his companions yet—all to the better. "Scal," Joros said, just loud enough for the Northman to hear him over the shouting, "it's time to begin earning your keep. Keep them safe," and he carefully pointed to the panicked twins so there could be no misunderstanding. "Do whatever you need to do."

To his credit, the Northman didn't hesitate. His feet touched the ground in the same moment he drew his wicked-looking sword from over his shoulder. He picked his way quickly through the crowd, a stone forcing a river to part around it, his blade never touching flesh—more a promise to anyone who thought to stop him.

"Shield them," Joros murmured to Anddyr, behind him on the horse. The mage twisted to get enough space free for his hands to weave their patterns, but his muttered spells sounded thick, clumsy. The casting took him entirely too long, and Joros aimed an elbow into his chest to sharpen the mage's focus. The merra had been whispering to him all week, still trying to take the skura from him; Joros hadn't been watching them carefully enough.

The barely-seen shimmer settled over the twins and Scal, who turned to face the torches and the shouts, his sword angled across his body, waiting.

"You're a monster," the merra spat. She, with her grotesque face, was so quick to accuse others of what she wore so openly.

Ignoring her, Joros said to his mage, "Get me the mob's attention." This spell came almost too quickly, almost an instinctive reaction, like a gasp from a falling dream. A crash like thunder rent the air, and the shouts turned to terrified screams. Joros growled a curse and drove his elbow harder into the mage's chest—but, granted, it had redirected the crowd's attention.

Joros lifted both arms into the air, standing in his stirrups, and tried to make his voice as loud as the spell: "Leave them." All the eyes turned to him, and all the torches. Anddyr was frantically muttering another spell; which one, Joros couldn't guess. "These two are now under my protection." Past the crowd, the male twin was on his knees, clutching at his sister's legs, eyes full of desperation. "Put away your weapons, and we will leave you in peace."

There was silence for a time, fear woven over the villagers like a spell, doubt creeping up their spines; and then, from somewhere, a laugh, hard and uncompromising. The fear popped like a bubble. A torch flew through the air, aimed not at the twins, but at Joros. It landed short, falling to the dirt road, but it was enough to make his horse rear, pawing the sky with panic. Anddyr scrabbled to get one arm around Joros, holding on as desperately as Joros clung to the horse. The crowd surged toward them, anger focused once more, fires bright against the dropping night. Anddyr's arm thrust past Joros's face, fingers bent like claws, and his shouted words were high with terror in Joros's ear.

And then, there was only fire. Screams, for one moment, but the fire swallowed them with everything else.

It was like waking slowly from a dream, the line blurred between what's real and what was dreamed. There was sobbing, and prayer, and neither seemed right. The glare faded from Joros's eyes, white drawing away from the center, and he pushed himself to sitting to see what was real.

Barely, he kept his gorge from rising. The fire was gone, fast-burning, no natural thing, but it had left destruction. The town square was black and burned, buildings beginning to collapse under charred timbers. The villagers . . . there wasn't much left of them. Charred corpses, if there was anything, as black and crumbling as the wood. In front of him, where the mob had been charging, was nothing but burned ground. At the far end of it all, where a handful of corpses stood frozen as scorched skin stretched taut over bone, there also stood Scal and the twins, within a half circle of perfect preservation, Anddyr's shield still a faint shimmer around them.

The merra knelt, head bowed over her hands, vehemently reciting prayer. Anddyr sprawled near her, sobbing and retching and screaming in turns, his face a rictus of horror. He clawed at his palms, as though he were trying to strip away his own skin.

Slowly Joros rose to his feet, feeling like an old man, feeling like half his mind had fled to somewhere else. Each step was like walking through water, but the sting of his hand connecting with the mage's face seemed to bring some sense back. "Bloody . . ." he started, but the words dribbled through his mind. His foot to Anddyr's stomach knitted them back together. " . . . fecking idiot." Another kick, drawing together the scattered pieces of his mind. "I'll kill you," he promised, but the words didn't feel right in his mouth.

He moved with more surety through the swath of destruction. He kept his eyes forward, focused on the Northman's expressionless face, trying not to breathe in the stench of burned meat. He stopped outside the perimeter of the shield, for he wouldn't be able to pass through it, but he held his hand down to the twins. They both knelt, clinging to each other, eyes wide in identical faces. "You're safe now," Joros said with all the softness he could muster. To his own ears, he just sounded tired.

"This is a bad thing," the Northman rumbled. Joros didn't know if he was referring to the burning or the twins, and he didn't elaborate. The shield around them flickered and faded; Anddyr had either cast the spell off or his reserves of power had been devoured to feed the flames.

The female twin loosened her arms from her brother, her eyes still wide but a hardness growing in them. He knew her, Rora, knew her as well as he could from the reports his shadowseeker Nadaro had sent years ago. She was a fighter, as strong as her brother was weak. "Who are you?" she demanded.

He had thought so carefully of what he would say to her, the perfect words, but his thoughts were strewn across the world, too fractured to pull together. "I am a shadow," he said instead, "and I know your name." A dagger flashed into her hand, one with a blue stone set into the pommel. The Northman's eyes flickered from Joros to Rora, sword still held ready. Joros felt a grim smile stretch his face, half sneer. "So you've met some of the others, then. I promise you, I'm a different kind of shadow." The words were flowing back to him, the cottony feeling fading from his mind. "Our shadows chase us, but a good shadow can hide you from sight, keep you safe." Moving slowly to keep from startling her, he reached into his robe; his fingers found the seekstone easily. He tossed it to her, and it was likely instinct that made her catch it, though she dropped it with a curse almost immediately. Her brother, Aro, snatched it up, and his mouth dropped open. Disorienting, no doubt, to have his sister's sight layer over his own. She'd likely been surprised by the flicker in her own sight when she'd touched the seekstone.

"Smash the stone in your knife," Joros told her, "and the shadows will never touch you again."

The two looked at each other, Rora and Aro, and their eyes spoke words no other could read. She pulled free a second dagger, used it to smash the stone in the first. Aro nodded, passed her the seekstone; there was something unreadable in her eyes when she looked back to Joros. "Who are you," she said again, and it was less a question this time.

"My name," he said, "is Joros Sedeiro. I have need of a few companions such as yourself."

"For what?" Rora demanded.

Joros spread his hands, the image of innocence. It almost felt obscene, surrounded by such destruction. "It's just the beginnings of a plan, really, but if I do need two such as yourselves, I want to make sure you're readily available."

"Two such as us," Aro drawled, and his voice was a near-perfect mockery of Joros's. It dropped to a normal register as he said, "You mean twins."

Joros granted him a small smile, a nod. "I mean twins."

"People aren't usually in the habit of collecting us," Aro said. "Unless it's heads. They like collecting twins' heads."

"It's actually hands, usually." He hadn't heard the merra approach, but there she was, venom dripping from her voice, and Anddyr trailing in her wake.

The brother snorted. "See?"

Joros could have strangled the merra; his hands clenched and unclenched at his sides, but he kept his eyes fixed on the twins—kept them on the woman, for there was more thought behind her eyes than her brother's. "I'm not a normal man."

Aro laughed outright at that. "Higher moral standing than the rest of the world, hey? How lucky for us."

There was a time for anger—hells, most times were good for anger—but there were times when a calm voice could carry a threat so much better. "You will die out here," Joros told them levelly. "Understand that. You will be hunted down for the rest of your short lives—not even by shadows, but by normal men with any amount of brains in their heads to see the truth staring at them. You'll be drowned, most like, or burned if there's no water nearby when they catch you. Stoned, if the mob is patient enough. You'll die, one way or another. However, as you have just seen," and he gestured expansively, in case they were too dense to catch his meaning, "I am very capable of preserving your lives."

"We've managed our own lives pretty well so far," Aro said, but his eyes flickered to his sister, his voice losing its confidence.

Joros held her eyes, and it was she who asked, "Why? Why d'you care if we live?"

"Twins are very important to me."

The merra spat at him, a wet gob that hit the still-healing side of his face. She spat again at the twins, and snarled, "Abominations."

"You're very fond of that word," Joros said, wiping the spittle from his face, keeping a tight hold on his anger. "One might think you'd use it more sparingly, considering."

Her scarred face flushed, but she stood resolute. "The Parents demand their deaths."

"I don't doubt it," Joros scoffed. "They'll have to wait, though. I've heard they're patient, and we can only pray that the merras and parros have spoken true."

She had one last mouthful of spit, this one for the twins again. "The Parents' curse be upon you," she snarled at them, her voice and ruined face cold, "that you be dead and drowned before the sun should rise again." She turned away, stormed through the destruction of the village. Only the Northman watched her go.

Turning his attention back to the twins, Joros held his hand out to them again. "I offer once more. You will have my protection if you come with me. Elsewise, you are free to die, as you wish."

They looked to each other again, eyes speaking, and slowly the woman's face settled, set. Her hand reached up, fingers wrapping tight around his own; less accepting his protection, and more a challenge. She made it sound like a death sentence as she said, "We'll go with you," and Joros gave her his best smile.

CHAPTER 24

Af ter her first contract, Rora'd hidden away topside, somewhere not even Aro knew about, because he hadn't been
training the same way she had. Tare knew, though, because
she'd shown the place to Rora. Tare'd found her there, hiding,
and just sat with her for a while. "It's a hard thing," the hand
had finally said, "to have no choices left."

It'd felt, then, like the worst thing in the world. Now Rora
knew how stupid and young she'd been. It was much worse to
have choices, and have all of them be shit.

She didn't trust the head man, Joros, with half his face
burned raw and a hard smile that *did* touch his eyes but was
all the scarier for it. She kept the stone he'd tossed her, the one
Aro'd whispered had let him see out her eyes, but it was just
like a normal stone since she'd shattered its match in her dagger. To be safe, she'd smashed all the gems in Aro's rings, too,
though it went against everything she knew to destroy good
money like that. Joros'd given them each a purse of coins,
mostly copper rames and sests with a few silver gids thrown

in. A man who had to pay you to stick by him wasn't usually someone worth sticking by.

That was where the shit choices started. Keep with the untrustworthy bastard and his collection of freaks, keep her and Aro's bellies full and their heads attached—or go back out on their own, where all the world wanted them dead and would do it without blinking. Shit choices, but one of 'em had more shit in it than the other.

So they had a new pack, probably the strangest pack Rora'd ever seen.

Aro liked the big bear of a Northman; he'd always made friends with the fists back in the Canals, admired the way they could just punch through life without spending a moment of it thinking. The Northman was like two fists put together, so big he could block out the sun if he stood the right way, but for all that, he wasn't just a fist. There was a brain behind his eyes, and it even seemed like he knew how to use it. Didn't stop Aro trying to make friends, though.

There was the merra, who no one except the Northman seemed to like, not that Rora could blame them. She was a mess to look at, the kind of thing that shouldn't exist outside stories meant to scare kids, and Rora got the sense that if she was ever stupid enough to be alone with the merra, one of 'em would likely end up stabbed. She kept glaring at Rora, and Aro, too, and spitting whenever they happened to catch her eye. Kept chanting prayers, too; seemed like her favorites were the ones about killing twins before their plague spread out on the earth, so there wasn't any kind of friendship to be made there, even if Rora'd been looking.

Then there was Anddyr. He stared at her even more than

the merra, and turned a bright red whenever she caught him staring. He never talked to her—then again, he didn't do much talking to anyone except himself. The merra'd tried to talk to him, the night they'd all made camp just out of sight of the burned-up village, but Joros'd stepped between her and Anddyr, and they'd had themselves a nice glare. "*That* is your doing," Joros'd said, pointing back toward the village. "Anddyr is weak, susceptible, and your corruption poisoned him, twisted his mind. Their blood is on your hands. You will not speak to him again."

The merra hadn't had anything to say to that, but she hadn't turned away before she'd glared and spat some more. Woman had so much spit in her mouth, Rora was thinking she was half water. Then Joros'd talked to Anddyr some, and Anddyr'd pulled out a little jar and eaten something from it and gotten so shaky and mumbly that Rora'd thought he was dying, but none of the others seemed to think anything was wrong. The merra'd glared, and Joros'd smirked, and Anddyr'd finally stopped shaking and spent the rest of the night staring at Rora with too-wide eyes. He was the mystery she couldn't crack.

Then there was the fact that every time she closed her eyes, she saw the fire shooting out of Anddyr's hands, and all the death it'd left.

She'd been trying to get up the nerve to ask him about it, because Aro wouldn't even look at Anddyr, so she knew he wouldn't ask on his own. It was left to her, just like usual. Took two days, but she finally tugged on her horse's reins to get it to drop back to where she could feel Anddyr's eyes. They'd found some horses in a part of the village that hadn't gotten burned, and there'd been no people around to tell them they couldn't take the beasts, so Rora'd gotten to learn to ride a horse. Hurt like hells when they bounced around, but she had to grant it was better than running on bloody feet. Aro kept falling off his, for no reason any of them could figure out, but the horse would go running off soon as it didn't have a rider, and the Northman always went to drag the sulky thing back. He almost smiled every time he did it, and that made Rora wonder if Aro's falling was such an accident. She'd never claim to understand the way men made friends.

She didn't look at Anddyr, even though she could feel his eyes bright on her face, because she was hoping he wouldn't be so shy if she didn't look at him. "I've been meaning to ask," she said, keeping her voice low enough no one else was like to hear. "The night you all found us. You . . . did something. With your hands. It was like you made fire . . ."

"I did." He had a nice enough voice, soft and solemn, the kind of voice that alone wouldn't make you any friends but wouldn't get you into any fights either.

"How?"

"I'm a mage."

Rora almost looked at him, but just glanced out the corners of her eyes instead. He was winding his horse's mane between his fingers, not looking at her for once. "What d'you mean?"

She felt his eyes again, real quick. He spoke a little slower, like he thought she maybe hadn't heard him: "I'm a mage."

She did look at him then, with her forehead scrunched up and a frown on her face. "What's that word?" she asked, in the nicest way she knew how. "Does it mean . . . Well, if I had to guess," and she was careful with her words here, didn't want to offend him or anything, "I'd guess you were a witch."

His nose wrinkled at that, but it sounded like he was talking just as careful as she was. "No, I am a *mage*." That didn't help Rora any, so she just kept looking at him. Tare'd taught her that was one of the best ways to get the answers you wanted, just let the silence go on long enough the other person felt the need to fill it. That was how she got anything important out of Aro. Finally Anddyr sighed the saddest little sigh, and he looked over at her with his eyes like a dog's, and he didn't even blush too much when their eyes met. "We don't like being called witches."

Rora grinned at that, as much to encourage him as anything, though her heart was beating a little faster. "I've never seen a wit—mage." She corrected herself real quick when she saw his eye start to twitch, and a smile pulled at his mouth. He didn't have a face that was used to smiling. "Never seen a mage before. Are they all like you, throwing fire around?"

His face went sad again, and he looked back down at his fingers in his horse's mane, turned them over so he could stare at his palms. She hadn't noticed it before, but they were reddish, looked a lot like the healing skin on Joros's face, and there were deep gouges crisscrossing his palms. "No," he said softly. "That was . . . I shouldn't have done that. I didn't mean to. I . . . I'm not always as in control of myself as I should be."

She could feel him slipping away, curling back in on himself, running away from whatever sort of bond they'd started to make. Quick, she asked, "What else can you do?" He glanced back up, and she flashed him a smile. Aro should've gotten up the stones to do this—he was so much better at charming people, pulling out answers slow and careful like pulling a worm from the earth, gentle so it came out whole instead of leaving behind broken pieces of itself. Rora could get good enough answers with the tip of a dagger, but that wasn't always the best way, not when answers were dug in deep. "I like to know everything I can about everything," she said, trying to sound all innocent, "and I don't know anything about mages."

Anddyr shrugged, twisting the horse's mane again. "I can perform many spells—there are more spells than any one mage could ever learn."

"Then how d'you learn to do any of 'em? Does it just . . . happen?"

"No—well, not usually. Control is the first thing a mage learns, so that it doesn't 'just happen.' That's the most dangerous thing for a mage . . . not being in control." He looked down at his hands again for a bit, then shook himself and looked up at Rora, like meeting her eyes was a test he wasn't sure he'd pass. "All mages are taught at the Academy. We learn as much as we can in five years, and then we're free to do as we please."

Rora didn't ask the obvious question, which was how Anddyr ended up with Joros when it didn't exactly seem to be by his choice. Instead, she asked, "So this place . . . the Academy, it's just full of mages?"

That little smile went on Anddyr's face again. "Yes. It's rather like an anthill. Everyone with a job to do, everyone helping each other out." That seemed like a topic he could warm up to, his face going clearer than she'd seen it yet, his eyes bright on hers even though there was still some red to his cheeks.

It sounded a lot like life in the Canals, truth told, except for the everyone-working-together part. It seemed like a strange thing, that Rora's life as Scum had been anything like this high-talking witch's. "So how'd you know?" she asked. "How'd you find out you were a witch?"

"Mage," he corrected, but there wasn't any anger behind it, just the same tone Garim'd always used when he'd tried to teach Aro to speak right.

"Mage, right. How'd you know you were a mage?"

Anddyr laughed, and that was enough to make Rora's eyebrows shoot up. She regretted it right away, because his face looked like it'd just realized how much his mouth had been talking. He turned that bright red again and wouldn't look at her anymore. "There's not much mystery to it," he mumbled. "A young mage . . . makes himself known."

"How?" Rora prompted when it seemed like he wasn't going to say any more.

He fidgeted a bit, but it seemed like he won an argument with himself to keep talking. "The signs started when I was young. It's usually fire—when I was angry, things near me would start afire with no reason, or fires would go out if I got scared. Pottery would crack if I got sad. The sorts of things that don't just happen on their own. My parents knew what that meant, and so they took me to the Academy. The masters tested me for power, and accepted me when they found it."

"So things would just happen, without you being able to control it?"

"That is what I said," Anddyr murmured.

Rora rode next to him for a while longer, trying to decide if she could dig out any more answers or if Anddyr'd break apart if she pulled any harder. Finally she said, "Thank you," and tapped her heels into her horse's sides without waiting to see if Anddyr'd look back up at her. She rode up next to Aro, but didn't look over at him either. She was sure he'd heard every word.

Time passed strange, traveling on the twisting roads. Rora'd never been outside Mercetta till now, and the days themselves seemed different. It'd feel like it'd only been a few days since Joros'd found them, and then she'd realize Aro had more'n a week's worth of beard growing on his usually smooth cheeks, that more time had gone by than she could keep a hold on. They rode into a village and the Northman rumbled that it was the last they'd find before they left Fiatera. It'd started to snow near right after he said the words, like the sky itself was giving them a warning. Didn't stop them from pushing on, after they'd bought as much food as they could. Rora got herself a nice cloak lined with fur, probably the finest thing she'd owned since what she'd stolen from Nadaro Madri, and stealing wasn't quite owning.

After they'd left that last village behind, the road faded away into scraggly grass that got covered by snow, and they slept on the cold ground, and didn't run into any other travelers, and had only each other for company. It got so cold that even talking got to be a chore, an open mouth like an invitation for the cold to seep down into your bones. They rode quiet, and slept around big fires. It seemed like the merra cared about having a fire more'n she cared about food to cook over it, and mostly the Northman seemed set on keeping her happy. Didn't seem like she ever was happy, but maybe he kept her from being a raging horror.

There was nothing to mark the change, but up at the head of the group, the Northman rumbled, "We are in the North."

"How d'you know?" Aro asked.

The Northman gave him a look that didn't seem to hold any emotion at all. "I know."

No one else questioned him.

"Anddyr," Joros called, and the witch rode up next to his master. Joros passed him a pouch and Anddyr held on to it with both hands, his eyes closed and his face screwed up. His hand shot out all sudden, finger pointing in a direction that looked no different'n any other. Joros took the pouch back, tucked it safely away.

"What was that?" Aro demanded, riding up right next to Anddyr. "What'd you just do?"

The witch just blinked like he was staring into the sun, and it was Joros who answered: "My servant and Northman friend share the task of guide."

"But what'd he do?"

Instead of giving an answer, Joros turned his horse to line up with Anddyr's pointing finger, and the journey continued.

Rora rode up, Aro a beat behind her, to ride next to Joros. "We're gonna start needing some answers," she said.

"Then you'd do best to seek them elsewhere," Joros said evenly.

"What is it you're looking for?" Aro asked. "What's in the North?"

"An item of personal value but of no meaning to you."

"Then what d'you need us for?"

"I don't know that I will." Joros wasn't looking at either of them, his words coming out with their ends clipped off like a caged bird's wings. "If I don't, you'll have received a few weeks' respite from being hunted."

"And what if you do need us?" Rora asked.

He did look at her then, and his voice was hard as rock: "Have you heard the expression 'don't test the gift of a blade'?"

"What's that supposed to mean?" Aro demanded, but Rora and Joros were too caught up with staring to answer him. "We need to know what we're doing here," he went on, but he was all bluster, and Joros knew it. They just ignored him, and even though Joros was the first one to look away, it didn't feel like Rora'd won anything. His eyes just stayed fixed on the direction Anddyr'd pointed, and there were no answers to pull out of him.

Quietly, Rora dropped back. The witch was there, riding just behind Joros like always. Pausing next to him, she kept her eyes ahead and her voice low as she said, "I suppose it'd be too much to hope you might have some answers?"

His face went red, then green, staring like her at a sick dog too stupid to know good food from bad. He swallowed a few times, then just shook his head. Rora nodded, and dropped back farther.

Time was hard to keep a hold on in the white blanket of the North. The sky turned to gray, like the clouds were huddling together for warmth, like even the sun couldn't reach through. The nights were darker than the days, but not by so much. Worst, the cold was like a live thing that found its way into any clothes, brushing against skin and stealing any warmth it could wrap its fingers around. It bit away at Rora, who was used to living in a packed-full city, where the air shimmered above the canals just with the heat of the day. The Northman, wrapped up in a cloak almost as white as the snow but dotted with old stains, he was the only one who seemed not to feel the cold. He gave it to Rora, that bear-head cloak, handed it over without a word as she sat shivering on her horse. That made the merra spitting mad, but she did it silently, just glaring murder at Rora's back even harder than before. She refused to speak to any of them for a while, even the Northman, who seemed like the only person in the world she didn't hate.

They saw heavy clouds in the distance the next day, but the closer they got, the clearer it got that they weren't actually clouds. Without any of them agreeing to it, they all stopped to stare. You could see parts of a wooden wall from so far away, but smoke covered most of it, and it didn't look like there was much wall left under all the smoke anyway.

"What happened here?" the merra asked softly, and it sounded like the first time she hadn't been happy to see a fire.

"A raid," the Northman said, and there still wasn't anything in his voice besides the words. "There is always a raid."

"It's one of the convict camps?"

"It was. It has been. Aardanel."

Aro piped up at that: "That's a Northern word?"

"Aye. A Northern name, but a southern place."

"What's it mean?" Rora asked softly.

"Lost hope."

Joros snorted. "We'll stop there," he said. "They'll give us fresh horses, enough supplies to last us."

"No," the Northman said. Just a simple word, and it made Joros's face go a bright red, but somehow none of 'em thought to fight against that one little word. Scal turned his horse, and the merra followed him. Rora was happier about sticking by the Northman than by Joros, and Aro would always stick with her, so they turned, too. Joros with his red face finally followed, the witch trailing after him like always, face and body frozen in a flinch like he expected to be hit any second.

With the nights as gray as the days, they stopped for sleep when Joros decided he was tired. The trees stopped like someone'd drawn a line on the ground that they couldn't grow past, and that meant no more fires. They slept cold, all lying close to try to hold on to what warmth they had. The merra would mutter her prayers all through the night, just loud enough to be annoying, just annoying enough to make sleep hard.

The Northman showed them how to find a hard, black berry that grew under certain patches of snow, and he could usually bring down hares with his shortbow. He got a fox once, white as the bear cloak he hadn't asked Rora to give back. They ate the meat raw, all slippery and stringy, but it made your stomach stop howling if you could choke down enough of it. Anddyr only ate the berries, until Joros ordered him to eat the raw meat. The witch got down a mouthful and brought it back up right away. They didn't give him any more after that.

Whatever it was, the witch did his magic with the pouch more often, finger always pointing off to somewhere that didn't look any kind of special. Joros already had a short temper, but it got shorter the longer they went without finding whatever he was looking for. He set to beating the witch one night, not for any real reason, and his elbow took Rora in the nose when she tried to pull him off. The Northman grabbed Joros by the neck and threw him into the snow, stood at the center of the huddled witch, the pissed Joros, and the bleeding Rora. Joros was no kind of idiot, so he just sat where he fell and glared for a while, and Rora kept her eyes sharp on him while blood from her nose froze on her face.

Aro's horse broke a leg, slipping on a spot of ice as Aro slipped from its back. The Northman cut the screaming horse's throat as Anddyr, sobbing, cradled the horse's nose against his chest. They ate horse meat that night, still warm enough that it steamed in the cold, all of them except the witch.

When they set off again, Joros ordered his witch to give Aro his horse. Anddyr trudged through the snow, far behind the rest of them. Rora finally rode back, holding out her hand to help pull the witch up behind her. Even through the bear cloak, his hands were gentle around her waist. They didn't speak a word, any of them. Opening your mouth let out too much warmth.

They'd stopped to sleep three times since passing by the burned-up place. It was hard to know just how many days that was, since it seemed like the sun was always fighting to break through the clouds and the snow, night and day the same flat gray. It was the second time since waking that Joros rode back with his face all fury to hand Anddyr the pouch. It seemed like the witch's whole body shook where he sat behind Rora, knuckles white around the pouch. It came all sudden, the weight of him suddenly gone as he fell clean off Rora's horse. He landed in a sprawl, but it wasn't enough to knock the air from him, and he used that breath to laugh and laugh and laugh, face stretched in a crazy grin and his eyes bright with triumph as they met Joros's.

CHAPTER 25

The sun was warm against his face through the waving grass, and Keiro had to admit that he enjoyed the bathing warmth of it on his skin. Modesty had caused him to keep his breechclout, but it really was impractical to wear anything else, when the sun beat so mercilessly down on the Plains. His skin was tanned a rich brown, almost as dark now as the plainswalkers' skin. He was hatch-marked with tiny, shallow cuts, the peril of walking through the Plains near naked. He hardly even noticed now when the grass sliced at him—his new-dark skin was tough as leather, and the grass never cut too deep.

They'd called him Pale for the first weeks, a gently jesting nickname, but they called him by his real name now. He'd earned that, somewhere along the way. It might have been after he'd caught his first groundbird, leaping up from a low crouch in one explosive motion, arms wrapping around the squawking fowl and neatly snapping its neck. The children had cheered wildly—they'd been trying to teach him to do it for days. The adult plainswalkers, who hadn't been there to see all the spectacular failures that had come before his success, had been duly impressed. He thought that was when they'd started to use his real name.

It may, though, have been after Poret washed his feet—or tried to. Keiro had lost his boots sometime in the span between the river-that-ran-from-the-sun and Algi's village. It had seemed as though everyone west of the river had gone barefoot, and so he had, too. His feet were hard as horn now, the soles so thick he hadn't felt when Kamat had jabbed a spear tip into his heel. They were colored an even deeper brown, too, from dirt and mud and all the years of walking. It had impressed the plainswalkers, who did all their walking in the safety and softness of the grass and mud. That could have been what gave him back his name.

His brown-stained feet were beginning to grow restless. It had been a very long time since he had stayed in the same place for so long, since his apprenticeship within Raturo so long ago, but it was growing harder by the day to leave these people who knew his tongue and shared his faith. That last had been a disappointment, though only a fleeting one—how could he do anything but rejoice at finding followers of the Twins, when he had expected his exile to be both physical and spiritual? They knew all the old stories, but they loved to hear him tell them still. They were a peaceful people, and innocent in so many ways.

There was, unexpectedly, a place for him here.

At his side Poret stirred, murmured sleepily. He stroked her hair, felt her contented sigh wash over his chest.

The moon would be rising soon, ascending from the hills

to the east. He'd been surprised by the hills, the ridges of land among the unfeatured Plains. The plainswalkers seemed to think the hills cursed, in some way, though he had yet to determine why. Perhaps a remainder of their old religion, whatever false gods they had worshiped before they'd learned of the Parents and the Twins. It would be night soon, and he'd lead the plainswalkers in prayer, thanking the Twins for their shelter from the sun that burned hotter here than it did to the north. He would tell a story, perhaps one of his journeys to the west, which they all seemed to love. Then he would sit up with the elder, Yaket, among the stars and try to find out the answers she was so unwilling to give.

How had they learned to speak the language Keiro spoke, the language of Fiatera? "It has been so," Yaket had said with a smile, "since the days before my grandmother's grandfather." How had they learned of the Twins? "They have been with us for as long as we have been worthy of them." Had there been another preacher, before him? "No, Pale," she'd said with a laugh, "you are the first of the black-robed to find us." How had they learned all the old stories, then? "My father taught them to me, and his mother to him." It was maddening, the same thing every night, no matter how he asked. "You will see, in time," she'd said, tapping his cheek below his ruined eye, and then she'd rolled up on her grass pallet and gone to sleep.

He shook Poret's shoulder gently to wake her. She rose, rubbing at her eyes, and gave him a little smile before walking into the grass. She knew his habits well. He liked to pray alone, back to the lowering sun, before he went to lead the tribesmen in prayer. He was rarely alone, among the tall grasses and short walkers; he had learned to take what time he could for himself.

It was Keiro's thought that, after a length of time, after enough prayers spoken, after so many steps taken, a man developed a less formal relationship with his gods. He had heard it all through Raturo, the oldest preachers casually calling on Fratarro for patience, or suggesting to Sororra that it might be time for a smiting. Speaking to the Twins as if in conversation with a close friend, a well-loved relative. So it had been for Keiro, these last few years, when there had been so few others to speak with. He liked to think the Twins, should they bless him by listening to his voice, would smile tolerantly, fondly, when they heard his words. He wasn't so sure of that anymore, after turning away from the desert, but it was the only way he knew.

"Thank you for bringing me here," he said tonight, to the faint red points of Sororra's Eyes growing slowly deeper as the light leached from the sky. "I don't know the purpose yet, but that's often the way of things, isn't it?" He paused, giving her a chance to respond, should she choose. The only sound was the wind brushing against the grass, so he went on. "There must be something more here. There's a mystery, but I can't find any more of the strings to pull, or think of the right questions to ask. You made me for walking, you know," he said with a faint, gentle reproach. "Not for standing. Not for staying." A sigh blew through him, an echo of the wind through the grass. "I know I'm meant to find something here. I can feel it. All my walking has led me here—but for what? I can't see the end to this path."

And then, for the first time Keiro could mark in his life, his prayer—whether formal or casual, spoken or silent—was given answer.

Sometimes the grasses played tricks with the eyes—reflected light strangely, fractured the vision, cast shadows where they had no business being. Keiro blamed some of it on only having one eye, of course, but every plainswalker had told him of the dangerous ways the grass could mislead. So naturally, he first thought that the two points of reddish light glowing within the grass, low to the ground, were just reflections of Sororra's Eyes above. Then the two near points loomed closer, and blinked.

Eyes, yes, but not any that lived among the stars.

The creature that came forth slowly through the grasses should not have existed. It moved like the spotted cat he'd seen in the great forest at the edge of the desert, lanky and graceful, stalking low to the ground. A long body, slender but broad-chested, a thick neck carrying a wedge-shaped head. It was black, black as a moonless night, save for the eyes that glowed with their own fire and never left Keiro's face. Scaled, Keiro saw by the last light of the sun, not furred. A tail, when it slid from the grass, that was longer than the rest of the creature altogether, slim and sinuous and forked at the end. It paced slowly around Keiro in the small clearing, the space of flattened grass that was barely large enough for two humans. As the sun vanished and the near-full moon dominated the sky, sending its wispy light washing down, points among the black scales began to glow, too, a perfect reflection of stars in the night sky. The head lifted, four long legs straightening to raise the barrel chest, eyes reaching level with Keiro's, and the creature opened its mouth, a black pit dotted with sharp white teeth. Keiro, immobilized by awe and fear, squeezed his eye shut and dared not breathe. He could not watch his own death come for him.

And then it spoke.

"Child," it said, in a voice high and lilting and otherworldly. *"Son of gods."* Another breath, washing his face with warmth, and then the softest of rustling sounds.

Keiro opened his eye to see the tips of the black tail disappearing through the grass.

He chased, not knowing quite why, diving through the grass, but the creature was gone. It left no track, no path of broken stalks, no sound. His heart pounding a desperate rhythm inside his chest, Keiro searched for an hour or more before he finally, achingly, gave up.

The children were the first to see him, of course, as he trudged into the tribehome. They showered him with questions and demands for a story that was much too late, couldn't he see the sun had gone down? He had no words for them—opened his mouth and then stood there looking a fool when no sound came out. He shook his head, the only apology or explanation he could give.

Yaket was sitting on her grass mat near the fire. She must have seen something in his face or eye, for she rose wordlessly, motioned the children away and for Keiro to follow. They walked back into the grass, a distance from the tribehome, silent in the night. She stopped at a place no different from any other and turned to Keiro. No words, but eyebrows raised expectantly, moonlight glowing on her wrinkled face.

The words came slowly to him. He could hardly do the creature or the experience justice, but he tried, chosing the words carefully. He was not a man prone to poetry, but there was a singing in Keiro's heart like he had never felt before.

Yaket smiled when he finished, a smile radiant as the moon, warm as the sun. "You have been blessed, Keiro. Keiro Godson."

"I don't understand."

"I will show you." She looked up into the sky, eye squinting at the moon, and smiled. "Three days, I should think. Three days, and all will be clear."

She left him there, standing in the middle of the grass sea, with no more explanation than that. Left him bereft, with a feeling of loss like none he had ever known. His eye, the one good eye, stared blankly into the grass. Behind the other eye, the empty one, a black beast danced, with glowing spots and deep red eyes.

Three days, she had said. The longest days of his life, which had been full of days of endless walking and little sleep. The days stretched longer than the years he had walked Fiatera with his father, longer than the precious years he had spent with Algi that had felt like a lifetime, longer than all the years he'd held the Twins in his heart. He felt a broken man, more misplaced than he had ever felt among all the people beyond the river-that-ran-from-the-sun who looked and spoke so differently. He couldn't even give name to the emptiness, the deep void that had grown within him.

Three days of the plainswalkers smiling and calling him Godson, touching his arm and then placing their hands over their hearts. "You are blessed," Yaket said simply, the only explanation she would give.

Three days, useless days where he could do little more than sit and stare and ache.

Three days, and at the sunset of the third, Yaket touched him on the shoulder and bade him rise.

They walked east, and Keiro, tall enough to see above the waving grass, saw that they were walking toward the hills, the lumps of land that were so incongruous among the flat Plains. The moon, full and proud in the sky, watched serenely.

Keiro asked no questions, for he knew the elder would give no answers. His throat was tight, constricted; he didn't think he could have spoken if he'd tried. His heart was like a trapped thing, desperate for escape. There was a heaviness in him, his limbs thick and uncooperative, and yet his whole being strained forward. A frenzy to know, and a dread of the finding.

The moon was high, almost directly above them as they ascended the first hill. With the night so well lit, Keiro could see the enormous mound that was the center of the hills, with the smaller knolls scattered all about. "We are in time," Yaket said as they reached the top of their hill, and she sat, legs folding neatly beneath her. A frustrated scream resounded within Keiro, but found no voice. He, too, sat, his hands shaking.

When the moon was at its highest point, throwing its glow over the rolling hills, it began.

One first, a solitary creature standing atop the highest hill, its black scales drowned by the glow of the bright points embedded in its skin that gave back the glow of the moon. It stood, muzzle pointed up at the sky, and it began to sing.

There was no other word for it, though it was like no singing Keiro had ever heard. One solitary sound, rising and falling alone in the night, weaving over and around and through itself. It was beautiful, heartbreakingly so, and the ache within Keiro's breast deepened, a weight so heavy he was sure he would be crushed.

And then came the others, swarming around the base and sides of the hill, joining their voices to the first, high and low, harmony and discord, joy and grief, beginnings and endings and an eternal balance. They sang to the moon, on the night when it rode fullest in the sky, and it was at once the most beautiful and the most anguished moment of Keiro's life. A cry burst from him, a sound of sheerest yearning to bounce off the woven music that spiraled up into the stars.

It ended, in time, as all things must. The voices left, one by one, the glowing creatures slipping slowly away as the moon began its descent, until only the first remained, the purest note among a night of more beauty than should rightly exist in the world. That voice, too, came to an end, a drifting closure, and something within Keiro broke.

He didn't know how long she let him cry, sobbing into his hands with all the sorrow and the joy he'd ever felt. At the touch on his shoulder he looked up, the tears still streaming from the only eye that could cry, and saw his face mirrored back in Yaket's, her mouth stretched in the sweetest smile. "It is good, Godson. Here," she said, patting his shoulder, "the old stories yet live."

CHAPTER 26

The looks the merra'd given her hadn't bothered her—Rora didn't give two shits about anything a merra might think. It hadn't been her glaring that'd made Rora give back the white cloak that was big enough to swallow her up—but she *had* given it back, and she was starting to regret it now as she lay on her belly at the top of an icy ridge, peeking out over the edge.

She didn't know if it'd started as a pit, but it sure was one now, a huge hole dug down into the snow and ice and stone, with what looked to be a hundred blond-haired men moving around below among the sounds of chipping stone. A hundred was the biggest number she knew of, and there were more Northman than she could count up to, so a hundred seemed as good a guess as any.

There were fresh holes dug down into the ice, new-made piles of stones reaching almost hip-high. Looked like the Northmen had been hard at work, digging down the floor of the pit deeper. "You people sure move fast," she murmured.

Scal grunted, but didn't do much more for a reply. Joros'd

sent them up together, not wanting Scal to go alone in case anything bad happened, or maybe because he didn't trust the Northman. Rora guessed he'd picked her because he didn't think any of the others were much use, and really, she couldn't say she disagreed. The witch had been so silly with excitement that Joros'd had to thump him on the head, and Joros and the merra weren't on any kind of good terms. And Rora knew her brother, so it wasn't hard to guess that Joros'd already pegged him as pretty useless. That left Rora, the best of all the people Joros didn't trust.

The others were all back a ways, back where Anddyr'd fallen off Rora's horse, hunkered down against the cold while they waited for her and Scal. The wind was loud enough and blowing the right way, so it seemed like Anddyr's laughing hadn't reached this far. Though Rora didn't like thinking about how close they'd all come to stumbling right into the pit and all the Northmen.

There was no telling what they were digging for, but they didn't look to have much idea of where it was either. Wide and deep, the pit was, and getting wider and deeper by the minute, with shovels and picks and hammers swinging.

"Any ideas?" she asked. She didn't know how much he knew about the North, but he had to have a better view of it all than she did.

He just shook his head, though. "There is no knowing. This deep North, it is all a mystery to me."

"You're a Northman, aren't you?"

He shook his head a little. "I do not know all of the North. I know the snows . . . but this is a place of ice." A pause, and she watched his face go hard as he stared into the pit. He said a word, hardly more'n a whisper, a word she didn't know. *"Iveran."* His hand went up to his chest, like he was grabbing at something under his tunic. "I will go find out what they search for."

Rora eyed him up. Obviously he could pass for a Northman, he was one after all. But that was part of what made her nervous. Everyone knew you couldn't trust a Northman, they were all animals in men's skins, bound to turn on you as fast as you could draw a blade. But Joros seemed to trust him, more'n he trusted any of the others—which wasn't saying much. Still, Rora'd gathered that the witch'd been around longer than Scal and didn't have near that amount of trust. That made sense, though you couldn't trust a madman, and there was no denying Anddyr was that. Northmen were said to be worse than madmen. "Joros won't like that," she said, "not without us reporting to him first. He said to come straight back."

She couldn't tell if he hadn't heard her or just chose to ignore her. "I will wait here until dark. You go back."

She'd tell Joros to have them move camp somewhere else. If Scal was like everyone said a Northman would be, and led all his brethren to come kill them in the night, Rora didn't plan on sitting around and waiting for him to do it. If he was worth the little bit of trust Joros gave him, well, then that was good for him, and he was hardy enough that some time wandering in the snow to find their new camp wouldn't do him much harm. If he wanted to stay up here and freeze, he was welcome to it. Rora started to shimmy backward, away from the edge of the pit.

"Rora." His voice stopped her. He was fidgeting at his throat, and finally pulled away the thick white cloak, letting let it slide across the ground to her. She raised her eyebrows, burying her fingers in the warm fur, and he shrugged. "It will mark me."

If he wanted to freeze even faster, that was his own business, too. She crept back, holding on to the cloak, and when she was far enough away to stand, she wrapped it gratefully around herself. She almost hoped he didn't die, or betray them, though either one was more likely than neither. He was a good enough sort, even if he was a Northman.

She was guided back to camp by a dull glow, and she felt a fire rising up in her to match it. She stomped into the camp, built in the shadow of the five most pathetic trees she'd ever seen, and then stomped on the sad little fire they'd built. Aro and Joros swore at her, the merra spit at her, and Anddyr cowered. "Just over that ridge," she growled, glaring at all of them in turn, "are a hundred fecking Northmen. No fire."

"But I'm cold," Aro said, snot dribbling from his nose over his upper lip like he was a kid again, "and hungry."

"No fire," she repeated.

"'The accursed shall fear the righteous flames,'" the merra quoted at her.

"Pathetic flames, more like," Rora snapped. "A mouse wouldn't've feared them."

A hand pawed at her leg. "I'm sorry," Anddyr whimpered, and looked up at her with the same puppy eyes as Aro.

"Tell me what you saw," Joros demanded.

"Whole bunch of Northmen digging into the ground. No sign of what they're looking for, but they're looking hard."

"Where's Scal?" the merra suddenly demanded.

Rora thought about not answering her, just because of all

the spitting, but Joros's face creased in a frown, and she could see the question in his eyes, too. "He stayed back. Said he was gonna find out what they're looking for." She spoke just to Joros then, trying to let her eyes do more of the talking than her words. "We should probably move camp. Just in case someone saw that fire."

Joros's eyes narrowed at her, and she knew she was being sized up just the same way she'd done to Scal. Finally he said, "She's right. Horses, everyone. We'll circle wide around the Northmen."

It wasn't pride that filled Rora, just the same sort of feeling she got from Tare or Garim or the Dogshead, the feeling of knowing you'd done right and been approved of. She still didn't much like Joros, but he was a man who knew what he was doing, there was no question of that.

So they rode dead east for a while, away from where Scal was probably still hunkered down, where all the other Northmen were digging for Parents only knew what. They turned north again when Rora suggested it, because Anddyr was in the middle of another one of his fits, and with Scal gone and Joros looking like he'd got lost in his thoughts, there wasn't really anyone else to play guide. So after a while she told them to stay put and ranged carefully out, making sure there wasn't any sign of Northmen nearby, and then they set up another cold camp, curling into miserable balls. Scal's fur cloak was big enough to cover her and Aro both, and they sat huddled together. Anddyr passed around hunks of near-frozen meat, but didn't keep any for himself.

Joros was still silent, hadn't said a word since they'd moved camp. Rora cleared her throat to get his attention and said,

"You know what they're looking for, don't you? All those Northmen."

"I may," he said, still seeming pretty distracted. "Anddyr. How long since we left?"

The witch glanced to the side, his lips moving like he was talking, but it was nothing Rora could hear. He looked back and said, "Forty-seven days."

It couldn't've been more than two weeks since she and Aro'd joined up with them, so they'd been on the road a while before that. Joros was nodding, talking to himself just like Anddyr did, and that almost made Rora smile. "They must have left directly, could have stayed on the main roads and moved much faster . . ."

"Who's they?" Aro demanded.

Joros gave him a withering look, but for once he seemed to be in a question-answering mood. "Some of my former compatriots. I don't know who. A number were sent out to find the . . . items Anddyr was able to track down."

"Former compatriots?" the merra repeated. "You renounced the mountain?"

"I did."

Her eyes narrowed, like she didn't quite believe it. "Why?" she demanded, but Joros waved her words away like they were smoke.

"What mountain?" Aro asked, but Rora touched his arm to hush him and ask a question of her own.

"This is the place where you figure out if we're useful or not, isn't it?"

"It is."

"Then you'd best tell us what we need to know."

The merra added, "Tell us all of it."

It was a dumb thing to ask, and Rora saw the same contempt on Joros's face. The head never told his pack *everything*. He did tell them some, though, enough to keep them from asking too many questions. Joros spoke straight to Rora and Aro, and though she knew he hated sharing any words, still he kept talking: "I would imagine you know of the Bound Gods." Aro snorted, but Rora's hand on his arm kept him from interrupting. "There is a group, the Fallen, dedicated to freeing the Twins and restoring them to power. I *was*"—and his eyes darted darkly over to Vatri—"a member of that group. Their purposes no longer suit me. They are, however, at a point in time where they may be very close to achieving their goal."

The merra laughed, the sound cutting through the snow and wind and words. "You're more a fool than I thought. The Twins can never be freed. They're destroyed, and buried."

"Buried, yes. But not destroyed. Gods cannot be killed, even by other gods."

"Their powers are gone," the merra went on, still laughing. "They're trapped for all of eternity. Doomed to watch the world they hate carry on while they dwindle."

"You're wrong," Joros said evenly, "about so much. You priests always are. There is a way to free them, and restore them. It can be done, and it will. The Fallen need only find them."

Vatri laughed again, eyes bright with mirth. She looked more horrible that way than she did frowning like she usually was. "Oh, I'm shaking. There's nothing more terrifying than a god with no limbs."

"You," Joros said, "are a fool. So sure of your invulnerability. I would almost"—and he gave a hard smile, the kind that didn't even touch his eyes, the kind of smile that made Rora hear *to the ends of the earth*—"be content to sit here and let happen what will, if only to see you proved wrong."

The merra smiled right back, as much a threat as his was. "I would gladly sit and wait with you for as long as it takes. My corpse will keep watch on the sun, even after all memory of the Twins has faded from the world."

"Perhaps it will."

"Enough," Rora said tiredly. She'd broken up enough pissing contents between Aro and the other boys in Dogshead Pack.

"I'll say nothing more," the merra said, turning away with a smirk. "I have no more words for a traitor."

Rora rubbed her hands over her eyes. It'd been too long since she'd gotten a good amount of sleep. "So what's the plan?" she asked Joros.

"We'll have to see what, if anything, Scal finds—"

"You think the Twins are buried there, do you?" Vatri interrupted.

Joros gave her a level look. "They just may be."

Again the merra laughed, long and loud.

Without a word, Joros pulled at the pouch on his belt, the one Anddyr always did his magic on, and tossed it to Vatri. She caught it clumsily, the flap falling open, and showing a flash of black. She pulled it out, a black chunk almost too big to fit in one hand. Rora couldn't figure out what it was, and the merra looked like she was having trouble, too. Then, all of a sudden, she started screaming, the black thing falling from her hands to roll in the snow.

Anddyr and Joros moved in the same moment. The witch to scoop up the black thing, Joros to clap a hand over the merra's mouth and cut off her screaming. She twisted away from him, disgust plain on her face, mixed in with raw horror. *"Don't touch me,"* she snarled, scrambling backward away from him. She looked like a cornered cat, hissing and desperate and ready to kill.

Aro stood up and grabbed the black thing from Anddyr, turning it back and forth in front of his face. She saw the moment he recognized what it was. His eyes went big as they could, face going white as the snow, and he dropped the black thing in shock.

It landed in front of Rora's feet, a big black chunk amid all the white snow, and she had to tilt her head back and forth a few times till she could figure out what it was. A knuckle, a nail, a little piece of sawed-off bone sticking out. A toe that was bigger'n her hand. Her stomach turned.

"Evil," the merra gasped, her face still twisted. "Abomination. Evil."

"What the hells is it?" Aro demanded. "Where'd it come from?"

Joros scooped the toe up off the ground, put it back into the pouch, and tucked it securely away. "It's a piece of a god, and it—and I—are the only things that can keep the Twins bound."

CHAPTER 27

There was little difference in night and day this far north, among the constant snows. Scal had not expected that. It was a strange thing, to be moving constantly through a swirl of gray. Worst when the winds blew whistling by. Screaming their rage. He was not sure, really, where was north. South. Up or down.

There was little wind, now. Enough to tug at his clothing. To whirl the snow into his eyes. No worse than he had ever dealt with.

Strangely, he missed the cloak he had given Rora. Not for heat. For the weight of it on his shoulders. The familiarity of it. One of the few things that had made it through more than one life.

Alone atop the ridge, he watched. Counted carefully. Twenty men, perhaps, at a time. He saw how they worked in shifts. Half of the workers leaving their places to go wake men who slept on hides in a sheltered space. The woken men would go to take the places of the men who now took the hide beds they had left. For a full shift he watched. Four hours, if he counted it right. Watched until the men who had been working as long as he had been watching woke the sleepers, calling them back to work.

Scal unbound his hair and scraped it down over the right side of his face. To hide the convict's cross that showed through his beard, that would mark him. There were beads, still, wound into his hair, and little bones. He had torn them out, long ago, after the first village where the men had pelted him with stones. The folk living in the northern reaches of Fiatera did not trust the Northmen. Scal had retrieved the beads and bones, though, where he had thrown them. It was not so easy to throw away the memories of a life. He had woven them back in, once he had grown big enough that men gave more thought to fighting him. When he could use his sword well enough to make any man who did not think carefully enough regret it. It was not so easy to be anything other than what life had made of him.

He knew he looked a Northman. It was the point, after all. Wagoneers and merchants would hire him because a Northman would strike fear in any contemplating the value of stolen wagons or goods. If he did not look the part he was meant to play, there would be no part for him.

In the blowing snow and gray light, Scal slipped away from the ridge.

He walked carefully. Circling wide. He could take his time. He had some hours. The noise came to him over the ice, soft, distant. Picks and axes chipping at ice and stone.

When he judged it was right, he turned, following the sounds of digging. Down the slanting, gentle slope that led into one side of the pit. More sound now, voices raised in tired jest. Speaking words he had not heard in years. The snow and the wind and the walls of the pit did strange things to the sounds. Bouncing and echoing and fading. Sounding one moment as if there was a man standing right next to him. The next as if that same man were shouting from miles and miles away. In that disorientation, Scal nearly tripped over a sleeping Northman.

It was the snow, the sound and the light. Impossible to get one's bearings. Scal beat a quick retreat. Circled wider, to make sure it would not happen again. When he drew close to the camp again, it was at a safe distance. At the edge of the sleeping place, but not close enough that the workers could see him either. There was a mound of snow, blown into shape by the unpredictable winds, and Scal sat behind it to wait. He could feel the cold. The icy ground could have been against his bare skin for all the difference his breeches made, but it hardly touched him. He could see, now, that some of the Northmen slept without furs, directly on the ice. It was the way of their people. The way of the North. Scal knew who he was, knew what blood ran through his veins. It was a thing he had accepted.

He counted the time so that he would not sleep. It had been a long time since he had slept much, but this, too, was a thing he had accepted. A man, truly, did not need so much sleep. A man alone, looking for work, sleeping in forests and fields, learned to sleep lightly or not at all. There were animals roaming at night, and brigands. So Scal counted, and he was only two counts off when the workers set down their tools and began to trudge to the sleeping place. When the sleepers rose and trudged the other way, Scal rose, too. Melted through the swirling snow to join their ranks. Just another Northman. Another blond face among all the others. He picked up a hammer, and began to pound through the snow and ice.

Little was spoken. It was hard work, this, and breath could be better spent. No one spoke to Scal. No one looked at Scal. Just another face. Just another worker.

"I can feel it, brothers. We are close."

His fingers slipped, suddenly loose around the haft of the hammer. It came free on the downswing, flying from his fingers to crash against the face of stone on which he was working. The eyes turned to him, he could feel them all on his back. He kept his face down, mumbled an apology as he retrieved the hammer. There was a snort, a suppressed laugh. No more.

And the voice from his last life went on, "Only a little longer. Then we will go home."

Scal paused in his work, feigned wiping at sweat that was not there. Turning his face to his sleeve, he looked over his shoulder.

There stood Iveran. Dressed all in white, as ever. Nearly hidden in the blowing snow. Shorter than Scal remembered. Though Iveran had always been short for a Northman, and Scal was much taller now. There was white streaked through his hair and beard, but little else had changed. There was still a white cloak hung from his shoulders, another snowbear that had given its life for the chieftain. The snowbear's head pulled up over Iveran's, bloody muzzle snarling. The same fearless feral grin mirrored below, teeth bared against the world.

Scal felt a child again. Lost, with no place or name that was his own. A boy on the verge of being a man. Blood of the North, gods of the south. A voice calling him little lad, another *ijka.* A Northern sword in his hand, and a knife in his boot with a chieftain's death promised to it. The bodies of a dead priest and a dead friend, the bodies of a stillborn child and the closest thing he had had to a mother. No clear answers. Only gray, swirling snow.

The hammer swung. Stone shattered.

A man must atone, Parro Kerrus had said, *for all the deeds in his life.*

The hammer swung. The hours passed. A hand touched his shoulder, briefly. Words of encouragement murmured against the wind. "Almost there. Dig deeper. Soon. Soon." Men faded into the snow to sleep. Apparitions appeared to take their places. Hammers fell. Picks clanged. Shovels dug. Axes screeched. "Just a little longer. My bones feel it. Home, soon. Dig a little longer."

"Iveran!"

The cry rang, pure and clean, echoes spiraling up and down through the rift. Heads turned, eyes seeking. Iveran hurried through the snow, legs taking him over scattered blocks of ice and stone to the man who stood leaning on his shovel, eyes bright. They spoke, and Iveran took the man's shovel, and he hurried off. "Dig!" Iveran barked to the rest of them, and they dug.

There came, at length, a woman. Stepping gingerly upon the ice, holding tightly to one of the two men who flanked her as her feet slid. They stood out sharply, those three dressed all in black, against the whirling snow. The woman more so, for the fiery hair on her head. She went to Iveran, and they spoke, and their smiles shone off the ice.

"Uisbure," Iveran called out. "Kettar. Isto. To me. The rest of you, go take your sleep. You have earned it."

There was no cheering, as Scal might have expected. He had forgotten, in some things, the way of the North. Tools were merely laid on the ground, and the Northmen turned to the sleeping place. Save for three. Two of them Scal knew, older versions of the men who had welcomed him roughly but honestly in his last life. He watched them, for a time, until standing would draw too much notice. He followed the others to sleep, but in the drifting snow he faded away and looped back. He would have liked to say he did it for Joros. That he did it to learn what he could, to earn the cets he had been paid. But Joros was far away in his mind. He was a child again, a boy not yet a man, and there was a space in his chest that had been empty for years. A need he could not name.

He could only get so close. There were few places to hide well in the dug-out pit. He drew as close as he could, concealed behind a block of stone and snow. They dug, the four Northmen. Iveran and Kettar and Uisbure, and the fourth whom he did not know. A man hardly older than Scal, white fur draped across his shoulders. They dug as the woman watched with her black-robed attendants. There was a hungry look their faces all shared.

He could not have said how long it took. He lost track of the minutes and hours, lost his count among the memories and the aching in his chest. It felt so open that he was surprised, each time, when his hand came away clean after touching the place over his heart. Time passed, shovels and axes chipping away at the stone and ice. The snowbear claw dug into Scal's palm, but he could not make his hand release it.

A good memory, Kerrus once had told him, *is a curse as often as it's a blessing. Pray, boy, that Metherra is kind enough to grant you short sight.*

Silence. Loud and ringing to his ears, that had become so used to the constant noise. A silence, split then by laughter. Words Scal could not hear, the woman pointing. Axes and shovels dropped to the ice, rumbling that was low and angry. The Northmen, turning.

Scal dropped low to the ground, huddling behind the shield of the rock. He prayed, silently but with feeling, to the Father that the Northmen would pass on the other side. Patharro was listening, or luck was with Scal. Uisbure passed first, swearing under his breath, followed by a scowling Kettar. Iveran and the other, Isto, walked together. Iveran's face was blank, betraying nothing. The younger man was full of fury, red points on his cheeks, fists clenched. The white on his shoulders, Scal could see now that he was closer, was a strip of snowbear fur. One enormous black-clawed paw dangling onto the man's chest. Scal's hand clenched. Around his snowbear claw, around his flamedisk.

They passed, and they did not see him.

The woman still stood over the place where they had been digging. Her men, now, had taken up the tools, struggling against the ice.

There was a pouch tied at Scal's belt, full of golden coins, more money than he had known there was in the world. It told him he should go closer. See what they were digging at, kill them if need be. Bring the knowing to Joros, who had brought him here just for this, perhaps.

The coins were quiet, though, near silent against the gaping in his chest.

He gave a brief glance to the two digging men. No more. Then he rose, shielded by the snow and the strange things it did to sound, and he followed the four men back toward a life he thought he had left behind.

Things were different, in the North. In Fiatera, the leader of a group such as this would have his own tent, guards posted to keep him safe, keep any from bothering him. That was not the way of the North. Iveran had a pallet, nothing more. No better than any of his men. He sat near a fire some of the others were beginning to build, Kettar and the man Isto to his sides.

The aching in Scal's chest drove him forward, the two pendants bouncing against the hole in him. Fire and snow, the two lives he had left behind. Belonging, truly belonging to neither, yet belonging more than he ever could in the life he lived now. So much had been taken from him. Some had been given back, and then taken again. It was a boy's hurt. A hurt that had never left him.

Scal reached out, fingers touching the white fur cloak. The man turned, eyebrows raised. No recognition, until Scal brushed back the hair from his right cheek. The convict's cross, the white scarred flesh standing ridged through his beard. Eyes widening, too many emotions flickering to follow or name. Mouth opening, shaping a single word. *Ijka*.

Softly, into the falling snows and crackling flames, Scal said, "I have *vasrista* to claim, Iveran."

Things moved quickly from there. A space was stomped out in the snow, a circle wide as two men laid heels to head. "You have grown, *ijka*," Iveran said with a roughness in his voice as Kettar took the sword from Scal's back. The sword he himself had given to Scal. "You look well. Strong." Scal could not look at the man he had loved and hated both, his eyes fixed into the snows.

"I will fight for you," the man Isto said to Iveran, eyes glaring.

There was a laugh, a sound that did not belong. The same laugh, once, had echoed through the blood and the ruins of Aardanel. "If there is to be a fight"—there was a question in the words, one meant for Scal, one he could give no answer to—"then I will do my own fighting. Perhaps I have *vasrista* of my own to claim."

There were words, words that should be said. Words that had bounced hollowly within Scal for all the years since the snows. Perhaps since the first snows, even. He had said some of those words, though, a claim for *vasrista*, and they had silenced all the other words within him. There was nothing more to be said, now. Words, lost among the snows and the ice.

"The weapon is yours to choose," Kettar said to Iveran. It was his right, as the one challenged. Hands were most common, for a simple challenge of honor. The blades were saved for the deeper challenges. One weapon with which to fight the other man. When the blades came out, only one of the men would walk from the ring.

The eyes were on Iveran, all of them. One pair only, fixed on Scal. Softly the chieftain said, "It will be swords, I think."

There was some outcry, some cheering. Little enough to matter. Mostly, there was silence. A waiting, a breath held. Kettar gave Scal his sword, for the second time.

"Must this be how we end, *ijka*?"

Scal had grown since Valastaastad, grown taller than Iveran. He could look clear over the other man's head. He found words, not the ones that should have been spoken, yet ones that needed to be: "It must."

And so it began. A circle formed by stomping feet, ringed by angry, excited men. Iveran at one side, Scal at the other, forced now to see him. To meet his eyes. To see the pain there, and the love.

Love your enemies, Parro Kerrus had told him, long years ago, in another life, *for they teach you what you'll never become.*

CHAPTER 28

Time crept by, measured in the slow fall of flecks of snow, in the steam of air that leaked out from noses and mouths, in the suspicion growing in three sets of eyes. They wouldn't stop staring at Joros, the merra with her ever-present anger but something new in her eyes as well, the boy-twin with his simple confusion and fear, and the girl with more intelligence in her eyes than he'd given her credit for. They watched him in silence, until they began to realize, one by one, how much time had gone by.

Rora, with her smart eyes and coarse voice that didn't match, was the first one to speak the new feeling rolling through their camp, covering the suspicion like a blanket of snow: "It's been too long."

"It has," the merra agreed quickly, her glare turning to Rora. "You never should have left him alone."

They were tense, all of them, and with good reason. The North was not a hospitable place, and their only guide out was, to all appearances, missing. Returning the merra's glare, Rora stood and brushed the snow from her breeches. "I'll go back for him."

Behind Joros, Anddyr made a choked little sound. Joros held up his hand to stop her. "I believe we *all* will go. It may be that something more important than we realize is happening."

Aro whined about it—it seemed as though he always found something to whine about, more useless than the boy-twin inside Raturo—but his whining stopped when his sister pointed out that if he didn't want to come, he could stay here *alone* and watch the horses. After that, they all moved in silence. The horses were reluctant to move, but enough of Joros's whip got his moving, and the others trudged on after.

Rora led them, eyes narrowed into the blowing snow. There was no knowing what sense guided her, but at some point she held up one hand to halt them, another finger held over her lips for silence. They all dismounted, staked the horses in a huddled ring. Rora led them on hands and knees up a slope, motioning them all to keep low. "This is where I left him," she said softly, and then her eyes grew wide. Drawing up next to her on his stomach, Joros soon saw why.

He had expected to see the pit as she'd described it. North-men crawling all over it, constantly digging. Instead, the Northmen had formed a press, the mass of them gathered around two of their number locked in combat.

"*Scal!*" the merra hissed, and Joros could hear the fear in her voice. It was one of the first emotions besides disdain he'd heard from her. No wonder, with the only person in the world who could tolerate her currently one too-slow movement away from losing his head.

"Idiot," Joros spat. He had no time to waste on fools, and if the Northman had gotten himself captured, he was certainly a fool. His eyes roved around the pit, an ancient place, perhaps made by men long forgotten, or shaped by the strange-swirling winds and melting snow—or perhaps by a forceful impact centuries ago. At the far end, surrounded by three high cliffs of stone and ice, three forms still dug, stark against the snow in their black robes. There was a strange twisting in Joros's stomach at a flash of red hair above one of those robes. "Stay here," he said to the others. "Anddyr and I have business to attend to." He fixed his eyes on Rora, flicked them at her brother as an afterthought. "I may have need of you two at a moment's notice. Anddyr will fetch you here, if necessary." He turned to his mage, then let his eyes drift back into the pit, to that damned point of red. The easiest way down would be to backtrack to the horses, circle around to where the Northmen were at the mouth of the pit, and slip around them while they were all distracted. That would take time, though, and there was a pounding in Joros's breast that said there was little enough time to waste. "Get us down there fast, Anddyr."

Since he'd burned the town, the mage had become unfailingly dutiful in taking his skura. His control was renewed, and his subservience, so Joros was pleased to see the mage already beginning to weave a spell. He recognized the cloaking first, that infinitely useful little spell. If anyone was persistent about looking, Anddyr had explained the first time he'd cast a cloaking, they'd be spotted in a second, but the Northerners fighting should prove a good enough distraction to keep persistent eyes away. When Rora's surprised swearing told Joros the cloaking had settled over him and the mage, Anddyr began another spell, fingers moving too quick to follow, so much of a distraction that Joros was taken entirely by surprise when the mage pushed him over the edge of the cliff.

Joros fell, the cold air whistling by fast enough to snatch the breath from his lungs, to keep him from getting out a good scream. The ground had seemed so far below from the top of the cliff, but now there was almost no space between it and Joros. He could pick out individual stones, guess which chunk of ice would crack his skull open. Screwing his eyes shut, he vowed to curse the mage with his dying thought. Yet it was that briefly glimpsed red hair that stuck in his mind.

The impact knocked the breath from him. Despite himself, his eyes flew open, determined to witness each horrid moment of his death. The ground was there, looming close— but no closer. He was stopped perhaps two handspans above it, something stretched around him like an unseen hand holding him safe. He wasn't dead, and he could move, and as Anddyr landed beside him, all of it made Joros irrationally angry. He scrambled to his knees—more difficult than it should have been, for the mage's invisible barrier moved beneath him like a blanket thrown over water—and fought toward the mage, growling curses. He saw the panic in Anddyr's eyes, but didn't see the mage's hands begin to move again. The barrier fell away beneath Joros, sending him sprawling to the cold ground. It was a gentler fall than it would have been from the cliff, but that did nothing to improve his mood.

"It's easier to fix the landing!" Anddyr squealed, scrabbling away as Joros rose. "The falling is the hard part. Please, cappo, I'm sorry . . ."

Joros stood over the mage, glaring down at the pathetic creature. There was no room in him to hate the mage more than he already did. His last thought, when he'd been convinced of his death, had been of red hair. The mage's punishment could wait.

The sounds of fighting—sword clanging against sword, cheering and shouting—were louder inside the pit, echoing strangely off the cut walls. Joros himself had laid the groundwork for recruiting this Northern tribe, sending shadow after shadow into the wastes to find a tribe both vicious and motivated by hard Fiateran coin. Clearly, the work of those long years had been stolen from him, too, bent for the benefit of another. He was almost glad his idiot Northman had stirred them all into a useless frenzy. Joros turned from the noise and stepped over Anddyr, moved toward the far end of the pit, where shovel and pick against stone and ice were softer sounds, calling to him. He and the mage moved like shadows over the ice, unseen, silent. The three came into sight, black-robed like Joros, their backs to him, two bent over and working at the ice, the third watching with a waterfall of hair the color of fire.

Joros was not a man given over to emotions. He was strong, stoic, staid. Anger, though, was not an emotion—it was a driving force, a thing to propel him forward in life, to make him great. The anger swelled in him now, always just below the surface, but this wasn't a pure anger. It was touched with something he had no name for, and that alone gave more breath to the anger.

His shortsword didn't come quietly from its sheath, the sound of it making one of the preachers turn, enough that the sword biting into his neck turned his head obscenely around like an owl's. The blade stuck in the suddenly limp body, and

Joros had to fight to yank it free. It gave the other preacher time to lift his shovel as a weapon, but his darting eyes couldn't see through the cloaking. His sword drawing a spray of blood as it finally let go the first man's neck, Joros brought the blade beneath the raised shovel and into the man's stomach, twisted, pulled it smoothly out. The man screamed, fell, clutching at the hole in his gut. Joros made a sign to Anddyr, who let the cloaking slip away.

Dirrakara's face was a mixture of horror and shock, eyes huge in her head. "Hello, love," Joros said levelly, the cold of his anger driving him forward. He took a step toward her, around the half-dug hole where the dead man and the dying man sprawled. She scrabbled at her hip, pulled out a knife to hold before her with both hands. Joros's sword was barely longer than his forearm, but that knife looked sad, pathetically ineffective. The thing that wasn't anger gave a twinge, and Joros shoved it down viciously, refusing to acknowledge it. There was only the anger, and his goals, and nothing would stand between them. The world would burn in the fire of his anger, if it came to it. There was no room for mercy. He took another step forward, Dirrakara stumbling back. "What have you found, hmm?"

"How . . ." She couldn't seem to compose more than the one word, her lips parted as she stared at him. There was always so much emotion in her.

"You've been busy, I see." She must have traveled hard to have gotten here so soon, and to coordinate with the Northman tribe so quickly, but she could never be faulted for being inefficient. "Thank you, for doing my work for me."

"How . . ." The knife shook in her hands. She'd never looked at him with such fear before. He knew his face was still a mess, littered with the fading folds and ridges of burn-scars, but he didn't think that was what put the fear in her eyes.

"You think you know me." He didn't know where those words came from or how they snuck out past his lips, but they spewed forth, propelled by the anger and the thing that wasn't. "You never knew me." She would have feared him long ago, if she had. He stepped forward again and she jabbed the knife toward him, more a spasm than anything. "We could have been great." Joros caught it easily, the fingers of his left hand wrapping around the blade. He felt the bite of it, but dimly, the anger running hot through his veins and pushing the pain aside. "You should have trusted me." Disjointed words, boiling up with the thing that danced with his anger. One hand still around her knife, his blood leaking warm down his wrist, Joros brought his other hand up, raising his sword so that its tip rested beneath Dirrakara's chin. "You should never have left me." The anger screamed for her blood, but he pressed gently, lifting her chin with the point of his sword so that her fear-wide eyes met his, and there was nothing else in the world. "You should never have loved me."

Finally, she found her words. They came out a whisper, her throat careful against the bare blade so close. "I wasn't wrong," she said, "not in any of it."

A twist of his hand pulled the knife from her fingers, flung it aside. Dripping his own blood that steamed in the cold air, Joros raised his hand to wrap it around her throat.

"Cappo!" Anddyr's voice rang out high, startling Joros so badly his sword nearly pierced through Dirrakara's skin. He had forgotten about the mage, forgotten the search, forgotten everything but her. He held her by the throat still, not hard enough to crush, as he turned to face the mage.

"What has our friend found in the ice?" His voice was rougher than he would have liked, and he let that feed his anger. Anddyr made an inarticulate little noise, and Joros walked to his side, pulling Dirrakara after him.

Anddyr had dragged the bodies of the two preachers from the hole and cleared away the loose snow and debris. The hole that the preachers had dug was smeared with their blood now, a red sheen already freezing over, but it was still possible to see, so very clearly, what they had been chipping carefully around.

There were two faces there, swallowed by the ice, skin desiccated and dry and flaking. Two heads, pressed together, one with long brittle hair, each face bigger than a man's could possibly be. All the old stories said the Twins had been giants among men.

And thus did Fratarro shatter upon the bones of the earth . . .

Joros's heart thumped in his breast, slow, steady. This was it. Finally. "Anddyr . . ."

The mage was already moving, fingers weaving so that heat radiated from his hands. His face was strained, he was likely close to the end of his power, but he wouldn't stop so long as he could keep doing *something*. He knew better.

The ice faded slowly, clinging to the dry flesh it had held for so long. A neck, and then another. More of the long hair, splayed out in a halo. A shoulder, an arm. Another arm, holding. A chest, a third arm, a hip. Legs, three, four. Two bodies, ancient, wrapped one around the other, larger than Joros, larger than men could be.

Over the ice, drifting with the sounds of fighting, a shouting began, voices raised in unfamiliar words.

There were two bodies, with four arms and four legs.

. . . his limbs flung to the far horizons.

In the silence above the hole, above the two bodies that could not be the Bound Gods, the distant screaming gave voice to the fury within Joros.

Anddyr made a choked sound. "It's not them," he whispered, and then flinched away, though Joros stood still as ice.

It was the mage who had led him here, led all of them here; it was Anddyr who had been wrong. Yet he was only a tool, and a broken one at that. It was no real surprise that a broken tool should prove false. He could turn his anger on a person who had performed only according to his own nature . . . or he could turn it to one truly deserving. There was a deeper hurt, here, than being wrong about the Twins.

Joros tightened his hand around Dirrakara's throat, his own blood dripping down her neck, and when he looked at her there was only the anger, burning pure like a furnace-flame, consuming the thing that wasn't anger. The anger would lead him, guide him, if he was strong enough to grab it with both hands and hold on to the bright flame of it.

CHAPTER 29

I t was the dumbest thing she'd ever seen, two men trying to kill each other while everyone else just stood there watching. The merra was cursing steadily under her breath—with phrases even Rora was impressed to hear—as she watched the fighting, her hands clenching around each other.

It'd only been a few minutes since Anddyr and Joros had disappeared into the air, but time felt like it was crawling by. It always felt that way when things were going on around you that you weren't doing anything about. It was one of the feelings Rora hated most. It wasn't helplessness, it was uselessness, and that was the worst.

Not that Scal wasn't handling himself well. He was bigger than the man he was fighting, but slower, too. It'd twisted her head, at first, to see the other man wearing a furry white cloak—she'd thought Scal'd shrunk, until she remembered his cloak was over her shoulders. Must be a Northern thing, those white cloaks. She didn't know how long they'd been fighting before she and the others had come up to watch, but she could tell they were both getting tired. They were a good match, that much was clear. She knew how it'd go. One of them would slip soon enough. It was what always happened in a fight like this, one of you got tired first. And because they were so matched, the other one wouldn't hesitate. Rora didn't much like the thought of sitting around and just watching Scal die, but there wasn't much she could do. It'd be stupid, risking her own neck for someone she barely even liked. You took care of yourself, that was the first rule in the Canals, the most important rule no matter what the packheads might say.

She looked over to see how Vatri was handling it all, since she seemed to have a liking for Scal, but the merra was gone.

There was a choking noise next to her, and Rora looked over to see Aro white-faced and pointing. *Down*. She craned her neck over the edge of the ridge and saw a yellow point skittering among the ice of the cliff.

If they were a pack, this little group Joros'd assembled, Rora knew that the merra was the expendable one. Joros didn't even want her along, he wouldn't care if she died. And to a point, Scal was expendable enough. He was a fist, a bruiser, and there were always more of those to find. A fist was only useful so long as he could keep fighting, and after that point he was less than useless. Joros'd left Scal to whatever stupid trouble he'd got himself into, so he didn't much seem to care what happened to the Northman neither. You did what your packhead thought was best, that was the second rule in the Canals, and even if Rora didn't know why, Joros seemed to need her and Aro for something. They weren't so expendable.

Down among the Northmen, she could see all the swords and knives and axes. Not new weapons, not by a long ways, but she knew they'd be plenty sharp. Men like them, trained fighters, they always kept an edge on their weapons. And the merra, halfway down the cliff now, it wouldn't take more'n one good swing to cut her in half.

In the Canals, you took care of yourself first, and did what you were told second. But there was another rule in the Canals that came in between the first and second ones, a rule that didn't ever get talked about. Between taking care of yourself and listening to the packhead, whenever you could, you took care of the rest of the pack. There were people the packhead could stand to lose, but that didn't mean you had to sit by and let it happen.

And if this group was her pack now, pretty soon she'd be watching about half her pack die and doing nothing about it.

She swore, using some of the words Vatri'd been using because they were so nicely descriptive, and swung to Aro. "You stay put, y'hear? Move one fecking hair and I take your whole head off." He nodded, wide-eyed, and stayed put as Rora swung over the edge of the cliff.

It wasn't much different from climbing down into the Canals, when it came down to it. The hand- and footholds weren't as clean cut, the ice was slipperier than bricks even after a good storm, and it was a longer climb, sure, but Rora'd had years of climbing down into the Canals fast as she could. Vatri'd got a good start on her, but the merra wasn't much of a climber, that was clear. Kept slipping or stopping, holding on tight to the ice like she was afraid of falling. Rora could just about see her regretting her choice, and every other choice that had led up to her clinging to an ice wall high above the ground. It didn't take too long for Rora to near catch up to her, just a few lengths above the ground, but that was when the cheering started.

Rora twisted around, saw all the Northmen waving their arms and weapons. From as high up as she still was, she could see down into the middle of the ring. Scal was on his back, tripped, scrabbling backward toward his sword. He wouldn't be fast enough. The other Northman had his sword lifted up in both hands, point aimed down right at Scal's heart, his face twisted up. Vatri screamed—Scal's name, just once, loud enough to ring off the ice louder'n all the cheering.

It distracted the smaller Northman for just a second, but that was all it took. Scal's hand moved, and then there was suddenly a little knife in his opponent's throat, blood spouting. The man's sword clattered onto the ice as he scrabbled at his neck. Faintly, Rora could hear his gurgling. Then it was drowned out by more screaming, raw fury, as all the Northmen surged in toward Scal.

He was already on his feet, holding a sword—his, or the other Northman's, it didn't matter, it was a blade. And then there wasn't any more standing and watching. There was just fighting, and Scal was going to die.

Rora pushed herself off the ice, dropped for a bit, rolled over her shoulder as she landed. There was a twinge in one leg as she sprang up to her feet, and she knew there'd be a big bruise on her shoulder in no time, but she didn't let those slow her down. She pulled her knives out, the long one with the broken blue stone and a plainer, shorter one Tare'd given her after her first contract. She started forward, toward all the huge, hulking Northmen who had their backs to her, and used a small person's best defense against a tall one: started slashing at the backs of legs, knees and ankles when she could get them, anything to slow or immobilize. Tare'd always told her to avoid fights like this, where bodies were pressed so close together you could hardly get any room to move an arm. Tare'd taught her how to fight a few people at a time—hells, once she'd had to fight off five Rats in an alley—but she wasn't used to this sort of fighting. It helped, though, being short. She'd never've thought she'd be thankful for it. She slipped in between the big bodies, hamstringing as she went, carving her way toward the center of the ring.

The first body she tripped over was the Northman Scal'd been fighting, dressed all in white with a little bone knife in his throat. Rora didn't give the body more'n a glance before righting herself and pushing forward again. There were more bodies littered on the ground here. Scal'd been busy. She still couldn't see him around all the big Northmen, but she had to think they wouldn't still be fighting forward if he was down and dead. It was hopeful, in a way.

And then someone crashed into her from behind, sending her toppling over. She landed half over a dead Northman, her face pressed into his spilled guts, and a weight lying across her back. She started struggling, kicking out with her legs, swinging her knives backward, anything to get free. Yellow cloth covered her head, and Vatri hissed in her ear, "Stay down!" Then there was an inhuman roaring, and the merra's scream ringing in her ear as she pressed Rora down into the dead man.

It got real quiet, after, or maybe all the sound was just drowned out by the echoes in Rora's ears. The merra was dead weight on top of her, not moving. Rora rolled and pushed up, shoving the merra off her back, and then paused on her hands and knees, gaping.

All the men who'd been fighting a second ago, stomping over dead men to get at the one Northman, were all down now, not a muscle moving. All down like dead men, except for the one still standing in the middle, his sword held up to block a blow that wasn't going to fall anymore. Scal looked over at Rora, the only other person moving, their eyes meeting over all the bodies. The place was quiet as a crypt, and maybe it was one now.

Rora turned to the merra. She was as unmoving as all the Northmen, but Rora pressed her hand against the side of Vatri's neck and there was still a thump there, under all the hard, ridged skin. "She's still alive," she said, expecting Scal to be at her side. He wasn't, though. He was just standing in the same place he had been, his sword hanging down and dripping blood on the ground, staring down at all the Northmen lying around like rag dolls. He was covered in blood, head to foot, and there was no knowing how much of it was his. Rora gave the merra a few slaps across the face, but it didn't wake her up. Muttering to herself, Rora stood up and picked her way over the bodies to Scal. "Hey," she said, but he didn't answer. His eyes were somewhere far off, somewhere she couldn't reach. She stretched up on her toes, reached up high as she could, and gave her arm a good swing. He reacted to the slap the way the merra hadn't, his eyes blinking and finally focusing on her, his hand reaching up to touch his cheek. "I need your help with the merra," she said when she was sure she had his attention.

He nodded, like his mind was still off wandering, but he wiped his sword clean on the nearest body and sheathed it over his shoulder, following her back to the spot of yellow. He moved slow, like he was walking through a dream, like he expected all the Northmen to get back up and start fighting again.

"She did this?" he asked. His voice was still the normal rumble, but it sounded different, somehow. Rora couldn't put a finger on it, not with her head spinning like it was.

"She must've. What'd *you* do, to make 'em all attack like that?"

He shook his head, avoiding her eyes. He didn't show emotion much, and Rora was a little lost to see it now. It didn't help that she couldn't really figure out what emotion he was finally showing either. He was a hard one to read, and he didn't give any kind of answer to the question. When they got to Vatri, it was like he put on a mask, his eyes getting sharp like normal, his face going flat and smooth as a slab of cut stone.

They hunkered down together next to the merra, and Scal lifted her up so that one of his hands was supporting her head, and with the other hand pulled the waterskin from his belt. It was as covered in blood as the rest of him, some of it dripping down onto the merra's face with the water he squirted out. It worked better'n the slapping Rora'd tried, because Vatri's eyes fluttered open, even if they didn't seem to focus on anything. The water dripped down around her gasping mouth, faint pink trails where it touched Scal's blood. "What did you do?" he asked her.

"Not me," the merra said weakly, and one of her hands lifted up to touch her chest. That didn't make any kind of sense to Rora, but it seemed like it was enough for Scal, since he gave a small nod. Vatri started pushing herself up, trying to sit. She shook her head, like she was trying to clear out something inside it. "We should go. They'll wake up soon."

"Then they are not dead?"

"No. Just . . . sleeping."

Scal stood, pulled Vatri to her feet. The merra swayed, held on to Scal's shoulder to keep from falling.

"Why am I not also sleeping?" Scal asked.

The merra reached out to tap a finger against his chest. "You have the Parents' protection," she said, and then her mouth stretched in a weird way. It took Rora a moment to realize it was supposed to be a smile. "I told you, I didn't do this. I *also* told you they have a particular interest in you."

"She must've hit her head," Rora said, but neither of them even seemed to hear her.

"What happened here?" the merra asked Scal, motioning to all the Northmen, and then grimaced. "I mean . . . before me, what happened? Why did they attack you?"

Scal frowned, and Rora expected him not to give her an answer either. Turned out he was just taking a long time to talk like he always did, like he was thinking his words over five times before he said them. "I did a thing that needed to be done, but should not have been," he finally said. His eyes drifted across the ground and Rora followed them to where they stopped on the Northman with the little knife in his throat. "It was a thing that was not the way of the North. I"— and he shook his head, his eyes leaving the dead man and going back to Vatri's face—"am not truly of the North."

Rora'd never felt more invisible, or less like she wanted to be somewhere. She looked up to the edge of the cliff where she'd come from, saw Aro's head poking over, his arms sticking out, one waving and the other pointing deeper into the pit. She cleared her throat to get Scal and Vatri's attention, pointed the same way Aro was. "Joros's that way," she said. "He might need some help."

And then there was a scream, echoing down from the way Rora's finger pointed. Rora looked at Scal and he looked back, and something passed between them—something that was shared by people who were used to *doing* even after they thought they couldn't move anymore. It was a look, a kind of test, that said something like *If we both go do this, we'll each have to do less.* A silent sort of agreement between people who were used to cleaning up the stupid messes others made. So Scal scooped Vatri up and held her over his shoulder, and he was right at Rora's side as they jogged deeper into the pit.

CHAPTER 30

There was a thing that kept a man going, after he should have rightly dropped. Once, Scal had seen a man fight with a dozen wounds, his own blood staining his battered armor as he fought. When the last bandit had fallen, the wounded man had stopped, looked around, and dropped. Dead at the very instant of victory. As long as there were things to be done, a man could force himself to do them. To push aside pain so raw it made a breath of wind feel like a thousand knives. To push aside the thinking, the thoughts that could make a mind or a heart crumble.

Later. There was screaming. There was another thing to be done, yet.

The witch-man knelt in the snow before a shallow hole, his hands scraped bloody as he pulled out things half frozen. There was a small pile on the ground next to him. One large piece, blackish-brown, bent in the middle. It was, Scal saw when he got closer, a giant's arm. There were two bodies nearby, newly dead, still steaming in the cold air.

Beyond, Joros knelt atop a third body. Scal guessed that she had been the one to scream, though she was screaming no longer. Joros's hand lifted, a shortsword in his fist whose tip was dripping blood.

Scal set Vatri upon the ground near the witch-man, told her softly to stay there, spoke to Rora with his eyes. She was competent. She knew how these things were done. She knelt down next to Anddyr, gently touching his arm. She would take care of him, and so Scal turned to Joros.

He was not a small man. Heavy with his age and too little activity. Tall enough, for a Fiateran. One hand, grasping him by the back of his clothes, was enough to lift him off the woman. Deposit him struggling on the ice. Pull the sword from his hand. Then Scal looked to the woman.

She was dead, well dead, a wide hole above her heart where the sword had gone in more times than Scal could guess. Joros had not aimed well, with the blows. Her chest was full of holes, her black robe blacker with blood. She stared sightlessly into the gray sky.

Scal did not like the mutilation of corpses. A dead thing should be left to whatever peace there was in death. *The dead have earned what little honor we can give them,* Parro Kerrus had told him. Before death had touched his own life, Iveran had said, *A dead man is nothing. Leave him, and let him rot.*

Joros's fist pounded against his back, wordless rage pouring from his mouth. One of Scal's hands, again, was enough to knock him to the ground. It left a print, the image of Scal's hand marked in other men's blood. Holding his reddened jaw, Joros gaped up at Scal. He was not, Scal knew, a man used to being hit, for all the hitting he himself did.

"This thing you did," Scal said softly, motioning to the woman's body with the other man's sword, "it is not a good thing. You will not do it again." He threw the sword at Joros's feet. Waited. If the man moved to threaten, he could reach his own sword fast enough. Joros did not move, though. The glare remained on his face. The raw fury, and the hatred. But he did not reach for his sword.

A laugh broke across the ice. High and wild. "I told you!" the witch-man cried out, and laughed again. "I knew it! Cappo! Oh, Cappo, come see!"

Joros stood, still glaring, and sheathed his sword. Pushed past Scal, the woman forgotten. Over her, Scal murmured, "Be at peace in the Mother's arms. Find shelter at the side of the Father." Then he, too, went to see what the witch-man had found.

There had been two giants in the hole, long dead, a cocoon made of their entwined bodies. The witch-man had torn them apart. Shattered the dusty bones. Ripped the dry flesh. Opened them like a cracked egg to show what lay within. All that was left, now, were the heads and the torsos, and the black thing curled between their chests.

"Abomination," Vatri said softly. She was distant still, since the thing she had done. He could see the fire returning to her eyes, but slowly.

"I found it," the witch-man crowed. Joros clapped him on the shoulder. Laughed. Coming from him, Scal could hardly recognize the sound.

Together Joros and the witch-man lifted the black thing from the hole. They struggled with the weight of it, the size of it, as big as Scal's chest. No one helped, or even offered. Scal did not want to be any nearer to it. Finally they laid it on the ground. Began pulling at parts of it. Uncurling it, slowly. Carefully. Making it nearly as big as Scal from foot to chin. When they had done, it was a hand. Blackened, and bigger than a hand could be, but a hand.

Eyes bright, Joros looked to the witch-man. "What do you think, Anddyr? Burn it?"

Vatri made a choking noise. "You're going to destroy it?"

"I told you." Joros smirked at her, the mirth still in his eyes. "I've sworn to keep them bound. With one Twin broken, they can never be whole, and the best way to ensure they stay that way is by destroying Fratarro piece by piece. The toe is all I need to find the remaining pieces—like calls to like. I don't intend to leave *this*"—and he tapped his foot to the great hand—"for any more of my old friends to find."

"I didn't . . ." Vatri closed her mouth. Frowning. Thoughtful. Tried to speak again, stopped. Finally she managed, "Fire. Fire is the way."

Scal did not understand any of it. He decided he did not want to. There was a feeling, deep in his stomach and his chest, that he could not name. He did not like to look at the hand. Instead he watched Vatri. Watched the thoughts whirl behind her eyes, the distant-seeing pupils. She was returning to herself, after the thing she had done, but her eyes still moved strangely. She would need watching. Need to stay awake. He had seen men die, after a hit on the head, after their eyes had gone strange. Talking, laughing, drinking, and then sleeping and dead. It was not the same with her, for she had not hit her head, but still she would bear watching.

The witch-man tried to make his spells, waving his fingers and hands, but he stopped. "I can't," he whimpered.

Joros would have been angry, a different time. He was not now. "Scal," he called. Sounded almost happy. "We need a fire."

He looked to Vatri, and she looked back. The strangeness was in her eyes still, and something else. She nodded, and so Scal pulled out his flint. He did not like having to get so close to the hand. The skin of it was hard, did not catch fire easily. There was no kindling. Only sparks falling onto the black palm, dancing for a moment, flickering out. Stars, falling in the night sky. Finally one landed and caught. The tenderest of flames, gasping against the unyielding skin. *Fire,* Parro Kerrus had said, *is the most powerful thing there is in this world.* It caught, and it held. Quickly, then, it began to eat. Scal backed away, to Vatri's side. She watched the glowing flames. The same way she always did. Searching in them, for the voice of her goddess. The fire rose, stronger. Grown fat on its feast.

"It's done," she said softly, though the flames still rose against the gray sky. Caught the falling snow and turned it to smoke. "We should go. I don't know how much more time we have."

"For what?" Joros demanded.

"Until the Northmen wake up."

There was too much to be explained. Too much Scal did not know, or understand. Time to leave, that he knew. That was a thing he could do. He rose, and he did not wait. He walked. Heard light footsteps following. Rora, it would be. Careful with her feet, careful with her words. Behind he could hear Vatri, trying to explain to Joros. Failing, because the words were rattled in her brain. The witch-man spoke softly to himself, the way he always did. Scal led them wide around where the Valastaa Clan lay sleeping among their dead. He did not want to see them again. Silently he prayed for them, for all the men he had known and killed this day. It was vengeance. Justice. Parro Kerrus and Brennon could rest now, be peaceful at the Father's side. It was a strange thing, though. He could not see Brennon in his mind's eye. When he tried to think of his friend's face, he saw only a still babe burning in his dead mother's arms.

He hurt, in every way a man could hurt. Later. There were things still that must be done.

Rora came to his side, took the snowbear cloak from her shoulders. Held it out to him. His hand reached for it. Stopped. He shook his head. "Keep it," he said, though he could not have said why. She put it back over her shoulders, the end of it dragging along the ground behind her.

They found her brother at the edge of the pit, at the top of the slope leading into its depths. He held the horses, looking too proud of such a simple thing, and there was wonder in his eyes. "I thought you'd be dead for sure," he said as Scal took Hevnje's reins. He did not answer. Simply mounted, though his leg could hardly hold his weight. Began to ride. He could hear the the five others following, their voices mixing together. "I told you to stay up there." "I knew it, I found it, right all along . . ." "The Parents work through me." "How's any of that possible?" "Anddyr has located four more." He did not want to listen. Time to leave.

The snow fell. It always did, and always would. Gray, this deep in the North. Sometimes a lighter gray, sometimes a darker. The sun did not truly rise or set here. It circled in the sky behind the gray snowy clouds, endlessly chasing the moon, but was never gone. There was always snow, and always gray. Little else. Little enough else to keep a man thinking. To keep his thoughts from going to the places he could not let them. Not yet. He was not done, yet.

Vatri rode next to him, after a time had passed. She startled him from a half-sleeping daze, though she did not seem to notice it. "I think I know now," she said. "Why Metherra brought me to you. You were meant to lead me here. For this. A black coal against the white . . ." She stopped. He could see her trying to sort the words. To make them come out right, when she was not even sure of the right way to spin them. "I thought he was evil, thought he was trying to free the Twins. That's what the preachers do, I didn't think he was any different. But now . . . I think he's doing the right thing, truly. He's trying to keep the Parents safe. Maybe not for the right reasons, or in the right ways, but . . . a good thing done for bad reasons is still a good thing, isn't it? He *knows* things, Scal. He says the Fallen really can free the Twins. I can't . . . not help. To stop them, I mean. And I think that's why Metherra showed you to me. If I hadn't found you, I never would have known about any of this. I never would have been able to *do* anything, and now I can. I can really help. Scal? Can you hear me?"

The words were trapped in him. Hard in his throat. So many things in all his lives he had never said. Too late, now. Always too late. There was a breaking here. A fracture in a slab of ice, spidering slowly but unstoppably outward. There was an ending waiting for him, somewhere. A fourth life he had built, in all these years. A life he had not liked. Not been able to change. The snowbear claw still hung around his neck, next to the flamedisk of the Parents. It would end soon, this life. Perhaps it already had. He did not think this was a new life he was in now. It did not feel like a fifth beginning. It was a space between. Another wandering. Another searching, in the end-less snow.

They camped that night, the moon a pale shimmer beyond the falling snow. Vatri collected twigs to build a little fire, with Joros helping. Rora said it was a bad idea. They were not so far from the pit. The Northmen might come looking for them. Her eyes went to Scal for support. He saw them, saw the plea there. He could not answer it. His throat was closed, holding back all the things that would come spilling forth if he did not hold them tight.

"The Tashat Mountains, I think," Joros said. "That one's the closest. We may be too late for any of the others, but we'll have to try."

"If they find the other pieces, though," Vatri asked, "won't they be able to free the Twins?" Her voice sounded clearer. The words coming more steadily. She would not need watching for much longer.

"Perhaps, but they'll be much weaker than their full poten-tial. Weak enough that, even unbound, they could still be destroyed. Fratarro is the key—in breaking him, the Parents broke both their children. It's only a matter of keeping them broken . . ."

A face loomed before Scal's eyes. Crinkles around the mouth, between the eyebrows. Concern, yet also a distance. "Hey," Rora said, touching his shoulder, "are you all right?"

They had stopped. There were things to do yet, but they were far-off things. Things that were too far away to see in his mind's eye. They were not things to keep a man going beyond his time. They had stopped. There would be no more pushing off. No more later. Nothing left to stop the inevitable. The walls dropped, and the world rushed in to break against him. There was too much pain. Body and heart, and it was too much. Scal was a simple man, and there was only so much a man could do.

"Gods, he's bleeding!"

There was a flurry, snow and hands and warmth. Peeling back the layers of his clothes, the layers of his self, to set the cold Northern wind against his flesh and all the wounds piercing it. Too much. It was more than a man could take. Scal closed his eyes, and there was a hope in him that beyond the snows, in whatever kind of life followed this one, he might find Parro Kerrus and Iveran, Brennon and little Jari, and that things could be made different than they were.

CHAPTER 31

Alone atop a little hill, Keiro watched the full moon crawl slowly up the sky. If he'd thought three days of waiting had been unbearable, he would laugh at his past self now. Thirty days, and every piece of his being had been straining forward toward this night.

He sat smiling, for though there was a need ready to burst within him, an unbearable sort of desperation, he could be no less than ecstatic on this night. It was in the air that washed over his skin, a touch of coolness in the breeze to calm and comfort. It was in the short grass he sat on, tickling against his bare buttocks, for his breechclout had finally fallen apart and the replacement he had made from woven grass had been a horrendous failure. It was in the stars, certainly, the white points flickering far off and the two red points watching low at his back. Mostly, of course, it was in the moon, the moon that had summoned him here. He watched it rise achingly slow, and there was a song in his heart that his voice could not give life to.

Finally, with the moon at its highest, proudest place in

the sky, the first of the creatures Yaket had called Starborn appeared at the crest of the tallest hill, and it began its song.

It was not the same song it had been before. It was different in many small ways, but no less beautiful for them. To Keiro, it sounded like walking, each note a step along a wondrous, looping path. The other voices joined in slowly and faded out again, fellow travelers coming and going, beginnings and endings. This was a song of passage, of the impermanence of people and things and places. It was a song of one winding life and all the other lives it touched on its way down the road. There was walking in the singing, and then there was stopping, for feet could only carry for so long. Always, there was an end to walking. There was only the one voice, the first voice, singing of the stillness, singing an end as the other Starborn left the hill, their glowing scales dimming, fading into the darkness. One voice singing, and as the moon slipped from its apex, across the distance between the big hill and Keiro's, two red stars shone, a mirror to the Eyes at his back. The voice faded away, the song ending, the walk over, but the grounded stars remained, the scattered points of white light and the two red eyes, locked on him across the expanse. There was a whisper in the wind that caressed his bare skin, and with pounding heart Keiro rose to his feet.

Walking had always been so easy. An effortless thing, easier than drawing breath. Walking was the thing he had been born to do. Yet his feet felt heavy now, each step a fight, the grass twining around his ankles to drag him back. He had a thought, briefly, that perhaps he should turn away, face the Eyes that were among the stars and not their red counterparts on earth, cross the Plains back to Yaket's tales and Poret's arms. That was as unthinkable, though, as not walking. His feet knew his path, and his heart.

It seemed to take a long time to reach the top of the highest hill, though truly the moon had hardly moved in the sky. The Starborn still waited for him, red eyes watching intently. Against the black sky, with its scattered flecks of glowing white scales, Keiro could certainly see why Yaket called them Starborn. To the rest of the world, to all those who thought them long dead, ancient history, older than the oldest stories, they would have been called *mravigi*.

For a long time atop that high hill, they simply looked at one another, Keiro and Fratarro's ancient creation. Then the Starborn turned and began to descend the hill, its tail flicking in what Keiro thought to be a beckoning sort of way. He would have followed even without that. There was a patch of scrub brush a few lengths down the hill, spare, thorny branches that picked at his skin as he wove through them after the thick-scaled creature. Its white scales had dimmed now, little more than a faint glow leading him forward through the night.

Even with the moon at its brightest, Keiro almost tumbled into the hole. He caught himself as the Starborn's forked tail tip slipped over the hole's lip into darkness. Even among the desolate Plains, underground would have been safest for them, though it made him ache to think of the high-soaring *mravigi* trapped so far away from the stars. They had not been made for tunneling, or for hiding. Nor had Keiro, but he had been made for following. He sat at the edge of the hole, feet dangling into the open air beyond, and didn't give it a second thought. He pushed away from the ground, and the thorns let him slip away.

His heels hit the ground first, and then his knees, and then his head. It was not the landing he would have chosen, but the tunnel was dug at an angle. Shaking his head to clear it, Keiro saw the Starborn watching him. It glowed again, dimly, just enough that he could make out the curve of walls and ceiling. A space big enough for the broad-chested creature to pass through comfortably on four legs, belly low to the ground, though it was not so easy for Keiro on hands and knees. His back scraped against the top of the tunnel, his forehead finding protruding roots in time to save his back from them, and his knees throbbed from the awkward landing, scraped raw by the rough-packed floor as he crawled. He could see the deep gouges left by claws, the marks of the digging for which they must have been so ill-suited. Pelir had told him that Fratarro had given his children wings so that they could fly among the stars. There was no sign of wings on the creature he followed, not even stumps where once they might have been. He couldn't imagine the Starborn passing through this tunnel with bulky wings.

At first he thought the thrumming was just the pain in his head from so many impacts. But he could *feel* it, feel the vibrations in his palms and in his shoulders when they rested too long against the walls. He thought, then, that it was the scared pounding of his heart, the knowledge of so much earth pressing around him, held back only by time and hope. It was a sound, though, distinct in his ears and in his bones. It was a sound like to drive him mad with its constancy and its mystery. Gradually it seemed to grow louder, as the tunnel angled ever downward. He had no idea how long he'd been crawling, following behind the faint glow of the *mravigi*. Sometimes there were other tunnels, gaping empty holes that blew warm air against his sides as he passed, but his guide never turned, and so neither did Keiro.

He would never have noticed the light had he been aboveground, had his eyes not been straining in the darkness. It was little more than the gentle glow of the Starborn that led him, but it *was* more, faintly more. The difference between one star and four on a no-moon night. Insignificant, unless it was all the light there was. The thrumming was louder, a low rumble that clenched around his lungs.

Keiro felt the space before he saw that the tunnel had opened up around him. For a moment he thought they had come full circle, passed back into the open night on the Plains. Only there was no moon here, just a hundred thousand stars punctuated, every so often, by two points of red. Their voices murmured, their claws scraped against the stone and earth, their bodies pressed against one another—the thrumming was loudest here, the sound of so many foreign creatures together in one space.

"*Home,*" a voice said softly, a whisper in his ear, the same voice that had named him the son of gods. The Starborn stood beside him, its eyes steady on his own, waiting. It didn't need to lead him farther; Keiro's feet knew the way now, and his heart. He started across the vast chamber, the false stars of the watching *mravigi* shining above and all around, watching. His feet moved with surety now, the steps coming as easily as they always had. All his life, every step, and there had been so many, had drawn him to this place beneath the hill.

A massive *mravigi* lay upon the floor, three times the size of the one who had led Keiro, all its scales white and bright as the moon. The red eyes watched him like drops of blood on snow, eyes nearly as large as Keiro's palm. More astonishing than the *mravigi*'s size, even, or the white scales, were the jointed wings folded tightly against its sides.

Keiro hardly had time to dwell on the wondrous creature, for what sat beyond it filled him with even more awe. His legs crumpled, the strength sapped from him by awe, and his good eye wept shameless tears as he looked upon his fallen gods.

They were burned, their skin charred black and patterned with cracks as all the old stories said, so that they were almost a part of the darkness that encased them. Sororra sat with her knees pulled up to her chest and her arms wrapped around them, head bowed so her brow rested upon her arms, a mound of contained sorrow. Hard iron, nearly as dark as her burned flesh, circled at wrist and ankle, and heavy chains snaked deep into the ground. Next to her leaned her brother, his slack face a mirror of hers save for the deep lines that pain, and not fire, had etched into his face. His mouth hung open wide enough to reveal the startling redness within, and the tips of white teeth. He looked almost peaceful in sleep, or in undying death— whatever horror the Parents had condemned him to. Almost peaceful, save for one thing. *And thus did Fratarro shatter upon the bones of the earth . . .*

It was raw flesh where his limbs had been torn away, red and sickly and dripping ichor. One leg was gone at the hip, the other halfway to the knee, and he sat in a pool of his own blood. No right arm, but his left was there, the sinewy stitching that held it to his shoulder rough and unpracticed, blood oozing around the edges. It ended in a ragged, ichorous stump, no hand to make it complete . . . . *and a shard of ebon pierced his immortal heart . . .*

Fully as long as the arm he had, the spiny shard went clean through him, pinning him against the wall he leaned on. Ichor dripped slow and steady from the wound, tracing familiar patterns down the burned crags of his chest and stomach and groin.

His Bound Gods, the fallen Twins . . . found, at long last.

"Thank you," he said, soft, a choked whisper. At his side the *mravigi* bowed, and even the white-winged beast inclined its noble head.

"Be welcome here, Godson," the one at his side murmured.

Keiro gazed at them, his beloved gods, more than he had ever hoped to find in all his wandering. "How?" he asked, and didn't know how to end the question.

"They fell here, long ago, broken and bound. We found them, and did what we could, those of us who were left. We have all waited a very long time." There were words unspoken as the Starborn's eyes fixed to Keiro's face, open and expectant. *Waited*, those eyes said, *for you*.

It was, suddenly, very hard for Keiro to breathe.

There was a touch, gentle, at Keiro's knee. Looking down, dimly visible in the faint starlight glow of the *mravigi*, one of the Starborn sat, no bigger than Keiro's hand and the color of smoke. It stood with one foot pressed to Keiro's knee, its head stretched up toward him, and tiny, translucent wings spread for balance.

Wonderingly Keiro leaned down, fingertips brushing against the soft scales between the *mravigi*'s small eyes. The little creature pushed back, eyes flickering shut in catlike contentment. Among all the wonders of this night, it was this one that gave him a moment to collect his thoughts, to gather his breath.

The moment was not to last. Keiro lifted his head to gaze

once more upon his gods, fingers lightly trailing down the little Starborn's spine. A red glow, brighter than the eyes of the *mravigi,* bright than stars on a moonless night, suffused the chamber. It was a sudden thing, as though a curtain had dropped away to reveal a thousand hidden candles. It was Sororra, ancient head rising from her crossed arms, and black-burned lids lifting from red eyes.

"Cazi likes you," a voice murmured, soft yet piercing, and the red light redoubled as Fratarro, too, opened his eyes. A smile split his face, wiping away the lines of pain.

Keiro fell forward with a cry that held no words, a sound of shock and joy and wonder and countless emotions beyond naming, a sound born of more than he had ever before felt in all his life. His forehead pressed against the warm stone, and beneath his clapsed hands his heart beat at a frantic pace.

"Rise, Keiro," said Fratarro's gentle voice. "You have found us. Rise, and see where your long patience has brought you."

Shaking, with tears streaming from his one eye, Keiro rose and faced his gods.

They were glorious, beautiful and terrifying, their faces matched, though the lines of Sororra's face were hard where her brother's were soft, and it was anger and not pain that was carved deep into her charred flesh.

Never in his life—standing before his living gods who towered above him, beneath the benevolent smile of Fratarro, who had suffered so greatly, in this enormous space beneath the earth—had Keiro felt so small.

"Be welcome here, fraro," Sororra said, and it sounded almost like a growl. There was an old story that said that Sororra's first words spoken, after Patharro had sent his children among the humans, had created winter.

"It's not that she's hateful or hostile," Pelir had told him so long ago. "Merely . . . distant, sometimes. And who can blame her? She suffered under the Parents even before they cast her out. They made her as she is, and then hated and denied what they had made of her. Who are we to say that she should be so easy to trust, or to love?"

Keiro pressed his fist to his forehead, between the good eye and the bad. "I am honored beyond words, my lady," he said. He knew that wasn't the right honorific, but what title did one give a god? "And my lord," he added quickly, bowing to poor Fratarro.

"We knew the faithful would one day find us," the god said.

"And you are the first among the faithful," Sororra said, her voice an echo of her brother's, though harder.

"The most faithful. Son of gods, my children have named you."

"Your collection grows, brother."

Keiro's head was reeling, the words hardly sticking in his brain. He wanted to kneel again, to cower, to prostrate himself and blubber devotions. He wanted to flee, scramble his way back up the twisting tunnel to the cool night air, to sit beneath the bright moon and not have to think for a time. He wanted to pinch his arm, to wake from this strange dream next to Poret, sleeping among the plainswalkers, and yet if this was a dream, he wanted never to wake. He wanted to glory in the sight of his gods, bound and unseen for centuries, *found* finally, but he could hardly bear to look at them, the smoldering fury and the raw painful love and the horror of all that had been done to them.

"We are in need of help," Sororra said bluntly. "My brother must be made whole again."

"I . . . I will help in any way I can," Keiro stammered. It was his life's goal, his purpose. It was a strange thing, though, to actually be faced with that purpose. Such distant goals, held for so long, made real and solid in the blink of one eye.

Fratarro smiled at him, the smile that was so gentle and full of understanding that it was like to break Keiro's heart, but even as the god opened his mouth to speak, his eyelids fell, closing shut the bright glow of his eyes. Sororra's head returned to her arms, and the starlight glow was once more all that filled the carvern.

"What's happened?" Keiro asked, and he could hear the panic in his own voice.

"They sleep, Godson," said the Starborn at his side. *"Be easy. They have little power left to them. It is all they can do, sometimes, to wake."* The creature folded its legs, setting its belly to the floor. *"Sit. Rest. They shall return."*

Hesitant, still feeling the touches of panic, Keiro sat beside the *mravigi*. The small one, the Starborn with wings whom Fratarro had called Cazi, scurried into his lap. He had small claws, but sharp, and he hooked them into Keiro's arm. A cry of surprise more than pain burst from Keiro as the Starborn scrambled up his arm to finally perch on his shoulder, snuffling curiously at Keiro's hair. That pulled another surprised noise from Keiro, though this one was a laugh.

"How often do they wake?" Keiro asked.

His Starborn guide lifted its head to regard him, and the small *mravigi* nestled on his shoulder. *"They wake when they are able. It is no easy thing, to fight the bonds placed on them. They shall—"*

The sudden brightness cut off the Starborn's words, the red glow bursting like the sun over mountains. Fratarro, eyes wide to the ceiling, his mouth open not in a smile but in the last breath drawn before a scream. The lines of pain that suffused his face were not smoothed away, but carved doubly deep. Sororra's eyes flew open, too, and for a moment, the space it took for a star to die, their faces were as a mirror. Fury and pain eternal, released from the place they'd been held tightly down. Fratarro's back arched, straining against the shard pierced through his chest, and the drawn breath burst from him in a scream, a sound that shook the earth, sent clods of dirt falling through the air. The *mravigi* began to scream, too, high voices raised in an echo of pain. Tiny claws dug into Keiro's shoulder. The stars began to flicker out, the *mravigi* going dark. Keiro saw Sororra move to her brother, hold his one arm that ended in raw flesh, the ichor flowing now down his arm in an unrestrained stream. "My hand!" he heard Fratarro shout, but no other words followed. Just a mindless screaming, an animal's dying wail. Before the last of the starlight died, Keiro saw Sororra hold her brother, straining against the chains that bound her, and he saw the white Starborn rise from its place at their feet, its enormous wings spread wide. Then all the star-specks were gone in a rush of scurrying claws, and all the red eyes, and it was only the darkness and the screaming, the small creature clinging to Keiro's neck, and the faint sound of flapping wings.

ABOUT THE AUTHOR

L iving in the cold reaches of the upper Midwest with her beast of a dog, Rachel Dunne has developed a great fondness for indoor activities. This, her first novel, was a semifinalist for the 2014 Amazon Breakthrough Novel Award before being picked up for publishing. For as long as snow continues falling in Wisconsin, she promises to keep writing.